W9-BLD-600

DOGISM

A Mark Anthony novel

QBORO BOOKS
WWW.QBOROBOOKS.COM
"QBB – We write them hot books! You didn't know?"

Q-BORO BOOKS
Jamaica, Queens NY 11434
WWW.QBOROBOOKS.COM
(For store orders, author information and contact information
Please Visit Our Website for the most up to date listings)

Copyright © 2004 by Mark Anthony

All rights reserved. Without limiting the rights under copyright reserved above. No part of this book may be reproduced, stored in or introduced into a retrieval system, or transmitted, in any form, or by any means (electronic, mechanical, photocopying, recording, or otherwise), without prior written consent from both the author, and publisher Q-BORO BOOKS, except brief quotes used in reviews.

ISBN 09753066-0-X
Revised Edition – First Printing April 2004
Library of Congress Control Number: 2004091683

"Scripture taken from the HOLY BIBLE, NEW INTERNATIONAL VERSION Copyright © 1973, 1978, 1984 International Bible Society. Used by permission of Zondervan Bible Publishers."

This is a work of fiction. It is not meant to depict, portray or represent any particular real persons. All the characters, incidents and dialogues are the products of the author's imagination and are not to be construed as real. Any references or similarities to actual events, entities, real people, living or dead, or to real locales are intended to give the novel a sense of reality. Any similarity in other names, characters, entities, places and incidents is entirely coincidental.

Author website: www.markanthonyauthor.com
Cover Photo & Art - Copyright © 2004 by Q-BORO BOOKS all rights reserved

Coming Soon:

Lady's Night

a **Mark Anthony** *novel*

This book is dedicated my mother:
- Dorothy -

Look Ma' I did it again!!!

And you know what? People thought it was a fluke a few years back but they didn't realize it was all part of a five year plan. Just when people thought it was over, I popped up on those best-seller lists. They didn't realize that I was just getting started. I can't stop and I won't stop! With all of the creative stories and ideas that I have inside of me, Ma' I don't know how to stop! You are a major part of my inspiration....

Thanks for teaching me early on to just work hard for whatever it is that I want out of life. You showed me how not to be a jealous, envious hater like so many people in this world who shall rename nameless...

You helped give me life and now I am part of your legacy. As I give life to the words that I write, know that my words and my books will out live me, my words and my books are part of my legacy and therefore they are also part of your legacy...

Everything that I do would not be possible if it were not for you and your numerous unconditional sacrifices that you made not only for me but for the rest of the fam'...

Ma' I hope that you're proud of the kid, your baby boy! I also hope that one day I will learn to love like you love...I love you Ma'!

Acknowledgements

To Jesus Christ – First and foremost thank you for loving me and saving me. Thank you for giving me this talent and creative ability to write and thereby impact the world. Thank you for teaching me and showing me what my purpose in life is. Thank you for showing me how any and all of the mistakes that I make in life are a'ight, just as long as I learn from them and teach people from my errors. And I definitely thank you for showing me and proving to me that when I am chasing my dreams and fulfilling my purpose that I have no room for fear and that I have to fill up every ounce of my being with unshakeable faith. Faith is what brings the invisible things into reality. In addition to being my God, you are my father, my brother, and my true homeboy! Regardless of what people think, I know that I am tight with you and I know that you have given me your clearances on what many people don't understand. I love you.

To Sabine: We made it out of the foxhole of our life. We've definitely enjoyed the summers but just know that the winter in our life is over and the spring time is just starting to bubble once again. We've both learned what it means when it is said that "true friends are made in foxholes." No one except for us will ever *really* know what went on inside the foxhole of our lives. Only me, you, and God will *ever truly know* what we share and what we have. *We define us, so therefore no one but God can judge us*. I love you. And I sincerely believe that angels can take on a human form. I believe that because you are my angel from God.

To Christian Cultural Center, Brooklyn, NY – I am glad that I am a member of the #1 church on the planet, hands down! Keep doing what y'all are doing because y'all are *positively* changing thousands of lives and that's why there are literally thousands of people walking through those doors every week. Among the countless things that I have learned from y'all is this: ***"The quality of your life depends on the quality of your decisions..."***

Author's Note:

As with everything that I write, I try my best to be conscious of what I put down on paper. I'm conscious of what I write because I realize that my words have the potential to touch, reach, and influence many people. One of my goals when I write is to simply use words to paint a picture of what I see or have seen happening around me. My goal has never been to glorify negativity of any sort, and if any of my stories or collective words ever give that impression then I apologize to all of my readers. If that be the case please accept my apology and understand that the spirit of the writer was not to incite, promote, or induce any type of negativity.

However, I do feel that I have a gift from God, the gift of writing. And one of the ways in which I use that gift is by portraying negative things that fixate people, but not just for the sole purpose of entertaining people, rather I do it in order to get my readers to read between the lines and *really* see what lessons lay beneath all of the negativity. My hope is that my readers will understand and see what I am usually trying to say is that even in the midst of negativity there is always a solution to the negativity. I think that in any type of media communication if negativity is always portrayed without providing some sort of solution then that can become problematic. Understand that even when there seems like no solution to the myriad of problems in our lives and in the world, that the solution always lies in the hands and in the mind of God.

In our individual lives we could be in the midst of what to us could seem like the darkest darkness, but understand that even in the midst of darkness if there is the smallest bit of light then there is hope. We need to look to that glimmer of light and trace it back to its source. And when we find the source of light we will have found all that we need to navigate through life's ups and downs. In closing I just want to add the following:

Many of the problems that we see in society is partly due to the fact that the majority of families are in a big mess, and aside from broken homes, the majority of families are in the big mess mainly due to the fact that most marriages are in a big mess, and most of the marriages are in a big mess mainly because God is truly not in the center of most marriages.

- Mark Anthony -

In The Beginning

I'm probably the only nigga in the world that would take a hoe and want to turn that hoe into my housewife. But when that hoe goes by the name of *Scarlet del Rio* and she has measurements of 36-24-48 many people would probably not agree with me, but based on those measurements I am sure that people would understand why I would want to turn Scarlet del Rio into my housewife.

36-24-48 will get any man open, at least any black man. Let me break it down so that you can see where I'm coming from. The 36 is important, but out of the three measurements it probably is the least important. Even if you throw the letters B, C, D, DD, or whatever letter or combination of letters after the 36 it still wouldn't hold that much weight. It is the second and third set of numbers that get the most weight, and it is specifically those second and third set of numbers that will cause a nigga to consider turning a hoe into a housewife.

See, the second number tells you what a woman's waist size is. The last number lets you know what size a woman's butt is. Whenever that last number is 40 and better, then a woman is "working with something." When that last number reaches anywhere from 50 to 54, then you know for sure that a woman is "really" working with something! If that last number gets above 54 it could either be a real good thing or it could be a real stomach turning nasty thing. The bottom line is that you always have to look deeper into the numbers.

When you look deeper into the numbers that's when you'll begin to understand that it is the ratio of those last two numbers that really gets a nigga wide open. The craziest ratio that a woman can have is a "one to two ratio." That means that for every one inch of waist that there is exactly two inches of booty. When that, one to two ratio exists, women walk around with an almost voodoo like power, and sometimes they don't even know that they have that kind of power.

I probably shouldn't be letting the "ratio-rule" out of the bag because it has long been one of those things that men have kept amongst ourselves, it has been something in which women have been kept in the dark about because if women knew what kind of power that the ratio held over men, they would become very powerful and dangerous with that type of knowledge. But for my sistas sake I'll make sure that the ratio-rule is very clear so that y'all can fully understand the importance of ratio.

If a woman's measurements were 34-25-40 that would be good. It wouldn't be great but it would be good. See the last number is a 40 which would meet the booty threshold, but the 25 would cause the numbers to miss the one to two ratio. Now if a woman was a 36-27-46 those would be good measurements because the 46 is way over the booty threshold of 40. So in this case, even though the waist is a 27, which also wouldn't provide that one to two waist to booty ratio, it would be ok because of the simple fact that the 46 is so much higher than the threshold of 40, and a bigger butt would overcompensate for the lack of the exact one to two ratio. But see if a woman had a 60 for the butt category and lets say a 36 for the waist category then that might be a scary thing because in this case the woman could be approaching the fat and sloppy side. Unless a brother is into the BBW thing (big beautiful women), then things can get scary when the last number reaches above 54 so you have to be careful.

The ratio rule is only an exact science when the ratio of waist to butt works out to be one to two. But when the ratio is not one to two, things get a little tricky because then you have to take other things into consideration such as how tall is the woman, or how much does the woman weigh, is she thick or slim, does she look good, does the first number (the chest size) along with the cup size make up for other variables that might not be on point?

The measurements game is not an exact science but it is fun when it is broken down. And all I can say it that when that ratio is one to two, most men will recognize it immediately. It is that ratio that has caused car accidents due to niggas "breaking their necks" to turn and look at a woman on the street when they should be focusing on driving their car, it has helped boost the AIDS and

STD rates, it has caused many abortions, and it is responsible for many one night stands.

In my case, I had seen many women with the one to two ratio. But I had never seen a woman where the ratio was perfect and everything else was bangin' from head to toe. By everything else, I mean height, skin tone, feet, hair, nails, lips, legs, chest, etc. And I'll be honest, in my short lived life I had never had a woman, sexually that is, who had those perfect measurements and all the other right variables. But that all changed on the night I was introduced to Scarlet del Rio.

When Scarlet walked through the door and entered my bachelor party she was with two other very attractive and scantily clad women, known as Joyce and Jasmine, who I later learned were sisters by blood in real life. And although I was high and I had been drinking, I was sober enough to realize that Scarlet was beyond just a nice looking woman, she was off the meter, off the chain, bangin', slammin', however you want to phrase it, she more than had it going on!

There was about twenty or thirty guys at my bachelor party and each one of them was open from the combination of weed and liquor and Scarlet and her crew. Scarlet, Joyce, and Jasmine immediately began their show. They stripped, drank liquor, smoked weed, and did all sorts of things including girl on girl routines.

Of course, since I was the soon to be groom, the majority of the strippers attention was placed on me. I enjoyed the attention, and although the bachelor party was like a seen from Sodom and Gomorrah I threw all of my religious and moral convictions out of the window. There was no way that I could think about God at a moment in time when three big naked booties were being thrown in my face.

Too much liquor always turns people into a different person and I know for a fact that I was a different person on the night of my bachelor party. They always say that when a person is drunk that is when the "real" person is seen and all of the hidden truths in that person come out to the light. In essence, liquor takes away all the layers of inhibition and keeps peeling back layers of shyness until the true person is shown.

Well the night of my bachelor party was one of the first times that the public, meaning my close friends and associates got to see a glimpse of the "real" Lance Thomas.

I was cursing, which was totally out of character for me, I was giving the strippers precise and detailed erotic instructions and suggestions and overseeing them to make sure that they were carried out to my liking. But one of the most uncharacteristic things that I did on the night of my bachelor party was I stripped butt naked out of my clothes. Yup, I had the family jewels and all just flappin' in the wind.

I was cheered on and jeered and encouraged by my friends. Reggae music was blasting and I remember dancing real freaky with one of the strippers, I think it was Joyce who I was freaking. It was like I had become the star stripper at my own bachelor party. I was actually turning out Joyce on the make shift dance floor.

I was fully aroused the entire time that I was dancing with Joyce and I could tell that the entire party was gonna be taken to the next level. Before I knew what was what, and with my encouragement, my bachelor party had quickly turned into a full fledge butt-naked orgy.

And while both Joyce and Jasmine were both also bangin' in terms of looks and body, all of the men at the party wanted to get with Scarlet. They were offering her all kinds of money and propositioning her to perform all kinds of sexual favors. But for some reason Scarlet was clinging to me as if I was her man. She did it in an exotic way as if to make the rest of the men jealous. At first I thought she was doing that in order to make herself seem more desirable to them, which would have meant that she could have charged them just about whatever she wanted to charge them if they wanted to be with her. Then I thought that she was making sure that she fully carried out her duties which were to please me, the bachelor, the groom to be.

As the party carried on I remember thinking to myself that Scarlet was feeling me in terms of "wanting me." I don't mean wanting me just because she was paid to be my hoe for the night, and I don't mean wanting me in the sense that she might have been turned on from the wild activities, but I mean that I really sensed that she wanted me in the terms of she wanted to "get with me." However I brushed that thought off because I knew that I was drunk and I knew that she also had been drinking. Plus I had no real proof that she really "wanted me," I mean I had only known her for about an hour, so how could I really "know" for sure that she was feeling a nigga?

The truth was that I didn't know for sure but I did have a good gut feeling and I was usually right when ever my gut told me something about a woman.

So as the bachelor party / orgy ensued in one part of my house, Scarlet led me by the hand to another part of the house, a more isolated area. She immediately began performing oral sex on me without me even requesting it. And it was at that moment that a thought of my fiancée flashed into my mind. But as I closed my eyes and cupped both of my hands behind my head and enjoyed Scarlet, I realized that I, at that actual moment in time was not literally married. After all, I had not walked down the aisle and I had not signed anything, so if the state of New York did not recognize me as being married at that point in time, then I was not married, which meant that I was able to do whatever the hell it was that I felt like doing. I mean regardless of the fact that I was gonna get married in about twenty four hours, the fact remained that I was not officially married and I was still free to do what I had to do and free to do whatever I wanted to do.

And Scarlet didn't make my moral decision making process easy for me. When she was done servicing me she kept asking what else did I want her to do.

"Just dance for me," I instructed.

"That's all you want me to do?" Scarlet asked, sounding a bit surprised as she began dancing in front of me.

"Yeah I 'm cool with that, I just wanna look at you."

As Scarlet began dancing she also managed to seduce me with her eyes, but her eyes were not what I was focused on.

"So how long you been dancing?" I asked.

After not getting an immediate response, Scarlet replied, "Don't worry about that right now," as she backed her butt up into my face.

"You sure that's all you want me to do is dance for you?"

"Yeah that's it for right now," I said as I began to get re-aroused.

"You can touch me if you want to, I'm not gonna bite you," Scarlet responded.

I didn't act on what she had said and she kept dancing.

"Lance, I don't think you understand where I'm coming from," Scarlet added, sounding very soft and sexy, "You can do *whatever* you want..."

After she said that I remember feeling so open, but I still didn't immediately act on what Scarlet was saying even though I knew exactly where she was coming from. I just licked my lips and kept the most devilish grin as I responded, "*Whatever* I want?..."

"*Whatever you want baby,*" Scarlet seductively whispered in my ear as she ran her tongue around my earlobe.

Still, I just sat and chilled.

Scarlet kept dancing in her red stiletto high heels that had long thin straps connected to them which criss-crossed up and down her legs all the way to the top of her thighs. It was as if Scarlet was trying to get more into her moves in order to get me more turned on.

"So where are you from?" I asked.

"Brazil," Scarlet replied, "But, Lance, baby, don't worry about that, take your mind off of questions like that... Just relax."

That's when the thought popped into my head that this was probably gonna be my last opportunity to get close to any other woman other than my wife, so I knew that I had to act on the opportunity that was presenting itself. Plus I had never been with a Brazilian woman before and I wanted to know what that was like. I was also infatuated with Scarlet's small waist which made her booty look extremely big and juicy.

"*Anything* I want?" I asked as I stood up.

"*Anything,*" Scarlet del Rio replied as she smiled and came close to me and put her hand behind my neck and placed her tongue inside my mouth and started kissing me. Only God knew where her tongue had been prior to our encounter but I had no problem letting her tongue me down!

I knew that if I were to proceed with moral courage and just end the bachelor party right then and here, then I would never feel guilty because I knew that up until that point Scarlet had only given me a blow-job, and as far as I was concerned, married or single, getting a blow-job or a hand-job didn't make me a cheater.

But before I knew it my rationalizations no longer mattered because I had threw every care out of the window and had turned Scarlet around so that her back was to me. Both of her hands were against the wall, she looked as if she was holding up my bedroom wall, and I was inside of her with no condom. I mean she did say "*anything*", and anything for me meant sex from the back with no condom. I *hated* using condoms!

I knew that I was literally buggin', but Scarlet held true to her word and she didn't even question me about not putting on a condom, so I proceeded to work it out. The liquor was definitely talking to me because I wasn't trying to reason at all with any type of sane thinking. I mean yeah she was a big-butt-very-attractive-Brazilian-stripper-in-stiletto's who I had just met for the first time about an hour ago, but I figured that she didn't have anything in terms of any STD's so there was no reason for me to take any precautions. I just continued to stand behind those measurements and with my "ruler" I worked out her numbers like a mathematician.

Instead of thinking about God, my fiancée, AIDS, and an unwanted possible pregnancy I was truly and honestly feeling like "the man" because this was a dime-piece of all dime-pieces that I was hittin' and I was enjoying it. I didn't have to wine and dine the booty, and I didn't have to trick no dough on the booty, in fact Scarlet basically begged me to hit it, so I was definitely feeling like the man. But what was wild was that Scarlet turned out to be a "*squirter.*" She was the first squirter that I had ever been with, and when she had squirted it freaked me out because I had never seen anything like that, and that just helped to further reinforce in my mind just how much of "the man" I actually was.

Scarlet and I had eventually returned to the rest of the attendees of my bachelor party which continued on for about another half an hour after the two of us re-joined the wild scene. However, before Scarlet and I had left my bedroom she made me promise her that I would keep in contact with her. In my mind I knew that after the bachelor party was over that I would never speak to Scarlet again in my life, nor did I really want to. I mean I was getting married the next day and I wanted this to be the end of my running around and the end of my trying to live out my sick sexual fantasies. I was only twenty two years old at the time and I had all of the intentions in the world of walking down the aisle the next day and remaining faithful from that day forward "'til death did me and my wife part."

But I fooled myself because that night I listened to Scarlet as she told me that other than myself, she had never kissed any of her clients in the mouth because she felt that kissing was an intimate thing that should be reserved for special people. I also listened as she told me that while she had had sex with many men due to her line of work, that she had never ever let anyone do it to her raw without a condom. I also listened and believed her as she told me that she never gives out her phone number to clients that she meets but that she wanted me to have it and for me to use it.

I listened as she told me how she was a stripper and she danced at two strip clubs, one called, "Sugar Walls" which is out in Long Island, and another strip club called "Blackjack" which was located in Queens.

For some reason I believed everything that Scarlet was telling me that night. And like I said, I had no intentions of ever seeing or speaking to Scarlet again. In fact after the bachelor party was over I even did the right thing and threw her phone number in the garbage.

What I didn't understand was, why, when I was on my honeymoon was Scarlet constantly on my mind? The honeymoon is supposed to be somewhat sacred and special, but I have to admit that each time I had sex with my wife on our honeymoon, that the sight of Scarlet squirting like she did on the night of my bachelor party was constantly replaying itself in my mind.

The way in which Scarlet had turned me out on the night of my bachelor party had a real lasting effect on me. And it was less than two weeks after I'd returned from my honeymoon when I first began regretting the fact that I'd thrown away Scarlet's phone number. But I knew where she worked and I made it my business to visit "Sugar Walls"

Like I said, it had only been two weeks since I'd returned from my honeymoon but I did mange to make my way over to the strip club to see Scarlet in action.

Her shocked and jubilant reaction when she saw me, confirmed what it was that I thought that I had sensed that first night I'd met her at my bachelor party. That being that Scarlet was genuinely feeling something about me. I didn't know what it was but it was something that I had which drew her to me.

So as I sat down at the bar and sipped on a Bacardi and Coke I watched as Scarlet turned the club out with her routine. Although there were other strippers in the club, Scarlet had every man's attention and money was literally being thrown at her. As I sipped on my drink at the bar I looked at a flyer that had Scarlet's picture on it, and that's when I noticed her measurements which were listed on the flyer 36-24-48.

"That's what it is!... I knew it!" I thought to myself.

I sat and smiled because I thought that I had finally figured it out. I mean that had to be what had trapped me, it was the perfect one to two waist to booty ratio! But I still didn't know why Scarlet had been so drawn to me.

As Scarlet worked the crowd I remember my ego skyrocketing as I thought of how every man in that joint would have wanted nothing more than to have raw dawg unprotected sex with Scarlet. And I knew that not only had I lived out all of those men's fantasies but I had lived it out without even using a condom, so I was really the man.

As Scarlet finished her routine, she walked her pretty twenty year old tight body over to where I was sitting and kissed me on the cheek. I sat with a tooth pick in my mouth amidst blaring hip hop music. Scarlet was sweating very-very slightly, but even her sweat looked good, as she began trying to talk into my hear over the loud music.

"What's up baby!?" Scarlet asked.

"Damn you look good!" I replied as I wiped some of the sweat from her forehead. "You turned the place out!"

"I'm just trying to do my thing and make this money... Lance I'm so happy to see you! I didn't think I was gonna hear from you again." Scarlet stated with a genuine giddy type of smile.

"Well actually I lost your number. I don't know what I did with it. I was going crazy trying to remember it but I couldn't. So I figured that I might as well stop by and see you."

"Well I'm glad you did... I was thinking that maybe your wife found the number and killed you or something." Scarlet said as we both started laughing.

"Nah it was nothing like that. But honestly I thought that you were just frontin' that night and that the liquor had been talking for you. I didn't think you was really feeling me like that."

"Oh, so in other words you thought I was a whore or something right!?" Scarlet said with an attitude as she did a Dr. Jekyll and Mr. Hyde.

"No, no, no, nothing like that," I replied as Scarlet cut me off.

"See, that is what's so frustrating about this business. It's that you don't want to get close to anyone because you never know what they're about. Most men are just about getting some butt and that's it. And at the same time some men don't even want you because they think that you're a whore. And then I don't want to be with someone who can't accept me for who I am especially if they can't separate what I do for a living from who I really am as a person."

Trying to put out a four alarm fire that I sensed was about to erupt, I asked, "So why don't you give me a chance to learn who you really are?"

I must have pushed the right buttons that night because later that evening Scarlet del Rio had once again given me her phone number. And that time I was sure as to not lose it.

****

Although I had been recently married, Scarlet and I managed to stay in very close contact. And I learned a lot about her. I learned that she was trying to become a nurse. I learned that she was making like $2,000 a week. I learned that she was trying to get away from doing the strip clubs and bachelor parties and trying to focus on producing, promoting, and selling triple X hardcore porno movies over the internet. I also learned that Scarlet had been sexually abused when she was younger and that she had been in at least two abusive relationships.

All of this I had learned during the *five years* that Scarlet del Rio and I had kept in contact. Yeah, it had been five years since Scarlet and I had met at my bachelor party. And during those five years you might as well say that Scarlet was "my girl." Although nothing was ever officially confirmed by the two of us, we acted as if we were a couple. Especially from her end, I mean many people will say that I am naïve to believe that Scarlet had not been with any other man sexually except for me during the past five years. But I know what I know, and I know that Scarlet, despite her line of work had been very loyal and faithful to me during the five years that we were involved, and despite the fact that my marriage was and continued to be a very limiting factor for both Scarlet and myself, I know that sexually Scarlet had remained loyal to me.

But early on in my relationship with Scarlet, I realized what it was that had caused Scarlet to be so drawn to me. See, number one, she was crazy! And number two she was a got damn psycho bitch! The stalker type... Scarlet really had all kinds of emotional issues, self-esteem issues and all kinds of drama in her life. And I think that from the time I met her that something in her told her that I was genuinely a good guy with good intentions that represented safety and security and emotional support which is what she was desperately craving and searching for in a man.

Scarlet definitely had her issues. But being that when it came to sex, she was like a female version of me, a literal sex freak and sex fiend who was willing to sex me at the drop of a hat without all of that unnecessary foreplay, I was willing to overlook a lot of her crazy stunts and her emotional issues. The sex was beyond good and because she kept her body tight and the ratio was always in proper proportion, plus she looked, and deep down she was really a good person at heart. Really she was.

During the five years that I've known Scarlet I always battled with myself and I tried my hardest to fight off the demons that drew me to women like Scarlet. During those five years I had come to know God more closer and I knew that I had to end things with Scarlet so that I could move on with my life and focus on my wife, not to mention that during those five years I had a baby boy who'd entered my life when my wife had given birth to our first and only child.

But it was a scary thing when I'd told Scarlet that things had to end between the two of us. I mean I was literally scared because she was down right crazy!

"Lance there is no way in the world that I am just gonna let five years of my life go like that! I don't believe in wasting time so therefore how are things just gonna end like that!? We haven't accomplished what we want to accomplish in this relationship! What happened to all of that talk that you use to kick to me, telling me that we're gonna have a baby together and that we're gonna go to Miami and live!? What happened to all of that, or was that all just game and lies!?"

"Scarlet, I'm married and you know that... You always knew that from jump street."

"Of course I know that! And I am not telling you to leave your wife! I've never told you to leave your wife, you're the one, Lance Thomas, that was always running your mouth about how you wanted to leave your wife and all of that. But I can tell you one thing, and that's that you're gonna be with me! That is for damn sure!"

"Scarlet it's over... I mean I've been wanting to bring this to you for a while but I just didn't know how."

"What do you mean it's over!? How can you just so nonchalantly say 'Scarlet it's over?' Don't you have any kind of feelings!? Lance what the hell is wrong with you!? You're coming across all cold, what did I do to you!? Tell me, what did I do to make you just wanna be all cold, and with no feelings and no reason what so ever come out and say 'Scarlet it's over.' Lance what the hell is wrong with you!?"

"Scarlet you didn't do anything. This isn't really about what you did or didn't do. It's more about me wanting to do right by Nicole."

"Nigga please! Lance you ain't getting over with that. How the hell after all of this time do you just wake up and wanna be faithful!? What about the past five years!? You can't change that so why are you trying to just switch up!? No matter what, from the time you met me you violated and ruined whatever you and Nicole had and you know that!"

"But Scarlet it's about more than just Nicole. I gotta do right by God."

"Oh my God! Lance come on with that. Where was God when you were sexing me for the past five years!? Where!? See Lance, let me explain something, you had options, you had a whole lot of options, but you chose to exercise the option of being with me and Nicole so you can't just back out of that that easy! Life don't work like that, at least not with me it doesn't!"

I blew air out of my mouth as I began to get frustrated. I guess I knew this was what I had allowed myself to nurture for five years. I always told myself and convinced myself that I was Scarlet's personal savior, I felt like she needed me, and that I was the only one who could help her with her emotional issues. But at this point I realized that I had only been making things worse by having strung her along and having led her on for so long.

I was an idiot for leading my hoe to believe that she could and would one day be my housewife. And you know what? Maybe she could have been my wife if I hadn't already been married, but since I was married she had to bounce because things had dragged on for long enough, and since I called the shots things were gonna be over when I said that they were over.

I had endured relentless verbal abuse from Scarlet for about an hour.

"Lance, if you leave me I will make your life a nightmare and I mean that!"

I knew that Scarlet meant it and I knew that she was fully capable of carrying out any threats that she made. I mean we had taped ourselves having sex, she knew my home number, my work number, she knew where my wife worked, she knew where my son went to school, she knew the entire routine of everyone in my house and she knew what kind of car that I drove. Not to mention that all she had to do was promise any thug cat some butt if he would agree to pump some hot slugs into my body and kill me. So needless to say, I knew that I was threading on very thin ice because Scarlet was such a ghetto-ticking-time-bomb-crazy-emotional-nut.

But I had to hold my ground. I mean I was getting more mature. Regardless of what people felt about my religious convictions I knew that there was a higher source that I ultimately would have to answer to. And I knew that there was more to life than a big butt and a smile. Not to mention that the ratio thing was not that important to me any more, in fact, lately I had found myself noticing less thicker women who did not exactly meet the one to two ratio. That however was beside the point.

I had to deal with Scarlet and I didn't know exactly how to deal with her. I did know however that I wasn't gonna back down from my stance because I had to leave this chick alone, even if it meant that I would have to be on guard for literally anything and everything.

"Lance, tell me right now if you're messing with some other chick!" Scarlet screamed. "'Cause if you are I will kill both you and the other bitch, whoever she is!"

"Scarlet you don't understand me. It is not about any other woman except for my wife and..."

Scarlet cut me off as she asked, "What!? The sex ain't good no more!? You don't want this cat anymore!?" She asked as she unzipped her pants and began pulling down her pants and exposing herself.

See, that was exactly what I could not deal with. Scarlet was cool but she was so got damn ghetto and raw and rough around the edges. Even though she was my Boo and she could be sweet as whatever and could cook like a chef, I couldn't deal with that wild unpredictable side of her that was mixed in with the real street side of her. Plus, like I said, I was married and she should have understood that. Period!

"Scarlet pull up your got damn pants!"

"What!? You scared of me or something!? You don't wanna come take this cat!?" Scarlet yelled while pointing at her exposed vagina. "You know my ish is clean so what's up!? Tell me you don't want this! You know you want this!"

I was two seconds from walking out of the door but then I took a glimpse at the booty and decided that I should just sex Scarlet one more time and just really kill it! And the whole time while I sex her I could remind her that it will be the "last time." But since Scarlet is such a ticking time bomb that might not have been the best thing to do, 'cause I was not trying to end up like John Wayne Bobbit with my penis chopped off.

Luckily for me I did end up getting out of her crib alive, in tact, and with my penis in one piece. But I was also called every kind of American and Portuguese four letter word in the book. When it all boiled down to it I had to end up following through with the plan of sexing Scarlet "one last time" because that was probably the only way that I was gonna get out of her house that day.

What I thought would be a potentially dangerous idea turned out to be one of the funniest sex episodes in the world! See, throughout the whole time that Scarlet and I were having sex, she did nothing but curse me out and tell me how much she hated me, and all I did was reconfirm to her that I did love her but that that was gonna be the last time that we were gonna see each other and be with one another. While we had sex she had the biggest attitude and like I mentioned, she cursed me throughout the entire ordeal, she even tried to repeatedly back her thing up unto me real hard in an effort to hurt me, all the while I know that she was enjoying the whole thing.

When we were done, Scarlet barely gave me enough time to get dressed and she was throwing me out of the house. I was scrambling to get up out of that piece before she decided to do something real crazy like get a knife or a razor or something. The whole scene was scary and it was funny because I didn't know what kind of sex to call that in which we had just had. I guess that you could have called it good-psychotic-break-up-rough-sex.

Scarlet continued to promise and assure me in a sick sounding fashion that she was not gonna let me go. But what could I do? I left her house that day and I promised myself, that other than my wife, that there were gonna be no other women in my life, ever.

****

As it turned out, aside from enduring Scarlet constantly calling me and having her stalk me and aggravate me for like the last three months, I had managed to keep my promise to myself.

But three months down the road was all it took for me to reconsider the promise that I had made to myself the day that I had left Scarlet's crib. I mean I knew that Scarlet was a psycho-nut-job and that I had to stay on the run from her in terms of avoiding her and not being in close proximity to her, but I really didn't think that I was ever gonna be entranced by another woman in the manner in which Scarlet had managed to keep me entranced for the past five years.

So I guess you could say that during the three months after Scarlet and I had had our psychotic-good-rough-sex episode which was supposed to mark our official break up, that I learned a few things. What I learned is to never ever fall in love with a hoe and try to turn her into a housewife, and I also learned to never ever make a promise that I could not keep, even if that promise was made to no one other than myself.

Needless to say, three months was all it took, yet I was about to break the promise that I had made to myself when I said that there were never gonna be any other women…

ONE

I once heard a brilliant saying. It went something to the effect of, "A successful person will always put himself in a position to take advantage of an opportunity when it presents itself. Not only will the successful person put himself in a position to take advantage of an opportunity, but when that opportunity presents itself he will be the first one, if not the only one to spot that opportunity. After he has spotted the golden opportunity he will pounce on it with the vigor of a hungry ferocious lion, allowing nothing to let that opportunity slip away."

As I drove down Pennsylvania Ave., I suddenly realized that a golden opportunity was presenting itself. It was in the form of one of the most beautiful females that I'd ever laid eyes on. The ironic thing was that this golden catch was one that I'd let slip away in the past.

As she drove in her black Convertible I made sure to ride right along side of her.

"What is her name?" I agonized trying to remember where I knew her from.

When the light turned red I had time to recollect my thoughts. After sitting through torture for a minute and a half, it hit me like a brick. "She's that beautician!"

The light turned green. I thought to myself, "Lance, don't let this opportunity pass you by."

It must have been fate that brought us to yet another red light. At the light I stared at the captivating woman. I glared with the most lustful, awe filled stare that I could muster up. I wanted her to know that I was looking. If she returned the favor and looked my way I wasn't gonna be a punk and quickly turn my head away.

She must have felt my passionate stare, because she finally did look my way. Unfortunately, she didn't look for very long because the light had turned green again. But she'd looked my way long enough to smile as she nodded her head to the music on Hot 97 FM. Her convertible top was down, she knew she was fine. The look that I gave her was the start of an affair. Although I didn't even know her name, in my heart, I'd just committed adultery once again.

Again, it must have been fate that allowed us to continue to travel in the same direction. It was the same fate that caused the light to again turn red. I thought to myself, "I got a smile out of her at the last light," now seize the moment. "Lance don't let it pass you by."

I had to do something quick 'cause this traffic light affair was bound to end soon. So again I lustfully stared. She knew I was clocking her but she kept her eyes fixed straight ahead as she continued to nod to the music.

"Wave to her Lance," I intently urged myself. "Wave!"

I could sense the light was about to change. So, very lightly but hard enough for it to give off a sound, I tapped on my horn. She still didn't look my way. So I ambitiously tapped on the horn two more times. That time she had to hear it because I'd hit the horn a little bit harder.

Yes, yes, yes! I was mad excited because she'd finally looked my way. Being as cool as I could be, with my bald head glistening in the sunlight and with my shades on, I lifted my hand and said very softly, "Hello.'

This time I got no smile. She just stepped on the accelerator and my ego all at the same time. But Yo, I was a hungry lion and I wasn't gonna let this sly fox get away.

"Come on, just don't turn," I earnestly hoped. "Please let me get one more red light, please," I begged to myself.

Fortunately for me, as fate would have it, four blocks later the light did turn red again. I moved in for the kill. Without any hesitation I pulled up alongside of her in my white Lexus GS300. Right away I tapped on the horn three times. She looked. So I quickly motioned with my index finger for her to pull to the curb. I'd motioned as if I was a cop instructing a speeding driver to pull over. She smiled but she shook her head no.

Feeling rejected, I put my hands together motioning as if I was begging or praying and I lipped the words, "Please." She again smiled and shook her head to say no.

Man! The light was turning green. Not only that, Pennsylvania Ave. was running out and we were both about to reach the Belt Parkway which was my point of destination and probably hers as well. I didn't want to enter the parkway's jungle because then my fox would have surely escaped the grasp of my claws.

As the light changed she took off. I too hit my accelerator, I managed to stay neck and neck with her car as if I was in the Indy 500. Feeling a sense of urgency I vivaciously tapped on my horn to get her attention, which thank God I finally did.

Seeming kind of annoyed she lifted her hands, arms and shoulders as if to ask, what did I want?

"Pull over, I have to ask you something," I said, as I motioned towards the curb. I waited for her reaction. She gave me a look as if she was gonna suck her teeth and keep going.

Fortunately her right blinker came on.

"Yes!" I wanted to piss in my pants I was so happy.

After signaling to pull over, she sped up to pass me. Finally, I'd lured her in. I pulled right behind her, put my car in park and turned on my hazards. Feeling like a State Trooper, I got out of my car as if I was preparing to ask for her driver's license and registration, the dark blue tank top that I had on revealed my dark chiseled physique.

"How you doin'?" I asked as I approached the driver's door of her car.

She answered with a hello, then she added, "I had to pull over or you might have caused an accident. What's wrong with you?"

"Nah, I had realized that I knew you and I wanted to see if you remember me?"

She looked at me as if to say, "You better have a better line than that."

As I looked at her I felt star struck and perplexed. Then I thought quickly and said, "Nah but for real though, I wanted to know if you could cut my son's hair."

"How do you know I do hair?" She asked.

The ice was broken as I reiterated, "I told you I know you."

"From where?" She asked.

"You work in "International Hair Designs" on Franklin Avenue, right?"

She slowly looked me up and down trying to figure out who the hell I was. Then she answered, "Yes I work there."

"See," I said as I smiled, "I told you I knew you… And you probably thought I was trying to kick game to you or something."

She looked at me confounded. Slowly shaking her head while smiling at the same time, she asked, "So you almost killed yourself trying to run me down, just so you could ask me if I can cut your son's hair?"

"Word…See I'm not satisfied with the barber I'm taking him to now. You know like most barbers, my barber doesn't clean his clippers and all that. And I'm sayin', you know what kind of diseases you can get from dirty clippers."

She looked at me and proceeded to nod her head but she didn't say anything. I was simply in adoration, because I was speaking to someone so beautiful. I don't know where on earth I'd pulled that haircut story from, but it was a start.

As I attempted to protract the conversation I said, "Besides, I figure a female beautician probably isn't cutting sweaty men's heads all day, so their clippers should be a'ight, you know what I'm sayin'?"

She answered with a laugh, "Wait, first of all what is your name?"

"Oh, my name is Lance," I answered. "Excuse me for being rude."

"Hi Lance, I'm Toni, but you probably already knew that…"

"Maybe?" I responded, with a smile.

"Lance, you don't even know if I'm any good or not."

Instantly my hormones went daft with thoughts of good sex. I thought to myself, "Baby, I would bet money that your stuff is good."

Holding my hormones at bay, I responded, "If your work is as beautiful as you look then there won't be a problem."

"Oh stop," she jokingly said as she batted her hand at me, "you're making me blush."

Inside, my hormones were cheering insanely loud, as I said to myself, "Yes Lance, yes, you are the man!"

"Here," she said, "let me give you my card."

With her seemingly soft hands and her butterscotch complexion, she reached toward her dashboard area and handed me a shiny black card with gold lettering. As I took the card I couldn't help but notice the gorgeous airbrush design on her freshly French manicured fingernails.

She advised me, "On certain days it's mad busy in the shop so just call me or page me before you come in and I'll let you know how long a wait you'll have."

"A'ight that'll work," I said.

As I went to take her business card, I made a conscious effort to reach for it with my left hand. The reason being, my wedding band was on that hand. I wanted to make sure that the gold and diamonds blinded Toni. I didn't see any rings on her beautiful hands which let me know that she'd definitely taken note to the fact that I'm married. If there's one thing that I've learned in my five years of marriage it's that a wedding band on a man's hand can be spotted from one hundred yards away. Maybe because it's such a rarity, especially amongst young good looking cats like myself.

By her seeing the ring it accomplished a couple of things. It put some doubt into her mind that maybe I wasn't just some sexy nigga trying to kick it to her. I needed that doubt because unless she had no class at all and if she didn't fall for that haircut game, she would've written me off the moment we pulled away in our cars.

Toni appeared to be a high maintenance female, and most high maintenance females ain't trying to give no play to some guy they meet on the street, especially a guy that pulls them over in his car. They might give a guy their phone number or they'll take a guy's number, but in their head it's a whole different ballgame. They'll be like, "This player probably has all types of women. I ain't trying to mess with him 'cause I ain't gonna be another notch on his belt. Besides, he looks too good anyway. He probably thinks its all about him."

At this stage I didn't need negative thoughts like that flowing through Toni's head. My ring played a big part in killing that negativity and it left open the opportunity to push the right buttons later.

As I prepared to walk back to my car and put an end to this traffic light affair, I said to Toni, "Conduit avec precaucion." Which in Haitian Creole means, "Drive with caution."

Taken aback she responded, "Vous Haitienne?" Which means "are you Haitian?"

Walking away I said, "No but I know that you are."

Those were the last words I spoke to her as I got in my ride and drove off. Inside my heart I knew that she would be thinking about me, especially after I'd freaked her mind with her native language. I must admit that I 'reached' when I spoke those words of broken French. See, I have a thing about Haitian women. To me they are all that and a bag of chips. I've dated many Haitian women and I just learned to pick up on the language. I'm not fluent in the language, but I figured that I should at least make the effort to vaguely know the language of such fine sistas.

Her card said Toni St.Louis, which was a tip off that she was Haitian. Last names like St.Louis, or as she would pronounce it, "St.looie", and names like Joseph or Pierre are instant giveaways to a Haitian decent. Hey, I reached but it worked.

On the ride back to my house I fantasized about Toni. I wondered what it would be like speaking to her on the phone. I pondered to know what her feet look like. My heart rate was slightly accelerated as I felt happier than a kid on Christmas Eve.

After the twenty minute ride to my crib was complete I had to switch gears. I had to take off the Mac attire and don the husband outfit.

****

"Hey baby," I said to my wife as I walked in the back door.

"Hi Honey."

"Nicole," I said, which is my wife's name, "I've been thinking about you all day. I couldn't wait to get home to see you."

As a smile appeared across Nicole's face, she replied, "Really baby?"

"Yeah," I answered, "now come here and give me some sugar you sexy thang."

After taking off my shoes I made my way to the living room to catch the last fifteen minutes of Oprah. My wife sat next to me.

"So Lance, how was your day?"

"It was a'ight. You know, same ol' same ol'."

"Lance…"

Before my wife could ask me anything else I interrupted her by diverting her train of thought.

"Nicole where's LL?" LL is our son. The letters LL is short for Little Lance.

"He's here somewhere, he's probably watching cartoons or whatever."

"LL!" I screamed out to my son.

A minute later he came running and jumped on my lap while simultaneously slapping me five.

"What's up little man?" I asked.

"Nothing, I was watching Barney."

My son is the most adorable kid that you would ever want to meet. And he's the splitting image of his daddy. I just hope that when it comes to the gene that controls infidelity, that his gene is not a clone of his father's. I was feeling a little guilty so I played with my son for the remainder of the evening. I didn't really want to look my wife in the eyes for the remainder of the day. Not that I'd cheated on her or anything, it's just that for today I belonged to Toni. Actually my wife would have had a hard time stimulating me. She looks good and all, a banging body and the whole nine yards, but this evening I wanted to be mentally stimulated by Toni and no one else, not even Scarlet.

While we were eating dinner my wife caught me daydreaming.

"Baby, what are you thinking about?" She asked.

Startled like a little kid caught with his hand in the cookie jar I quickly responded, "Huh?... Oh, nothing. I ain't thinking about anything, just something that happened at work today."

"Oh, tell me what happened, was it funny?" She inquired.

"Nah. It was nothing," I said as I, like a boxer tried to back my way out of a corner. I'd just gotten caught out there thinking about Toni. I quickly excused myself from the table as I sought out a solitaire environment.

Later that night when the lights were out and my wife and I lay in the bed, we cuddled and pillow talked. I was hoping that she would go to sleep so I could reminisce about the traffic light affair that I'd had with Toni. Unfortunately my wife had other plans in store for me. Nicole's period had ended a day ago. Usually she's in the mood right after her "friend" departs, and tonight she was holding true to form.

Nicole began to kiss on me and caress my chest. Her friskiness showed signs that unfortunately she was in the mood. Uninterestingly I played my role as husband. I was praying that Nicole wasn't physically in the mood for an all star performance because I wasn't in the frame of mind to deliver one. No foreplay, no massages and all that. If she wanted it, she had better get me aroused, hop on and do her thing so I could go to sleep. Hopefully she'd climax before I did, but if not, I could have cared less.

TWO

More than a week had passed since I'd pulled Toni over in her car. She was out of my sight but she was always on my mind. I must have looked at her business card a hundred times. I had the beauty shop's phone number and Toni's pager number glued into my brain's memory. Just about everyday I've had to wrestle with myself to keep from calling Toni.

Saturday finally rolled around and I had an excuse to go to Toni's shop. Although LL was not in dire need of a haircut I decided to bring him to the shop anyway. Like always, LL objected to getting his hair cut. However after a little coaxing and a McDonald's Happy Meal, we found ourselves in the jam packed beauty salon.

I immediately searched for Toni. After I'd spotted her working at her chair, I calmly walked over to her.

"Remember me?" I asked.

Toni was in the process of doing someone's hair so she looked into the wall mirror that she was facing. She paused and thought for a second. Then she turned around with a curious smile and said, "Yeah, I remember you."

There was another pause of silence. Then I asked, "Do you have a lot of customers?"

"Well its Saturday, so it's always packed in here…"

"I brought my son with me to get his haircut, do you…"

"Oh that's right… Is this your son?... Oh he's so cute… Hey cutie. What's your name?" Toni asked while reaching to pinch LL's cheeks.

In a shy voice my son answered by saying, "LL."

"Oh he is so adorable… Didn't I give you my card? Why didn't you call before you stopped by?"

"Actually I wasn't gonna come today. It was a spur of the moment type thing."

"Lance, right?"

"Yeah."

"Well Lance you can wait if you want but I am mad busy. I should be able to squeeze LL in, in about an hour and a half. Is that alright?"

"That's cool we'll just chill. I might get a manicure to kill time, I don't know."

LL and I took a seat in the waiting chairs and I contemplated whether or not I should get a manicure. As I sat I couldn't help but stare at Toni. She had on a pair of navy blue spandex pants and a white tee shirt that was tied into a knot. With her belly button exposed, I noticed that Toni had what looked liked a red rose tattooed near her navel, and she also had another large exotic tattoo which was located at the base of her back right near the crack of her butt.

I knew damn well that I shouldn't have used my son as an excuse to go to see Toni, but hey. I was there and there really wasn't a regretful enough bone in my body that would have made me leave. As I sat with LL, I constantly kept glaring at Toni. I don't know why I'd done it to myself. I mean I'm married and all, yet here I was on a Saturday afternoon checking out a beautician.

I always told myself and believed that nothing would happen as far as me literally cheating, and so far in my marriage it hasn't, except of course for the five year thing that I've had on the side with Scarlet del Rio. But to me the "Scarlet thing" shouldn't really count against me because for one, I had got involved with her before I was actually married, even if I had only met her on the night of my bachelor party it was still before I had said "I do." And plus Scarlet was like my dual wife. In the hood she would be known as Wifey. And everyman, married or single, whether he is willing to admit it or not has someone other than his wife or his girlfriend that he would consider to be wifey. Wifey is the one he calls when things aren't going right at home. Wifey is the one who will have his back no matter what. Wifey is the one who will be down to do whatever, whenever, and wherever. Wifey is the one that knows about the real wife or the real girlfriend and doesn't flip out about it, in fact Wifey remains faithful to him even though he is tied down. Wifey "puts it on him" like no other woman.

But it just gets harder and harder to stay faithful especially when I keep feeding my lust hormones with women like Toni. I mean here I was trying to distance myself from Scarlet and permanently end things between her and I, and I've been doing a good job at that for the past three months, and yet I still let myself entertain and act on the thoughts of being with yet another woman.

Toni caught me gazing at her and she kind of down played it by waving to LL. Yeah I was busted, but any man in there right mind would be staring at Toni. Man, everything about her was turning me on. It's like every move she made was erotic, even if it was just her reaching for a pair of scissors.

"You're not getting your nails done?" Toni asked.

"Nah, I think I'm a just chill."

"Why not? I think that's cool when men take good care of their hands. It says a lot about them."

The girl who was sitting in Toni's chair getting her hair done, abruptly objected to Toni's statement.

"Any man with manicured nails is about one of two things. Either he's gay, or he's all into himself which means he ain't nothing but a good smelling - pretty dog."

Another beautician responded, "That's right girlfriend!"

Toni took the floor as she said, "That is not true. Just because y'all dealt with the wrong brothers in the past, that doesn't mean that a good man can't treat himself to a manicure."

This conversation was about to erupt into a full fledge debate. Therefore I'd decided to get up and just get the manicure. As I walked over to the nail technician, I gave Toni a high five for sticking up for the brothers. "You go girl!" I jokingly said as I walked past her.

The other beautician sucked her teeth, and sounding as ghetto as ever, she said, "Whateva! Men ain't nothing but dogs."

LL was still in his seat and after seeing my hands in two bowls of warm water he asked, "Daddy what you doin'?"

"I'm getting my nails done?"

"Ill that's for girls! Ill!" LL remarked as he frowned his face.

With half of the shop amused and laughing at my son, the comedian, I felt mad embarrassed. It was cool though, because the laughter also made me feel very relaxed in the ambiance of Toni.

After about thirty minutes of getting my nails cleaned, pulled pricked and tucked, I sat back down next to my son.

"Daddy let me see."

I showed LL my hands and he replied, "Your nails ain't all that."

Those who were in close proximity burst out into laughter as LL was slowly melting the hearts of every woman in the place. The boisterous beautician, whom I later found out was named Shaniqua, egged LL on.

"Good men don't get their nails done right?" She asked LL.

"Nope?" LL replied as he shook his head from side to side.

"See, even little shorty knows what time it is. I'm telling y'all, if you want a good man you better find a brotha with some rough, ashy, jacked up, mechanic type hands."

"And Shaniqua what is your man's name again?" Toni asked.

Shaniqua rudely snapped back, "I don't have a man!"

"Oh yeah, that's what I thought... Anyway, um Lance don't even listen to Shaniqua. She's just going through something."

I laughingly replied, "Nah I ain't sweating the small stuff. I'm sayin', I'm a secure brother. You kna'imean?"

I want to believe that I'm secure, but in actuality I am the most insecure man on this planet. It seems that all I do is done so that I can receive positive attention from females. All the time I spend in the gym working out and all those protein shakes that I drink, that's definitely not for me alone, and sadly to say, but it's not even just for my wife's pleasure when we're in the privacy of our bedroom.

What I wear, how I smell, how I'm groomed, the car I drive and how much I bench press is all done for particular moments, moments when there is nothing but nice looking women around and I'm able to make good eye contact with them.

See, women are not as blunt as men in terms of making the first move. Sisters are sly with their game. Excluding the women that are just out there whoring around, most women have game slicker than Luster's Pink Lotion on a Jheri-Curl. But with women, I've learned that it's all in the eyes. That's why I am all about eye contact.

After I'd sat back down, I continually tried to look into Toni's eyes to see what kind of vibe I would get. I looked in a way as to not make her feel uncomfortable, but at the same time, I wanted our eyes to lock.

Toni kept busy at her work as did the other beauticians. As Toni worked, the salon became increasingly crowded. I'd always heard good things from females about this salon. I was beginning to see first hand what all the hype was about. This salon, which has a great reputation, was often frequented by female stars such as Lil' Kim, Mary J. Blige and Faith Evans to name a few. The salon is also a Spa, and it is very spacious and elaborate. It's decorated with dazzling mirrors, leather couches, a nice big screen television and a surround sound stereo system.

There was a buzz that filled the air as women canvassed the parquet floors. In that buzz I was able to decipher some outrageous conversations. I wish that I had brought a tape recorder to tape some of the things that were being said. Some of the conversations and gossip was fit for a trash talk show. Other conversations actually taught me a thing or two. You had your "inspirational speakers," and of course you had your, "Amen / You go girl," conversations.

The women involved in those, "You go girl, slapping each other five conversations," made me think that they were auditioning for a part in the movie <u>Waiting To Exhale.</u> Like most women, these women had no mercy when it came to the way they were talking bad about men. Brothers that were not there to defend themselves were being labeled everything from dogs, to cheap, to no good in bed.

To me, that kind of talk gets sickening after a while. Throughout my life, I've learned something about women who participate in those "slapping each other five conversations." What

I've learned is that their memory is way too short. Most of those women are constantly complaining about being dogged, hurt or disappointed by men in the same way. To me, you would think they would remember the warning signs and realize when they are dealing with a dog. But no, they always con themselves into thinking "this one" or "that one" is *different*. And when this one or that one turns out to be the same as the rest, women turn around and label all men as no good.

Whether or not men are the problem, one fact remains about the "Amen / You go girl" women. That fact is that these women are always dishonest with themselves. They are dishonest because usually right from jump street they see the warning signs of a dog, and yet they con themselves and say, "But he's different."

To me, the "You go girl" conversations are nothing but a big justification party. Women need to start owning up, and accepting a big chunk of the responsibility as to why many relationships have no substance.

During the many conversations that were going on I managed to finally lock eyes with Toni for about three seconds. After those three seconds I felt as though I was a crack fiend who had his hit of crack for the day. I was convinced that Toni's eyes hadn't just caught my eyes in a passing glance. Rather she wanted to look my way. Her look let me know what she thought about me. In those three seconds she told me that she likes dark skin guys. And as far as my looks were concerned, her eyes told me that she thought that I had it going on.

Before long, it was time for LL to get in the chair and get his hair cut.

"LL can I cut your hair now?" Toni asked.

LL didn't respond.

"Come on LL don't show out in here! Let Toni cut your hair," I admonished.

As LL made his way to the chair I remarked to Toni. "That was fast, it didn't even feel like we were in here for an hour."

Toni responded, "Well, I figured while my other customer is under the dryer I'd take care of LL. I mean she's gonna be under there for about a half hour. Plus, my other appointment called and said she was gonna be late."

As Toni adjusted an apron around LL's neck, she asked, "So LL how old are you?"

LL kept silent but he managed to put four of his fingers into the air.

Toni responded in an alto tone as she said, "Wow, four years old! You're a big guy…"

LL smiled. Toni was making him feel very comfortable.

"So LL, how would you like your hair cut?"

"I want it like my daddy."

"Lance, he is sooo adorable! Toni said while smiling in my direction.

Toni quietly asked me was it alright for her to actually cut his hair the way my hair was. She wanted to make sure, being that I have a Michael-Jordan-style-bald-head. Unknowing to Toni, I seductively made my way closer to her and said, "yeah, it's no problem."

I was standing as close to Toni as I possibly could. The smell of her "Red Door" perfume was like an aphrodisiac. As I pointed out to Toni the sensitive areas of LL's head, I contemplated just pulling her close to me and giving her a kiss. Fortunately I had enough self control to not do that, but my heart rate was definitely accelerated so I decided to stand back a little.

LL was very calm in the chair. He's not like most kids that cry, kick and scream when they get their hair cut. As I stood next to Toni and watched her work, she advised me that I could take a seat if I wanted to.

I responded, "That's ok, I like being close to beautiful women."

After I said that, Toni looked at me, she didn't smile or respond. I was wondering had I just blown my cover. I had to change the subject quick.

"So Toni how long have you been doing hair?"

"Oh, for years. But I really got serious about it when I turned 18."

"That's good. And you're how old?…"

"I'm 24, why?"

"No reason. I was just asking. You know, being that you said you started seriously doing hair at 18."

"Yeah, I really just do this during my breaks from school. I'm in graduate school at Howard University."

"Oh word. That's kinda fly, an ambitious, intelligent, and talented woman."

Toni smiled. "Whew," I thought to myself. "Back on track."

LL was just about finished. It didn't take long to shave his little head. Toni asked was it alright if she put alcohol on his head to prevent any infections or bumps. I nodded in agreement. As Toni sprayed the alcohol onto LL's head he squinted in pain for about ten seconds. She then sprayed hair spray onto his scalp and applied powder to his neck.

To make LL feel good she said, "Now let me see my little man… Um, um, um, you gonna have all the little girls going crazy over you now."

LL replied, "The girlies are already sweatin' me!"

The other females in the shop fell out in laughter.

"Oh he is too much," Toni said while laughing. She reached for a bowl of candy and she gave LL a Blow Pop and a pack of Now & Laters.

"Thank you," LL said.

"You're welcome sweetie."

I asked Toni how much did I owe her. She informed me that they charge $7 for children's haircuts.

As I reached into my pocket I advised Toni that I would be bringing LL back in about two weeks. Then I nonchalantly handed her $30. After cordially telling her to take care, I took LL by the hand and prepared to leave. As we were walking out, LL stopped at a wall mirror to verify that his haircut was tight. With LL having no objections we continued on our way out the shop and headed towards my car.

LL and I were about to start the car and pull off when I heard Toni yell my name. She got my attention and ran over to the car.

"Lance, you know his haircut was only $7 right?"

"Yeah I know. And I gave the rest as a tip."

Toni asked, "Are you sure?"

"I wouldn't have given it to you if I didn't want you to have it."

Toni was quiet for a second. Then she looked at me and said, "Thank you... So, you're gonna be back right?"

"Definitely!"

Toni smiled her million dollar smile as she reached into the passenger window and pinched LL on his cheek. After which I started up the car but I didn't pull off until Toni had vanished out of my sight. As I drove off I was feeling good. My calculated moves were working. The radio in my car was blaring and I had a Kool-Aid grin on my mug. I was happy because I was envisioning all of the possibilities between Toni and myself.

THREE

My wife thought that LL looked cute, but she had objections to me having let LL get a bald head. Her reasoning was that if we allowed his hair to be cut too short at such a young age then there stood the possibility of his hair remaining short in the future. I simply told Nicole that LL had wanted a baldie, and that her theory was not a proven medical fact, just some old wives tale.

Fortunately for me, my wife didn't put up much of an argument. She isn't the argumentative type and neither am I. I would have to say that, that is one of the reasons why we have remained together for so long. However, that isn't the only reason that our marriage is healthy. My wife and I are both God fearing Christians. Yeah I know I don't come across like the God fearing type but "in my own way" I really am. My wife and I attend church service every week, but by far, we are not just Sunday Christians. Rather we are quite active in the ministry. We often lead bible studies, we open our house for Christian fellowships, and we regularly pray together.

I might not look like the religious type but I know the Bible from cover to cover. Yet the struggles that I have with lusting over women seem to keep me entrapped. My wife and I can talk about anything. I often tell her about my struggles, but my insecurities keep me from being totally honest. I'll tell my wife about women who might have come on to me at work. Or I might tell her about a past girlfriend that called the house to say hello, but never deep details, or dark secrets, dark secrets such as my affair with Scarlet. See, I'll tell my wife "insignificant" things because I know that she is a very secure person, actually she's too trusting. But then again, if according to God, a man and a woman become "one" at marriage, I guess she is only doing what is natural by trusting me.

By me only telling Nicole part of the real deal, subconsciously I'll feel as though I am confessing to her all of my shortcomings. But half truths are what have done man in since the time of Adam and Eve. I would never tell my wife about the many times I've sneaked and watched porno movies or the many times that I've found myself gazing at the dirty pictures in the X rated magazines at the local candy store. Not to mention the few times that I've found myself placing dollar bills into the garter of some naked, big butt, hips-gyrating female at the booty bar.

One thing that I'm certainly not proud of is the fact that I have a unique ability to hide my dirty deeds from everyone. Yet even though I am not proud of that unique ability to be a double person, there is something that I can guarantee and take to the bank right now and throw away the bank book because it is never gonna come out. In fact it will probably go to the grave with me, and that is all the dirt that me and Scarlet have rolled around in. Rest assured that I will never spill the beans to Nicole as far as Scarlet is concerned. Besides, now that I am ending things with Scarlet there really would be no future reason to bring it up to Nicole.

What is funny is, the relationship my wife and I have, make us the envy of many. We have financial stability, a house, two cars, a healthy child, we're young, educated, good looking, and the list goes on. As for me in particular, I'm viewed as the most positive black man aside from men like Michael Jordan, and Jessie Jackson.

It's scary, because although no one knows about the dirt that I do, it's as though I'm leading a double life. The thing is, I don't always consciously realize the possible consequences of my split life. I just find myself "doing things" that I have been conditioned to do from the past. Not that that's an excuse, but hey, I don't ever want to be viewed as just a little better than Satan.

****

Well, like every week, Sunday rolled around and I found myself in the front row of the church pews. I was singing songs, praising God, praying and the whole nine yards. Yet I still found myself thinking about Toni. Toni wasn't the only female that crossed my mind. I also found myself looking at the bodies of some of the sisters in the congregation (that too was becoming commonplace for me). It's mad wild 'cause the sexual thoughts just pop up out of nowhere.

Fortunately, throughout my sexual fantasies I also had a chance or two to pay close attention to the sermon, and I was very convicted by what was being said. But just how long would that conviction last?

After service was over, I did like I usually do, and that was, I sought out visitors of the church and made them feel welcome. I thanked them for coming and encouraged them to come again. I extended to them the opportunity to study the Bible and I was there to answer any biblical questions that they might have had. If one didn't know better, one would have thought that I was a pastor in training. Yeah, I had the charm and charisma of O.J. Simpson, but the guilt of being a Christian, slash sinner, was becoming very draining. I always wonder how long I'll be able to keep this up. I know that eventually I'm gonna either have to repent or just give in to my desires 'cause I can't keep playing both sides of the fence.

That evening after Sunday dinner was over, Nicole, LL, and myself were in the living room. LL innocently asked me if Toni could cut his hair from now on. His question sparked some curiosity in Nicole.

"Lance, you switched barbers?" My wife asked.

"Yeah," I nonchalantly replied.

"I like the way Toni cuts my hair," LL joyfully inserted.

My wife replied, "LL sure is crazy about this *Tony*."

"That's just because he got free candy when he went. Baby I forgot to tell you that I decided to try a new barber. A guy on the job got some type of infection on his scalp from dirty clippers, and he was using the same barber that we have been taking LL to."

"Really?" Nicole inquired.

Knowing that I was lying through my teeth, I jazzed up the lie by adding, "Yeah, these ghetto barbers don't take good care of their blades."

Then LL totally blew up my spot when he smiled and devilishly said that he thought that Toni was pretty.

"LL what are you talking about?... Wait a minute. Tony is a female?" Nicole asked.

Trying to down play it I simply said, "Yeah, women know how to give men hair cuts, you didn't know that?"

"I know that, I just didn't know that they had a woman working in the barber shop. I guess that unisex name threw me off."

I replied, "Oh, Toni doesn't work in the barber shop, she works in a beauty salon."

"Oh, where at?"

"In Brooklyn," I answered.

"Brooklyn? You went all the way out to Brooklyn for LL to get his hair cut?"

I had no idea where this line of questioning was going so I was trying to think of an evasive statement. Fortunately, LL spoke up.

"Yeah, and Daddy got his nails done like a girl." He said.

My wife smilingly asked, "Honey you got your nails done?"

That was my out. I had to divert Nicole's attention because I knew she was gonna ask who was Toni and where I'd known her from. I didn't want to be forced to lie.

"Yeah, I got my nails done. And you didn't even notice," I jokingly said. "Baby, I'm trying to make this marriage thing work, but if you can't even notice when I go out of my way for you and get my nails done, well I don't know..."

As my wife playfully slapped me, she gestured for my hands so she could examine them. Without warning, I took her hands and pulled her close to me and gave her a real passionate kiss. Although LL was in the room it didn't matter because we were always lovey-dovey around him. After the kiss my wife smiled at me. We both knew what time it was. I left the room and my wife proceeded to take LL to his room to prepare him for bed.

Later that night my wife and I made passionate love for about a half hour. Throughout the whole sexual encounter, passion was bouncing off the walls. I was hoping LL hadn't heard us or heard the bed constantly squeaking...

When we were done, I felt great because not once during sex did I think about Toni or any other woman for that matter. Nicole was the only person on my mind that night. We had a stimulating conversation as we cuddled in the dark and kissed each other until we fell asleep.

FOUR

My wife, who has a Masters degree in Forensic Psychology, works for the New York City Department of Probation. Basically, she is the boss to about fifteen probation officers. She has a very stressful job, it's like she is constantly taking on all of the stress that the probation officers feel. Plus, she has to deal with obnoxious judges, lawyers and district attorneys. Despite the stress, Nicole loves her job. But if it were up to me I would have her stay home with our son. Unfortunately, she sees her career as a very high priority in her life.

I work as a Service Technician for Con Edison. I started the job as a "co-op" when I was in high school and I stayed on and became a full time employee after graduation. Basically, I respond to all types of gas and/or electrical emergencies as well as regular service calls. The blue collar job is definitely not a glamorous job but it pays extremely well and with the benefits, I would be a fool to leave for something else.

I received my bachelor's degree in business by going to college at night. The company paid for the whole thing, so it was like I went to college for free. In the future I might look to move into management with the company, but right now I am more than happy with the position that I have. It's like I'm my own boss. I'm out in the field driving around all day by myself, except for the days that I ride with a partner. The beauty of the job is the freedom that it affords me while I work. Unfortunately though, the job can also get me into trouble. I say that because everyday I go into houses with gorgeous women and the temptation to flirt is always there. I also have to deal with seeing nice looking ladies when I drive around on the street. The battle that I have with preventing myself from approaching many of these females is enormous! But I would be lying if I said that I have never succumb to my hormones while on the job.

As a matter of fact, after searching the database in my brain, I realized that it was on the job that I first encountered Toni. A couple of weeks ago I'd received a service call for "*no hot water*" at International Hair Designs. When I responded to the beauty salon, I walked into the midst of chaos. There were about seven women who were mad as hell because they had to get their hair washed in ice cold water. I was like some sort of savior when I walked into that shop. I quickly put everyone at ease and I explained to them that it probably was just the pilot light that was out and needed to be lit.

Being that the spring was in full swing and the summer was right around the corner, it meant that it was time for me to show off my body. I accomplished that by cutting the sleeves of my uniform very high, about to the top of my triceps. That way whenever I carry my tool box, the weight of the box naturally would make my muscles flex.

I'd recognized Toni as I made my way to the dark basement to examine the water heater. She really hadn't paid me no mind but I was whipped from the moment that I walked past her and saw her. As for the other females that were in the shop, I heard them whispering and making remarks about how I looked. They were saying things like, "Girllll!" and, "Um, um, um!"

The comments were flattering, but I really didn't sweat it because I was zoning off on Toni. She had a real exotic look. What struck me the most was her butterscotch complexion, her nice eyes and her hair. I immediately noticed that her hair was the type of hair that doesn't even need a perm in order for it to be straight. Her hair looked as though if she were to wet it, it would be wavy. Her body was slamming from head to toe. She wasn't like bam! Bam! Boom! She didn't have one of those ghetto butts with a 1 to 2 waist to butt ratio or a chest like Dolly Parton, but she was very well proportioned and had more curves than an hour glass. I would say that Toni's measurements were about 34-25-40.

When I'd left the shop that day all I could think about was Toni. The first thing I did when I had reached home was I called my man Steve to let him know about my day.

Steve and I have been tight for years. In fact, he was the best man at my wedding, the man responsible for throwing me the wildest bachelor party on record. The bachelor party where I'd met and sexed Scarlet. The cool thing about Steve is that I can tell him anything. He knows that I'm trying to be sincere in my

Christianity, yet he doesn't trip if I join him on a visit to the booty bar. He understands what it is like to be a man. It's bugged because sometimes he says that I should have never gotten married, and then sometimes he'll say that I am the stupidest man in the world for even looking at another woman.

I feel mad at ease around Steve because when I'm around him I don't have to put on a front. I mean the majority of my other friends, who unlike Steve are from the church, they don't keep it real. By them not keeping it real it forces me to put up a front whenever I'm around them. If I ever mentioned to a church member that I looked at another woman, they would be ready to crucify me. But on the inside, I know that 95% of the men in my church if not 100% of the men have the same lust and sex problems that I do. It's just one of those things that no one talks about.

It's like masturbation. If you had one hundred men in a room and asked those in the room that masturbate to raise their hand, I would be surprised if five men raised their hand. What would happen is, you would get one hundred men who, in an attempt to hide their embarrassment or insecurity, would start laughing and looking around at each other. Very few, if any would dare to raise their hand. Yet, if you took an anonymous survey of the same one hundred men and asked them the same question, where absolutely no one would know the results, I bet you 95% of those that responded to the survey would indicate that they masturbate, married and single men.

To me it's like I know that I'm not alone in my struggles, because what on earth could these men be masturbating about? It has to be about the women around them that they are lusting over. Some of the men in the church keep it real, but not enough. So that's why I am always hanging out with Steve. My wife encourages me to hang out with men in the church, but I don't. I feel like its work just hanging out with people who don't keep it real. Then again, I guess that I am just as afraid to keep it real with them. After all, it's not like my struggles are a good thing.

I had called Steve and told him that I was coming by his crib to kick it with him. The moment I got to Steve's house, I flooded him with excitement.

"Yo Steve, it's over kid. It is over! I'm telling you I think it's over!"

Steve curiously questioned, "Man what's up? Whatchu' talking about? Get at me dog."

"Steve I saw the baddest female ever! Hands down the baddest. I mean slammin' from head to toe!"

Steve nonchalantly down played my excitement as he responded. "Yeah, and?" While looking at me as if to say he'd seen this routine before. "What else is new? Lance you tell me that ish on a regular. And I keep telling you it don't matter how good a woman looks because there is always someone else out there that will top her. It's a bottomless pit. There ain't no end to the madness!"

"Steve but yo, I don't know? I had a job in this beauty parlor today and I'm telling you, there was this female, man she was all that and a bag of chips! Yo she had that fly Brazilian look that I like, you know?... Her look was different than Scarlet's, but man... Her hair was slammin', her complexion, her shape, her eyes..." I paused, then I devilishly laughed as I added, "Yo, I know that her toes have to be the bomb! I'm sayin', as good as she looks, her toes must be all that! Steve you know I'm a foot man, no doubt."

Steve sarcastically replied, "So let me guess. You're coming to me with your sob story about how you don't know how it's gonna last between you and Nicole. And you feel mad guilty about creeping because you're a Christian and all that ish, but yet you're ready to turn this new hoe into your housewife."

"Steve, yo like I said when I first walked in the door, I really think that this time it's over between me and Nicole. I love her and the whole nine, but I can't keep putting myself through this."

"Through what nigga?!"

"Through what?"

"Yeah, through what?... First of all, did you get the digits from this new chick?"

"Nah but…"

"Did you even kick it to her?"

"Nah see, you…"

"Lance, tell me that this chick was at least flirtin' with a brotha?"

"Nah, yo let me explain."

"Lance, you never seen this chick before today, you didn't kick it to her, you got no phone number, and she wasn't even giving you any rhythm. What I'm trying hard to understand is why the hell are you ready to leave your wife?... I hope it ain't over this chick! Wait, hol' up, tell me you at least know her name?"

When Steve got no reply from me, he burst out into belly ache laughter. His laughter was uncontrollable. Watching him come to tears in laughter, I too had to give in to the humor of the situation. After almost regaining his composure, Steve laughingly said, "See, that's exactly why that marriage thing ain't for a nigga. Lance, you got a dimepiece wife and yet you ready to leave her for someone who you never even spoke to! Lance you still getting skinz at home. I can understand the married men that have reluctantly become recycled virgins. I can see them wanting to creep or bounce. But you… Ha ha ha ha ha… Yo!"

Steve continued in his laughter.

"Steve you keep laughing. I bet you you'll be in my shoes one day. Watch!"

Steve tried to keep a straight face but he couldn't. He started laughing again as he said, "There ain't no way in hell I'm gonna be in your shoes! Why the hell am I gonna get married if I'm gonna cheat? I can do that by staying single! Plus I'm not the church going type or anything like that, but if there is one thing that I have learned from Jesus, it is to stay away from that marriage thing. I mean think about it, if marriage was all of that then why didn't Jesus get married? He didn't get married because he was smart enough to know that niggas need to avoid that *marriage thing* like the plague!"

"Whateva kid. Just mark my words, I'm gonna bag that chick and when you see how she looks, that's all that will be necessary. I won't have to say a word 'cause the joke will be on you."

Although Steve took my feelings for Toni as a joke, I became determined to prove him wrong. As a matter of fact I was determined to keep Steve in the dark about Toni until I was at least up to bat with her. I haven't even told him about the roadside encounter that I had with her and that had been like a week ago.

FIVE

When the start of the work week rolled around, I realized that I had to refocus and take care of the home front. I started the week by waking up early and surprising Nicole with breakfast in bed. I carried a tray that held a plate of scrambled eggs, French toast and a small glass of orange juice. When I woke Nicole up, she was truly surprised.

"Ohhh, thank you baby. You are so sweet!"

My wife proceeded to sit up properly in the bed and she reached for the tray. As she reached for the tray she simultaneously closed her eyes and puckered up in a request for a kiss. I on the other hand, purposely caused my lips to miss her lips and instead I planted a kiss on her cheek. Then I jokingly informed, "The breath baby. The breath is kickin'! Let's keep it real, it is six in the morning and you haven't seen a toothbrush."

With that, we both started laughing. Nicole snapped back at me and she said, "Yeah, that's why you still got eye boogers caked in your left eye."

Again we burst into laughter. I playfully tapped Nicole on the head with my pillow before making my way to the kitchen to grab my breakfast tray so I could join her in eating. When I made it back to the room I said grace and we began to eat.

"Lance, I love when you surprise me like this."

"I know. That's why I did it. There's gonna be a lot more surprises like this so be prepared."

As we ate and talked, I realized that marriage was made for moments like the present one. I constantly need to remind myself of such. As we ate we discussed the highlights of the passionate sexual encounter that we had engaged in about eight hours ago. We told each other how much we loved each other and how we wished we could spend the whole day in bed. But we knew that Mondays were never fun and we were actually spending too much time in bed as it was. If Nicole didn't catch the 6:59 train she would definitely be late for work. So we put the trays out of the way and we rolled around in the bed and hugged for a couple of more minutes. Then Nicole went to take her shower and to get dressed.

As Nicole got ready to leave, I woke LL up so he could see his mother off to work. And as was the case every morning, after LL kissed his mom good-bye, he ordered a bowl of Fruity Pebbles and proceeded to make his way to his usual location which was in front of the television to watch cartoons. With Nicole out of the house it seemed as if the morning was flying by. I got LL dressed and I too got dressed. Before I knew it, it was time to drive LL to the daycare center. LL and I would have a ball every morning during our ten minute ride. I enjoyed our morning rides because LL and I would always converse. Our conversations allowed me to teach LL so much about life and answer all of his poignant questions.

We made it to the daycare center and I signed LL in for the day. LL's teacher was married and although she was about ten years older than me she had it going on. I was always thoughtful enough to let her know it. His teacher would always smile and laugh whenever I flirted with her. She also would warn me that she was gonna tell Nicole, but I knew she was just playing. See, the way I figured it, my flirting was definitely healthy for the both of us. Healthy in the sense that the attention that LL's teacher got from me had to be flattering being that I'm a younger man and all. She is probably very much in love with her husband so I knew that nothing would come of my flirtatious ways. And for me, it was healthy because it allowed me a good way to keep my game sharp. I was never rude to LL's teacher or obnoxious, so to me it was always a harmless and playful thing.

After I dropped LL off I attempted to make my way to my car so that I could head to work. Notice that I said that I'd "attempted" to make my way to my car. When I'd walked out of the daycare center I noticed that Scarlet del Rio was leaning against the drivers' side of my car. She had her butt pressed up against the glass and her arms were folded in a defiant confrontational manner.

My heart kind of dropped to my stomach because Scarlet had shocked me with her presence. She was the last person that I had expected to see.

Even though my heart had dropped to my stomach I calmly prepared myself to walk across the street to my car and confront Scarlet. But I knew that I had to play things cool in order to diffuse any possible violence on Scarlet's part.

"Well isn't this a pleasant surprise," I said as I leaned and kissed Scarlet on her right cheek as she continued to stand with her arms folded across her chest, displaying all kinds of attitude.

"Lance don't come at me like that!" Scarlet barked.

"Oh boy, here we go!" I thought to myself.

"Come at you like what?" I asked.

"Like everything is cool between us, you all kissing me on my cheek and talking about 'isn't this a pleasant surprise,' yet your ass don't know how to call nobody!"

As Scarlet began to raise her voice I didn't want her causing a scene because I didn't know who was around, and the last thing I needed was someone at LL's day care center calling Nicole and telling her about the huge confrontation that her husband and some beautiful voluptuous Brazilian woman had in front of the building.

"Scarlet go to the other side of my car and get in so that we can talk," I said as I pressed the button on the remote to my car's alarm.

"I don't feel like sitting in your car! Why can't we talk out here in the open!?"

"Because, Scarlet you're causing a scene! Now either get in the car or I'm outta here, I don't need this!"

"Oh you don't need this!? And I suppose you think I do need this!? I don't need this either and I don't deserve to be treated the way you've been treating me!"

As I brushed Scarlet out of the way in order to attempt to open the driver's door of my car she started flippin' out, she began screaming and started attacking me like she'd lost her mind.

"Don't you put your hands on me! Who the hell do you think you are!?" Scarlet yelled as she started throwing a series of right hooks to my head. She wasn't exactly a small woman that couldn't hold her own in a street fight. She was a heavy handed momma who was originally from Uptown who could practically hit like a dude. So needless to say, I was feeling every punch that she threw, not to mention her accuracy was right on point as each blow that she threw was landing flush in my face, head, and neck.

"Scarlet get in the car!" I screamed. "Are you crazy or something!?"

"Lance you're gonna talk me and you damn sure are gonna apologize for putting your hands on me!"

Although I knew that I had not put my hands on her, I had merely bumped into or brushed her body as I attempted to open my car door, I simply wanted to put water on this fire ASAP because people had begun to take notice of the two of us.

"OK OK! I'm sorry for putting my hands on you... Now please calm down! We can talk but lets just do it like civilized people. So please, just go to the other side of the car and get in and we'll talk about whatever it is that you want to talk about."

Scarlet was breathing a little heavy from the anger that had built up inside of her. She didn't respond verbally to me, she simply pulled down the tight skimpy short sleeve shirt that she was wearing which had managed to ride up a bit and expose her stomach. The shirt actually looked like it could fit my twelve year old cousin, but that was beside the point.

As Scarlet got into my car she made it a point to slam the door as hard as she could.

"Come on Scarlet, it doesn't take all of that!" I said in a raised voice.

"Lance you are so wrong! How could you be so cold? It's like I might as well have fallen off the face of the earth because you just completely cut me off and I don't think that is fair because I haven't even done anything to you. I'm always leaving messages on your cell phone and paging you and you never return any of my calls! Lance I don't deserve to be treated like that!"

"Baby... First of all calm down. Both of us need to just calm the hell down! I mean its way too early in the morning for all of this. Like I said when I first saw you, it is a pleasant surprise to see you. But what isn't pleasant is all of the yelling and screaming and punching. Don't you know that you don't hit like the average woman?" I asked in a joking manner as I took hold of Scarlet's hand and gently pulled her closer towards me.

As we hugged, I remember the smell of her Gucci perfume turning me on like crazy!

"See doesn't this feel good?" I asked.

"Lance of course it feels good. And that's why I'm so hurt. I don't get to touch you, kiss you, feel you, talk to you, and you seem like you don't even wanna give me *none* anymore."

I moved my lips close to Scarlet's lips, and after our lips were perfectly aligned I began tonguing her down. She was acting like an animal that had been caged up for weeks and was ready to go on a sexual rampage.

As I kissed her I managed to slip my hand in her pants and get her even more turned on. I didn't know where things would lead to so I wanted to quickly move from in front of LL's day care center. Even though I had dark tinted windows I still didn't want to take a chance of freaking Scarlet right in front of the day care center.

"Baby I want you so bad," Scarlet moaned.

"I want you to," I replied, "But we just can't do it right here in front of the building."

So as Scarlet sat up in her seat and adjusted her pants, I started up the car and I drove around the block. And before I could find a real good secluded spot to park, Scarlet had unzipped my pants and she had my privates in her mouth and she was getting busy.

See, I had genuinely wanted to sit and talk things over with Scarlet but apparently she had other plans and I wasn't about to interrupt her. I simply sat back closed my eyes and enjoyed every minute of the early morning surprise blow job.

When she was done, *swallowing* and all, and asking me if I enjoyed it, she wiped her mouth, looked at me and said, "Lance, don't just shut me out of your life like that."

Now what was I suppose to say? I didn't really want her feeling like a cheap two dollar hoe, and I didn't even feel that she was, I had strong feelings for her, I mean she was still Wifey, but I just had to stop seeing her and being with her. Five years was way too long and I had to hold my ground.

But like an idiot I replied, "Scarlet I'm not gonna shut you out and you know that."

"You promise?"

"Yeah I promise."

Scarlet attempted to move closer in order to start kissing me again, but I wasn't trying to hear that. I mean she had just went down on me, and I didn't wanna be tasting all of *that*, even if it was mines.

"Baby I gotta bounce, I'm gonna be late for work," I quickly blurted out in order to avoiding her tongue from landing in my mouth.

"Lance forget that job! I keep telling you that I make enough money to support us. You don't even have to be bussing your ass everyday the way that you do. Just play your cards right with me."

"Yeah I know. That offer always sounds tempting but... I don't know... See, Scarlet why do you do this to me?... I gotta hurry up... But I promise you, that we will speak. I'm gonna call you and we'll hook up. I promise. But you just have to promise me that you're not gonna be popping up and flippin' out on me like you did today. That's what scares me about you. I mean how do I know that you're not gonna do that when Nicole's around?"

"Lance you know that I wouldn't do that to you. I mean I accept the fact that you're with Nicole. She's number one to you and I know that. But I damn sure am gonna be *number two*, you better believe that! And as long as I don't see you with some other chick you don't have to worry about me. Just keep me happy and satisfied."

My head instantly began spinning from Scarlet's twisted logic.

"OK, Scarlet I hear you. But *trust me*, there is no other *number two*. A'ight?"

"OK I trust you, but I'm just putting you on notice. I know you gotta hurry up and go to work so just drive me to my car around the block."

I quickly circled the block and made it to Scarlet's pimped out black Mercedes Benz S600.

As she got out of my car she kissed me on the lips and said, "I better here from you."

"You will. Don't worry," I said as I watched her walk to her car with her 36-24-48 measurements. "Damn! Look at that!" I said to myself as I shook my head and lustfully stared at Scarlet's body.

I quickly gathered myself and rushed off to work. I knew that I would have to think of something in order to get Scarlet del Rio completely out of my life. "But then again," I thought to myself, "I could really be a hoe and stay with Scarlet and Nicole and still try to bag Toni all at the same time."

I knew that it would take a lot of hard work but I didn't have too many other options. Otherwise Scarlet was bound to throw all kinds of monkey wrenches into the whole program that I had planned for Toni. My head was spinning from the pressure so I told myself to just keep Scarlet completely blocked out of my mind until I could think of a good enough plan.

"Yeah Lance. Just forget what you just told Scarlet. Keep things the way they have been for the past three months. Don't call her, don't see her or anything. Just block her out."

I tried to take my mind completely off of Scarlet as I wondered if there was any plausible excuse that I could muster up to see Toni later on during the day. I drove myself crazy trying to think of something. Finally I realized that it was Monday, and in New York City, most beauty salons are closed on Mondays. As I continued to drive to work, I thought to myself that during the work day, while I was on my work route, I would drive past the beauty parlor just to make sure that the shop was definitely closed.

By the time one o'clock in the afternoon pulled in I decided to make good on my promise. I drove past the shop and everything held true to form, the shop indeed was closed. Inside, I kind of felt real empty. It was like I had built up all this excitement and anticipation of possibly seeing Toni, but with the shop closed, I felt like a deflated balloon. For the remainder of the work day I had the most dejected feelings running throughout my body. I couldn't even concentrate fully on my work. I felt like a Crackhead that needed a hit in the worse way. I kept telling myself "just call her." I wanted to at least speak to her but I really had nothing to say. It wasn't like she was a friend of the family or whateva. And if I called her, I didn't wanna call her with no "Mac of the year," player lines. I simply decided to scratch that idea.

Enough was enough. I had to convince myself to stop sweating this "Toni chick." I had to get the thought of her out of my head. It was almost three in the afternoon and I still hadn't taken my lunch break. So I decided to pull into a McDonald's drive thru. As I spoke my order into the menu-board I realized that the female that was taking my order sounded very sexy. I was wondering how she looked. I told myself, "I bet you one hundred dollars that when I pull around to pick up my food that she will be the most busted looking female you ever wanted to see." I loved placing bets like that with myself just to test my theory. It's called the "McUgly / McSlammin' Theory."

The theory states that any female that takes your order at the drive thru and sounds sexy, is almost guaranteed to be ugly. But if she sounds regular or even if her voice sounds a little masculine, then it's highly probable that she will be slammin'. So after placing my order I pulled around to the pick up window. And man was my theory wrong! The girl that came to the window definitely had it going on. Although she looked as if she was barely old enough to have her working papers she still had it going on.

She was a young Spanish chick with crazy long hair. She was even able to fill out those stiff but loose polyester pants that are part of the McDonald's uniform. When she reached for the money I held onto it so that she would have to tug on the money when she grabbed for it. After she realized that I wasn't going to let go of the money she looked at me and repeated the price.

"Yeah, I know how much it is," I replied. "I just wanted to look at you a little longer. You don't mind do you?"

She didn't respond. She just smiled and took the money.

When she came back with my food and the change, I noticed that her name tag said Carmen.

"So Carmen how old are you?" I asked.

"Sixteen," she replied with another smile.

"Would your man mind if you gave me your number and I took you out?"

"I don't know?"

"Listen my name is Lance. Carmen, I was thinking, why don't you just give me your number and I'll call you? I mean I don't wanna hold up the line or get you in trouble."

Carmen quickly wrote down her number and gave it to me. As I drove off she instructed me to take care. I put her number on the dashboard of the work van that I was driving. I placed it there like I've done with literally hundreds of phone numbers in the past. I knew I wasn't gonna call her. I mean I'm not one to rock the cradle or anything. She was a little cutie so I'll just make sure I stop back at that McDonald's and I'll go inside next time to take a better look at her body. If the body is whack then I can still gas her for some free food or something. I knew that sixteen years old was way too young for me. For some reason I would always bug out with myself and think stupid thoughts about young girls like Carmen. I just hope my thoughts won't get me locked up one day.

Well at least Toni was out of my mind. My lunch break was over and as for my cupcake job, I only had to sit around and do nothing for another twenty minutes and after that I would be on my way home. I decided to past the twenty minutes by digging into the pile of my X-Rated <u>Black Tail</u> magazines. I gazed at the magazines and got my heart racing a little and then I was ready to bounce for the day. The remainder of the day passed with no unusual occurrences. The only unusual thing that happened during the remainder of the day was Scarlet blowing up my pager and my cell phone like some deranged nut job. She had to have left like twenty messages for me and I didn't return one of her calls. I knew that would really just piss her off but hey, what could a brotha do?

Finally evening time rolled around and I could have won an Oscar for the way I romanced my wife. As I romanced Nicole I was feeling like a little kid on Christmas Eve. I couldn't wait to go to sleep and wake up the next morning and open my present. I just hoped that Santa would bring me Toni in some form or the other. Toni was the last person that I thought about after my wife and I said our prayers and lay waiting to fall asleep.

SIX

Tuesday was upon me and I was as vibrant as an aerobic instructor. I was ready to conquer the world. Even my wife, before she departed for work had commented on what a good mood I was in. I guess I was subconsciously excited about the prospect of seeing or speaking to Toni.

Unfortunately as the day played itself out, I still had no plausible excuse to go see Toni or to call her for that matter. I thought that at least if I went by her shop while I was working, I could play it off like I was just in the neighborhood and had dropped by to say what's up.

But that was how I would approach going to see someone like Carmen or any average female for that matter. I had to pull out all the stops with Toni. I decided to go ahead with something that I had been contemplating for the past two days. I called up 1800FLOWERS and had them send Toni two dozen roses. I told the operator of 1800FLOWERS that I wanted the card inside the flowers to read:

Dear Toni,
> *Just the thought of you brightens my day. So I hope that the smile on your face from being surprised will brighten your day.*
> *-With love, from Your Secret Admirer-*

I didn't care what the cost of the flowers were. All I knew was that I really felt good about having them sent. In my mind I was convinced that Toni deserved the flowers. It makes me feel good just knowing that I would be making someone else feel good. Women melt from things like flowers and love letters and the like. I think that they melt more so due to the fact that someone took time out just to make them feel special. Hopefully Toni would be melting over my anonymous gesture.

****

I have to admit that later on that night as my wife, Steve, LL and I watched the NBA playoff games I felt a little guilty about having sent Toni the flowers. But I blocked out the guilt and went on like everything was normal. I was cheering my team on. I had my Heinekens and a full tray of Buffalo wings so in actuality everything was quite normal. I was giving LL and Steve high fives and kissing my wife whenever a clutch basket was made. The beer was giving me a little buzz, and coupled with the elation of having surprised Toni, it made it easy for me to block out the guilt.

Earlier that same evening, I had caught Steve up on all of the latest details between Toni and myself. I told him how I was planning on calling her the next day and seeing if she'd received the flowers. Steve's response, well, he simply shook his head and laughed at me. But again I warned him that he wouldn't be laughing when he sees Toni.

Nicole, who is very comfortable around Steve, had on some tight shorts and a tee shirt, just your regular relaxing type of gear. When she got up and went to answer the phone Steve tapped me, and while pointing to Nicole he asked why would I cheat on, "That." Having no reasonable response, I smiled and responded with, "Yo kid, I'm just sayin'."

It's mad ill because it's like men have this un-penetrable code of silence when it comes to cheating. Like, I could have just told Steve that I had had sex with Toni an hour ago. Yet he would be able to look Nicole in the face as calm as ever, kiss her on the cheek and comment on how great her food is and the whole nine. Similar to what he has been doing. See, like any other guy, Steve knows how to play the game. And if roles were reversed I would play the game the same exact way. Men never took a class on this stuff and we don't even have to discuss how to do it. But we had to have learned it somewhere 'cause it just oozes out of us too damn smooth. I would bet that LL was subconsciously learning how to play the game by just being around us and we didn't even know it.

When Wednesday showed up I couldn't wait to call Toni. I'd been wondering if she'd actually received the flowers. I was starting to lose my mind. I was thinking thoughts like, "what if she chose not to come in to work on Tuesday? What if she thinks the secret admirer is some other punk that's sweating her?" All kinds of thoughts were rambling through my mind.

As usual, when I work I carry my cell phone with me. Today was no different. I decided to wait until around 11 O'clock in the morning to call Toni. I figured I would catch her before she was real busy with customers. I felt a little nervous about calling her, but those jitters were normal. I would say that most men are a little nervous when they make that first call to a female that has got it going on. I had no idea what I was gonna say or how I was gonna say it but that usually works better for me. I knew that I had to just come at her as myself so that she would at least sense the sincerity.

I dialed the shop's number and it rang twice. But before someone picked up, I quickly pressed the end button on my cell phone. In turn, what I decided to do was I decided to page Toni and put in my cell number for her to call me back. My reasoning was, by having Toni call me it would help break the ice a bit. So after I paged her I simply went about my business as usual. I didn't want to be sitting around with sweaty palms and all that. But I did however keep an eye on my watch, and noticed that it was only ten minutes later when my cell phone rang.

I answered on the first ring but I tried not to sound too eager as I said, "Hello."

"Hi, did somebody page Toni?"

I was screaming inside. Toni had actually called me back! She sounded sweeter than ever.

"Yeah, how you doin' Toni? This is Lance."

"Oh, Lance what's up Boo?"

"Boo?... Ah man! That was all I needed to hear," I reasoned to myself. If I never spoke to Toni again it would have been a'ight 'cause she called a nigga Boo. Yo, plus she knew right off the bat who I was. I decided to get right to the point and not beat around the bush. So I donned my Mac voice and replied.

"Nothing much, I was just calling to see how you were doing. And I wanted to know if you liked the flowers that I sent you?"

There was a quick moment of silence. The silence was followed by a childish sounding laughter of embarrassment.

"Lance, you sent those flowers?... I was trippin' the whole day, trying to figure out who they were from. Yes, of course I liked them! That was so sweet... But..."

Before Toni could mess up the flow and throw acid all over my program, I interrupted her by macishly playing down the situation.

I picked up Toni's words in stride. "But, but, but... What? What was you gonna say?... Listen, before you say anything, I just wanna say that I'm glad that you liked the flowers. And I also wanna ask what if I drop by your job tonight and pick you up? And after I pick you up, why don't me and you go to Juniors restaurant?"

Toni chuckled and said, "Lance, whoa, slowdown. Slowdown... I heard of being straightforward, but man... Lance, like I was saying, the flowers were very nice and thoughtful... But I can't go out to eat with you."

"Why not? All I wanna do is take you to get some cheesecake. That's it. No strings attached... A'ight? We can eat cheesecake and talk about a few things."

"Talk about a few things like what?"

"Things..."

There was another brief pause. Then I heard a sigh, followed by a short laughter.

"Oh my God, Lance... Alright, I'll go get some cheesecake with you."

"Yes, yes, yes, yes, yes!" I screamed in my head.

Toni then pessimistically added, "Lance, I don't even really know you. I mean..."

I quickly interrupted. "Toni, like I said, no strings attached, I just wanna talk to you about a few things."

"But Lance, by the time I get off I'll look too through. You don't even wanna know how busted I'll look by the time I leave here... Plus I ain't even dressed to go out."

I responded, "Toni, don't worry about how you'll look. See, you making this more than it is, we just gonna eat some cheesecake, you don't have to be dressed for that, right?"

"Yeah ok... Lance I gotta go. It's getting hectic in here."

I joyfully said, "Oh no problem, so what time does the shop close?"

Toni replied, "I'll be leaving here around eight."

"Eight O'clock is good. I'll pick you up from the shop."

"Lance, why don't I just meet you in the lobby of Juniors, at let's say... eight thirty? ... It doesn't make sense for me to leave my car here and then afterwards have you drive me back to the shop to pick it up."

"That's true. OK so I'll see you at eight thirty. You know where it's at right?"

"Yeah on Flatbush Avenue, downtown."

"OK, so I'll see you later."

"OK bye."

After that conversation I had to check to see if my pants were still dry.

"I knew it!" I confirmed to myself. I knew I could bag that. I knew it! Ever since I looked into Toni's eyes at the shop that day, since then I knew I had it locked. Yeah, if I was some busted nigga that had nothing going on, Toni would never have accepted my offer. But she saw the face, the Lexus, the muscles, and the bald head and that's why she accepted. This date had been confirmed ever since the day I pulled her over on Pennsylvania Avenue.

I tried to calm down and concentrate on the rest of the day, but it was extremely difficult.

About fifteen minutes after having confirmed the date with Toni, I called my older sister Tiffany to make arrangements for her to pick up LL from the daycare center. Tiffany had no problem with doing me the favor. In fact she often looked out and picked

LL up for me when I would work overtime or something. When I was done speaking to my sister I immediately called Nicole.

"Hi Baby."

"My wife, sounding very excited and surprised said, "Lance! Hi honey. What's up? I'm glad to hear from you."

"I just had to hear your voice so I decided to call you."

"Really?"

"Yeah. You know how much I love you?... Right?..."

Nicole responded with a laugh and I added, "What?... You think I don't love you or something?"

Nicole giggled then she replied, "Nah, I know you love me."

"OK, just making sure. I have to stay on top of those kinda things, you kna'imean?"

After telling me that I was crazy, Nicole laughed. I interrupted her by saying, "Oh yeah... Listen, baby I wanted to let you know that Tiffany is gonna pick up LL. So you can pick him up from her house when you get off?"

"Why, what happened?"

"Well, my supervisor just asked me if I could work until about ten tonight."

"Until ten? Lance, tell him you can't do it. Did you forget about Wednesday night Bible class at the church?"

"I knew it! Man! I knew I had something to do. Man! I already told him I would work late. See we had this big Gas Main that broke and we have to restore about eight hundred homes that have no gas."

My wife, sounding disappointed said, "Well, if you already told him you would, and being that it's an emergency, I guess you have to work. So I'll see you around eleven, right?"

"Yeah, that sounds good. Oh Nicole, don't worry about dinner 'cause I'll just eat Chinese food or whateva."

"OK, but Lance you know we've already spoken about your work hours interfering with other things. I don't mean to be nagging you but you can't keep putting your job before God."

"I know baby, but I really can't help it tonight. A'ight? We'll talk about this later ok? I love you."

"OK, I love you too, bye."

It's not easy, but lying comes so natural to me. It's to the point that when I lie it doesn't even feel like I'm lying. It's especially hard when it comes to lying to Nicole. But like always, I just mentally block out the wrong that I do. As for missing Bible class so I can creep with another woman, I definitely feel horrible. But I block out the feelings of guilt, the guilt of leading my wife to think that I'm "husband of the year", when actually I'm using my skills to dis her. Yeah, that guilt I block out very well. I mean I don't let those feelings sit in my conscious mind 'cause if I did there would be no way that I could carry out my devilish actions. Yet the dark side of me wants to go ahead with the evil deeds. It's that dark side that rises out of my subconscious and plays itself out consciously. But the guilt and all that, I always quickly force it back to my subconscious so I won't drive myself insane.

When work was over I rushed home. I was excited like crazy. I blasted the basement stereo as I showered and changed clothes. I knew that I had to be in and out of the house quickly so that I wouldn't get busted by my wife or anyone who might see my wife later on in the evening. Before I left the house I called the dispatching office at Con Edison and informed them that if my wife called that they were to call me on my cell phone and let me know, but by no means were they to tell her that I had already left for home. In reality I knew that if my wife needed me that she would just beep me or call me on the cell, but I still had to cover all my bases.

Before I knew it, it was a little past seven and I was already parked and waiting near Juniors. It's so ill, but as was the case with any given day, as I sat in the car I found myself thinking some sick sexual thoughts. I would say that I easily think about sex, some six times or more every hour of the day everyday. I'll fantasize about a woman that I saw during the course of the day, a sexual encounter I had when I was seventeen, the topless dancer that I saw, it didn't matter, sex of some sort was always on my mind.

Being that I had some time to kill I decided to try to reach Scarlet so I called her at her house. When she picked up I stated,

"See, I kept my promise. I told you that I was gonna call you and I did."

"Lance?"

"Yeah this is Lance. Oh you done forgot my voice that quick or are you confusing me with some other cat?"

"No I didn't forget your voice. It's just that I only paged you and called you like two days ago and now you wanna return my call!?"

"Scarlet you know that if I ever don't return your call it's because I'm with Nicole. You know that."

"Oh so you're saying that you have been with Nicole for 48 hours straight!?"

"Got damn Scarlet! Damn!... Why do you always come at me with so much drama!? It's like lately every time I speak to you or see you, you come at me with some rage and drama! And you expect me to wanna eagerly gravitate to that!?"

"Lance listen! Don't even go there! Because it is not about me and you know that! You are an expert at spinning the situation and making it seem like I'm always the one to blame. But how the hell do you think I'm supposed to feel? You didn't have no problem with me going down on you the other day! Did you!?... Of course you didn't! I guess that wasn't no 'rage and drama' at that moment because you was getting something out of it! And then you got the nerve to not even return my calls. You tell me, how the hell am I supposed to feel?! Tell me because maybe I got this whole thing twisted!"

Well she did have a point. I mean I guess that was foul, considering that she had serviced me quite lovely that morning I could have at least called her during the day or even the next day so that she wouldn't feel so cheap and whorish. But at the same time Scarlet was forgetting that I had told her that we had to stop seeing each other. Why couldn't she just get that through her head? And she must have had some short term memory lost because I had never asked her to go down on me.

In a very calming tone I replied, "Scarlet, see you are getting things twisted. I had never asked you to go down on me. You took that upon yourself to do that and plus…"

Scarlet immediately and rudely interrupted me, "What!? Oh my God! Lance I can't believe you would even say something like that! You were the one that was reclined back and enjoying it! Why the hell didn't you tell me to stop!?"

"Come on, you know that no man in his right mind would tell a woman to stop in the middle of some head unless it wasn't good!"

"Lance you know what!? That just proves that you think it's all about you! You really are only thinking about yourself and looking out for yourself so I guess that I should just do me and not even worry about you."

"Finally!" I thought to myself. Scarlet was finally getting it.

"Scarlet, see it might come across that way but deep down you know that it is not even like that."

"Lance I don't know what to think. But I guess that deep down you don't even know what you want. 'Cause I know that this has nothing to do with Nicole, because Lance I know and you know that you can't ever be faithful to her so why are you even fooling yourself? Lance just admit it. This is all about you getting with somebody else. You think that I'm stupid!?... Yeah when everything was new and exciting and I was the hottest stripper in New York you had no problem being with me! Right!? But now that the whole fantasy is wearing off you feel like it's time for something new, and you figure that you'll just dump me and move on to the next best thing!"

"Scarlet, that is so far from the truth and you know it! Because if it was about wearing you out and moving on to the next best thing then tell me how did I stick around for five years? I could have easily moved on to the next best thing much sooner. Why can't you just respect my wishes and know that the best thing to do is to give me some space, permanent space, and we'll just see how things turn out!"

"Lance, I have told you this time and time again. And I will tell you again. I am not gonna be your third option and I know that that is all that this whole 'space' thing is about. Now I'm gonna end this conversation by telling you this: You better start spending more time with me! And be very clear on this, when I find out who this *other chick* is, Lance it is gonna be on! Let me find out! I am telling you Lance you better handle you business because the moment that I suspect some sloppiness I am gonna be right there all up in your ass!"

And with that Scarlet hung up the phone on me.

Man I needed that type of drama like I needed a whole in my head. I knew that I could not be *sloppy*, there was no room for not even one false move. I knew that for my sake, and for Nicole's sake, and even for Toni's sake, in fact, especially for Toni's sake because up until now Toni was mad innocent and totally oblivious to all of my ways, and the last thing I needed was for Scarlet to find out about Toni and roll up on her or something. And believe me Scarlet would have no problem in *rolling* on Toni.

Although I had to keep Scarlet in "cut-off status" I knew that I had to use the only weapon against her that I had. And that weapon was between my legs. Yeah in my mind, Scarlet was history and she would remain history in my mind. But so that she wouldn't cause World War III I knew that I would have to keep Scarlet satisfied with some good sex. Spending quality time with her was really not an option, because after all there is only twenty four hours in a day, and I was determined to get things jumped off with Toni which was sure to occupy a lot of my time. But I guess for the sake of peace, that I would have to make time to break Scarlet off some pipe here and there.

When eight O'clock came, I decided to make my way inside Juniors. I went to the bar and ordered a rum and coke. The drink helped me relax. While I sipped on the drink I contemplated taking off my wedding band but I knew that Toni already knew *what time it was*. Besides, I ain't even trying to play no, "I'm single and available crap," because that requires too much work. I'm a keep the marriage thing real with her.

Being that it was a Wednesday night the restaurant wasn't that busy. The Wednesday night waitresses weren't all that either. But that didn't matter 'cause I knew my girl would have it going on. I must admit that for a moment I started to get paranoid. I was thinking, what if Toni stood me up? She didn't seem like a no class lady, but on a first date I knew to expect anything. Deep down I doubted that she would stand me up. Besides, if she was gonna stand me up I know she would have had the decency to call me on the cellular. Again feeling paranoid I thought, what if she'd erased my number from her pager and had no way of reaching me? I looked at my watch and noticed that it was seventeen past eight. My phone hadn't rang so I thought it was safe to assume that Toni was on her way.

I finished my drink and I just parlayed. I had on a pair of black jeans with a beige short sleeve tight fitted shirt, and some casual shoes that looked like ankle boots. I didn't want to be too dressy being that Toni was gonna be coming with her work gear on.

Well at least work gear was what I thought Toni would be wearing. As I made my way from the bar and to the restaurant's lobby I saw Toni looking as good as ever. She had on black high heels with stockings, and she had the bomb dress on. It was some kind of slinky material that clung close to her body. Her outfit almost caused my mouth to have to be scraped from the floor. After having picked up my fallen jaw, I walked over to Toni and hugged her.

We both were smiling as we greeted one another.

"Look at youuu... You certainly look very lovely. Now what was all of that, 'I'm gonna look through. And I won't even be dressed to go out?' Yeah, y'all sisters are all the same. Always tryin' na make a brotha look bad."

The ice was crazy broken. I always seem to make women feel very comfortable around me.

Toni smiled and responded by blushingly saying, "I know, I know but I just can't go out looking busted, so I went home real quick and changed."

"Um, um. That's cool. I'll let you slide this time. I mean I definitely ain't mad at that dress."

Toni laughed.

"Lance, I'm sorry I'm late. Were you waiting long? There was so much traffic on Atlantic Ave., that's what took me so long to get here. If I hadn't gone home to change I would have been here on time."

"Oh nah, don't sweat that. I was chillin'. Do you want a drink before they seat us?"

Toni decided that it would be best for us to just order drinks once we were seated. The restaurant isn't the classiest of places but it's one of those good first date places. The ambiance is mad cool, with nice music in the background, its a'ight.

When we were seated I said, "Now Toni, you look very gorgeous and I know you had a long day at work, so I hope you don't tell me that all you want is cheesecake. I mean it's a'ight if that's all you want, but I'm a keep it real and let you know that I am starving."

Toni laughed and she waved her hand at me in a "Sister-Girlfriend" kinda way. "First of all, that cheesecake thing came out of your mouth. A sista definitely ain't shy, so you better believe I'm gonna order some real food and we can have cheesecake for dessert."

We both laughed and I said, "Yeah a'ight, there's definitely nothing wrong with a sista with an appetite."

As we both studied the menu I found out that Juniors was one of Toni's favorite places to eat. I on the other hand had been to Juniors on a number of occasions but I never actually ate the food, I would always order their world famous cheesecake. When the waiter came to take our order we decided to get Buffalo wings as an appetizer. For the main course Toni ordered shrimp parmesan with linguine. I decided to go the traditional route with pork chops and rice. Although it was way too early to order dessert, we decided to get it out of the way. So we both ordered small cheesecakes. As far as drinks went, I ordered a Long Island Iced Tea and Toni requested a Strawberry Daiquiri.

When we were done ordering, Toni shot right at me.

"OK Mr. Lance, so why did you send me the flowers?" She said while smiling.

I smiled as I explained, "I just wanted to do something nice for you? I like making people feel good."

"Oh, so you go around sending everyone flowers?"

"Nah, I'm not saying that. I mean, I do that for people that I feel are special."

Toni laughed and asked, "Oh, so you feel that I'm special. Why, because of the way I do hair?"

I tried not to smile or laugh, I wanted to get things on a more serious note. After all, I had no idea as to how long this opportunity was bound to last or if I would get another opportunity like this again.

"Toni, I'll be honest. I really don't know you at all. But I do know that you seem like a very unique person, and what I'm sayin' is, I feel as if something special could happen between us."

By this time the waiter had come back with our drinks and our Buffalo wings. Toni smiled her beautiful smile, sipped her drink and then she proclaimed, "You know what Lance? If I was younger I would be falling head over heels for you. I mean you're a very attractive man and you seem like you have a lot going for yourself. But I'm not as naïve as I used to be."

I had a feeling as to where Toni was going with this but I played dumb. I took a sip of my drink and I looked right into her eyes as I commented, "I don't understand what you're saying."

Toni replied, "Well, let me not jump to any conclusions. What I mean is that I think you have a lot of game?"

Sounding astonished I asked, "Why do you think that?"

Toni reached over the table and grabbed my left hand. Her hands felt as soft as cotton candy. While playing with my wedding band Toni asked, "Lance is this a wedding ring?"

Without hesitation I confidently replied, "Yeah."

Toni let out a quick chuckle and she asked, "So you are married?"

Again I confidently replied, "Been married for five years."

I guess Toni wasn't expecting my confident answers. Sounding confused she questioned, "So Lance what are you doing here with me?"

"See Toni, I'm here because of questions like the one you just asked me."

Toni responded, "Come again, you lost me."

By now the waiter came with the main course. We both adjusted our seats and place settings to make ourselves a bit more comfortable. After commenting on how good everything looked we began to eat. I continued with my explanation. I was trying to cause Toni to have sympathetic feelings for me.

"Toni, what I'm saying is that it gets frustrating being married, because everyone expects you to conform to some set of rules or what have you. As soon as you go out of bounds they want to crucify you. Take tonight for example, what's wrong with me taking you out to eat? I mean it's not like anything sexual is gonna happen. Can't a married man go out to eat with a female?"

After chewing her food, Toni responded, "See, first of all does your wife know that you're here?"

"That doesn't matter," I replied.

"Yes it does matter. Second of all do you find me attractive?"

"Toni there isn't a man alive that wouldn't find you attractive."

Toni continued, "OK, so your wife doesn't know that you are having dinner with someone that you find attractive, that right there is a problem. Let's not mention that I happen to find you attractive. See you're right, it's not a crime for us to be here eating. But Lance, why play with fire? You're an intelligent man. You know exactly what can come about when two attractive people of the opposite sex go out to eat. Especially when the married person's spouse has no idea he's where he is, doing what he's doing. Plus you even said that you feel something special could happen between us or something like that."

I knew that I had to switch subjects so I did.

"Well, Toni let me ask you, are you in a relationship?"

"Yes. As a matter of fact I am. But it's a long distance relationship and you know how those relationships go. I mean I'm trying to make it work but he's all the way in Las Vegas. We met in grad school but he's finished with school so he won't be coming back for the fall semester."

I could have made a stupid comment by asking her, why, if she was in a relationship, was she here with me? But I didn't want to go that route. I iterated, "Well, long distance relationships can work if you want them to."

"Yeah I know that, but Lance he's similar to you. He's young, has a lot going for himself and I have to be realistic. I mean I know he's probably with some whore right now dropping the same bull that most men run. I look at it like this, I am not tied down to anyone and I don't have to live as if I am."

"See Toni, you just hit my situation right on the head. I mean I always feel like I locked myself down at too young of an age. I didn't get all of the game out of my system before I committed to marriage. When I got married I really loved my wife. Matter of fact, I still love her. But at the time I wasn't ready for marriage. I thought I was, but I just wasn't. Plus she got pregnant and all. You know how that goes."

"Lance, I understand what you're sayin', but you made a commitment so honor it. I think that when it all boils down to it, it's just about self control."

I cut a piece of my pork chop and I said, "Yeah that's true. See Toni this is all I want from you. I just want a friend. You can help me out with my feelings."

By now the drinks were getting to both of our heads, we were both feeling a little nice. Toni laughed and said, "OK, I'll be your friend. But you probably got a million other 'friends'."

"Nah, that's not my style."

Toni stated, "Lance, when you left the shop with your son, the women in that place were going crazy. They were ready to take off their panties and throw them at you for you to autograph. I know you probably get women going crazy over you wherever you go."

I was feeling like the man. But I down played the comment. Acting better than Denzel Washington, I looked Toni in her eyes. I shook my head and frowned as I explained, "Nah, Toni, honestly I'm not about that. I'm not out here trying to get off with every woman I see. By no means am I an angel, I mean I know I have things about me that I have to deal with. But I'm not a dog. I'm past that dog stage of chasing women or catching them when they throw themselves at me. See you're stereotyping me, and if anything, I think that I and many other men are just misunderstood."

We were both just about finished eating our food. I requested the bill from the waiter, and I asked him to put Toni's cheesecake in a box because she was not gonna finish it but she wanted to take it home.

The bill came to fifty three dollars, so I handed the waiter $60, leaving him a seven dollar tip. It was now about half past nine. As we made our way out of the restaurant, my ego felt crazy good because I had this trophy walking by my side and mad brothers were clocking her.

Toni had parked a couple of blocks away from the restaurant. So being a gentleman, I walked her to her car. We talked as we walked. Toni defended the comment that I had made about her stereotyping me. I on the other hand was trying to be as charming as possible. When we got to her car I asked if she'd enjoyed herself. She informed me that she had.

"So Toni can we be friends? That's all I want."

Seeing right through my game, she smiled and said "Yes, we can be friends but Lance you better…"

Toni stopped in the middle of her sentence. I begged for her to continue.

"I better what?"

"Nothing. Nothing Lance." Toni said as she, being as classy as ever reached to shake my hand. I placed my right hand into her right hand and she said, "Thank you for everything Lance. Get home safe ok?"

Feeling cocksure, I asked, "Toni, can I have a hug good night?"

My heart started to race. It wasn't racing in a nervous way, it was racing in anticipation. Kind of like when you're just about to have sex for the first time with someone. Toni held open her arms which meant that she had accepted my proposition. Toni is about five feet six inches tall, but the heels that she had on brought her to about five feet ten inches. Me being six three meant that when we hugged, her face was planted just above my chest. I hugged her firmly so that she could get an idea of how hard my body was, but not too tight as to hurt her. Toni's long wavy, which was let out, came down to about her shoulder blade. So while hugging her I simultaneously stroked her hair a couple of times with my right hand.

While still hugging her I cautioned her, "You make sure you get home safe too. A'ight?"

Toni replied "OK," and she prepared to step into her car.

Trying to show as much chivalry as possible, I closed Toni's driver's door for her. She waved goodbye and I walked off and headed toward my own car. I felt like doing cartwheels or jumping and kicking my heels together. I was ecstatic. I blasted a slow-jam tape as I drove home in my Lexus. Everything went great. I couldn't have asked for anything more. Inside I knew that Toni was mine if I pushed a few more buttons. However, I would be walking on thin ice being that I'm married and all. So one false move and I could ruin everything. I was excited but I was also kind of scared. See it wasn't even Toni's intentions to have me falling head over heels, yet I knew I would sell my soul for her.

As I approached my Colonial home which was located in a beautiful middle class section of Queens, called Cambria Heights, I noticed that the kitchen and bedroom lights were on. I didn't want my wife to see me because I looked to clean to be coming home from nearly a double shift of hard work. Plus I still had Toni's beautiful scent on my clothes. I definitely was not going to activate the automatic garage opener because that would make too much noise and I would be busted. So I parked in front of the house and I sneaked around to the seldom used side door. My heart was palpitating 'cause I had no idea if my wife was looking out of the window watching my every move, nor did I know which part of the house she was in.

I opened the side door and headed straight for the smaller bathroom which was located near the kitchen.

When I'd safely reached the bathroom I yelled real loud, "Hi Honey. What's up LL? I'm home."

Then I locked myself in the bathroom and immediately began to run water in the sink. I could hear my wife's footsteps coming from upstairs. I sat on the toilet bowl even though I didn't have to use it. My wife reached for the bathroom door and tried to twist the knob but it was locked.

"Lance, open the door?"

Speaking over the running water I replied, "Baby you know I don't like you watching me when I'm using the bathroom. I had to go real bad, I've been holding it since about eight O'clock."

Nikki responded, "Lance, how long have we been married? You know I don't care how you look when you use the bathroom. I miss you, I haven't seen you all day."

"A'ight baby I'll be out in a minute. I'm sayin'. I'm not doing a number one, I'm doing a number two."

Nikki sucked her teeth and responded, "Just hurry up."

I immediately stripped naked, and turned on the shower. I took probably the quickest shower on record, dried off and walked upstairs to my wife. When I saw her she didn't look like she was in a good mood. I immediately became suspicious. What if somebody saw me at Juniors? What if Scarlet had called the crib or did something sick and twisted in order to raise Nicole's suspicions? What if this? What if that?

"What's wrong baby?"

Nikki quickly and bluntly said, "Nothing."

I walked out of the bedroom and went to check on LL but he was already fast asleep. I went throughout the house and turned out all of the lights. When I came back upstairs I tried to make conversation.

Sounding very anticipating I asked, "So baby, how was Bible class?" What did y'all learn?"

My wife looked at me and rolled her eyes.

"Nicole what's wrong?" I asked.

"Lance how are you gonna just walk in the house and not even greet me? I haven't seen you all day. At least come and kiss me when you walk in."

"Honey I'm sorry. Really, like I said I just had to go real bad. It was one of those hard number two's."

I know my wife very well and I knew that at that present moment all she wanted was for me to shower her with affection to prove that I was really sorry. So that's exactly what I did. I rubbed her body and kissed her all over.

"Come on baby, at least give me a smile. I said I was sorry. Please…"

Nikki just looked at me and acted as if she was pouting. I knew that she wasn't really mad so I began to tickle her. "Come on let me see a smile," I said, as I vigorously tickled Nicole. Nicole finally gave in and started laughing. "Yeah, see I got you laughing now," I said as I continued to tickle her. "You gonna tell me what Bible class was about? Or do I have to keep tickling you?"

My wife couldn't take it anymore and she yelled while laughing, "Ok, ok, stop, I'll tell you."

I stopped tickling her and she kept laughing. She finally calmed down and explained that the class was about a passage in first Corinthians which explains how it is wrong for there to be divisions in the church, and that there should be no favoritism at all, just one church united in doctrine and way of life.

"That sounds like it was a deep class." I exclaimed.

Nicole affirmed that it indeed had been a deep class. Then she added, "See, Lance that's why you can't miss the classes. How are you gonna grow spiritually if you're not around for the lessons?"

Feeling very convicted and knowing that my wife was absolutely right, I put up no argument. "Honey you're absolutely right and I have no excuses. All I can say is that it won't happen again."

Nicole added, "That's what I wanted to talk to you about tonight."

While Nicole was speaking, I turned off the lights and we lay in the bed talking in the dark.

"Lance, we have a good marriage but I want it to be perfect. I feel that if we both are truly committed to the same spiritual things then we won't have no problems at all in our marriage. What I'm saying is that I can sense that in the past month or so you have just been going through the motions spiritually. And if there is something wrong or something that you're holding back, then you should tell me or at least speak to one of the older brothers in the congregation."

I responded, "Nah baby I'm ok. It's just that I haven't been as focused as I should be. It's all a matter of having the right focus and lately I've been focusing on things other than God. I can't blame it on the nice weather that we've been having or on my job, nothing like that. It's just me, I have to refocus and I promise you I will."

My wife explained that she didn't want it to seem like she was making a big deal out of nothing, she just wanted us to be on the same page. I told her that I understood exactly where she was coming from, and I thanked her for caring about me in that way.

Nicole then switched subjects and asked, "So was it good?"

I immediately got suspicious. Nervously I asked, "What? Was what good? What are you talking about?"

Nikki replied, "Your number two."

Realizing that Nicole was joking, I replied, "Oh! You silly fool." I grabbed my pillow and playfully smacked Nicole in the head as I said, "Don't worry about what I do on the throne."

We both began laughing. When we were done horsing around we hugged and kissed and we said our prayers for the night. When the two of us were done praying together, I continued to quietly pray on my own. I prayed real long and earnestly then I just stared into space. I knew that my preoccupation with Toni was affecting my whole inner being. My preoccupation was bound to start manifesting itself in other areas of my life. I thought about being honest and telling my wife how I really felt about Toni. I also thought about talking to a neutral person as to how I was feeling on the inside, a neutral person other than Steve. Someone like the pastor of my church, 'cause unlike Steve I know that the pastor would hold me accountable for my actions.

The reason that I felt like spilling the beans to someone was because Toni was causing feelings in me that literally scared me. She caused something more than infatuation. It was a totally different feeling than I ever got from being around Scarlet. I was scared because deep down inside I knew that the feelings that Toni was causing me to have were the type of feelings that would make me seriously contemplate getting a divorce and starting over with Toni. Scarlet or no other woman had ever made me seriously consider that, because with Scarlet and anyone else for that matter I always knew that it was really nothing more than serious lust and infatuation.

I lay in thought for nearly a half hour. And I came to the conclusion that it was way too early to start confessing, because when I truly observed everything I realized that I hadn't done anything wrong. I mean for all I knew, there stood a good chance that nothing at all would jump off in terms of Toni and myself. With that in mind my thoughts switched to how good Toni had looked this evening. I thought about the fact that she actually told me that she was attracted to me. I was so happy. Again I managed to block out everything my wife and I had just spoke about. I blocked out my religious convictions and I just envisioned the possibilities between Toni and myself.

I looked over at Nicole and I noticed that she was sound asleep. I wasn't really horny or in dire need for sex, but the thought of masturbating came into my head. I contemplated doing it... Then I changed my mind and just lay there. I could have awakened Nicole for some sex but like I said, I wasn't really feeling horny.

After about five minutes of not being able to doze off, I found myself gently removing the covers from on top of me. I quietly snuck out of the bed, I was praying that the box-spring wouldn't squeak. At that point the last thing I wanted to do was awaken Nicole. After I'd made it out of the bed I softly walked to the bathroom. I pulled down my pajama bottoms and sat on the toilet bowl.

It must have been that demon that has been inside of me since I was twelve years old that conned me to do it. He sprang to life and caused me to close my eyes and make love in a ménage-a-trios with Toni and my sister-in-law as I masturbated.

SEVEN

During my 27 short years on this planet, I've learned that women are one big ball of emotions. Not that they break down and cry at every sad moment, nothing like that. Rather, what I've learned is that, the way to a woman's heart is through her emotions. In a relationship, women need to know that men care about them. They need to hold hands. They need to receive the flowers, the cards, the letters and the romantic dinners. But women, more than anything need conversation before they can truly *connect* with a man. Men on the other hand are completely the opposite. What drives men are all of the physical things.

See I knew that in order for me to really bag Toni, I would have to put my physical needs aside, and concentrate on her emotional being. The evening after our dinner date I decided to page Toni. It was very late in the evening, probably close to eleven thirty. But I had to speak with her in order to start developing that emotional bond. The reason I had waited so long in the day before I called was because I wanted Toni to wonder whether or not I was gonna call her. If in fact she had been wondering about my phone call, it would only have caused her to be filled with anticipation of my call. Hopefully when she hears from me, that anticipation will turn to excitement.

Being that I didn't know Toni's home telephone number I couldn't just call her at her crib. Also I didn't want to page her and have her call me back at my house. After all, my wife was sleeping and how would it look if she were to answer the phone and hear Toni's voice on the other end? What I did was, while my wife was sleeping I snuck downstairs to the basement of our house. I decided to page Toni from the basement and have her call me back on my cell phone. The basement is the area of the house we use when we want to entertain a large number of guests. Our basement is hooked, we have the big screen television, the bar, the Jacuzzi and the whole nine yards.

Anyway, I was hoping that Toni hadn't fallen asleep or went out for the night. Fortunately when I paged her she returned my call right away. My cell phone rang and I quickly answered.

Cautious, as to not speak very loud I kept my voice kinda low, which actually made me sound "Barry Whiteish."

I answered the phone by asking, "How you doing Toni?"

Toni sounding as if she was half asleep, responded, "Lance?"

"Yeah this is Lance. Were you sleeping?... I was calling to check up on you."

Toni quietly laughed and she replied, "No, I wasn't actually sleep. I was watching the VIBE show, but I was just about to fall asleep."

"Can you talk?" I asked.

"Yeah. I can talk."

Then I asked, "So, did you make it home alright yesterday?"

Toni now seemed to be a bit more alert as she replied, "Yeah, I had no problems. I'm a big girl, I can take care of myself."

I laughed as I asked her had she eaten her Juniors' cheesecake. She informed me that she'd tried to eat just one slice of the cake and save the rest for another day but she couldn't. Shamefully she admitted that she became addicted to the Juniors cheesecake and had eaten the whole thing in one sitting.

"Lance, that cheesecake was calling my name! I tried to put it down but I couldn't. I was like a dope fiend or something. I felt so bad, but I just kept eating and eating. It was like I would close the box and attempt to put it back in the refrigerator, but I just couldn't. It was so sad... I definitely gotta get my ass to the gym this week!"

"So what," I exclaimed. "It's not like you're fat or anything. You can splurge every now and then."

Toni agreed, "Yeah, that's true... So Lance, where are you at? Why did you get in touch with me so late?"

"I'm at home."

Toni asked, "Where's your wife? And, by the way, did you tell her about our little date last night?"

I purposely wanted to avoid Toni's first question but I was willing to bounce around her second question with a politician like answer.

"Well, let's just say that indirectly my wife had an idea of where I was at."

I could feel that Toni was smiling as she asked, "What does that mean?"

"Don't worry about that…"

There was a brief silence. Then I asked, "So are you happy to be hearing from me?"

"Yes, actually I am happy to hear from you. But had you really cared whether I'd made it home safely you would have called earlier."

I knew Toni wasn't serious, so I just laughed and explained to her that I had been busy.

"So Toni, is it alright for me to call you at home?"

Toni laughed and replied, "Lance you're married."

"Come on Toni."

"Lance I'm serious! I see we have to have a serious talk because I can see where things might be heading."

"So let me have your number and we can have our serious talk over the phone."

Toni, seeming as if she must have been smiling while at the same time shaking her head asked, "Do you have a pen?"

"Yup."

Toni gave me the number and I copied it down. Then I instructed her to get a pen as I gave her my pager number. I tried to give her my cell number but she told me that she already had the number in her pager's memory. Then for some stupid reason, I told Toni to take down my home number. I guess I was trying too hard to falsely convince her that I only wanted to be her friend.

"You're giving me your home number? Lance what about your wife? What is your wife gonna think?"

"Toni why are you sweating it? My wife will be cool with it."

Toni asked, "What's your wife's name again?"

"Her name is Nicole."

"Oh, so you mean that if I call with my soft sounding voice that your wife wouldn't flip? Imagine me saying, 'Hi Nicole, this is Toni. I'm a friend of Lance, can I speak to him?'"

I laughed and explained, "Toni you can call whenever you want to call. I wouldn't have given you the number if it wasn't a'ight."

Toni sounding confused and unsure said, "OK if that's what you say."

Switching subjects I asked, "So who do they have on VIBE tonight?"

Toni told me that Patti Labelle had performed on the VIBE. Just like everyone else was accustom to doing, Toni explained to me that she had been switching back and forth, watching both Keenan Ivory-Wayans show and the VIBE. She was irate over the fact that the two shows aired at the same time. Toni also mentioned that Michael Jordan had been on Keenan's show.

"You know, you kinda look like Michael Jordan." Toni remarked.

I laughed as I said, "If I had a dollar for every time that I heard that, I would be a millionaire."

Toni explained, "No really, you do look like him."

I responded, "Yeah and if it's not Michael Jordan, people tell me that I look like Malik Yoba. All it is, is that people see me, a dark skin brother with a bald head, and automatically I look like some bald headed superstar. Soon people will be telling me I look like R. Kelly."

Toni began to laugh, "That's not true. It's not just because you have a baldie. I don't think you look like no R. Kelly or Malik Yoba but you do look like Mike. And Mike has it going on!"

Just craving to have my ego massaged, I asked "So then you must think that I got it going on too?"

"Lance I already told you that I think you're cute. But you're married and I ain't down with OPP."

I didn't want to go back in that marriage direction. My mission was accomplished, I had my conversation with Toni. Subconsciously I could tell that Toni was being drawn to me. I wanted to end the conversation here so as not to spoil anything.

"A'ight Toni, I'm a bounce. But listen, I'll probably be bringing LL by the shop in a week or so."

"No problem sweetie. Just call me and let me know. So yeah I'm a hang up too and get some sleep... Alright, so good night."

I pressed end on my cell phone and just sat there. I couldn't believe that I had balls enough to give Toni my home number. I wasn't too worried because I didn't think that Toni would actually ever call me at my rest stop. Plus I knew that Nicole wasn't the type to yell and scream and get ghetto if another female were to call. I just couldn't believe that I had let myself get to the point where I would stoop low enough to freely give out the home digits. In the back of my mind I was thinking how I wanted to sex Toni in the worse way. I knew that it could be a reality but I would just have to wait on it.

Until that time of glory came, I would just have to get off on the times that Toni tells me that she thinks I'm cute, or when she calls me boo or sweetie. I could always reminisce about the hug she gave me after we ate dinner, or the way her hands felt when they touched mine. As I turned out the lights and proceeded to walk upstairs, I wondered when would the need for phone calls to Toni wear off? When would the thoughts of her hugging me, not be enough?

My heart began to race as I pondered kissing Toni. I thought to myself. "I bet you her tongue feels like a water fountain." I couldn't wait to make love to her. I wondered how soft her thighs would feel. I fantasized about performing oral sex on Toni the first time I got the chance. Usually a female would have to wait for that privilege. That is a privilege that is reserved for only the elite. Toni was elite material and I knew that her cat was clean and disease free so it wouldn't be a problem. I smiled like a pervert just thinking about the possibilities between Toni and I. The last thought that I had before I laid down next to my wife was I visualized Toni in a pair of red thong panties and no bra preparing to make love to me.

As soon as I lay down, my wife turned over and hugged me. My wife had unknowingly, but tragically interrupted the fantasy I was experiencing with Toni. Being that the fantasy had been interrupted, I willingly kissed my wife and I began to caress her body. Just thinking about Toni had turned me on to the point that I was ready to have sex. I woke my wife and asked her if she wanted some.

Sounding very tired and despondent she asked, "Now?"

Seeming as though I was some sort of freak, I responded with a desperate plea, as I said, "Yeah. Now!"

Then I kissed my wife on the forehead and tried to set things in motion but my wife wasn't having it. "Nicole. A'ight?... Wake up."

"No baby." She said while pushing my hand away from her crotch. "In the morning."

After being rejected, I was irate. My blood pressure was raised to its boiling point. Had I been a cartoon character you would have seen steam flowing from my skull. I didn't know what to do with all that pinned up energy. My hormones were going wild and all I wanted to do was have an orgasm. I thought about going to the living room and popping in one of my porno tapes that I had hidden in my closet. I even considered sneaking to my basement and calling Scarlet to see if she would be willing to sneak into my basement and hit me off. Then I thought about just masturbating right next to my wife and putting sperm on her butt so she could know how much of a freak and a fiend I really was.

I just lay there vexed like crazy. I thought about praying to take the temptation away, but what good was that gonna do? After all, I wasn't even in the right frame of mind to pray.

EIGHT

Before I knew it the month of May was just about over. I had brought LL into the shop for a haircut so he would be freshly dipped for the Memorial day cookout that my wife and I had planned. It's so funny because now I felt much more comfortable being in the shop with Toni as opposed to the first time. To me the whole atmosphere felt more relaxed and loose.

Toni seemed to be excited because I was around. Unlike the first time I had visited the beauty salon, Toni was very talkative around LL and myself. She even picked up LL and paraded around the shop with him. It was kind of like she was showing him off as if he were her own son. She and LL had conversations ranging from what he'd been learning in daycare to his favorite toys. Toni actually took time away from her customers to sit down and talk to LL, that's what made the situation seem odd but sincere. LL had game like his daddy and he managed to slip in that his fifth birthday was in two weeks. Toni melted and promised to buy him whatever it was that he wanted.

With Toni looking as sexy as a Soul Train dancer, I felt like a proud peacock that was basking in the sun. I sat back and just clocked Toni's beauty. I knew that in a matter of time I could claim her if I wanted to. And believe me, I wanted to.

As I sat and received another manicure I noticed that Toni had on some slip-on sandals. They were the type of sandals that had a very slight heel to them. All of her toes were exposed, and there was a thong between her big toe. You could tell Toni was into cosmetology, because even her toes had an air brushed design. Her red toenail polish made her feet look like succulent appetizers. They reminded me of pigs in a blanket. I couldn't wait to suck on them.

For the first time I'd noticed a little ghettoness in Toni. It was cute because I knew that she wasn't really ghetto at all. It was probably just the beauty salon's environment that was causing her to be a little louder than her normal demeanor. In her winsome ghettoness, she seemed to be claiming me. I guess that she was starting to get a little attached to me. Toni also could have been slightly jealous, knowing that other very fine women were in the shop and I wasn't holding back from looking at them.

Toni began commenting on how addictive the Juniors cheesecakes are. She made certain to mention to another beautician, that *she and I* had gone to Juniors the other night. She also seemed to need my confirmation on a lot of petty things. She would project her voice in the direction of where I was getting my manicure and ask, "Right Lance?" Or "Lance, am I lying?"

When I was done with my nails, Toni summoned me and wanted to see how my manicure looked. To my surprise she wasn't happy with the way they had turned out. She made sure to let the nail technician know it. I tried to let Toni know that it was alright, but she again, with her fetching ghettoness, was like, "Nah, it looks a'ight but your nails are still a little suspect."

After rinsing the head of one of her customers, Toni grabbed me by the hand and sat me at an empty manicure table. She quickly went to work on my cuticles. When she was done buffing and plucking, and stroking I had to admit that my nails did actually look better. I just felt funny that Toni had kind of played the other technician in front of everybody. There wasn't any confrontation or nothing but Toni just embarrassingly voiced her opinion on the other technician's skills, which she felt weren't up to par.

Honestly, I just thought that Toni's actions were a ploy to let people know that she was thinking about claiming me and that no one else had better had the same idea. I have to say that her actions definitely made me feel good. See, I knew that she didn't consciously realize what she was doing. Still, something was driving her to act the way she was.

By the time LL was finish with his haircut it was around two O'clock in the afternoon. Once again I gave Toni a very unselfish tip. Toni took it upon herself to walk us to my car. While we were walking I asked, "So Toni what are you doing for Memorial Day?"

Toni looked at me curiously and asked, "When is Memorial day again?"

I responded, "I guess you ain't doing nothing 'cause Memorial day is two days away. On Monday."

Toni laughed and said, "Oh man. I was supposed to go on a boat ride but I forgot about it and I didn't RSVP, so I don't even think I'll be going... Why did you ask?"

I answered, "Well I'm having like a barbecue- slash-party at my house. You can come if you want."

Toni smiled and looked at me as if to request some more assurance.

"Toni there is no problem. You can come."

I reached into my glove compartment and retrieved a piece of paper. On the paper I wrote down my address as well as the directions to my house. I also wrote the time everything began. Then I handed it to Toni.

Toni looked everything over.

"So you'll be there right?" I asked.

Toni nodded her head, and said, "Yeah I'll be there." Then she pinched LL on his cheek, which was full of candy. "Cutie can I have a good-bye kiss?" Toni asked.

I was playfully but extremely jealous because Toni was requesting a kiss from LL and not from me. LL smiled as he planted the stickiest kiss on Toni's cheek. Toni then stepped away from the car and waived good-bye. As Toni walked off I noticed that her butt was actually rounder than I had previously thought. I guess it looked that way because of the satin looking white pants that she had on.

"One day," I thought. "One day."

When I reached home I realized that my wife and I had to go to Costco so that we could purchase the food for Memorial Day. Being that the Knicks and Bulls were playing game seven of the eastern conference finals, the very last thing that I wanted to do was go food shopping. However, I didn't put up a fight. I just did what was responsible.

****

The next day I found myself in a familiar location, church, and as always, the sermon was very uplifting and at the same time convicting. The Pastor was preaching about, "What good is faith if it is not backed up by deeds?" He said many interesting things. For example, he asked everyone in attendance to raise their hands if they believed in God. As you would have guessed it, everyone in the place proudly raised their hands. Then he asked everyone that believed in Jesus to raise their hands. Again everyone in attendance raised their hands.

After doing that little demonstration he informed everyone that they now had something in common with Satan. People began looking at each other as they began feeling a bit uncomfortable. The pastor knew exactly what he was doing because now that he had everyone's attention, he told them, "That's good that you say you believe in God and the son of God. But I am going to tell everybody in this building something. Satan also believes in God. Yes, Satan believes in Jesus Christ. As a matter of fact, I would dare to say that Satan's belief in God is probably stronger than the belief that some of you sitting here today profess to have."

The pastor, who now had everyone riled up, went on to explain that there is a big difference in saying that one believes in God as oppose to *believing* God. I paused and I began to think about what he was saying. After pondering for a few seconds, I realized how deep his statement was. The pastor asked us to turn to John 3:16, which is a very famous verse. To paraphrase the verse, it states that whoever believes in Jesus, shall not perish but rather they will have eternal life.

The pastor went on. "Now let me ask each one of you something. When it's all said and done, when Jesus returns, do you think that Satan will have eternal life? Or do you think Satan is going to perish?" After asking the rhetorical question, he went on to explain that according to John 3:16 which states that whoever believes in God, which Satan does believe in God, would not perish, rather he would have eternal life. "Whoever believes!" He reiterated. "Satan believes so is he going to have eternal life or not?"

Of course, after having asked a radical question like that, everyone began to snicker and laugh because they were feeling uncomfortable. Then the pastor explained that people can be easily deceived into thinking that all it takes is a belief in God and you will be saved. But he warned that we can't take scriptures out of context. If we do take scriptures out of context we are only setting ourselves up for a rude awakening in the end.

The pastor shouted, "God is not a liar! He has already condemned Satan! Satan will have eternal life but it will be an eternity spent in hell. If you read your Bibles and tie in other scriptures you would know the answer to whether or not Satan's belief in God alone is enough to grant him a quality eternal life! Obviously this scripture in John 3:16 isn't talking about just *any* kind of belief in Jesus! It's talking about a belief that causes one to have settled attitudes about how they are now going to live a new life for Christ, due to the fact that they believe in the son of God." That belief, he explained, will be shown by the things you do.

He added, "Are you doing the things God commands you to do? Like going into the world and telling the lost about his son? Are you committing adultery? Are you not forgiving those that sin against you? Are you still getting drunk? Are you envious of people? Do you crave the things of this world? Have you been baptized?"

The pastor who had stopped shouting was now calmly explaining that, depending on how one answers the questions that deal specifically with areas in our everyday life, that is what will show the type of belief in Christ that one really has. He explained that anyone can profess a belief in Christ, just as Satan professes a belief in Christ. Yet as Satan is hell-bent on deceiving people and doing evil, we must not be like Satan and profess a belief in Christ while we continue to get drunk, while we continue to commit adultery, or for that matter, while some of us continue to procrastinate and have never been baptized.

Later that evening my wife and I talked at length about what we had learned from the sermon. I was the first to admit that I was one that claimed to believe in God but I wasn't truly willing to let him be Lord of my life, in the sense that I wasn't willing to give up certain things that I craved. I admitted to Nicole that I did want eternal life. I also admitted that because of the evil things that I continued to allow myself to do, I wasn't sure if I'd actually make it to heaven.

I didn't fully explain to my wife what I meant by "evil things." But obviously if I really loved and believed God, I wouldn't willfully lust the way I do. I wouldn't be so ready to commit adultery. If I truly believed Christ, then I would listen to His warnings that He gives me via the Bible. Especially when He warns and says that the people who do things to please their sinful desires will not inherit the kingdom of heaven, rather they only have a fearful expectation of the fires of hell.

NINE

Monday arrived and Memorial Day was upon us. Our party which had started at about five in the afternoon, had now been underway for about two hours. There were many people who showed up to get there eat on and to get their *swerve* on. The party was shaping up to be a nice event. Throughout the whole day I had been wondering when and if Toni would actually show up. Deep down inside I knew that she would show, but I was wondering how I was going to react in her presence.

I also was praying that Scarlet wouldn't pop up and make a surprise visit. See, I knew that Scarlet was the stalker type, so knowing her, she was probably camped out in her ride right down the block from my house with a pair of binoculars and a baseball bat ready to attack. And believe me, the last thing I needed was for her to see me with any woman that she didn't recognize because she probably wouldn't have hesitated to disrespect Nicole and march her big round butt into my party with a Louisville Slugger and cause a confrontational scene. Hopefully she had to strip at a party somewhere. Being that it was Memorial Day and all that was more than likely the case, so I figured that I shouldn't get too anxious about any Scarlet drama unfolding.

My wife and I had debated over whether or not there should be any liquor at the party. Actually Nicole objected to it. She figured that people didn't need liquor in order to have a good time, and she didn't want someone to get drunk and spoil everything. My wife also argued that many brothers and sisters from the church were going to be there and it wouldn't look right for us to have a *"worldly"* party.

I went against my wife's objections. Although, summer didn't officially begin until another three weeks, I still felt that Memorial Day marked the beginning of the mood that the summertime brings. So how on earth were we going to have a party with a summer feel to it, yet have no liquor? I went out and purchased so many Heinekens that I had to place them inside of two garbage cans that were filled with ice.

The party was being held simultaneously in our backyard as well as in our basement. I took some of the liquor from the bar in the basement and placed it on one of the picnic tables that were in the backyard. I left the rest of the liquor in the basement so people would have open access to the drinks regardless of where they were.

Although Nicole was disappointed in my decision, she didn't let it stop her from having a good time. As a matter of fact Nicole, who you've probably figured out by now that I also call Nikki, was the life of the party. She made sure that there were no wallflowers. By the time 8 pm rolled around, people were filled with liquor and everyone was getting their swerve on out on the make-shift dance floor. The music was bangin'. I was hoping that none of the neighbors would get annoyed by the noise and call the cops.

We had huge blue and red flood lights in the backyard, so that everyone could see what they were doing. Way more people showed up than I expected. I didn't even know many of the faces that were at the party. When I walked to the front yard of my house I noticed that the block was filled with double parked cars. I also noticed what looked like Toni walking up to the house. She didn't recognize me as she and a friend, made their way to the backyard.

With Toni and her friend unknowing, I followed right behind them with a drink in my hand. When they reached the backyard, the DJ was blasting the smash Bad Boy Entertainment record, Mo' Money Mo' Problems. That's when I made my move and let Toni know that she was definitely in the right place. I walked right in front of Toni and started dancing with her. I began yelling, "Ah yeah! Ah yeah!" While happily raising both of my hands in the air, I was careful not to spill my drink on her.

Toni began smiling and slowly bopping her head and moving her body, trying to get in rhythm with me. Then she held open her arms for a hug. I was still dancing and raising the roof, so she just grabbed me and hugged me, nothing seductive or anything, just a hello kind of hug. Then she introduced me to her friend whose name was Kim.

Kim was a'ight but she didn't really rank in the looks department. She was a four drink kind of chick, which means that I would have to have at least four drinks before I would kick it to her.

While being introduced to Kim, I noticed my wife looking at me. I didn't want to act suspicious, so I just kept dancing with Toni. Trying to talk over the music while still dancing I asked, "What took you so long?"

Toni explained that she and Kim had stopped at another barbecue before they came to my house.

As the DJ switched up the record and threw on another Bad Boy smash hit, The Benjamins, I playfully told Toni, "Y'all are so wack. Y'all should have come here first. Which party has it going on more? This one or the one you just left?"

Toni smiled and yelled into my ear, "Your party of course!... Y'all got it going on! And the music is tight!"

I stepped away from Toni and pointed her in the direction of where the food and drinks were. I told Toni that I would be all over the place, but I instructed them both to still have a good time.

I mingled and tried to talk to everyone to make sure that everybody was having a good time. As I mingled I made sure to stay clear of my wife so she wouldn't ask me who Toni was. Before I knew it Steve came up to me panting like a horse and emphatically asking, "Yo Lance who is that!?" He was pointing in Toni's direction.

Bobbing my head to the music, I just held out my fist for a pound. Steve tapped my fist with his fist as I proclaimed, "Yeah nigga! What!? Am I the man or what!? I told you all of that laughing was gonna come back and bite you in the ass!"

Steve asked, "That's the chick?"

"Word is bond," I replied.

Steve put his hand out for a pound while simultaneously grabbing me and giving me a ghetto hug. He informed me that I was officially the man, which was something that I already knew but I didn't mind hearing it again. "Yo, you are the man! Lance that chick is off the chain! She even looks better than Scarlet... I mean the trunk isn't as big as Scarlet's but man! She is bangin'!" Steve commented.

I macishly smiled and walked off.

Fortunately, as the night went on, no one got to the point where they were sloppy drunk. As the DJ threw on reggae music I searched out my wife and I began dancing real close to her.

Nikki immediately asked, "Lance who was that woman I seen you dancing with earlier?"

I knew exactly who she was talking about but I played dumb. "I don't know baby. I mean I been dancing with a lot of people."

Nikki seemed a bit peeved. She then made it clear as to who she was talking about, as she explained, "I'm talking about that exotic looking woman with the tight sarong skirt and the long hair, the one that was hugging all over you... Lance don't play dumb! I know everybody here except for her, so who is she?"

"Oh you mean Toni?" I said while trying to put water on the fire.

Nikki sarcastically mocked me and replied, "Oh you mean *Toni*?... Yeah I mean Toni! Who is she?"

Nonchalantly I replied, "I told you about her. She's the lady that cuts LL's hair."

Nikki sucked her teeth and warned me to watch how I was dancing with her. I thought to myself, "ah man, this is not what I need." I wanted to make sure that I squashed any friction right from Jump Street. So when I was out of my wife's sight I found Toni.

"You still enjoying yourself?" I asked.

"No doubt." Toni replied. "Some of my Soros are here."

"Oh yeah? What Sorority are you in?"

Toni explained that she was a Delta.

"You?" I questioned. "You look more like an A.K.A." I said as I playfully did the annoying A.K.A. call, "SqueeeeeWheeeee!"

Toni rolled her eyes and said, "Whateva."

Then I popped the question, or should I say I instructed Toni on what she would be doing next. "Toni come, meet my wife."

"Lance, I don't wanna meet your wife! Not now!"

"Come on Toni. Don't trip 'cause it ain't nothing. She already told me she wanted to meet you."

Toni was hesitant but she went along with me.

As we searched for my wife I felt as if I was bringing my fiancée home to meet my mother for the first time. I decided to check the basement. On the way to the basement I stopped and introduced Toni to many of the guests. I also managed to introduce Toni to Steve, who was gawking at her like a dog in heat. With everyone that she met, Toni smiled her million dollar smile and extended her right hand for a handshake as she would say, "Hello, nice to meet you."

So that Steve wouldn't totally jack up my flow, after introducing him to Toni I sent him to go and find Toni's friend Kim. I instructed him to keep her company as Toni and I continued searching for Nicole.

Finally, I spotted my wife and I yelled for her. "Honey, come hear…"

Being that the music was also blasting in the basement, my wife didn't hear me, so Toni and I walked over to her.

"Nicole, I wanted to introduce you to Toni."

My wife's back was towards Toni and I. When she turned around I noticed that she had a jar of barbecue sauce in her hand. I think I had kinda caught her by surprise.

"Oh," she said, as she quickly looked Toni up and down, but not in a way to make her feel uncomfortable. My wife didn't say anything. I guess she was just trying to check Toni's steelo.

I was about to butt in and break the uncomfortable silence, but Toni used her charming ways and spared me the chore. Toni's gold and diamond bracelet slid from her wrist to about half way down her hand as she extended her hand to Nicole for a handshake.

"Hi, I'm Toni. Nice to meet you Nicole."

I didn't know what to expect from my wife, but she wasn't a bit out of character as she smiled and said, "Oh, so you're the one that my son has been going crazy over?"

Feeling very uncomfortable and not knowing what to say, like a dummy I said, "Yeah Honey, Toni is the one that has been cutting LL's hair."

My wife paused and she gave me a look that said, "*NO DUH*." Then she replied, "Yeah Lance, I know that." To my surprise Nicole complemented Toni for doing such a good job with LL's hair. She also asked her if she was enjoying the party.

Maybe it was just in my head, but I felt that there was so much tension in the air that I could cut it with a knife.

Then, being as polite as possible, my wife excused herself from the introduction as she explained that she couldn't talk long because she had to check on the grill. She departed by telling Toni it was nice meeting her. Toni responded, "Likewise."

After Nicole walked off, Toni seemed a bit surprised as she remarked, "Lance your wife is very pretty!"

"Yeah I know," I replied.

I didn't want to make more of the situation than was necessary. I mean there probably was no tension or friction at all. Maybe it was just my guilt that I was feeling. Then I thought about it. I realized that I really had no reason at all for feeling guilty. I hadn't done *anything* with Toni.

As the night went on everyone continued to have a good time. Although I was enjoying myself, I didn't appreciate being separated from Toni for the majority of the night. Hours seemed to be flying by, and before I knew it, it was getting pretty late. Unfortunately most people in the party, including myself had to go to work the next morning. I didn't want the party to end but I knew I had to start winding things down at around one in the morning. I went to speak to the DJ, and I instructed him to go low key on the music so people would get the hint to leave. I advised him to start playing more R&B as opposed to the party jams that he had been lacing everyone with.

After speaking to the DJ, I noticed that Steve seemed to be really clicking with Kim. The two of them were hemmed up in a cozy corner of the backyard. Being that Kim was still here, I knew that Toni had to be around somewhere. I wanted to go look for her but I also wanted to make sure to speak to as many of the people from the church as possible. I guess it was obvious to them that I had been acting totally different from the way I act when I'm in church. My actions made it evident that I wasn't trying to be warm with them at all. But at that juncture in the party I definitely wasn't going to try and repent for the way I'd behaved. I just wanted to show my face to them and politick.

After politickin' and making my final rounds in the backyard, I realized that Toni had to be in the basement 'cause I hadn't seen her outside. So I headed straight to the basement to scoop her up. When I reached the basement I instantly became insanely vexed. I saw Toni standing near the bar smiling and talking to some cat that I didn't know. I had plans to march right up to Toni and snatch her up by the arm and ask her who the hell was she talking to and why was her smile so sparkling and wide! I began thinking, what if the kid slipped a Mickey in Toni's drink? What if he was an old boyfriend? I wasn't trying to hear thoughts like that. I psyched myself to just walk up to the cat Toni was talking to and just punch him dead in his grill.

I couldn't believe how angry I was. It's not like I have a short fuse or anything like that. I just felt like I was a dog who'd stepped away from his food for a hot second and here was some other dog putting his mouth in my food bowl.

Immediately I stormed towards Toni, but then I stopped in my tracks. I didn't get any closer to Toni 'cause I knew that I was about to do something that I would probably regret later. After pausing, I realized that it would not have been wise at all to cause any kind of an altercation. And believe me, if I were to snuff this cat, it would have caused a major scene. I thought against resorting to violence because first of all I had no idea who the cat was that Toni was talking to. For all I knew, the guy could have been Toni's cousin or what have you. Then I would've really played myself like a roach. Imagine me carrying on an all, only to find out that the guy really wasn't trying to kick game to Toni.

I yelled Toni's name from a distance. She looked up and spotted me. After putting her drink on the counter of the bar, she looked as if she'd told the guy she would be right back. Toni walked over to where I was standing. I had to remember to remain calm as I spoke quietly but with a sternness in my voice I asked, "Yo who the hell is that nigga!?"

Toni seemed shocked by the tone of my voice. She frowned and replied, "Ill!"

I knew that I had to quickly put my jealousy aside, so I smiled, trying to play it off, I said, "Ah, I got you. You thought I was trippin' right?"

Toni seemed unsure as to whether I was serious or not. She explained that the guy she was talking to was a Q-Dog that she'd known since her undergraduate days at Hampton University. She went on to explain how the Q-Dogs are the brothers to the Deltas. I played along like I was interested but I really wasn't impressed at all by all of the fraternity and sorority garbage. I've been tired of hearing about that fraternity crap since I was nineteen years old.

I remarked, "Toni you're making me jealous."

Toni who seemed a bit open from the alcohol laughed and she hugged me and seductively said, "Baby you know I'm all yours, so why you trippin'?"

With the snap of a finger, my jealous rage had worn off and was replaced by a Kool-Aid smile. That hug turned me on something crazy! I knew that I had to be very careful because I had no idea where my wife was or who was watching me. I quickly surveyed the basement which was starting to empty out. I couldn't locate my wife, so I kept Toni close to my body and gently caressed her back. In the worse way I wanted to take Toni upstairs to the guest room and try to get some. I had no idea if she would be with it but I definitely was gonna try.

I took Toni by the hand and tried to persuade her as I said, "Come on Toni, let me show you the rest of my crib."

Toni seemed as if she was about to hesitate but she didn't put up a fight as she followed right behind me. That corny, punk ass, Q-Dog nigga that was still at the bar waiting for Toni to return, looked at the two of us and just stared as he picked his face up from off the floor. I figured that Toni probably hadn't objected to me taking her on a tour of the house for a couple of reasons.

See, she had been given my home number, plus she'd met my wife, she liked my kid and she enjoyed my company. All of that had to make her feel very comfortable with an uncomfortable situation.

In a ploy to make it to the guest room as soon as possible, I hastily showed Toni the first floor. The first floor included the living room, the dining room, the kitchen and the den. Toni nodded her head and commented how nice the furniture was, and how spacious all the rooms were. I wondered if she was thinking to herself similar thoughts that I was thinking. I thought about how all of my material toys, such as my laced out crib, could very easily become Toni's if she played the right cards.

We finally made it upstairs away from everyone. This is where I wanted to be so I could attempt to make my move. I continued with the tour as I showed Toni the bathroom, and the master bedroom. Toni commented that she loved the satin sheets that were on my king size bed.

Like a pervert I said, "Yeah I like satin too. It feels good when you make love on satin sheets."

Toni smiled and playfully punched me but she didn't respond. We continued on the tour and we next came upon my son's room. His door was closed, so I slowly opened it and peeked in. To my surprise LL was sound asleep. I didn't understand how he could sleep through all of the noise. He must have been drained from all of the dancing that he had been doing. When he's on the dance floor he swears that he's Puff Daddy. As I showed Toni LL's room, she remarked how peaceful LL looked as he slept. "Yeah that's my dog," I replied as I closed the door to his room.

Our next destination was the guest bedroom. I continued to hold Toni's hand as we walked into the room. Jokingly, I told her that the guest room was the room I often slept in when I was in trouble with my wife. Acting very cautious as if she was anticipating something, Toni didn't respond to my last comment. She just nodded her head. Then I softly closed the door and stood with my back against it. I lustfully stared at Toni and I made sure not to say a word. I took Toni by both of her hands and guided her closer to me. After pulling her close to me I hugged her, closed my eyes and attempted to kiss her. Toni resisted and she quickly pushed away from my body.

In a loud whisper Toni asked, "Lance, what are you doing?"

I held Toni so that she couldn't walk away from me. I was careful not to hold her in such a way that would suggest I was trying to rape her or something.

"Come on baby, just one kiss," I pleaded.

Toni sounding a bit nervous asked, "Lance are you crazy!? I can't be kissing you in your house with your wife downstairs!"

I didn't reply. I just pulled Toni closer to me and began to kiss her. Magically her reluctance had disappeared. I could tell that she wanted to get into a real deep kiss, but at the same time she showed signs of apprehension. Her apprehension was probably why the kiss didn't last for as long as I'd wanted it to. Nor did the kiss lead to where I'd wanted it to lead. We did manage to kiss for about thirty seconds and I was aroused throughout the whole time. The kiss felt far better than I thought it would when I'd often fantasized about it. Toni's mouth was sweeter than an apple Blow-Pop.

Toni backed away from me. She seemed as if she was breathing a little heavy as she said, "Lance we can't be doing this!"

Like I said, I understood Toni's apprehension but I was more than ready and willing to lay Toni on the guest bed and take things to the next level. I was still blocking the door and Toni demanded that I move out of the way so that she could exit. Swiftly coming back to reality, I complied and moved out of Toni's way. Toni aptly walked out of the room. I wanted to run behind her but I just let her go.

After she'd left the room I slid down the wall of the hallway that was just outside the guest room. I sat with my butt on the floor and I let my knees rest near my chin. I thought about what I had just done. I knew that once again I had crossed that line that I'd promised myself and my wife that I would never cross. To justify the wrong that I'd just done, I abruptly convinced myself that it wasn't me who had tried to kiss Toni. Rather it was all of the alcohol that I had been drinking that led me to kiss her. I sat for a few minutes but I knew that I had to get back to the party and see the remaining guests off. I also knew that I would be up until about four in the morning with my wife cleaning up, so I had to get a move on things.

TEN

More than a week had passed since I kissed Toni. During that week, the shame of what I did seemed to intensify with each passing day. Having known what I did, I was getting tired of looking my wife in the face and having her see me as a do right man. I didn't want to feel depressed but I couldn't help it. The guilt was no joke.

I didn't feel comfortable expressing to anyone how I was being eaten up inside. I could have spoken to Steve, but all he would have given me was more head shaking laughter. With the way I was feeling, I really was in no mood to be laughed at. Within the past week I hadn't spoken to Toni. In fact I hadn't spoken to her since the party. That too was also ripping a tear into my heart. The rip in my heart was so big that I found myself in the booty bar three times within this past week. When I was in the bar watching the sexy women take their clothes off, it was like all of my worries would leave me. I wanted to pay the biggest butt dancer two hundred and fifty dollars to go to a hotel with me. Yet, I didn't want any sex from her. All I would've wanted was for her to sit with no clothes on and listen to my problems.

I actually propositioned a couple of dancers with my offer, but sadly I had no takers. The dancers explained to me that they made way more than two fifty a night, so if I wanted some takers, I would definitely have to up my price. They also didn't believe that I wanted to go to a hotel "*just to talk.*" They assumed that once we got to the hotel that my plans would change. That certainly could not have been further from the truth. But I simply settled for inexpensive lap dances. It was funny because as soon as I would leave the strip clubs, my depressive state would return. However, when I would reach home I would continue to combat the depression with masturbation.

During the week, Scarlet had acted as a good outlet for me to release some of my depression. I had called her and purposely patched up some of the comments that I had made to her. I was so stupid because I knew that I was only leading her on even further.

Plus I knew that I was only setting my life up for more drama. Things were starting to get a little bit thicker with Toni, so I should have definitely stayed away from Scarlet but I just couldn't. I mean regardless if I was trying to break up with her and distance myself from her, I still felt like I *needed* her during the past week.

Yeah, even with my trips to the booty bar, and with my depression, and with masturbating almost everyday during the past week, I some how had found the time to have sex with Scarlet like four times during the week. And the sex wasn't none of that psycho-love-hate type of sex. It was much more *ghetto-passionate*. Scarlet and I had finally been able to sit and talk like sane human beings. I guess that was because there was no talk of me leaving her.

Scarlet had been working real hard on this big project in order to get her website, www.braziliancoochie.com, fully completed and ready to launch. And since I have always had a thing for business I was able to give her some very helpful insight on how to effectively market her website and totally capitalize on the hardcore internet porn industry. Being that the two of us were able to connect on the whole website project, it sought of helped to distract us from all of the drama that we had been going through as of late. I knew that Scarlet *needed* me and I definitely felt like I *needed* her but I would be a fool if I tried to juggle three women, God, and a son. So although I didn't remind Scarlet of my decision to split from her, I knew that after the week was over that I would have to revert right back to my disappearing act and continue to distance myself from Scarlet.

****

On Monday evening my wife finally confronted my gloomy mood. "Lance what's up with you?" I know something is bothering you, I mean you haven't lifted weights this whole week, you're not eating as much. Something is bothering you."

"Nothing's wrong Nikki. I'm okay."

"You sure?"

"Yeah I'm sure."

I wanted to talk because I knew that just talking about anything would help my comatose state of mind. I just didn't want to be specific as to what it was that was bothering me, therefore I remained silent. Fortunately my wife was persistent as she looked at me with compassion and replied, "Talk to me baby. What's on your mind?"

Reluctantly I'd decided to give in and I explained, "Well, I don't want to be making a big deal out of anything, but do you remember last week when you saw me dancing with Toni?"

"Yes I remember. Why?"

I started to spill the beans right there. But all week long I couldn't even bring myself to think about how my wife would react if I told her that I'd kissed Toni. So now I certainly didn't want to witness her reaction first hand. I took my train of thought onto another track. "Well were you jealous?" I asked. "I mean was it alright for me to be with Toni?"

"Lance you know that I trust you. I mean I wouldn't even think twice about leaving you in the room with my sister if she were half naked."

I liked the thought of that suggestion. I was gonna joke and ask my wife if we could actually test out that experiment. But I had to remain serious as I interjected, "Well, it just seemed to me that you were a little peeved at me. I just don't want you to be thinking that I would be flirting with some woman right in our own house. I love you too much for that. I know you know all this but I want us to always be able to speak about anything that is bothering us, no matter how insignificant it may seem."

Nikki added, "Lance, you mean to tell me that you were feeling down because you thought that I was jealous of you dancing with another woman?"

I lied as I simply replied, "I guess so, yeah?"

Nikki defensively answered back, "Well, like I've always told you, I trust you Lance. I didn't have a problem with you dancing with Toni. It's just that she's a beautiful woman and I had no idea who she was. See I trust you, but these women out here are trifling. People say that men are dogs but women are just as bad!"

"Oh, so you didn't have a problem with Toni?" I asked.

Nicole explained, "No I did not. Nor do I have any reason to have a problem with Toni. All it was, was that I didn't know her, that's all. After you introduced me to her I had no problems with her. I mean from what I saw of her she seems to be a nice lady."

I replied, "A'ight, just making sure that we're always on the same page."

Nicole added, "By the way. Lance why don't you invite Toni to church? You should find out if she is saved? Because honestly, that is the way I'm learning to look at people, in more spiritual terms."

It was like magic. By just talking, I was able to slowly but surely slip out of my depressive coma. I knew that my wife was the most beautiful human being in terms of qualities and character that I had ever met. Here I was messing with Toni right under her nose and she was asking me whether or not the chick was born again. I felt a bit contrite when she asked me about Toni's spiritual condition. Her spiritual condition was something that I really hadn't pondered. I definitely wanted to dodge the question about whether Toni was saved. And there was no way in the world that I was gonna invite my mistress to church. If I were to do that, I might as well have applied for membership as one of Satan's demons.

In response to my wife's question I stated, "Well I don't know if she's saved or not. I mean I don't know her that well."

My wife shot back, "Well if you felt you knew her well enough to invite her to the party, you could have just as easily invited her to church. Lance you have to start learning to be more evangelistic."

I readily responded, "Evangelistic? I'm not trying to look like no Jehovah's Witness!"

My wife shook her head, "Don't worry about how you're gonna look. It's not about trying to look like somebody. You should be reaching out to lost people trying to tell them the gospel. Forget about the Jehovah's Witnesses. In the Bible, Jesus tells us to be evangelistic."

For good reasons, I didn't respond to my wife. I mean, I didn't feel like debating religion. Man, I was trying to get over the depression that was caused by my dogish mentality, and my wife was lecturing me on becoming the next Billy Graham or Creflo Dollar. At that point I really didn't need to be reminded of my week Christian faith.

Although I didn't care for the religious twist that the conversation had taken, the quick conversation with my wife did manage to cheer me up a great deal. After all, it appeared to me as if Nicole was giving me the green light to be with Toni. I mean she did say that she wasn't jealous of the relationship I had with Toni. My wife is even openly secure with the fact that Toni is a gorgeous woman. So to me it was like Nikki had OK'd the attention that I'd given Toni at the party last week. Man I felt so stupid. All week long I'd been having suicidal thoughts, and as soon as I talked to my wife about the situation, I find out that she's secure with the whole ordeal.

"Nicole, you know what I was just thinking?"

"No. What were you thinking?"

I answered, "I was thinking. Nah, actually I should say that I was admiring you because I know that the loyalty that you show me is genuine. It's authentic. Nothing or no one can compare to you Nicole. To me it's like that's one of the reasons why I love you so much. Come here give me a hug."

As my wife gleamed, I hugged her tight. I wasn't just dropping her some line of BS. I meant every word that came out of my mouth as I exclaimed, "Baby I'm so glad that you're not an insecure woman."

My wife and I began to kiss each other very deeply as I jokingly asked, "Wanna go make a baby?"

Nikki giggled and grabbed me by the hand and led me upstairs where we made love on our green satin sheets.

ELEVEN

Wednesday night, on our way home from Bible class my wife and I stopped at Carvel's to get some ice cream for LL. LL is mad cute but I am convinced that he is the most clumsiest kid that I have ever seen. Not once, but twice, after purchasing our ice cream and in the process of leaving the store, LL managed to drop his ice cream cone, sprinkles and all, splat right on the floor. I warned him that I was gonna buy him one more cone and he had better not drop it or he wouldn't be getting another one.

I didn't want to hold the cone for him, because I wanted him to learn independence. It was a scary ordeal watching him perform a Houdini act of licking the cone while walking to the car all in one shot. Fortunately for LL it wasn't three strikes and you're out. He made it to the car with the ice cream running all over his right arm but he was happier than a pig in slop.

As we drove home, my pager, which was on vibrate, went off. When we came to a red light I looked at the pager and it had 911 displayed along with a phone number which I didn't recognize. As I reached for my cellular phone I thought to myself that it was probably Steve giving me an update on the NBA championship game. He was probably at some chick's house, sitting pretty like a fat cat. I knew that all he wanted to do was rub in my face, the fact that I was missing the game because I had to go to Bible class. Although I didn't want to hear any of Steve's sarcasm, when we came to a red light I quickly dialed the number. After two rings, I heard a female's voice on the other end.

"Hello Lance? Can you talk? This is Toni."

I had to play things cool and not show my excitement to my wife.

I was cool and collected as I said, "Yo, what's up? Listen. Um, actually I'm driving right now. I'll call you back when I get home a'ight?"

Toni replied, "OK, but make sure you call me."

"Yeah a'ight, no doubt." I replied.

Yo, I put the cell phone down and I really thought I was about to have an orgasm in my pants. Toni actually called me before I called her! Either she was calling me to tell me she's upset with me, or the kiss got her hooked. Even though I haven't spoken to her since the party, which was about a week and a half ago, I doubted that she was upset. If she was she wouldn't have called at all.

"Lance, who was that?" My wife asked.

"Oh that was Steve. He was calling to give me an update on the game," I replied.

When we reached home we entered the house like one big happy family. I was starving and couldn't wait to eat. In addition to being hungry, I also knew that eating would help me to take my mind off of the fact that Toni was waiting for my phone call. As my wife and I ate we talked about the lesson that we had learned at class. I was into our conversation but at the same time I was also chomping down my food so I could get away from the table as soon as possible.

When I was done eating, I was easily able to jet from my wife. I used the excuse that I had to take LL up to his room to put him to bed. After I'd done that I made my way to the solace of the basement where I knew I would be able to get my "talk on" with Toni. But of course, this had to be one of those nights that my wife wanted to stay up and talk. I was pissed off because I couldn't wait for her to go to bed and leave me the hell alone!

Nicole, who was smiling, came down the basement stairs and said, "Guess what honey?"

Unaware at the time as to what my wife had up her sleeve, I nonchalantly asked "What's up?"

Sounding very excited my wife replied, "Well, I thought about how I don't spend enough time with you watching sports. So I'm a stay up with you tonight and watch the rest of the game. I've been thinking, and you're right, me watching the games is the only way I'm ever gonna learn to really get into it on the same level that you're into it."

"Damn! Damn! Damn! Damn!" I thought to myself as I wanted to scream. After all of the invitations in the past that my wife had not accepted, why did she have to choose this particular game to wanna watch? Why?... Damn! Now I knew that I would have to sit and explain to her every little detail about the game. Explaining sports to Nicole is something that I have longed to do. I want us to be husband and wife basketball fanatics. Had it been any other night I would have fallen in love with my wife's enthusiastic suggestion. It was just that I had to call Toni as soon as possible.

Luckily for me, when I turned on the game, I realized that the game was nearing the end of the third quarter. Which meant that I only had about thirty minutes or so before the game would be over. My wife was in true student form. The only thing she needed to do was whip out a pad and a pencil in order to take down notes. She began right away with the damn questions. I hated doing it, because I knew that I would probably turn her off from basketball forever, but I burst my wife's bubble right away.

As soon as she started with the questions, I interrupted her and said, "Baby, see, let me explain... You can't be asking questions now! The game is too close! I have to concentrate or else my team is gonna lose! This is an important game. A'ight?!"

Sounding like a sweet innocent kid, my wife asked, "Well how am I ever gonna learn if I don't ask questions."

Trying to brush her off I said, "Shhh, be quiet!"

After seeing my team commit a crucial turnover, I barked at Nicole, "See! Because you were talking, my team just made a costly mistake!"

My wife sucked her teeth in disappointed rejection.

I explained, "Baby don't take it personal that's just how it is. This is a big game."

I could tell that Nicole was mad. Whenever she's mad she becomes as cold as ice. She won't touch a nigga, she won't speak to a nigga or anything. Nicole was definitely mad as she sat there for ten minutes, faking like she was interested. But as soon as a commercial came on Nicole abruptly removed herself from the couch. Without saying a word to me she walked upstairs.

As she walked out of the room, I thought to myself, "well it's about got dam time!" I knew that she wanted me to chase after her and say sorry and all that garbage but not tonight. I couldn't wait for her to leave.

My wife had been upstairs for only five minutes, but I felt that that was long enough. I quickly rushed and called Toni. Her phone rang about five times, then her answering machine came on. Feeling disappointed, I left a message as I said, "What's up honey it's Lance? Just returning your call. Sorry it took so long for me to get back to you but, um, just call me when you get in. A'ight?"

Realizing that Toni wasn't home, I decided to take a chance and try the number from earlier that was in my pager. I dialed the number and it rang a couple of times. Toni picked up. Fortunately I didn't have to worry about my wife over hearing me because I had the sound from the game drowning out what I was saying. When I began to speak I was trying to be as apologetic as possible, "Toni, I'm sorry. Listen, I was dead wrong for trying to kiss you. I mean I respect you more than that, it's just that I had too much to drink that night. You understand right?"

My heart nervously pounded as I waited for Toni to respond.

Toni replied, "Lance, listen. First of all, I accept your apology. I wasn't exactly upset with you per se. It's like, well it's just like I've been telling you. We need to sit down and talk about what's been going on."

Just knowing that I wasn't on the hook for my actions led me to want to thank Toni. I thanked her as if she had just saved me from a raging river that was about to take me under. "Toni, whatever you say. The sooner we talk the better. What's up with tomorrow?"

Toni replied, "Tomorrow is fine."

I really didn't know what to say so I asked the common question, "So how have you been? How's Kim?"

"I've been alright. I was wondering when you were gonna call me or if you were ever gonna call me at all… As for Kim, she's chillin'. Matter of fact she told me to tell you that she had a good time at your party."

"Oh word, that's good. And what about you? Did you enjoy yourself?"

I could tell Toni was trying to sound very serious and the whole nine. But I knew that she was just as happy to be hearing my voice as I was to be hearing hers. I made sure not to address her comment about me not having called her. I could sense Toni was smiling as she said, "Yeah, you know I enjoyed myself."

I replied, "Good. That's real good."

Toni was starting to lose that serious tone of voice that she had when we began our conversation. She added, "Lance, baby it is hot as hell in my house."

I asked, "Are you in your crib? I just called you and left a message on your machine."

Toni replied, "Nah, I'm on my cell piece."

I laughed and I playfully responded, "Check you out. Sounding all ghetto. 'Nah I'm on my cell piece' … What do you know about a cell piece?"

Toni laughed as she explained, "Nah, but for real, I'm just driving around with my convertible down, I'm trying to cool off before I go to sleep, it's just too hot in my house!"

"Well what's up with the AC?"

Toni explained that that was the problem. The AC wasn't working.

I advised, "Listen, if you want, we can talk at your house tomorrow and I'll fix your AC for you while I'm there."

Toni didn't believe I was for real and she responded, "Yeah right."

"I'm serious! What do you have? Do you have central air? Or do you have separate air conditioners in each window?"

Toni replied, "Yeah we have central air but nothing is coming out of the vents."

"I'll take care of you. I'll hook things up," I assured.

Shortly after that our conversation ended. I made my way upstairs, where I found my wife greasing her scalp and rolling her hair.

Nikki rudely exclaimed, "Lance if you didn't want me around while you were watching your game all you had to do was tell me!"

I purposely ignored Nikki. In my mind I felt like telling her to shut the hell up. She knew where she could go for all I cared. Nikki glared at me while she continued to sit on the bed fixing her hair. I don't think that she was upset, but I know that by me ignoring her it didn't help to diffuse the situation. I stripped naked and made my way to the shower. Just to irk Nicole, I made sure to leave my clothes in a ragged pile right where I'd stepped out of them. As I walked out of the bedroom and headed towards the bathroom, my frustrated wife yelled, "Lance pick up your clothes and stop being lazy! I'm tired of picking up after you!"

That was the reaction I'd wanted. I mean if I had to be frustrated because I couldn't stay on the phone and kick it with Toni, I was gonna do my best to make sure that my wife was just as frustrated.

I stopped dead in my tracks and yelled back, "What did you say!?"

Nicole screamed, "I said pick up your clothes!"

I reiterated, "Nah, nah! Before that. Did you say you're tired of me?!" I knew that that wasn't what Nicole had said, I was just trying to create an atmosphere of drama.

I continued on, "Nicole I know you didn't say you were tired of me! Matter of fact I don't give a damn! 'Cause I'm tired of you too bitch!"

After saying that I stormed into the bathroom and I slammed the door. I slammed the bathroom door so hard that the entire house shook. Nicole became enraged and she bolted to the bathroom door and demanded that I unlock the door.

"Lance open this damn door right now! Lance!... Lance! Lance you're gonna apologize for cursing at me! Open this door!"

I knew my wife had truly blown her top. She sounded madder than I'd ever heard her sound and for good reason I guess. I mean, that was the first time in my life that I had ever cursed at her. Although she was highly upset, I made matters much worse by running the water in the shower. That move on my part sent a signal that I was ignoring her. However, it only caused her dramatic screams to get louder and louder.

After being in the shower for two minutes, I no longer heard her yells. I guess she'd worn herself thin from yelling. It's wild because before I purposely started the confrontation, I wasn't the least bit upset. But although I knew that this whole argument had no basis, or substance, I was really starting to get upset. After all, I ran the show in my house. Nicole was way out of line when she'd raised her voice to me.

I continued to wash my body, and I became angrier by the minute. All I knew was that when I was done showering, Nicole had better slowed her role. I thought to myself, if she keeps nagging me she's gonna get smacked before the night is over. Word!

I stepped out of the shower and dried off, I continued to prep my mind for battle. I stopped moving around for a moment so I could listen closely to what it was that I thought I'd heard. Yup. I was right. I heard my son crying in the background. His tears didn't help the atmosphere, as I thought, what did Nicole do to him?

I wrapped a towel around my waist and violently ripped open the bathroom door.

Heading in the direction of LL's room I yelled, "LL! LL where are you? Why are you crying like you've lost your mind?"

When I made it to the entrance of his room, I saw my son sitting up in his bed being consoled by his mother. "Nicole what did you do to him?" I rudely asked.

Nicole barked back, "What did I do!? The question is what the hell is wrong with you!?"

I screamed, "Nicole let me explain something to you! I wear the pants in this house and you better start respecting me!"

As we raised our voices at each other, LL tried to mediate the situation, "Stop!" He cried as he hugged Nicole as hard as he could. "Mommy stop! Stop Daddy!"

Fortunately for me it took the sound of LL's voice to snap me out of what felt like a hypnotized and psychotic state. I pulled my son from Nicole's arms and hugged him. As his precious tears rolled down my bare chest, I caressed his back and assured him that everything was ok. I knew that he was crying because he had never seen the two people that he trusts and loves the most go at it like cats and dogs.

It was at that point that I realized how stupid my actions had been. I'd made LL feel that same hopelessness that I used to feel as a child when I would witness my father verbally and physically abusing my mom.

Nicole kissed LL and reassured him that everything was gonna be alright. Sensing that the battle was over, LL began to calm down. Nicole made her way out of the room. But before she left she gave me a stare of death and said, "I hope you know why he's scared and crying like he is."

Nicole made her way to our bedroom but I decided to stay with my son. I put him on the bed and placed him under his Superman bed sheets. LL didn't ask any questions and he looked so peaceful as he began to fall asleep. I kissed him on his cheek and turned out the lamp in his room. His night light was on and I just couldn't get myself to leave his room. I pulled one of his little chairs from the corner of his bedroom and sat and watched him as he looked so serene in his sleep.

Many thoughts came into my head as I watched my son. I was hoping some of the serenity of the room would wear off on me. I knew that I wasn't gonna sleep in the same bed with my wife. I probably would stay in LL's room and sleep. As I stared at LL I began to talk to God. With all that I had in my soul, I prayed that LL wouldn't grow up to see women as objects that feed and satisfy his lustful cravings. I hoped to myself that LL wouldn't even have the problem of lust like I do. I knew that he would grow up to enjoy sex as just about every human being does. But hopefully he won't let the need for sex dominate his every thought like his father does.

Tears were on the verge of welling up in my eyes. The tears were due to the sad fact that just the other day I was feeling deeply depressed because I had kissed another woman. In fact, on Monday, and all of last week for that matter, I didn't even know if my depression was a result of the fact that I loved my wife and I knew I'd done wrong, or if the depression was due to the fact that I had an uncontrollable desire to be with other women.

I definitely didn't want that depressive state of mind to creep back up on me. Sadly enough, I knew that it probably would return if I again chose to let days pass by without speaking to Toni, and Scarlet for that matter. Deep down inside I knew that if I wanted to save my marriage and my soul, then I would have to muster up the will power to fully avoid all contact with Toni. Yet, like a drug addict, I knew that it was the rushes that I received from Toni and Scarlet that was making me feel sane. So how was I gonna just put an end to the cravings of the cocaine-like rushes that were causing a war to be waged in my mind and producing all kinds of irrational actions on my part?

TWELVE

When the morning rolled around I woke LL up and got him dressed and ready for the daycare center. My wife was already awake and dressed. She hadn't cooked any breakfast and being that she was ready to walk out of the door I doubted that she had any plans on preparing breakfast. I knew that she was still upset from the previous night. But I couldn't believe that she was gonna just walk out of the house without speaking to me.

My wife didn't even acknowledge me when she saw me. I said good morning to her, but she was as cold as ice and didn't return my greeting. Nicole whisked past me and searched out LL's whereabouts. She found him at his usual location, in front of the TV. Nicole kneeled down to LL's eye level and said, "Mommy is leaving for work now, but you be good today and don't give your teachers a hard time, ok?"

LL who was deep into his cartoons didn't really look my wife in the face as he answered, "OK."

Nicole added, "Now give mommy some suga'."

LL finally looked in my wife's direction as he wrapped his arms around Nicole's neck and gave her a kiss on the cheek. Nicole who looked like a stunning woman of Corporate America, in her skirt suit, again walked passed me without acknowledging my presence. Only this time she kinda bumped me as she brushed by me.

"Good morning to you too Nicole," I said.

Nicole gave no reply and she headed straight out the door. I slipped on my slippers and ran out the house after her. When I caught up to her I grabbed her by the arm and said, "Alright Nicole. I'm sorry!"

Nicole didn't look me in the face, but as she tried to twist loose from my grip she replied, "Em uh, OK."

I hated grabbing Nicole in the manner in which I did, but what else was I to do to let her know that I was really sorry.

"See Nicole, I said I was sorry and you're not even acknowledging my apology, that's not right."

Nicole responded, "Lance can you let go of my arm!? You're gonna make me miss my train!"

As I gave in to her demand I lifted both of my palms face up and said, "Fine. But don't say I didn't try to apologize."

I got no reply from Nicole. She prepared to unlock her car door and I didn't want to give up, so I tried to play on her feelings by adding, "See, we shouldn't have even went to sleep last night if we were angry with each other. But honey I don't want us to go to work still upset. I mean what if something happens to you today and I never see you again? I wouldn't be able to live with myself knowing you didn't forgive me. Or what if something happens to me?"

Nicole finally looked in my direction but she still didn't say a word. She started up her car and drove off to the train station. I was left standing there like a lamenting fool.

One thing that I wasn't going to do was let this whole argument thing keep my mind bogged down with worry all day long. I'm the master at mind games and mental abuse, so I knew exactly what game Nicole was trying to play.

The remainder of my day flowed on as usual. I thought about Toni and wondered how things would go when I was to see her later on in the day. I had a gut feeling that Toni would want to discuss things like, how wrong she feels for wanting to be with me. I also knew that I would kick some garbage as to how I really care for her and how I will do whatever I have to do in order to prove it to her. Yeah, it didn't take a rocket scientist to know what we would talk about. I just hoped that I would be able to get over like O.J. Simpson with my game.

As my work day whisked by, I decided to go back to the McDonalds where I had met Carmen to see if she was working. On my lunch break, although I wasn't hungry, I headed straight for a Big Mac. When I reached McDonalds I decided not to go to the drive thru because I wanted to go inside and get a better visual of Carmen. After I ordered my Big Mac and Sprite, I asked the cashier if Carmen was around. To my disappointment I was told that Carmen wasn't scheduled to come in until 5 pm. I simply advised the cashier to tell Carmen that Lance had stopped by to see her.

As I walked out of the restaurant and got back into my truck, I convinced myself that I would in fact give Carmen a call sometime in the near future. While eating my food, I was thinking of how much easier it would be to deal with a much younger and innocent chick like Carmen. It would be a piece of cake.

The Big Mac had filled me up. I wanted to relax for about five more minutes so that the food could digest but I remembered that I also wanted to send Nicole some flowers. Actually I didn't want to spend the money on flowers, but I was like hey, I haven't surprised my wife like that in a while and plus it would be a good way to get back in good with her. My break was ending soon so I quickly called 1800FLOWERS and placed my order.

I knew that I had to have the card read something spiritual. A scriptural passage would definitely brighten my wife's mood, and it would let her think that maybe I was trying to be more focused on God. I knew which passage of scripture I wanted to accompany the flowers, but I wasn't exactly a walking Bible so I didn't have the passage memorized. I told the operator from 1800FLOWERS that I would have to call her right back.

I hustled from the pay phone that I was using and went back to my work truck. I knew that somewhere in my truck, amidst all of the filthy pornographic books, that I had a pocket Bible laying around. I found it and turned to the "love chapter" of 1 Corinthians, chapter 13 which reads:

Love is patient, love is kind. It does not envy, it does not boast, it is not proud. It is not rude, it is not self-seeking, it is not easily angered, it keeps no record of wrongs. Love does not delight in evil but rejoices with the truth. It always protects, always trusts, always hopes, always perseveres. Love never fails.

After reading that passage I hurried and closed the Bible and I ran back to the pay phone and put in my order. When I was done placing the order, in my head I was like "Yeah." See I knew that after my wife were to read the card, along with the smell of fresh roses, that I would be in like flynn. That scripture said exactly what I would have wanted to say, but only much better than I could have ever said it. What I really needed to do was memorize more verses and have them ready and at my disposal for times when I want to kick some serious game to my wife. Man, if I ever started spitting out Bible verses, my wife would be all over me.

****

It couldn't have been no more than fifteen minutes from the time I was done ordering the flowers for my wife, when my pager went off. I recognized the number right away. It was the number to International Hair Designs. Without delay I became ecstatic. Unfortunately I was in the middle of a job and I hadn't brought my cell phone with me. I was in the process of conducting a gas leak investigation, but I felt the urge to neglect my duties and find the nearest pay phone. Fortunately, I was sane enough as to not risk a gas explosion just to satisfy my insatiable urges.

The gas leak investigation was taking much longer than usual. After twenty more minutes had passed by, my pager went off again. Once more, International Hair Designs' phone number was in my pager but this time it also had 911 after the number. I became intensely impatient. I rushed through the paper work that went along with the gas leak investigation and I made a somewhat confident conclusion that the gas leak was confined and not an imminent and dangerous threat. As quickly as I could, I made my way to a pay phone and called Toni.

After the owner of the shop picked up and relayed the phone to Toni, I heard Toni say, "Well it's about time."

I replied, "Yo I'm sorry. I was in the middle of a job when you paged me and I couldn't get to a phone right away."

Toni informed, "Yeah, I called your cell phone but no one picked up."

"Oh nah, I left the house this morning and I forgot to bring it with me," I explained.

Toni in her sweet soft sounding voice replied, "That's alright, as long as you're OK. Listen, so am I still gonna see you today?"

"Of course," I answered. Knowing that I had to be home this evening in order to put in "brownie" points with Nicole, I added, "Toni, it would really help if I could see you when I get off of work, say around five."

Toni responded, "Yeah five O'clock is cool. I'll just leave the shop early. Plus it's slow today, so that'll give me another excuse to leave."

After a brief pause I was like, "A'ight, so I'll see you at five, at your crib right?"

Toni replied, "Yeah. You still gonna see if you can fix the AC for me right?"

"Yeah that's not a problem."

Toni tried ending the call, but I reminded her that she had never told me where she lives.

She began laughing, "Oh, I'm sorry I didn't even realize that."

I have to admit that I felt like I'd been to Toni's house before. I know that she forgot to give me her address because she too was probably feeling mad comfortable with me as if she'd known me for years. After letting Toni know that I had a pen, she gave me her address which was, 99-01 Chevy Chase Rd.

"You live in Jamaica Estates?" I asked, sounding kind of surprised.

Toni answered, "Yeah." Then she started giving me directions on how to get there.

Being that I work for Con Edison, I was forced to know just about every street in Brooklyn, as well as every street in Queens. I interrupted Toni, "You don't have to give me directions, I know how to get there."

"Oh OK, so I'll see you there. Just ring the bottom bell," Toni instructed.

When work ended I sped to the daycare center and retrieved LL. After picking up LL I dropped him at Tiffany's house and asked her if she could watch him for about an hour or so. I explained to her that I had to run by someone's house to fix their Air Conditioning. As usual, my sister had no problem with watching him.

I would have preferred to have gone home, taken a shower and changed before I went by Toni's, but being married didn't afford me that luxury. Like me, my sister also lives in Cambria Heights, so I wasn't too far from Jamaica Estates which is only about ten minutes away. I was actually surprised to be going to Jamaica Estates. That would have been one of the last neighborhoods that I would have guessed that Toni lived in. See, Jamaica Estates is a very high class wealthy neighborhood. Not only that, but it's a predominantly white Jewish area. Many dignitaries like politicians, lawyers and CEO's live in the Estates. The most famous resident is probably Fred Trump, Donald Trump's father.

As I weaved my way through the curved tree lined street, I marveled at the mansions and the manicured lawns. The time was nearing five O'clock, so I was right on time. I made my way onto Chevy Chase Rd. and I looked for Toni's address. I came upon a very immaculate looking white brick house with huge pillars that reminded me of the white house in Washington D.C.. The lawn had statues and water fountains and the whole nine yards. Being that the day was bright and sunny, it only added to the beauty of the house. I was sure that this was the right crib because I saw Toni's convertible parked in the circular driveway.

Since I had on my blue collar attire, I felt a bit insecure. But I wasn't sweating it 'cause I knew that I had dough. Maybe not enough dough to live in Jamaica Estates but my bank account held mad weight. I parked my car along the curb. I got out of the car and after carefully surveying the grounds I made my way to the front door. As I got closer to the door I was feeling nervous. I felt as though I was going to pick up my prom date or something. When I reached the door I gathered myself, took a deep breath, exhaled and rang the bottom bell.

After waiting for a minute or so, Toni, who had came from the rear of the house, snuck up behind me and jumped up and grabbed be in a headlock. Being that she caught me off guard, I lost my balance and fell on my butt, yet Toni still had me in the headlock.

Toni began asking, "Yeah, what's up now? What's up punk?"

I couldn't help but laugh, as I tried to pull her arms from around my neck. The scene was cute because Toni was squeezing with all the strength she had and she really thought that she was doing something.

"Yeah you're too weak to break loose right?" Toni asked, trying to sound as if she was in a schoolyard scuffle.

Still laughing but sounding as if I was being strangled I said, "You got it. You got it."

Toni squeezed tighter as she demanded to know, "You give!? Hah? You give!?"

I was still laughing as I managed to say, "Yeah I give, I give..."

Then Toni loosed her grip and mushed my head. I lay on the ground looking up at the sun while laughing. Toni too was laughing.

"Toni, you crazy," I exclaimed as I picked myself up from off the ground.

When I got up, I became instantly aroused. I noticed that Toni had on some tight Daisy Duke shorts, slippers, a tank top and she also had her jet black sumptuous hair pulled back. I made sure not to make any lewd comments about Toni's shorts. Toni stared at me and smiled. She was breathing a little hard as she asked, "So what's up Mista Lance?"

I licked my lips like LL Cool J, smiled, and while squinting from the bright sunlight I said, "Nothing. Same ol' same ol'. But yo, I am digging this crib!"

Toni asked a stupid question, but I guess it was rhetorical, "Oh so you like it?"

"No doubt," I replied.

Toni took me on a tour of the house. She started by showing me around the outside of the house which had all of the extra's, like the tennis court and the in-ground swimming pool. We talked as we walked and Toni explained to me that her father was a surgeon and that her mother was a very successful real estate broker.

As we made our way inside the house I viewed the plush marble floors and the very expensive furniture. Seeing how Toni was living on a whole other level, material wise, I felt like I had played myself by trying to impress her when I'd showed her around my house. Compared to Toni's crib, my house, as nice as it is, was like comparing a Hyundai to a Mercedes.

One thing I quickly noticed was that Toni was not joking when she said it was hot in her house. I was only in there for about two minutes and I was already beginning to sweat. I cut Toni off as she was explaining to me who was in the pictures that were on her mantle in the living room.

"Toni you wasn't lying. It is beaming up in this piece!"

Toni replied, "You see how I'm dressed right? I told you it was hot up in here."

I wanted to let her know that she didn't have to keep her clothes on just because I was there. But again, I didn't want to mess things up with a coarse joke.

"Toni, where's the thermostat?"

"What's that?"

"Come on now... You mean don't know what a thermostat is?..."

Toni, seeming as if she was in a very good mood due to my presence, looked confused as she said, "I don't."

I looked at her and didn't say anything. Toni continued to look at me dumbfounded. Then suddenly her confusion disappeared as if she had received a revelation. "Oh! You mean that square thing that controls the heat?"

I couldn't help but laugh as I shook my head and said, "You are just like a woman. Yeah, where is the square thing that controls the heat?"

Toni laughed and as she directed me to the *square thing*, she explained that she wasn't into *technical stuff*. When we walked up to the thermostat, I instantly diagnosed the problem to Toni's air conditioning woes. Toni looked at me and asked if I also needed to see that *short round thing* that was in the backyard.

"No Toni, I don't need to see the *compressor*," I sarcastically said. "I think I already know what's wrong."

"Well excuse me *Mr. Con Edison*!" Toni exclaimed. Then she shot back like she'd just received her second revelation. "Con Edison!... Wait a minute. You work for Con Edison?"

I replied, "Nah. I just like wearing the Con Edison uniform."

"Shut up Lance," Toni said as she slapped me on the arm. "No but for real, I knew it. That's where I know you from. Didn't you come into the shop one day while you were working?"

I smiled because I knew exactly which day Toni was referring to. "Yeah I was there. That was me."

Toni had her mouth wide open as she laughed and said, "I knew I wasn't trippin'. I was trying like crazy to figure out how come you looked so familiar. And you! Oh my God! That day you pulled up to me on Pennsylvania Avenue, talking about, 'I know you.'"

I laughed as I said, "Don't front, you know I was smooth wit' mines that day. My game was tight!"

Toni shook her head and she was about to say something else but she stopped in the middle of her sentence when she felt a whiff of cool air. She paused and looked at me with a confused look as she said, "I know that's not cool air that I feel."

Feeling like the chief and master of my trade I simply blew air on my finger nails and made like I was buffing them on my shirt.

"Lance, you mean to tell me that I've been suffering in this house, in this ghetto heat for days, and you come over here and fix it that quick?"

"Yeah, there was nothing wrong with the AC?" I explained.

"What do you mean? 'Cause my father is gonna wanna know exactly why it wasn't working. I think he has some repair company coming to look at it."

I went on, "I won't even attempt to explain what I did, 'cause I know it will be too technical for you to understand. But just tell your pops that someone must have accidentally moved the switch from AC and had it in the Heat setting. He can call and cancel whoever he had coming to fix it because it's already fixed. I personally guarantee that y'all won't have anymore problems."

Toni looked at me and said, *"Well excuse me."*

I felt good because I guessed that with my handy skills I had impressed Toni. But if only she knew how easy what I had just done was. I mean it was just a matter of moving a switch.

"Oh my God it's already starting to feel good in here. Thank you Lance," Toni added.

Toni's tanned looking and toned body was driving me crazy. It seemed as though we were the only two people in the house so I asked for a hug. Toni put up no argument and she gave me a hug. I didn't let her pull away as I looked her in her eyes and asked, "So you ready to talk or what?"

Toni looked up at me with her puppy dog eyes and nodded her head up and down. Toni was pressed very close against my body. She was feeling and smelling as sweet as ever, so sweet that I was beginning to wonder if she could feel something poking her. I knew that no matter what happened today, that Toni and I were definitely gonna talk. Regardless of whether what we talked about would prove to be positive or not, I realized that now was the perfect time to attempt to kiss her. So without asking for permission I just closed my eyes and allowed my lips and tongue to find Toni's soft lips. As my tongue touched hers, it felt like a wafer was just melting on my tongue.

Not only didn't Toni object, but she was actually getting into the kiss. She began caressing the back of my head as we kissed. She also caused her face to turn into the kiss a couple of times to make it more passionate. Toni finally pulled away from me. She didn't look directly at me as she shook her head and looked towards the floor. There was silence of passionate disbelief. The silence was broken when Toni said, "Lance come on, we definitely have to talk right now!"

Toni grabbed me by the hand and led me to her apartment. Her apartment was sectioned off from the main quarters of the house. She had a separate entrance that led to a door in the backyard and the whole nine.

We reached her apartment which looked as if it could have been in an IKEA catalog with the way it was decorated. Toni sat me at a chair in front of the kitchen counter top. She prepared iced tea for the two of us and then she got right to the point.

"Lance what is going on between us?" I mean you're married and all and here I am kissing you?"

I had no clue as to what I was gonna actually say, but I knew that I had to be as convincing as a con artist. I was still coming off of the high that I had received from the kiss, I felt like plastering one of those nervous smiles on my face, but I wanted Toni to know that I was serious and that I wasn't just taking this serious talk time as a joke. I didn't want to be distracted by Toni's face, her body or anything, so I looked to the floor as I began to speak to her.

I began by slowly shaking my head and saying, "See. Toni it's like this. I'm not saying that I have the worse marriage in the world. Nor am I saying that I don't love my wife. What I am saying or should I say, how I feel is, I feel like I have to be real with myself and if not I'll drive myself insane."

Toni who was standing up said, "I'm trying to understand you but…"

I interrupted her and said, "OK, I'll try to explain myself better. Toni there is something in me that just knows that things are not gonna work out between my wife and myself. You don't know how frustrated I feel inside my heart. I feel like I am constantly living two lives just to make things work between my wife and myself. My marriage is going on five years and I have felt like this since six months into the marriage. I just can't keep this up and that's why I know that there is nothing wrong with me being with you."

I knew that I was jacking things up. I wasn't being convincing enough. I also realized that if I wanted to sound confident, then I would have to feel confident and act confident. From that point on, I sat straight up and began to look into Toni's eyes. Thoughts of my wife were creeping into my mind but I swatted those thoughts away like an irritating fly.

Toni responded, "Lance I think I know what you're trying to say. But like I told you at Juniors, you still made a commitment to your wife and you should try to honor it."

I butted in, "Toni that's just it. I have been trying and it's not gonna work!"

Toni asked, "So how is being with me gonna change things?"

"Being with you Toni is gonna change everything. Because I know that if things work between me and you, then that proves that my marriage was destined to end. Toni, why else would I even be pursuing you if things looked mad bright for the future between me and Nicole?"

Trying to pull out all the punches I continued on. "Toni I don't want you to think that I'm a dog or anything like that. Don't think that at all because if I was a dog I would have cheated on Nicole a long time ago. But I have been faithful for all this time. I was doing what you suggested, in that I was trying my hardest to honor my commitment. But Toni think about it, why should marriage, day in and day out feel like such a laborious chore? Marriage shouldn't be like that, it's not fair!"

I think I was beginning to get through to Toni as she shook her head and explained, "Lance, since I've met you, I have been breaking all kinds of rules that I said I would never break. Rules, that if I were to see another woman breaking, I would label her as a skeezer or a chicken head. Lance, I really do think I understand where you are coming from, but I don't see how things can work between me and you."

"Yes," I thought to myself. I knew I had Toni steered in the direction that I wanted her to go. I just had to continue to bait her. Sounding like Keith Sweat, I came off like I was begging or pleading as I went on.

"Toni I know I don't have all of the answers. I don't know exactly how this is gonna work between me and you. But I know that with every absolute ounce of my being that I want things to work. Toni, listen to me, 'casue I am not trying to run game on you, I'm too old for that. But I promise you that I will do everything that I have to do in order to make this work."

At that point Toni sat down. I knew that I was causing her to consider crossing a line that she thought she could never cross. Toni remained quiet. I knew that I had said enough and I didn't want to interrupt her thoughts. I thought about saying something stupid in reference to Toni's man out in Las Vegas, but that would definitely have been a major error. I wondered what she was thinking about so I asked her.

Toni informed, "I'm just thinking, you know, about your wife and stuff like that."

That was the last thing I needed Toni to be thinking about so I had to come up with some serious game very quick!

"Toni you ever been on a scary roller coaster?" I asked.

Toni replied, "Yes."

Just as I was gonna expand on my game, I felt my pager going off. The pager was on vibrate so Toni didn't have a clue that I had been paged. I looked down and checked the number and it was Nicole. I paid it no attention and I went on.

"Toni I asked you that question because I see the wheels turning in your head. You're thinking about every scenario. You're thinking about how are we gonna speak on the phone. You're asking yourself, when are we gonna have the time to go out? You're thinking about, what if Nicole and I end up getting a divorce?"

I took Toni by the hand to reassure her, as I said, "Toni, I have had those same thoughts for five years but I've finally been able to honestly answer a lot of my own thoughts and questions. Toni think of that scary roller coaster, or bungy jumping, or skydiving. You know it's scary, you know the dangers but deep down inside you still want to experience it. And Toni the thing that stops people from experiencing the joys of the ride is the fact that they stand in front of the roller coaster and they think. They don't have to say anything all they have to do is just think. Then before you know it they back out and say, 'nah, nah it's too scary I'm not getting on.' See Toni, when people do that they rob themselves of experiencing the things that deep down inside they want to experience."

After saying that, I was like "damn!" I mean I was even shocked as to having pulled that game out of my hat. I wanted Toni to think about what I had just said and at the same time I didn't want to keep rambling on to give Toni the impression that I was gassing her. So after having said all of that, I asked Toni if I could use her phone. As she went to her bedroom to retrieve her cordless phone I realized that it was already a little past six O'clock. When Toni came back with the phone I called my wife.

I didn't want Toni to know who I was talking to so when my wife answered the phone I asked that common question, "Yo, you paged me?"

Nicole, who finally sounded like she was in a better mood said, "Yeah, I paged you baby."

"What's up?" I replied.

"Thank you for the flowers."

"You're welcome," I nonchalantly replied.

Nicole went on to say that she was sorry for not speaking to me this morning. She added that she knew that I was also sorry for what had happened last night. Then she asked about my whereabouts and LL's whereabouts. Toni was still standing right next to me and I didn't want to lie. I played things off by saying, "Oh. I had to fix my friend's Air Conditioner so I went there right after work, but LL is at Tiffany's."

Nicole asked, "When will you be home?"

"Oh, in like a half," I replied.

Nicole who wanted to verify my response asked, "You mean a half an hour?"

"Yeah."

"OK so I'll see you later."

I hung up the phone and placed it down on the counter. Of course Toni asked me who I had been speaking to. I knew that she didn't know who my sister was so I simply lied and told her that I had been speaking to my sister. Knowing that I had to leave soon I immediately asked Toni if she understood what I had been trying to get across to her.

Of course she still lacked a little confidence. But she told me that she did indeed understand what I was trying to say. I wanted to remove all of Toni's insecurities and leave her house knowing that a relationship had been officially fostered from this point on.

"Toni you want things to work between me and you. I know you do because if you didn't you wouldn't have suggested that we talk about things. I'm trying to get an understanding between us. I have to leave so I'll get straight to the point. From this point on I don't want you overly thinking about things... A'ight."

Toni shyly nodded her head in agreement.

I added, I ain't trying to back you into a corner or tie you down but I want us to establish a relationship."

Toni shook her head and smiled, as if to say she still had some things to think about.

I smiled too, as I said, "See there you go again, thinking. Stop thinking. Don't think about anything except for the fact that I am gonna do my part in trying to make things work between me and you. Toni all I want is for you to tell me that from this point forward you'll do your part in helping us make this work."

Toni still was smiling as she walked from out of the kitchen and into her living room. I followed right behind her and I hugged her from behind. I asked again, "You're gonna try right?"

Toni didn't respond.

I had to jet and I asked her to walk me to my car, which she did. We walked to my car without saying a word to each other. When we reached the Lexus I got in and sat behind the steering wheel. Toni was standing right besides the driver's window which was rolled down. I started up the car, looked at Toni and asked her again, "You're gonna try right?"

Toni nodded her head up and down to show me her agreement. Then she bent over and gave me a peck on the lips. After the peck we both seductively looked at each other. Toni stood back and waved as I pulled off. I was in a slammin' mood for the remainder of the night.

My wife and I had made up. I managed to explain to Nicole that the reason I was upset and had snapped at her was because I had bet a lot of money on the game and I lost. That was a total lie but my wife, who after reprimanding me for gambling, told me that she understood.

So with things good on the home front, and things John Blazin' between me and Toni, I was on cloud nine. I knew that I had a great dilemma to solve. That was, which of my two faces was I gonna wear around my wife? I knew that the face of evil was way too painful. All it caused was arguments, stress, and anxiety. But the face of good, required tedious hypocritical work. See, I didn't have the gall to do like some men do, in terms of just walking away from my wife and kid. I didn't even have the guts to get a divorce. Internally I knew that I cared way too much to just walk away from things or to get a divorce. Actually it wasn't even about that, because my family is still the most important thing to me on this planet.

It was more about feeling satisfied. I realized that just like prior to Toni, when I *needed* both Scarlet and Nicole in order to maintain my sanity, that I would now need both *Toni and Nicole* in order to maintain my current sanity. I was willing to put in the hard work. Just as Toni had made a vow to make the relationship work between her and myself, I also made a vow to myself. That vow was that from this point on I was gonna be the best Christian family man that ever walked the face of the earth. And at the same time, I was gonna blow Toni away and be the best lover since Casanova.

THIRTEEN

Nicole and I have worked out a system that is designed to combat boredom in our marriage. We looked at many older couples such as our parents and tried to figure out why they weren't as happy as they appeared to be in their youthful wedding pictures. Our brainstorming produced many hypothesis. But one major conclusion that we came to was the fact that many couples had stopped *dating* each other after marriage.

For Nicole and me, either Friday or Saturday was always set aside for just the two of us. On one of those two days we would do things that led us to continue wanting to spend the rest of our lives together. Whenever we would go out on dates we would make sure that we kept things spontaneous. One week we would go to a comedy club. The next week we would go out to Yankee Stadium or to a restaurant, you name it, we did it.

Lately I've noticed that we have both been letting other things take a higher priority over our marriage. Nicole, who always has great intentions, is becoming very one tracked. Her every thought is church, church, church. Believe me, as the husband I know that I have to be on a higher spiritual page than she is, but I can't see how that's genuinely gonna happen. I mean I'm gonna put forth a hypocritical effort to make it happen, however with Nicole's church-church-church mentality, she is causing me to resent the fellowship of the congregants.

See, what has happened between Scarlet and I, that really shouldn't count against me, I mean yeah I'll admit that I'm doing wrong in the sense that I'm creeping with Toni, but Nicole is no better because she is establishing a relationship with a mistress of her own, *the church.*

For example, grant it that my supervisor had asked me a week in advance to work late on Friday, I still knew that I would be home by ten O'clock this evening. I really wanted my wife and me to go out and do something. It's been over a couple of months since we've truly dated. Unfortunately Nicole turned down my request to take her to a late night movie. She'd informed me that the church was having a special Friday evening service and she had already made plans to attend. Nicole explained to me that the service wouldn't end until midnight. At which time, she knew that she would be exhausted and only looking forward to bed. Her suggestion to me was that I either stay home or use the night as a night out with the fellas.

"Yeah, a'ight," I thought to myself.

On my way home from work that evening, I knew that I definitely wasn't trying to go home and go to sleep. Man it was Friday night and I wanted to unwind from a week of work and stress. I contacted Steve and some of the other fellas to see what they were getting themselves into. Most of my friends were split down the middle. Half of them were just chillin' for the night, while the other half were planning on going out to a club. It's been a while since I'd been to a club and I thought about joining them, but tonight wasn't really a club night for me. First of all I wasn't feeling real Macish. I wasn't in the mood for dancing and I didn't feel like spending dough or buying drinks for some whore.

Yeah I didn't feel like kicking it to females tonight, and that was the main reason that I would not have gone to a club, so I was like forget the club thing. Scarlet was supposed to be stripping, or as she would put it, "dancing" at this club in Harlem, so I thought about surprising her by going to the club and checking her out and then maybe chillin' with her afterwards.

Although I was trying to avoid it, subconsciously I knew that I hadn't exhausted all of my options for the night. I still had the opportunity to call Toni to see if she wanted to take my wife's place and join me in seeing a movie. While still on my way home from work, I called Toni on my cell to see what plans she had for the night. And it felt sooo good to hear her voice! A voice that gets lively and excited because she is speaking to me. Yeah, and it feels extremely exemplary when Toni starts telling me that she missed me and the like.

"So what's up? What are you doing tonight?" I asked.

Toni explained that since it was a Friday, the shop had been extremely busy. She told me that she had just walked in the house after a thirteen hour day in the salon.

"Oh so that means your pockets are full of dead presidents and you're gonna take me out tonight right?" I asked.

Toni laughed as she said, "Yeah baby I'll take you out. My treat. Where do you wanna go?"

"Well I was thinking about seeing a movie, especially being that it's so late and all."

Toni responded, "Well you know what? Actually I'm exhausted from today, and I know that I have to be back at the shop at seven in the morning, so I was gonna just come home and get in the bed."

Sounding kind of disappointed because I had a feeling that Toni was trying to reject my offer, I replied, "Oh so you trying to front on me?"

Toni laughed and said, "No no. Of course not. I was just thinking, being that I'm tired and all, why don't you rent a movie and come over here and we can just hang out."

Toni definitely wasn't gonna get any objections from me. I informed her that I would be at her place within the next forty five minutes.

"What about <u>Men In Black</u>? Have you ever seen that?" I asked.

"<u>Men In Black</u>, with Will Smith right?" Toni asked.

"Yeah."

Toni added, "Nah I never saw that. Yeah, so rent that."

"A'ight, so I'll see you later."

I knew that I didn't have to stop at the video store, because I had purchased <u>Men In Black</u> for LL. He liked the movie so much that I bought it for him. I simply had to rush home, get showered and dressed and I could jet over to Toni's. The "Toni" rushes that I get were already starting to kick in. It's the same rush that I used to get back in the days when I knew I was gonna see my wife who was my girlfriend at the time.

I dug deep into my romantic repertoire to see what I could come up with to compliment the movie. In no way shape or form did I want Toni to be bored while she was with me. Being that I was still in Brooklyn, I decided to drop by the Canarsie pier. The Canarsie pier was a spot along Jamaica Bay just off the Belt

Parkway. It consisted of restaurants and boats and the whole nine that any pier would have. You had your people that came to the pier to fish. Others came to relax and enjoy nature as they would sit on the benches, bicycle, walk or rollerblade on the boardwalk and the like.

At the pier you could also purchase all kinds of seafood. I am no cook, but the dishes that I do know how to cook usually come out slammin'. I perfected my ability to cook certain dishes simply because I wanted to impress women. My plan tonight was no different. I wanted to impress Toni, so I purchased three live lobsters. I knew that Toni liked seafood because she had ordered shrimp when we went to Juniors. I couldn't wait to surprise her.

After having showered, I trimmed my goatee and my mustache to make sure my grill was on point. My attire was very casual, Air Jordan's, baggy jeans and a short sleeve button down rayon shirt. Before I left my house I grabbed the movie and I also retrieved the Old Bay seasoning for the lobsters. Just to cover my tracks, I left a note telling Nicole that I had gone out and that I would be back home around two or three in the morning.

I hopped in my car and before I knew it I was at Toni's place. When Toni answered the door she looked as if she had just come out of the shower. She had a towel on her head and she had on this sexy short silk robe. After hugging one another, Toni invited me in and she explained that she had in fact just come out of the shower. She told me to have a seat in her living room while she excused herself to go change. At that point all kinds of sexual thoughts were running through my head. The natural high that I was on began to elevate.

Then all of a sudden, both my cell phone and my pager started vibrating almost simultaneously.

It was Scarlet!

"Oh damn!" I thought to myself. "Not now!"

Being that Toni was out of the room, I decided to just quickly answer my cell phone and tell Scarlet that I would call her back. I knew that that was a real dangerous move because I was taking a chance that Toni might over hear me talking on the phone and then later question me as to who it was that I had been speaking to. But I also didn't want Scarlet blowing up my cell phone and pager throughout the night, so like I said, I decided to answer the cell but I knew that I would have to take control of the conversation and make it quick.

I answered my cell phone and I immediately started talking in a way that would not allow for any small talk, "Yo what's up Scarlet? Listen, let me call you back in about an hour, ok?"

"Nah that's not OK!" Scarlet rudely shot back, which sought of caught me off guard. "You're gonna speak to me right now and explain to me what the hell you're doing in Jamaica Estates!"

At that point my heart started pounding so fast and hard that I thought Toni was gonna hear it in the other room. I immediately started looking under the couch, and underneath the table and inside one of the closets in Toni's apartment to see if Scarlet was staked out in the joint with a butcher knife or something.

"Jamaica Estates?" I replied trying to sound ignorant as to what Scarlet was saying.

"Yeah nigga don't play stupid! That is exactly what I asked you. Jamaica-Got–Damn-Estates! On Chevy Chase Rd., whose house are you at!?"

At that point I felt like screaming out loud the words "Damn! Damn! Damn," as if I was the character Florida Evans from that famous episode of the TV Show <u>Good Times</u>. But instead I just slightly whispered to myself, "Ahhhhhhhhh Damn!" What could I say? I was just gritting my teeth out of both fear and frustration. I wish I could have just jumped through that cell phone and strangled Scarlet!

I walked to a very remote part of Toni's apartment and I began talking in a very low and stern voice.

"Scarlet del Rio, you listen to me! I don't know what you are up to or where you're calling me from or what the deal is! But I'm gonna say this one time and I am not gonna be arguing with you here on the phone... I decided to go out with the fellas tonight but I had to make a quick stop and drop off something for Steve

real quick. I didn't even know that this was Jamaica Estates, all I had was an address."

"Lance don't give me that!"

"What do you mean don't give you that!?"

In my mind I was panicking like crazy because I knew that Toni would be coming out of her room at any second.

"Who is the seafood for Lance!?... Oh let me guess. Steve called you at work and asked you to stop in Canarsie and get some seafood and instead of dropping it off at his house, you decide to go home and get all dipped out and then drop off the seafood before y'all go out... Right? Is that it? You must really think I'm a stupid Brazilian bitch! Or something!"

I knew Scarlet was heated because her accent started to come out as she spoke.

Scarlet was truly pulling my card. Now I was scared because I knew that Scarlet must have been following me and I didn't want her ringing Toni's doorbell or anything ghetto like that. So like my years of experience had taught me, I knew that when the evidence is strongly stacked against you, it means that it is probably a good time to cop a serious plea bargain deal. *Copping a plea* is basically admitting that you are guilty, and when you do that it's like saying that you're at least not trying to insult the prosecuting party's intelligence. And in this case, Scarlet was the prosecutor, the judge, the jury, and she would have had no problem being the executioner!

"A'ight listen!" I angrily and nervously whispered.

"Scarlet I'm not going out with the fellas. I lied about that. See, I'm admitting that. But I just can't explain to you right now what I'm doing because you wouldn't understand."

"I wouldn't understand what!? That you're screwing some rich white lady!? Only rich white folks live in Jamaica Estates! So Lance what don't I understand about that!?"

Since my plea bargaining strategy wasn't working I now only had one final option and that was to throw myself on the mercy of the court and beg for leniency.

"Scarlet I am not with no white woman! But please just listen to me. Please... I know exactly what you're thinking.

You're thinking that I'm with someone else and that that someone else is gonna take your spot. Baby that is just not true and I'll prove it! See, I'm about to say something that I have never ever said before and I am not just saying this because I want you to believe me...   But tomorrow, if you give me the chance I will explain everything to you face to face as far as what it is that I'm doing here in Jamaica Estates. And if after I explain and prove to you the legitimate reason why I was here, you still don't believe me, then I tell you what, you can take every sex video that you and I have ever made, you can take any picture that we have ever taken together, you can take all the letters and cards that I have ever given you, along with all of the gifts and whatever, and you can personally hand deliver them to Nicole."

Scarlet was silent as she thought about what I had just said.

"Scarlet, you know how fiercely adamant I have always been in terms of keeping you a secret from Nicole. So if I'm telling you that I am willing to break that veil in order to have your trust, that should be telling you something *baby*," I made sure to stress the word baby.

I don't know where on earth I was getting all of that *loose lip* pimp game from. And I knew it was damn sure risky pimp game that I was loosely throwing around. Everyone knows that it is loose lips that sink ships, but I had Toni right where I wanted her and I was willing to risk and do just about anything and say anything and to go to any lengths that I had to in order to avoid fouling things up with Toni.

Fortunately I had somewhat broken through to Scarlet as she angrily and reluctantly replied, "WhooooUuuughhhh! I can't stand you Lance! You better thank God that I'm in a rush! I'm dancing at this new club in Harlem for the first time tonight and I don't wanna stand up the promoter. Otherwise I would sit my Brazilian ass right here on Chevy Chase Rd. and wait to see which house it is that you come out of!"

Man, I didn't even know that Scarlet was actually camped outside! But that's just how gangsta and gully she is with hers.

"Scarlet remember what I said, a'ight?"

"Lance, you are getting real sloppy with yours Lance! Remember what I told you. If I can't be you're number one then I am damn sure gonna be your number two!"

"Scarlet I gotta go aayite," I very nervously whispered in a rushed tone.

"Oh you're rushing me off the phone!? Matter of fact I do have a few minutes... I tell you what. If you ain't with no other woman then bring yo' black ass outside right now and come sit in my car for a few minutes! I'm parked right next to your car."

As Scarlet was calling my bluff, out of pure disgust I blew air into the phone and I simply told Scarlet that I had to go. I hung up the phone and I quickly made it back to where I had been sitting in Toni's apartment.

Before I could sit back down Scarlet was again blowing up my phone. But this time I didn't dare to answer.

As my heart pounded I remember thinking to myself that there was no way that I was gonna be able to relax with Toni. I was too worried that Scarlet was gonna start ringing doorbells in the neighborhood in an attempt to find me or something.

But I knew that I had to relax and just deal with the drama that came along with being a *rolling stone*. If I was able to safely make it through the next ten minutes without Scarlet doing a *drive-by shooting* on Toni's crib then I figured that I would at least be cool for the night.

As Toni was still in her room changing, and thank God she had taken longer than I expected, she yelled out to me, "So did you have a problem getting the movie?"

I yelled back, "Nah I got it."

Before I knew it Toni had come out of her room wearing a tee shirt, sweat pants and those thick socks that bunch up around the ankles. She was also in the process of brushing her hair as she sat down next to me. Toni smiled at me and asked "So Lance how was your day?"

Not wanting to mention the drama that could quite possibly unfold if Scarlet were to figure out which house Toni lived in and rang the bell, I responded, "My day was cool. I didn't think it would turn out as good as it has. You know being that I'm with you and everything." Then I went on to tell her that I had a surprise for her.

Toni inched closer to me in excitement. "Really? What is it?"

Totally forgetting that Scarlet was camped outside, I added, "its outside, wait right here. I'll go get it."

While I got up to make my way outside, Toni turned the TV on. She then pulled her hair back and placed a silk scrunchy around it to hold it in place as she relaxed on the couch and expressed her love of surprises.

After first tip toeing up to a huge oak tree that was located near Toni's driveway and hiding behind it, I poked my head out from behind the tree to see if the coast was clear. Feeling like I was playing *hide and go seek* or some type of game like that, I nervously made it to my Lexus. With my heart pounding a mile a minute I scanned the entire block with my eyes looking for Scarlet. Fortunately she wasn't anywhere in sight. But knowing her, she probably was in a tree with a pair of night vision binoculars along with a gun and a red scope targeted dot pointed at my head waiting to pull the trigger. I knew that going outside was crazy and bold on my part but I also figured that even if I had bumped into Scarlet it would have made me come across in a much more credible manner to her.

Luckily for me I was able to safely retrieve the lobsters which were loaded in the trunk of my car inside of a box of ice. The lobsters were still very much alive and moving. I carried the box back to Toni's apartment and I checked over my shoulder one last time to make sure that Scarlet was not in sight, which thank God, she wasn't. Before I walked back into Toni's living room I told her to close her eyes. Toni was smiling from ear to ear. As I approached her I instructed her to stand up, and to make sure that she kept her eyes closed. When I got directly in front of her I quietly opened the box and I raised the box of lobsters up to her chin.

Toni, who couldn't see a thing, began to laugh and she asked, "Lance, what are you doing?"

I replied, "Nothing. Just relax, and keep your eyes closed."

Toni continued to smile and giggle while I remained silent for about ten seconds.

Then I said, "A'ight you can open your eyes now."

Toni opened her eyes. She saw the lobsters, and instantly let out a scream as she bolted for cover. When she was out of harms way she put a hand across her chest. Breathing heavy and sounding fearful, she asked, "Lance what is that?"

After witnessing her reaction I fell to the couch in belly ache laughter. Still terrified, Toni asked again, "Lance what is in that box?"

Still laughing, I got up from the couch and walked in Toni's direction in an attempt to show her what was inside the box. But as I got closer she ran and demanded that I get no closer. Finally my laughter was beginning to come to a close and I explained, "it's just lobsters baby."

Toni looked at me with an untrusting look. So to prove it I held the box down and tilted it in her direction. Toni proceeded with caution. She inched closer and closer to the box and attempted to look in. I thought about screaming and scaring her one last time but I decided that enough was enough. I didn't want her to think that I was childish or anything. When Toni was close enough to confirm that it was in fact lobsters, she let out a sigh of relief and began laughing. She punched me on the arm and asked was I trying to give her a heart attack.

"Just trying to have a little fun," I advised.

Toni informed me that she loves lobster but she had no idea in the world how to properly cook them. While walking towards the kitchen I confidently informed, "Well I didn't expect for you to cook them. I was planning on cooking for you… That's if it's OK with you."

"Uh oh, look out now!" Toni jokingly replied. "There is definitely nothing wrong with a man that can cook."

I instructed Toni, "give me the largest and deepest pot that you have."

As Toni searched for a pot I explained to her that cooking lobster was as easy as boiling an egg. Toni, who seemed to be delighted by the whole idea, informed me that she had to run up to her parent's to get a big pot being that all of her pots were of average size. While Toni went to locate the pot I made myself very familiar with her kitchen. To make things look good, I put on an apron that I saw hanging from the side of her range. I also placed a big wooden spoon on the table along with cooking gloves. I searched inside of her refrigerator to see if she had the necessary ingredients to make a salad.

As Toni returned to the kitchen with the pot, she asked, "Is this big enough?"

I reached and took it from her hand while letting her know that it indeed was big enough. Toni laughed and said, "Uh oh, look at Lance... Got his apron on and the whole nine, I'm afraid of you. Let me find out!"

"Just have a seat and watch. I'll show you how to be a chef," I replied.

Toni pulled out a chair from her kitchen table. She sat in the chair with her legs curled underneath her butt and her forearms on the glass kitchen table. As Toni sat with her hands folded, she smiled with excited anticipation. I began to demonstrate my skills as I said, "A'ight, the first thing you do is fill the pot up with water. That of course is assuming that the pot is clean, 'cause if the pot isn't clean the first thing you would do is clean the pot. I'm assuming y'all don't have no roaches or anything... Do y'all?"

Toni laughed while shaking her head no. By now she had her right elbow on the table and her right palm was cupped underneath her chin. Toni kinda spoke through her teeth as she assured me, "No, we don't have any roaches... You sure got nerve!"

"Just checking baby, just checking," I said. I then went on to explain the process. "OK, after you fill the pot with water you add your seasoning to the water. Then you bring the water to a boil. When the water starts boiling that is when you place the lobsters into the water... And that's it."

Toni seeming to be a little baffled, asked, "That's it?"

"Yeah that's it," I replied.

"So how do you know when the lobsters are ready?" Toni questioned.

"Oh. Well let me back track a bit. I forgot to tell you that you have to put the lobsters into the water while they are still alive."

Toni frowned and remarked how cruel it was to scorch the poor lobsters to death. I gave no weight to her feelings as I told her, "Don't worry about that. Better them than you right?... But to answer your question, you'll know that they're ready when you see their shells turn bright red. After they turn bright red you can then take them out of the pot, dry them off and put butter on them. Once the butter is on them you can place them in the broiler for a while."

"Does putting the butter on them add flavor or something?" Toni asked.

"Nah it just makes the shell easier to crack," I explained.

During the time I was explaining all of this to Toni, I had the fire under the pot and the water was at its boiling point. Toni cringed as I dropped the lobsters into the water.

"Lance that's so mean! Oh look at the poor things… You can tell that they're in pain 'cause they are moving around so crazy," Toni commented.

Again I brushed Toni's remarks to the side as I replied, "They'll be a'ight. Besides, you won't even be thinking about how they're feeling when you're eating them."

Lobster doesn't take that long to cook, so while they were boiling in the pot I began to prepare the salad. Toni expressed that I seemed like I was comfortable and that I knew my way around the kitchen very well. Trying to big myself up, I gloated as I sliced the tomatoes, "Yeah, cooking ain't all that. If I put my mind to it there isn't anything that I can not do. I'm multi-talented."

Toni was smiling. She became inquisitive and wanted to know more about my "multi-talents." I informed her that some of my talents couldn't be spoken about due to their explicit contents. With the expression on her face, I could tell that Toni didn't seem too amused by the nature of my comment. I quickly recovered by adding that I also knew how to do hair.

Toni became instantly amused, as she said, "Yeah right. What do you mean you know how to do hair?"

"I'm sayin'. I can do wraps, doobies, and all that," I confidently proclaimed. "Matter of fact, I'll even take care of your split ends."

Toni began laughing and then she looked at me with her head slightly tilted and asked, "Can you really do wraps?"

"Yeah, wraps are easy. All you need is some setting lotion, a brush, a comb, and a hair dryer, and you're good to go." As I cracked a smile, I advised Toni not to sleep on my skills. Toni demanded proof, and I assured her that I would prove it to her, just as long as she would be willing to be my guinea pig.

I was just about done with the salad so I asked Toni where would we be eating. She suggested that we eat in the living room so we could watch the movie while we ate. After looking in the pot I noticed that the lobsters were almost done.

"See, Toni come here a minute." As Toni walked towards the stove, I added, "This is what I was talking about when I said they'll turn bright red. They should be ready to go into the broiler in about two more minutes."

Toni got two plates and two trays. Then she asked what would I like to drink. Being that I wanted the evening to be as romantic as possible, I asked her if she had any wine. Unfortunately she didn't.

"You ever drank Alize?" Toni asked.

"Whaaat!" I cheerfully replied. "That's my drink. Why, you got some?..."

To my excitement, Toni did indeed have a whole bottle of Alize. Before long we were in front of the television watching the movie and eating. We were having a good time. Toni admitted that she wasn't very experienced at eating lobster. I watched her make a mess but I coached her as to how to properly eat the lobster.

I told her, "Yeah it will be mad messy if you don't know how to eat it. But when you eat it right, you'll be able to enjoy it better."

Toni did get the hang of it rather quickly. While she was eating she told me that she had no idea that lobster was so easy to cook and that she would definitely be treating herself to them more regularly. While we ate, we really weren't paying attention to the movie. We began talking about ourselves.

"Lance you know what?... I don't even know your last name. Knowing a person's last name is important you know. I can't be getting all close to you and not knowing the simple things like that."

I informed her that my last name is *Thomas*.

Then from out of the blue, Toni asked me how did I know that she was Haitian when we'd first met? I went on to explain to her that it was because of her last name. After sipping on her Alize she agreed that her last name was a very popular Haitian name. Toni informed me that she was born in Haiti, and she didn't move to this country until she was five years old. The delay was because her father was in medical school in the United States and he wanted to finish school before he sent for his immediate family members who were still in Haiti. Toni also told me that her mother was Dominican.

"Oh, so that's why you know how to do hair," I replied.

"What does that have to do with anything?" Toni questioned.

"You know that Dominican women are famous for knowing how to do hair very well," I explained.

Toni was surprised and explained that she really hadn't heard of that stereotype. I simply told her to ask the other beauticians in her shop and they would confirm it. Then I playfully teased Toni about certain Haitian stereotypes. It was good that she wasn't very sensitive. Toni seemed more than willing to joke with me as I asked her about Haitian voodoo and things like that.

Before I knew it, Toni and I were finished with the lobsters and we began to feed each other salad. Toni was in a playful mood. With the fork that she was using to feed me with, she caused it to miss my mouth, which in turn caused salad dressing to get on my face. Of course I didn't mind the joke, as I too began to put salad dressing on her face. Toni's playful mood ignited a flame in the back of my head.

See, when I initially came over to her crib I had no intentions of going any further than kissing Toni. But being that she was so happy I began to wonder if in fact I could fulfill my dream and *"hit it"* tonight. I knew that the Alize would be a big help so I made sure that we both drank as much as possible.

Toni continued to put salad dressing on my face. So out of nowhere, I informed her that if she was gonna keep doing that then she would have to lick it off. To my surprise and without hesitation Toni pressed her body up against mines and she ran her tongue from the area near my lips, all the way to my ear, where she stopped and began to kiss my ear.

Chills ran through my body and I became instantly aroused. I knew that I couldn't over react, so I kept my hormones at bay. Toni stopped kissing my ear and she just looked at me. I was desperately trying to translate her look into words. I was wondering to myself, "should I make my move now and try to hit it or what?"

The obvious thing to do was to kiss her. So I proceeded to do just that. It wasn't a very deep kiss, it was a kiss to test the waters. This time after we kissed, Toni broke some of the ice with a smile. She then stood up from the couch that we were sitting on and walked towards her bedroom. The voice inside of me was going bananas. In my mind I knew that the present atmosphere, combined with Toni's mood, was exactly what I had been pursuing ever since I first laid eyes on her. My heart began racing because I had a good feeling about what could possibly take place.

I was hoping that Toni would return from her room with a skimpy outfit, or a garter belt and high heels. That would have definitely more than fulfilled every fantasy that I've ever craved to fulfill. To my disappointment Toni returned from the bedroom and asked, "Lance, how late are you staying?"

I instantly got nervous. Here I was, thinking I'm about to get mines off, and Toni was wondering how she could get me to leave.

"Well what time is it now?" I asked.

"It's a quarter to one," Toni replied.

Sounding very dejected, I replied, "I guess I can bounce now. I mean I know you have to get up in the morning and all."

Toni injected, "Oh no. I wasn't trying to give you a hint to leave. I'm just saying I hope you don't think I'm doing those dishes."

Inside I was like, "Whew!" I let out a laugh of relief as I said, "Come on, I'm sayin', I cooked you the bomb seafood meal, and you're gonna make me do the dishes too?"

In actuality, I knew that Toni could have cared less about the dishes. I told myself that she definitely wanted it, and I had to make my move as soon as possible to give it to her.

Toni went on, "I don't care how late you stay, but all I know is that those dishes better be done before you leave!"

"OK mommy," I playfully said. I added "Toni, come over here so we can finish watching this movie. I promise when the movie is over I'll do the dishes for you."

I realized that the reason Toni had went to her bedroom was to retrieve a bottle of nail polish remover and some cotton balls. Toni came back near the couch and sat on the floor. She let her back rest against the sofa. Toni who was sitting between my legs took off her socks, exposing her sexy feet. She applied nail polish remover to a cotton ball and she began to take off the toenail polish.

I took a sip of my Alize and I commented, "Toni you have the most sexiest toes that I have ever seen!"

Toni blushed with embarrassment, as he laughed. Then she questioned, "Well what about you? How are your toes?"

"My feet are a'ight, but that's not important 'cause I'm not a female," I informed.

"Oh no, that is not true!" Toni emphatically remarked. "I know I do hair and nails, but one thing I can't stand is some jacked up feet on a man or woman. Oh my god! Ill! That just makes my flesh crawl."

After witnessing Toni squirm and shake her body, I knew that it was a good thing that I did have a set of nice feet. Toni asked me to pour her some more Alize, which was something I was more than happy to do. After I'd poured her some, she drank a little and continued doing her toenails. All of a sudden and from nowhere, Toni violently shook in disgust as she described how she definitely could not tolerate ashy feet or long crusty toenails. She especially hated toenails that, in her terms, are so horrible that they are at the point where they have started to turn black. We both laughed and agreed that bad feet are definitely a no no.

As Toni continued to discuss other pet peeves, I started to massage her shoulders and her neck. I was sure to be subtle about the way I massaged her. After about two minutes or so of massaging, Toni stopped talking and began expressing how good the massage was feeling. She moaned and let me know that she hadn't had a good massage in a very long time.

"That's not good," I replied, "you work too hard, your muscles need to be cared for."

Before long Toni had disregarded removing the nail polish from her toenails and she was totally into the massage. With her eyes closed she tilted her head upward towards the ceiling and seductively told me that she could get used to treatment like this. I was feeling like a Don. I laughed and informed her that she deserved treatment like this.

When one has been married for as long as I've been married, one learns what pleases a woman. All women are similar and although I hadn't *dated* other women in a while per se, I knew that I was making all the right moves. My marriage taught me how to be a great masseuse, and boy were those skills ever coming in handy.

I requested that Toni get some baby oil so I could give her a hand massage. She was very hip to the idea. In fact she was very eager because she had never had a hand massage. As Toni went to her bedroom to get the baby oil, I was going wild on the inside. See Toni, like most women, didn't know how erogenous the hands are. But again, from being married, I've also learned all the right places to touch a woman. I was thinking to myself how Toni had no idea how good she was about to feel.

When she returned with the baby oil, she proceeded to turn off the television because we both were not into the movie at all. Instead, Toni turned on her CD player and began playing Kenny

Lattimore. When she was done adjusting the CD player I asked her to join me on the couch where I started to massage her hands. As my slippery hands delved into every nook and cranny of her hands she began to voice her appreciation.

"Lance this feels so gooood!" Toni remarked.

I replied, "I'm surprised that you've never had a hand massage before, especially since you do nails and all."

Again Toni closed her eyes and enjoyed the experience as she said, "Yeah, I didn't know what I was missing."

I continued to massage Toni's hands for about five more minutes. It was getting late and I knew that I now had her where I wanted her. As I laid Toni's back onto the couch, she smiled and puppy doggishly asked what was I doing.

"You'll see," I devilishly answered. So after laying Toni on her back, I reached for her legs, which I lifted onto the couch. The laugh that Toni gave let me know that I could continue on with what it was that I had planned. With Toni's entire body now lying on the couch I quickly rubbed some more baby oil into the palms of my hands. After my hands were nice and slick I took Toni's left foot and began to massage it.

"You ever had a foot massage?" I asked.

Toni, who looked as if she was in heaven, didn't say a word. She just kept her eyes closed and shook her head no. To myself, I couldn't believe that guys weren't smooth enough to have never given Toni a hand or foot massage.

After a couple of minutes of massaging the left foot, I took her right foot and repeated my technique. Toni then lifted my ego by remarking that "I had it going on." I made sure that I put my all into the massage and I could tell that I was working wonders.

Needless to say, one thing was leading to another. And all I know is that Toni smartly asked did I have a condom. I was glad she'd asked because I knew that my dumb ass was ready to run up in her raw. I confirmed that I did indeed have a condom, and before I could blink, I was taking my sinful ways full-scale into the next level.

I can't front, my wife was on my mind at that very moment. Regretfully, I hadn't thought about my wife up until that point. It's sad, but there was no way in the world that I wasn't going to finish what I had started on Toni's couch.

When *it* was over, I was utterly speechless. For about twenty seconds, I had felt that feeling that I'd been searching and fiendin' for. Believe me, I couldn't remember "*it*" ever feeling any better. But after that feeling had subsided I realized that I had never felt lower or dirtier in all my life. While Toni and I were both still breathing hard, I was wondering what thoughts were running through her mind. We lay cuddled on the couch. Toni's back was pressed against my stomach and for some reason she remained as silent as a mouse.

Something needed to be said but no one spoke for close to ten minutes. I then kissed Toni on the cheek. In my mind I was like, I had better hurry up and get home to my wife, but at the same time I wanted to spend the night with Toni. In no way did I want her to feel cheap. So I simply laid there with her and thought about my adulterous ways. Before long, we were both knocked out on the couch.

FOURTEEN

I was fortunate that I managed to wake up when I did. It was ten minutes to four in the morning when I awoke. I had been sleeping *real good*. When I awoke, I wasn't exactly sure as to where I was at. But when it finally hit me that I was still next to Toni, I was like "oh my God!" I couldn't believe that I had let myself fall asleep. Instinctively my panicked state of mind almost caused me to make a bee-line for the door. But in my haste I didn't want to wake Toni. Although I was feeling shook, I didn't want that to come across to her.

Being as quiet as possible, I eased away from the couch and made my way to my pager which was on the kitchen table. My worst fears were confirmed when I realized that my wife had beeped me five times in a row. My dumb behind had the pager on vibrate. I had fallen asleep butt naked so there was no way that I could have known the pager had been going off. No way was I gonna allow myself to get even more rattled than I already was. I was gonna have to be a man and just go home and face my wife. Deep down, I knew that I would have no problem lying my way out of explaining my whereabouts for the night.

As I put on my shirt and prepared to leave, I made sure that I got every last drop out of what had been a very savoring evening. Toni was still on the couch asleep and naked. I stood there just gazing at every inch of her body. I was regretting like crazy that I had no camera. I analyzed Toni from head to toe and I couldn't come up with one flaw. Not one flaw. She was more than I had imagined she would be, and she looked better than a porno star. By watching her, I was starting to get very aroused. The thought of waking her up and trying to get some more ran through my mind. I also was two seconds from masturbating right there on the spot when Toni woke up.

She was a bit out of it so she didn't bust me looking at her. At that point I was almost done getting dressed. While walking over to Toni, I zipped up my pants and when I reached her I sat next to her and kissed her on the forehead. In a whispering tone I said to her, "Toni it's getting late so I'm gonna leave. A'ight?"

Toni didn't respond with words she just nodded her head up and down as she began to fully sit up and gather herself.

As I stood up and prepared to make my way to the door, I voiced those famous words, "I'll call you."

Toni still remained silent. I couldn't understand why she had become so non-verbal. I didn't wanna leave without her saying something, so I returned from the door and moved towards Toni's direction. When I reached her I sat back down on the couch and gave her a nice warm reassuring hug. As I held her close to me, I blocked out how good her velvet soft skin was feeling, and asked, "You ok?"

Toni finally opened her mouth but she didn't look me in the face as she said in a tired sounding voice, "Yeah I'm ok."

I gave her one last peck on the lips and I departed. Yeah I thought about telling her that I loved her, but that would have been lying. And besides, there was no reason for me to make such a statement.

By the time I actually walked out of Toni's crib and made my way to my car it was 4 in the morning so it was still dark outside. When I got to my car I noticed that a little note was on my driver's side window. It actually was a little yellow <u>post-it</u> that was stuck right in the center of my window and it read:

Lance it is 3:30 in the morning and you are still here! I should have smashed all of your windows, but your tire was a better option for now! I can not believe you!

The note did not have a signature or an identifying name at the bottom of it but as soon as I looked at my front tire I knew that only Scarlet could pull off such an act as actually slashing a nigga's tire at 3:30 in the got damn morning! Man!

I needed that as much as I needed a hole in my head. Fortunately for me Scarlet had only slashed one of my tires. Being that I had 20 inch tires and some chrome rims, changing the tire was not that simple, especially considering that I didn't have the special key to unlock my rims. My only option was to drive home with a flat. I knew that I was probably gonna damage my four thousand dollar set of rims but I really didn't have many options.

Anyway, I slowly chugged home in a very controlled manner. Scarlet had got me real good! I began to wonder if she had actually sat on Toni's block for the entire night. I wasn't sure, and to be honest I was more worried about what other trail of destruction, if any, had Scarlet left behind. My blood pressure instantly shot up as I became shook like crazy wondering if Scarlet was gonna go a step further than simply calling my bluff by actually blowing my cover with Nicole.

My heart was racing and I was nervous as hell. I mean here I was after having just had the best sex of my life with one of the finest chicks on the planet and I couldn't even savor the moment. Instead, I was chug-a-luggin' home at like 5 miles an hour, scared like I don't know what! Who needed this type of stress!? On one hand I had some psycho-stripper-mistress ready to blow my brains out if she could get a clear shot at me, and in addition to that I had to try to come up with an excuse for Nicole as to why I, as a married man, was coming in the house at damn near 4:30 in the morning.

This is definitely not how things were supposed to be playing themselves out. I am the first to admit that I can't handle drama and pressure, which is why I try so hard to be smooth with my game. But this was one bumpy road that I was seriously contemplating getting off of as soon as possible. The only thing that was making me consider staying the course was Toni. Especially now since I knew that the sex with Toni was off the meat rack!

Realizing though that if I was serious about pulling off this balancing act of being with both my wife and Toni, then I couldn't allow myself to get all worked up, worried, or bent out of shape over the evil I'd just done, and all of the minor setbacks that come with the territory of being a dog, setbacks such as dealing with a slashed tire and trying to pacify a good looking full bodied bangin' stalker in Scarlet del Rio.

When I pulled up to the front of my crib, the house was in total darkness. While unlocking the door, I felt as if I was an intruder or something. For some reason it was like every step that I took was magnified. Although I was trying to creep as quiet as a cat burglar, I still heard every crack and every squeak on the floor as I walked. I thought about jumping straight into the shower but I really didn't want to wash Toni's scent from off of my body, not just yet anyway. Like a little teenager I couldn't stop sniffing my fingers simply because they had Toni's dried up juices on them.

After reaching my bedroom, I switched the lamp on very dimly. I was trying to be as silent as possible but Nicole woke up. She immediately asked, "Honey are you alright? You had me worried sick? Where were you?"

Again, I didn't allow myself to get rattled. Her line of questioning was only par for the infidelity course. There was no reason to have fear because I knew that all fear really is, is False Expectations Appearing Real. Like my expectation of Scarlet having called Nicole was more than likely false, so in an effort to down-play things I sat on the bed and reached over and kissed Nicole on the lips. I was giving off the brightest mood that I could muster up as I responded, "Ah man, baby you wouldn't believe me if I told you what I've been through tonight. I got your pages but I couldn't call you back 'cause I didn't have my phone in my possession at the time. And I definitely had no time to stop at a pay phone."

As my wife laid in our king size bed, she curiously asked, "Well what happened?"

I answered back, "Me and some of the guys from work went to this comedy club in Manhattan, and guess what happened?"

Nicole began to sit up as she nervously asked, "What? Did somebody get hurt or something?"

I responded, "Oh nah, nothing like that. See, we all drove in this guy name Mike's car, 'cause his car is not that flashy and we didn't wanna get harassed by the cops. But when we came out of the club we couldn't find Mike's car."

"Oh Lance, don't tell, me somebody stole his car?" My wife sadly and genuinely asked.

I answered, "Well that's what we originally thought. But we found out that his car had gotten towed! We thought that we were parked in a legit parking spot but you know how it is in the city with those million and one confusing parking signs. And get this, they charged him two hundred dollars to get his car back! Yo this city is a criminal empire, charging people that kind of money and I mean we weren't even parked illegally! They had this stupid sign that was on top of like a million other signs that read 'Night Regulation,' that's it, it just said Night Regulation and it had a picture of a moon on it, the cop told us that whenever we see that sign it means that they have the right to tow a car on any night that they choose to start towing cars. Can you believe that!? That ain't nothing but straight up extortion! But there was nothing that we could do though. There was no way that the impound yard was gonna give us that car without us first paying the cash. They didn't even take credit cards or ATM cards, just cash. We all chipped in and helped Mike out, but it took us almost three hours to get his car back."

Nicole expressed what a shame it was that the car had gotten towed. Since she was expressing feelings of compassion I decided to drop another bomb on her, so before making my way to the bathroom and hopping in the shower, I added, "Oh yeah! And Nicole things got a little bit worse."

"What do you mean?"

"After all of the towing and getting the money together to get the car out of the impound, we finally make it back to Queens and I get in my car and start it up and pull off, and all of a sudden I here this crazy wobbling sound... I get out of the car and my tire is flat! Can you believe that? It's like when it rains it pours. And I'm not talking about a slow-leak-type of flat. I am talking about a serious major flat, a time to buy a new tire type of flat."

"Lance you're kiddin' me!"

"Nah I'm straight up serious! And I didn't have the key to unlock my rims, I mean if I did I would have at least put the donut on until I got home, so I practically drove home on the rim and probably ruined it. That's just more money that I gotta now kick out."

"Why didn't you just call me to come get you?"

"'Cause I figured that you and LL would be sleeping. And then after dealing with aggravation all night long it's like I just wanted to get home as quick as I could. So even if I had called you I wouldn't have felt like waiting for you to come pick me up... But anyway, I just wanna take a shower and I'll deal with getting the tire fixed tomorrow," I said as I made it to the bathroom and began running the water for my shower.

"You see how easy that was," I told myself. "I need to change my name to 'Lance B. Smooth" I devilishly thought as I prepared to step into the shower.

I hated to be washing Toni's body oils from off of me, but hey. I knew that I had to distract any subversive thoughts from Nicole's mind, and what better way to do that than becoming one with her by making love to her.

Love making was exactly what my wife and I did when I was done showering. And while we made love, all I kept envisioning was Toni's naked baby oiled body lying on her couch. I guess it was that thought which allowed me to perform so well with Nicole. Yeah, when we were done making love, I'll admit that I felt like a dog. But I felt like a very happy and satisfied dog. A dog who had had more than his fill for the day and was now ready to go to sleep.

FIFTEEN

A little more than a week had passed since the sexual encounter that Toni and I had. My wife hasn't been suspecting a thing, mainly because I have been on point spiritually. Nicole has seen an increase in my motivation to read the Bible, attend Bible class and the whole nine. But see, one thing that I've learned is that when you overcompensate in a particular area, there is bound to be another area that is being neglected. In my case, over the last week or so, Toni has been that area which has been getting neglected.

If I was a true dog I could have been like, "to hell with Toni." After all, I had already hit it and I'm married. So I didn't actually have to kick it with Toni anymore. I could have very easily moved on to pursuing Carmen or some other piece of meat. It's just that I wanted to continue to hang around Toni. I knew that the sex was good, and that definitely played a big part as to why I wanted to hang around and continue to please Toni. But the main reason that I couldn't see myself bouncing on Toni just yet was because I didn't have that sense of closure.

I didn't feel as though Toni and I had exhausted all of the possibilities that stood to exist between the two of us, and it's bugged because I always initially feel that way whenever I get involved with a female, only with me that initial feeling seems to never wear off. That's probably why I yearn to stay in touch with old girlfriends from as long ago as my early teenage years. Those past girlfriends can be married and my mind still manages to come up with "what if" possibilities. The only female that I feel like I have ever had a sense of closure with is Nicole.

That is also probably the reason that I have allowed Scarlet to hang around for so long. But even with her I never felt as if there was a since of closure, like we still had so much more to explore and conquer. See, with Scarlet, she has always caused a chemistry inside of me which constantly makes me feel like I have to hit it "one last time." The problem is, one last time has turned out to be five years of countless sex episodes with her.

During the week, Scarlet has been causing all kinds of turmoil. But I quickly began to realize that she was just hungry for my attention and that she wouldn't really go as far as blowing my cover. For example, she has been constantly calling the house and hanging up, real childish type stuff that happens with high school teenagers. It's as if she wants me to constantly me on guard, but if she was really serious she would have spoken to Nicole by now and I knew that. But regardless, she was a loose cannon and I had to make sure that I didn't scorn her in anyway. Because any woman that feels scorned is capable of some serious destruction!

I did however, manage to worm my way out of that thick situation that had ensued when Scarlet had apparently followed me to Jamaica Estates on the night that I first had sex with Toni.

I had made sure to simply not just call Scarlet the first thing in the morning of which I'd found my tires slashed. Rather I made it my business to go visit her! And when I made it to her crib I knew that the attention was gonna squarely rest on me so I had to try to deflect some of that attention in order to decrease the tension that was sure to be in the air.

When I saw Scarlet my first words were, "Now Scarlet, just explain one thing to me. Why were you going for my jugular vein by slashing my tire, especially when I had told you that I would explain everything to you?"

"Lance, the way I look at it, there is really nothing to explain. I know that whoever you was wit' that y'all ended up having sex that night. I went all the way out to Harlem... Matter of fact it was past Harlem, practically in Yonkers, and I performed my show and came back to Queens and your car was still there! So how do you expect me to not do something!? Apparently you were trying to play me and you were being straight up blunt and rude about it! I'm sayin' out of respect you could have at least got up and moved your car and parked it somewhere else to try and give the appearance that you had left, you had to know that I would double back and check out your sloppy lyin' ass story!"

"Scarlet I thought that we had an agreement. You was supposed to at least hear me out, so why would I think that you would double back on me and do something as low and gully as slashing a nigga's tire?"

"OK Lance. I'm sorry for slashing your tire. Now let me hear your tired explanation," Scarlet said with some mouth-twisting attitude.

"A'ight. Baby listen, I was with a chick. And I did try to get some… I mean…"

"Lance you know what!? You really are disgusting! I should just spit in your face right now!"

"Scarlet just let me finish… She was just a girl that I knew from high school and the only reason that I was there was because I was just trying to gas her into doing a three-some with me and you."

"What!? A three-some?"

"Yeah you know, a ménage-trois."

"Lance!"

"Scarlet how many times have I told you that I wanted to do that? So why would you even flip?"

"Why would I flip? Because it's always about you Lance! It's always about what you want. Yeah, you've told me about your little three-some idea before, but how many times have I told you that I don't do that!? Lance, you know how many girls come on to me at these strip clubs because I am always telling you about that! And whenever I tell you about those stories, I always make it a point to tell you and assure you that I don't swing like that and you know that I don't get down like that!"

"Yeah but see Scarlet, those women that come on to you are into that Lesbian thing, which is cool with me, don't get me wrong, but I'm not asking you to necessarily be down with the lesbian thing, I'm just sayin'…"

Scarlet interrupted me and added, "Yeah you're just saying that you want two women at the same time and that you would be willing to take them any way that you can get them! You'd be happy if they both just pulled their pants down and bent over and let you do your thing! Lance I know exactly where you're coming from, and like I already said, and I've been saying it all along, it's always about what you want!"

"Baby that is not true, 'cause if it were true then I wouldn't even want you to participate in the three-some! I mean of course I would want you to enjoy it and get something out of it! But can't you see that I'm at least being straight up with you?"

"Lance, what is this chick's name?"

"Why do you need to know that?"

"What is her name!?"

"Tina! Her name is Tina," I barked.

"OK let me break it down for you. Lance, you wanna get into Tina's pants, which you probably already did, but to pacify me you're trying to suck me into your little fantasy. Lance I am not stupid! This is all about you and that's it!"

"Would you stop saying that! First of all nothing happened between me and *Tina*. She wasn't with the idea and I was just trying to convince her."

"Lance that is a bunch of BS! You mean to tell me that you haven't spoken to this chick or seen her since high school, and out of the blue you decide to buy some seafood, get all dipped out before going to see her, and when you do see her all y'all do is talk about a three-some until the wee hours of the morning!? It just doesn't add up. Lance it is always about what you want!"

"See I never said that I hadn't spoken to her since high school."

"Lance you know what? Just forget about it. I ain't got time for games!"

"What do you mean 'just forget about it?'" I asked in an attempt to keep this ridiculous argument going. See I wanted to keep the argument going in order to distract attention from really having to explain who "*Tina*" was.

"I mean forget about it! Because you know what, this is how I know and can prove that you are full of it; if you *really* wanna do a three-some then why won't you try to convince Nicole to do it? Matter of fact I tell you what. If Nicole agrees to it then I'll be with it!"

"Now Scarlet you know good and well that I ain't asking Nicole to do that!"

"Why not?"

"Because she's my wife!"

"Yeah and…"

"And I know that she wouldn't go there!" I shot back as I started to sense myself really getting vexed.

"So your wife wouldn't go there and you wouldn't try to get her to go there, yet you would want me to go that route? How the hell am I supposed to interpret that Lance!?"

Throwing my hands up in the air I said, "Scarlet you should be a lawyer or a doctor because you are an expert at spinning things around and taking things where it is so irrelevant!"

"Irrelevant? No,no,no, I don't think so! My point is very relevant! Or maybe I need to spell it out for you. Lance if you want me to do sexual things that your wife wouldn't do then basically you are calling me your hoe!"

"See, now why are you even going there Scarlet? I ain't even call you no hoe or nothing like that and I never have viewed you like that! But like I said, you're a good spin doctor!"

"Lance you noticed that I haven't attempted to hit you or smack you or anything like that right!"

"Yeah so?"

"I realized something when I slashed your tire. See I was gonna slash all four of your tires but then I was like 'what the heck am I doing?' It was like something had all of a sudden clicked off in my brain and I was like 'Scarlet del Rio are you crazy or something? If Lance can't be faithful to his wife then how the hell can you expect him to be faithful to you?' Yeah I finally realized it Lance... I realized that you are a dog and I don't need to be playing myself the way I do. I mean why am I slashing your tires and hitting you and screaming and all of that when I can have just about any man that I want?"

"Scarlet come on with that! You know what you got in me! You know that no other man who looks as good as I do could treat you and sex you the way I do. You know that!"

"See that is exactly what I mean, there you go again thinking that it's all about you! You know what? I used to like that cockiness in you because I took it as confidence, and I'll admit it, most men are intimidated by me, so you have an edge in that area, but believe me and trust me Lance, there are much finer looking men than you out there who sex a *whole lot better* than you do and who have a whole lot more going for themselves than you do… Lance you know what? You are not worth all of the drama!"

"What drama baby?" I said as I attempted to move closer to Scarlet and show her some affection.

"Lance please don't touch me…"

"Oh so now you're gonna act all cold and stand-offish?"

"Lance, you know, you were right when you said that we need to end things. I mean why am I holding on to you and stringing myself along like I have no other options? You're the one who is frustrated, married, oversexed and has a kid and not many options. I'm young, sexy, I got money, and I can do whatever."

"Scarlet that was low," I commented, and I truly did mean it because Scarlet was taking big stabs at my ego.

"I don't care if it's low because it's the truth!"

"OK lets just back up a minute. This all started because you think that I'm treating you like a hoe simply because I won't ask Nicole to take part in a three-some, yet I would be willing to get you involved in one. But see that's because I know how religious Nicole is and I know that she wouldn't compromise her faith in God for something like that."

"Oh and I'm a spin doctor? Lance, you know what? We don't even have to take the conversation back there. I'm just gonna take you up on your offer, an offer which I now realize is in my best interest, and I'm gonna leave you alone…"

I didn't know if Scarlet was playing mind games with me or what. But I was feeling mad confused. In fact I was starting to feel hurt. Yeah it's true that for the sake of my marriage I had decided to leave Scarlet alone, but the end of the relationship clearly had to be on my terms, otherwise I knew that future problems would lurk because of the lack of closure that I would feel.

"Scarlet listen."

"No Lance you listen! Enough with all the games, I'm gonna give you what you want and what you requested. I mean you might be used to having your way with Nicole, but I am not Nicole, so if you're gonna be with me you can't be playing me for a fool and that is exactly what you're trying to do!"

As Scarlet said that she reached in her pocket and pulled out a drug dealer like wad of cash. She peeled off twenties and tens and said, "Here, this is five hundred dollars. This is for your tire that I slashed."

"Yo this chick is dead serious!" I thought to myself.

As I laughed a very insecure laugh I said, "Scarlet put your money away. Why are you trippin'?"

"Lance just take the damn money. And I am not trippin'! What is wrong with you? Isn't this what you wanted for some time now? So I am simply granting you your request, so the real question is *why are you trippin'*? Now here, take this money!"

I reached out my hand and I took hold of the cash and put it in my pocket.

"Scarlet…"

"Lance there really isn't much else to say. Things were real, we had some fun times and some real good sex over the years, but all good things must come to an end… So you make sure you take good care of yourself. OK?"

"Scarlet you are really buggin' out," I said, sounding very astonished.

From the drift of that conversation you can get a clear understanding as to why my ego was crushed. The remainder of the conversation continued on in a similar manner. I began to wonder if Scarlet had linked up with some other cat that was breaking her off with better *pipe* game than mines or was she really just fed up with me? I mean man, I hadn't even really done anything wrong. All I did was have sex with Toni one time, so I didn't know why she was trippin' the way she was.

I wasn't one to get dumped and get played so I knew that I would have to *bang* Scarlet at least one or two more times in order to put some real closure to the situation. And when I set a goal I won't stop until that goal is attained and fully achieved.

I also knew that I had to quickly correct the situation of neglect that I had been dishing Toni's way. I guess that my confidence was slumping so bad to the point that it had become one of the main culprit's as to why Toni and I had only been managing to speak on the phone. Unfortunately we had only been able to see each other once since we had sex. In my heart I felt as though Toni not only wanted to see more of me, but rather, she *needed* to see me more. I felt like I owed my presence to her. And since Scarlet had basically dissed me, I too was starting feel like I *needed* to see more of Toni in order to confirm in my own mind that I was still "the man."

The day after we had sex, Toni in her own way expressed to me that she wants to be around me as much as possible. I had finally got a chance to ask her why was it that she had remained dead silent right after our sexual encounter. What she told me was that although she was physically feeling real good, mentally she was actually feeling worthless, cheap, and dirty at that point. Yeah, she confirmed what I knew, which was the fact that I'm a great lover. But she also added that, to her, sex was more than just a physical thing.

Toni went on to explain that she had never made love to anyone without first getting to know them for a very long time. She added how she really trusts me, but at the point right after sex she felt vulnerable. Vulnerable in the sense that she knew that I could hurt her like she'd never been hurt before. All I had to do she explained, was never speak to her again and go on with life thinking that she was some cheap trick. Toni also wondered if I would drift out of her life just as quickly as I had drifted into it.

Toni had me completely misunderstood. See, yeah I'll admit that the day after we had sex, that I was second guessing myself and wondering if Toni was just some nice complexion, good hair whore. Or if she'd really felt so good about me that she just felt an urgent need to express her feelings by letting me have some "na-na."

During our conversation the day after sex, I made sure that she didn't have me misunderstood. The first thing that I explained to her was that if sex between the two of us wasn't supposed to have happened, then it would not have happened. I assured her of the fact that since we did in fact *make love*, it said a lot about how we feel about each other. I explained to Toni, that in the same way she probably couldn't explain why she'd gone against her normal rules and made love to me, I too was unable to explain why I'd gone against moral rules to be with her.

With that in mind I also explained to Toni that there was no way in the world that I was ever going to look at her as just some cheap trick. Just as I was confident that she wouldn't look at me as a typical male dog. I gave Toni my word that I was going to sincerely do everything that I had to do in order to allow the trust that she feels for me to get stronger and stronger.

There existed a catch twenty two in the sense that if I started over compensating to make Toni feel good, then my wife would be neglected and vice versa. To combat this dilemma, I came up with a well thought out plan of action. Actually, the well thought out plan turned out to be a no brainer. To solve my dilemma, all I had to do was switch my work schedule. Or at least I should say that all I had to do was create the illusion in my wife's mind that my schedule was going to be changing.

I was prepared for my wife to flip out, but I knew that if I had wanted things to work out then I would have to be straight forward with her. When she came home from work I told her, "Honey I know you're not going to like this but I've thought about it and I realize that it is gonna be the best situation."

Nicole prodded as she asked, "What are you talking about?"

Being confident and straight forward, I blurted out, "I switched my schedule at work. I'm gonna be working the graveyard shift for about a month or so."

Nicole raised her voice as she asked, "You mean twelve at night until eight in the morning!?"

"Yeah, that's what I mean. But like I said, it's only going to be for a month or so. Actually it might be less time than that."

"Lance why didn't you speak to me about this before you actually did it?"

Lying through my teeth I answered, "Well, baby I knew that you would have objected. And, but, honey listen... I already worked everything out. The bus will pick LL up in the morning so that's not a problem and I'll still be able to make it to Bible class and all..."

Nicole shot back, "Well when am I going to sleep with you? We're married and we should be together at night!"

In my head I was like "oh boy here we go again." My wife isn't a nag but lately she had been getting on my nerves, constantly objecting to *this and that*. I could already see that that was one good thing about Toni in comparison to Nicole. Toni seemed like she would be more than willing to let me wear the pants in the relationship. She seemed like she knew her place and would be more submissive like a woman should be.

I put my wife's fears aside and told her that we would spend our nights together on the weekends. Again I let her know that it would only be for a few weeks. Unfortunately the new nag in Nicole wouldn't let things die as she stated, "Well I don't...I mean, you still haven't told me why all of a sudden you decided to change your schedule."

Enough with this nagging I thought. I calmly but sharply snapped at Nicole. "Look Nicole! I'm switching my hours alright! That's it! If you want to know why I'm changing my schedule it's because I need to spend more time by myself. I figured when I get off work in the mornings I'll be able to relax by myself. I can hang out, sleep or do whateva it is that I want to do by myself!"

Nicole was about to cause me to drive my fist through the kitchen wall as she would not let up. "Oh, so you're trying to say that I'm stressing you out? Oh, what, you would rather spend as much time away from me as possible!? Is that it!?"

I looked towards the ceiling and slowly counted to ten before I responded. I didn't want this to escalate and I knew that it would if I kept adding fuel to Nicole's fire. I calmly answered in the softest tone of voice that I could muster up.

"No honey, that's not it at all. Listen, I don't want this to escalate into a big argument or nothing. All I'm saying is that I want to spend some time alone for a few weeks."

Nicole sucked her teeth and asked, "Well when do you start this new shift?"

"Sunday night," I replied. "I'll be working it Sunday nights through Thursday nights, and we can still spend Friday and Saturday together."

My wife didn't respond and I was glad that she didn't. I was expecting Nicole to remind me of the fact that I have a son who I should have thought about before I made my decision to switch shifts. Man, I was getting all this static and I hadn't even cleared things with Toni. See what I'd really planned to do was, I'd planned to continue working my normal eight AM to four PM - Monday through Friday schedule. But see, Nicole would be thinking that I'm home during those hours. When in actuality I'll be coming home from work like normal at four O'clock and go about the remainder of my day like I would on any other day. Then at night all I would have to do is get dressed like I'm going to work and head straight for Toni's crib and spend the night there every night... Yeah, I know it is a brilliant plan. A plan that only a dog in heat could think of...

One of my biggest concerns was the fact that I wondered if Toni's parents would object to me spending the night with her every night. I knew from experience that Haitian parents are mad old fashioned and strict. However, my concerns were eased as I remembered that Toni had already told me how hard her parents work. They are rarely home during the week, and when they are home they usually come in very late, eat and go straight to sleep. So in reality it's like Toni lives by herself, especially considering that she has a separate apartment and a separate entrance to her apartment. Therefore, I doubted that her pops would even be home to object to anything.

SIXTEEN

Steve and I had not hung tight in a while. So when Friday rolled around I decided to go by his crib after work and kick it with him. When I reached Steve's house I put him up on all of the latest details between Toni and myself. I especially made sure to tell him about the "sexcapade" that Toni and I had. To my full satisfaction he admitted that he was grossly jealous. Although Steve gave me my props, I made sure to remind him of how, only a few short weeks ago he had been laughing at me. Revenge is so sweet, because now I was the man.

As I gloated and rubbed my success in Steve's face, there was one thing that I didn't like. That was the fact that Steve, from out of nowhere started talking subversive. He began talking like I'd never heard him talk before. Grant it that he asked me about every nook and cranny of Toni's body, including wanting a detailed description of her vagina, but that was only normal for him to ask. But then Steve totally flipped the script.

He started kicking this mess about how he was really starting to feel for Nicole. He asked me had I ever really considered what I was doing to my wife. Steve also managed to throw in a bunch of *"what if"* statements. Statements to the effect of, "What if Nicole happened to find out about me and Toni or me and Scarlet?"

For the first time that I could remember I felt like col' punching Steve right in is ugly mouth! I mean, from one playa to another, Steve was breaking all kind of playa rules. I knew that he was probably just jealous. Jealous 'cause he didn't have the ability to scoop women like I did. Then I started thinking. "What if Steve had plans of snaking me?" Yeah, he probably saw how easy I *tapped* Toni, and had secret thoughts of doing the same.

If there's one thing I hate, I mean hate to the core of my insides, it's jealous, envious niggas. As I spoke to Steve I was getting more vexed by the minute. He was sounding worse than those male bashing women in Toni's beauty salon. Steve was just ripping into me and totally blowing up my spot. He was blowing me up so bad that I almost blew my top.

For a split second I really had thoughts of murdering Steve. Not because he might be trying to snake me for Toni. But rather, what if Steve was trying to back door me and play in my own backyard? Yeah Toni is all that, but Nicole is my true dimepiece. And I knew that Steve, like any other of my so called homeboys, if they had the chance, they would run all up in my wife.

After Steve had gotten all of the pertinent details that he needed in order to satisfy his own innate desires, such as asking about Toni's nipples, he once again, uncharacteristically began ripping into me about how I should be thinking about LL. He started saying that although LL is young, that he still probably understands what is going on with me and Toni. He asked me if I wanted LL to grow up and do the same things that I was doing.

I couldn't take it anymore. Who the hell did Steve think he was?! I'm sayin', he was coming at me all self righteous and all. Sounding ticked off I asked, "Yo Steve, get at me! Where the hell is all of this coming from?"

"Steve seeming as if he had no idea what I was talking about asked, "Where is what coming from?"

"Steve don't play stupid!" I barked. "I ain't never heard you talk like this in my life! Now all of a sudden you trying to label me as a dog or something!"

Steve immediately came on the defensive, "Yo Lance come on man. You know you my boy. Why you trippin'?"

I yelled, "Why am I trippin'!? What do you mean why am I trippin'?!" Now I was really beginning to believe that Steve was hiding something from me. I yelled, "You know exactly why I'm trippin'!"

Steve raised his arms in the air to show surrender. He proceeded to acknowledge me by my street name, "Yo L what's up? You lost me brotha. All I'm saying is that sometimes as men we have to…"

I interrupted Steve 'cause I knew exactly where he was headed. With a screw face I angrily said to Steve, "Yo Steve check this! I ain't stupid man! Nicole is bad and the whole nine. She's got a big butt and all that. Her head is on her shoulders and she's making dough. I see the way you be looking at her…"

Steve swiftly interrupted me, as he yelled, "Oh hold up! Hold the hell up!"

Like a lion I roared right back, "Nah, you hold up!" After Steve realized I was a more powerful lion he backed down. With his lips twisted, he looked at me and didn't speak.

I continued, "Steve, I'm sayin'! I see the way you be looking at my wife! But see I always let it slide 'cause I know that she has a bangin' body and niggas probably can't help but to look. But Steve I'm sayin', I never thought twice about you back-dooring me."

Steve, who now was seething with anger, yelled, "Lance I know exactly what you're thinking and I can't believe you would..."

I cut him off again. "Yeah you can't believe I would think you would try to snake me right? Steve, come on man! I'm a man and I know how men think!"

I got closer to Steve, and in an attempt to intimidate him, I let him know straight up, "Steve, I don't know where all this 'I should think about Nicole crap' is coming from. But let me tell you this, if you ever try to snake a nigga, I'm telling you, I'll murder you! Word is bond!"

I prepared to leave Steve's crib and I could have cared less if I ever spoke to him again. As I made my way to my car I knew that, like a woman, Steve would be determined to get in the last word. I was about two seconds from knocking him flat on his back, when he added, "Lance, man you don't even know who your boys are anymore. All I'm saying is that I personally know that I ain't ready for marriage. But it comes a time when we have to just stop thinking about the booty, 'cause there is more to life than that."

"Yeah, whateva!" I snapped back.

I jumped in my car and was about to pull off. And just as I figured he would do, Steve made sure to throw in the last statement as he said, "Lance, all I'm doing is telling you the same words that you used to kick to me. And I know that you know exactly what I'm sayin', 'cause remember you're the one who used to kick all that religious holy roller BS."

With Steve having dropped his final line, I took off in my car. I made sure to make the loudest screeching tire sound that my car could muster up. I couldn't believe Steve was acting so shady. Although I knew that he might have been right, all I'm sayin' is that he shouldn't have come at me like that. I mean I don't think that he has plans for Toni 'cause he knows that she's out of his league, but I know that he might have had plans of creeping with my wife. I was just making sure that I had deaded any of that before it began. As for our friendship, I really could have cared less if I didn't speak to him again.

Steve had me heated, but I wasn't gonna let that situation undermine the rest of my evening. Later on, while it was still early in the evening, I played Nintendo with LL for about a half hour. One thing about children is that whatever they engross themselves in they manage to bring with them a sense of solace. If they are playing Nintendo, it's like nothing else in the world matters. The same goes for if they are watching cartoons, it's like to them at that moment the only thing in the world that matters is cartoons. I really needed to spend more time with LL just to learn that same sense of serenity.

I couldn't play Nintendo with LL for very long because Nicole and I had to drop him at my in-laws. The reason being, Nicole and I had tickets for the Kenny G / Toni Braxton concert. The concert which was being held at radio City Music Hall was scheduled to start at eight thirty. By the time we'd left my in-laws, who live in Brooklyn, it was seven forty five. Believe me. When you are driving into Manhattan, a forty five minute cushion is nothing. So to say the least, we were running late.

I have a bad habit of getting angry whenever I'm running late for something. That anger usually leads to a lot of horn honking reckless driving which Nicole hates. The fact that I was still kind of ticked off because of what had transpired between Steve and I, coupled with the fact that we were now running late, I had to make a concentrated effort not to let my anger show. I simply focused on how great it was that Nicole and I were actually going out on a date.

With the Manhattan skyline in full view, we drove across the Brooklyn Bridge and my wife commented on how beautiful the New York City skyline looked.

I joked as I said, "Honey do you realize that every time we come into the city you say the exact same thing?"

Nikki replied, "Well, it's true."

Then from out of left field I asked, "Baby do you ever think about cheating on me?"

Taken aback, Nikki asked, "What? Where did that come from?"

I tried to down play things with laughter, as I added, "Not that I'm accusing you of anything, but I just be thinking sometimes… Thinking about whether or not I'm good enough for you. I mean, I know everyday you have to interact with successful Judges and Lawyers and what not. I just be wondering if you ever thought about… Well you know… cheating on me."

Nicole frowned as she sincerely replied, "Lance I would never ever cheat on you. Never. You mean everything to me."

Although I knew that Nicole would never really stoop to the infidelity level, I just wanted to hear it from her lips. Her words relieved me a great deal. Then Nicole blew up my spot and asked, "Well since you brought it up, have you ever thought about cheating on me?"

I wanted to blurt out the fact that not only had I thought about it, but I had come full circle with it. As I continued to drive, I thought to myself that it probably would have been better for me to jump into the East River and commit suicide, than to come clean with Nikki.

So as not to lie, I answered my wife's question truthfully, "Yeah baby. As a matter of fact I have thought about it. That's why I asked."

Nicole seemed shocked as she said, "What!?"

With Nicole staring at me and waiting for me to expand, I began thinking to myself, "man why did I open up this big can of worms?"

Nicole asked, "Well is there something wrong between us, something that would make you think about cheating?"

Being a master of deception I managed to twist my words around. But even I didn't expect to smoothly get out of this one.

"No, no, baby. I'm not talking about myself having thought about cheating on you. I was trying to say that I've really been thinking about whether or not you've cheated on me."

Nicole looked at me with a serious look. I remained silent and I guess my silence caused Nicole to feel a little uncomfortable. Then she laughed and asked, "Lance what's going on?"

As I blew air out of my cheeks I replied, "OK, baby I'll just put it out there."

"Yes, please just put it out there so I'll know what you're talking about." Nikki begged.

Backing myself out of an almost fatal situation, I explained, "Well baby, today me and Steve got into this big yelling match. I screamed on him 'cause I noticed that he looks at you a little to close, like he be wanting to do you or something."

When I was done speaking Nicole burst out into tear jerking laughter. She could barely get the words out of her mouth as she said, "Lance you thought that...Ha ha ha ha..." Again she began laughing. She laughed so much until she caused me to start laughing.

Then finally, after wiping her tears away, my wife said, "Lance you got me laughing so hard that you're causing my make-up to smear." She laughed again as she said, "I can't believe that y'all are best friends and y'all got into a shouting match over me. Baby listen to me. I'm flattered that you still get jealous over me, but come on now. Steve?... Baby I would never cheat on you, especially not with your best friend, a best friend that happens to be a dog at that. Lance you should know me better than that."

Yeah, I began to feel extra stupid about how I had acted toward Steve. But there was no time to dwell on that. We were practically right around the corner from the concert and it was already eight thirty. I had to park in one of those expensive as hell parking garages that are found all over New York City. But it was either pay through the roof and park in a garage, or have no peace of mind at all and risk getting your car towed by parking on the street.

Fortunately for us we were able to park the car and make it to our seats before the show started. Nicole and I were both excited like little kids. There was a buzz of anticipation that filled the air in Radio City Music Hall. Being a man, I had to hold back some of my excitement because I didn't want to seem soft like a sissy. But I was thoroughly enjoying the atmosphere of the concert. It was a mature crowd and everyone was dressed up. Sadly enough, I couldn't help but think how my mistress Toni would have greatly enjoyed an evening like this if she were with me.

It was nearing 8:45 when the people running the show informed us that the show would be starting in about ten minutes and that everyone should take their seats. I used the ten minutes to hug and kiss on Nicole. I also sweet talked her and whispered sweet nothings into her ear. Nicole was very giggly and happy. The whole time reminded me of how it was with Nicole and I years ago when we first met.

The ten minutes flew by. Before long the curtain on the staged parted and the diva, Ms. Toni Braxton came strutting out onto the stage with her dancers while singing her hit song <u>You're Making Me High.</u> The crowd went crazy. The first thing that I began thinking about was how good Toni Braxton was looking. Toni Braxton is sexy as hell as it is, yet she had the nerve to have on a dress with a split that was about up to her hip bone. Every time she walked all you could see was thighs for days. In my head I was like "Yeah kid!" Of course I was singing and cheering like the rest of the crowd, but I definitely was cheering her body more so than her voice. One thing that I hated was the fact that she'd let herself loose so much weight. I mean she is still the bomb as "Bony Toni," but she was *all that* when she had weight on her.

The concert was on point. Kenny G ripped it down as did Toni Braxton. Nicole and I had a bomb time the whole night. Again, the night was scarred by me not only lusting over Toni Braxton but I was going crazy over all of the other women that were in attendance at the concert. During intermission my wife and I were on line at the bar in the lobby waiting to order drinks, and that is when I saw some women that were more than capable of winning the Miss America pageant. There was this white woman, who I mean had it going on! Unfortunately, she was with somebody or otherwise I might have tried to flirt with her.

That night, after having seen bad white women and even fly oriental chicks, it proved the theory that is held by most dogs. That theory is that there is no such thing as the baddest woman, and every time you think that you've seen the baddest female, you'll manage to see someone that can knock them out the box. I don't know about knocking my mistress Toni out of the box, but that night at the concert, I'd definitely seen one or two women that would have given my mistress Toni a run for her money.

On the ride back to Queens with Nicole, I made sure not to spark any more dumb conversation. I really didn't have to worry about that because Nicole, who was out of her seatbelt and all over me, definitely had my mind preoccupied. Very uncharacteristically my wife had unzipped my pants and was playing with my goods as we drove. A couple of times she almost caused me to crash, but I managed to keep my composure. Just the thought of having sex in any unconventional location with Nicole had always been a running fantasy of mine, and what better time to fulfill it than now with my wife?

In the worse way I wanted to pull over on the side of the highway and do her right there, but I was scared that she might view me as a super freak, so I put my desires aside and waited until we were in the privacy of our own home.

SEVENTEEN

During the past few days, I'd set aside time so that I could read the Bible.   I have a very good knowledge of what the scriptures are all about, but I had been reading so that I could try to understand how I should deal with my adultery affliction.   No, I was not just reading the Bible as a *spiritual front* for my wife. Rather, I was trying to search the scriptures to see what on earth was wrong with me.

I realized that in the case of adultery that I had many Biblical companions who had been plagued with the same disease of adultery.   I was shocked when I read the story of how King David had committed adultery with Bathsheba.   David not only was pulled down by his own lustful desires but his desires for Bathsheba led him to lie and cover up what he'd done.   He also went as far as having Bathsheba's husband murdered!

As I studied that ordeal of David's, I saw many similarities in comparison to my ordeal.   See the scriptures refer to David as a man after God's own heart, yet he was still afflicted by the same thing that I was going through.   I justified in my mind that if someone as righteous as King David had been creeping around with women, then I must not have been as bad as I thought I was.

When Sunday rolled around I found it very ironic that the pastor's sermon was about the exact same account of David and Bathsheba.   I could hear that voice inside of me telling me that God was trying to say something to me.   No, I'm not superstitious but sometimes I think that things happen for a reason.   I definitely felt that it was no accident that the pastor's sermon was about adultery.   They always say that the best sermons are the ones that seem as if they are being spoken directly to you and specifically for you to hear.

There were certain things that I had failed to read when I read about David and Bathsheba.   The pastor mentioned those things in his sermon and the words that he spoke made me look at the account of King David and Bathsheba in a totally different light.   The pastor pointed out to the congregation just how angry God became with David after he'd committed adultery.   The pastor also showed how sorry David was when he realized the extent of his sin. He read the scriptures which conveyed David weeping bitterly in his repentance. The pastor also mentioned that although David continued to be tempted with adultery, he didn't continue on engaging in it. Rather, David's regret was made evident by the righteous things that he chose to do after he'd committed adultery, and from that point forward. What he did was he managed to put adultery behind him and he led God's people, the Israelites, like no other King had ever done.

When service was over I realized with even more intensity that I could relate to the dirt that David had done. But in no way shape or form did I fear God like David had, nor was I as repenting as David had been.

Sunday night was quickly approaching. And faced with the choices of doing right, or continuing with evil, I didn't know which way to turn. I found myself in that gloomy state of mind that I am usually in just before I get depressed. There was no way in hell that I was gonna let myself get depressed. I knew that I had to confront my demons head on and start correcting the nonsense.

Toni had already consented to the idea of me spending my nights with her. That present Sunday night was supposed to be the first night of many nights that I would start spending with her. Reflecting on what I had learned from the word of God and remembering the piercing words that Steve spoke to me, in my mind I was like *"forget Toni."* Enough damage had been done. I convinced myself that there was no way I was gonna be at Toni's house Sunday night or any other night for that matter. Scarlet had basically removed herself from the picture so now was a perfect time to just make a clean break from Toni and I could be done with all of the drama, lies, and cheating.

Yeah, although I'd promised Toni that I would start spending more time with her, I would just have to let her know that I would now be reneging on the spending the nights thing. I convinced myself to not worry about the fact that Toni might think that I'd just gamed her for a piece of butt. I had to really get angry with myself for feeling that I *owed* something to Toni. After all, she was a responsible adult and she should have known the consequences before she opened her legs for me. I laughed to myself as I thought, "word up I don't owe that whore anything."

My gloomy mood was starting to subside, and I prepared to eat dinner with my family. Being that my schedule had never really changed, I knew that it would be very easy to tell Nicole that I'd come to my senses and decided not to work the graveyard shift. I knew that I could gas Nicole by saying to her how I realized that being home with her was more important than spending time by myself. I thought to myself, I could really get in good with Nicole if I also mentioned that I realized that it was important for LL to see me and that the graveyard shift would hamper that father and son time.

Right before we started to eat I made sure to turn off my pager. I also turned off my cellular phone. Therefore Toni wouldn't be able to get in contact with me at all. Finally, I was beginning to realize that the only way to rid Toni was going to be for me to go cold turkey and have no kind of contact with her whatsoever.

During dinner that evening, my wife had reminded me of the conversation that we had had on our way to the concert the other night. She tied it into the sermon that we'd heard earlier in the day. She told me how she felt that it just doesn't make sense to cheat, because just like with King David, cheating only leads to lying and a whole host of other sins.

Our conversation was flowing very smoothly. I was agreeing with my wife and I was letting her know what particular points that I had managed to pick up from the sermon. As we ate I wondered if I would ever tell my wife about Toni. I knew that I would want her to know one day, but I had no idea how I would tell her.

The food that Nicole cooked was definitely hitting the spot and I was in such a good mood because I finally felt, even if just on a small scale, a sense of freedom from my distorted sexual desires. I was just about to drop the surprise on Nicole and let her know that I had decided against the graveyard shift, when the phone rang.

Sounding upset I said, "Man! Can't we ever have a peaceful moment without the phone ringing?"

Nicole shot back, "Don't answer it. Just let the answering machine pick it up. If we keep answering the phone at all times of the day and night people will think that it's ok to call here whenever they want."

The answering machine usually picked up after the fourth ring and our phone was already on its fifth ring.

"Man the answering machine ain't even on!" I said sounding disgusted.

"Just let it ring," Nicole instructed.

The phone was approaching its tenth ring and I was getting very annoyed. I told Nicole that I would answer it because it had to be important if someone would let the phone ring for that long. I pushed my chair from the kitchen table and proceeded to answer the phone which was hanging on the kitchen wall. Although the phone had ticked me off, I didn't want my anger to come across when I answered the call.

I commented to Nikki, "Watch them hang up as soon as I get to the phone."

Picking up the phone I politely said, "Hello."

To my complete surprise Toni's voice was on the other end. Inside my head I was like, "Ah man.' My heart raced but I played it cool as she spoke and said, "I didn't think you were home 'cause the phone rang so many times."

I replied, "Yeah, I was eating dinner."

Toni apologized for interrupting my meal. I told her not to worry about it. Then she proceeded to ask all kinds of personal questions, like why was my cell phone and pager off? I lied and simply told her that I didn't know that they were off. Toni was kind of annoying me. Here I was with my wife standing right beside me and practically breathing down my back, and Toni was running off at the mouth. I was hoping the she'd hurry up and get to the point of her call. Then it happened... Toni melted me with her words.

She seductively said, "Baby, when I couldn't get in touch with you I got scared. I started thinking that you might be trying to avoid me or something."

Talk like that was not what I needed. So I said, "Oh no. Nah I'll be there."

Toni asked, "So you are still coming tonight, right?"

"Yeah definitely."

"So what time are you coming?... Lance I miss you. It feels like haven't seen you in so long and... I don't know why I'm telling you this but, it's like I can't stop thinking about you."

Trying hard to not get totally wrapped up into Toni words, I responded, "I'll be there at eleven thirty."

Toni ended by saying, "OK just don't disappoint me."

I hung up the phone and just like that I had been roped back into my destructive cycle. I know that I've said and felt like this before, but this time I really and truly felt like a crack addict and to me Toni was that big bright vial of crack.

As I hung up the phone my wife asked, "Honey who was that?"

In my true dog form I replied, "Oh, that was my supervisor, he was reminding me that I had to come in at twelve tonight."

I could hear the disappointment in Nicole's voice as she sucked her teeth and dejectedly said, "Oh yeah, I forgot you were starting that new shift tonight."

Luckily Nicole let the issue rest. She did suggest that we put LL to bed and go make love before I left for work. Wanting to satisfy Nicole's every need, I complied with her wish. Yeah, my wife and I made love that evening and I made sure to put an asterisk next to tonight's sexual performance. The reason being, I almost cried while making love. See, Nicole literally burst out into tears as we were having sex and I didn't know what was wrong. As my wife rode on top of me, her tears trickled off my chest, the tears were flowing from Nicole's eyes like a leaky faucet. With her voice cracking from emotion, Nicole told me that she'd just became overwhelmed with joy because she was feeling so close to me and in love with me at that moment. She also added that the tears were because, as he put it in her words, "she just loves me.'

Like I said, I too almost came to tears. I'm rotten to the core but I did have some *human* feelings in my body. I wanted to cry because I knew that without a doubt I was still gonna listen to that demon inside of me, and in about an hour or so I knew that I would be cuddled up with Toni and possibly getting my freak on with her.

EIGHTEEN

When Toni greeted me at her door I could tell that she was jubilant over my presence. Toni who smelled fresher than a bed of roses, had on silk pajama pants and a silk pajama top. She hugged me and wouldn't let me step into her apartment until I'd first kissed her. Although her mouth felt very refreshing, I just wasn't into the kiss. I had been thinking about my wife's tears of joy for the entire ride over to Toni's crib. Sadly enough, my wife's tears weren't enough to make me turn around and go back home.

Yeah, I was already at Toni's and I figured that I might as well make the best of it. Toni could sense that something was wrong with me, I guess because I wasn't acting as happy to see her as she was to see me. When she asked for the reason for my somber mood I lied and told her that everything was "A-OK." To myself I was like come on, what did she think was bothering me? She knew that I was a married man, couldn't she just put two and two together and figure out what was troubling me?

One thing about Toni that I noticed as of late, was the fact that she hadn't been mentioning Nicole's name at all. I wondered if she'd just decided to block out the fact that I'm married. Since our "sexcapade," Toni hadn't mentioned anything about me being married.

Toni was smelling good and looking good. She was also playing to a tee, the role of an adulteress. As all kinds of thoughts were running through my head, Toni was busy sweet talking me and making me feel like a king. Before I knew it, she had my shoes off and she was feeding me grapes. Toni also took it upon herself, as she put it, to relieve me of the stress that I was feeling. Roles were drastically reversed as compared to the last time I was at Toni's place. Now it was I who'd become the recipient of the massage.

Toni was doing a very good job on my shoulders as she reminded me once again of how much she'd missed me. Then before I knew it she was on my lap and we were kissing. Again, roles were reversed as Toni began kissing my neck and kissing my ears. I'm human, and to boot I'm a man, so I was definitely getting turned on. Toni was operating smooth as hell. Like magic, she had my shirt off quicker than I could blink.

I couldn't believe it. Here was Toni, feeling all over my muscles and I hadn't done a thing to try to turn her on. I knew that Toni wanted to establish a relationship with me, but now I was beginning to have some serious reservations. All this time I had been thinking Toni was a respectable high maintenance lady. But lately all she'd been revealing to me was that she was nothing more than a two bit whore!

The thought ran through my head that maybe it would be in my best interest if Toni proved to be a whore. 'Cause then I wouldn't feel as bad if I were to dump her. Plus, who was I fooling? I knew that I wasn't gonna marry her or nothing like that, so actually I should have been happy that she appeared to be a whore.

One thing that I decided to do differently as compared to the first night that Toni and I made love was I decided to take my time. I sat back and began to really enjoy every touch that Toni placed on my body. I caressed and squeezed all over her body as well. We weren't like two rabbits in heat 'cause we did manage to converse as we made out. I definitely felt more at home this night as opposed to the last evening that I'd spent with my beautiful sexy mistress. This time I was no longer on her living room couch. Rather, on this late evening, I found myself stretched out across Toni's bed.

I don't remember where Toni's silk pajamas had disappeared to, but my plans of taking my time and enjoying things quickly went out the window. The smell of Toni's "choochie juices" had set me off. Before long, and like a deranged sex addict I couldn't believe what I'd brought myself to do next. But one thing is for sure, and that is, I was enjoying every moment of what I was doing.

The sex lasted about just as long as it had lasted the first time we performed together. This time though things were much different on Toni's part. When we were done having sex she placed her head on my chest and she expressed how she was starting to fall in love with me. To myself I was like "Oh boy here we go." Why does it seem that after performing oral sex on a woman, they start talking about *love*? Maybe they confuse multiple orgasms with love... I don't know.

However, I knew that it was just a matter of time before that topic of love would come up. In a way, I was prepared for it so I just made sure not to respond.

As we lay in her room with the lights off, Toni expounded on her statement. Talking in a quiet and still tone of voice, Toni said, "Yeah baby, I've just been really thinking. I mean everyday you're the only thing on my mind. Lance it's like you have a spell over me or something."

My ego couldn't help but feel gassed, as I chuckled like a pimp.

Toni quieted me by saying, "No Lance I'm serious. I really have been thinking about our whole relationship. See, after we made love the first time I didn't know what to think or how to continue on in this relationship. I was thinking about just not allowing things to go on any further between us. But I realized that that would have been too hard for me to do.

As Toni spoke I managed to remain quiet because I wanted to let her speak her mind. It's sad but I was feeling so good about all that Toni was saying. Yet at the same time I felt like the game was over. I had captured my kill and devoured it. To me, the hunt was always the most enjoyable part of the game. Unfortunately, in Toni's case, that particular part of the game was over.

Toni continued, "Lance I know you're married and I don't even like thinking about that. But I have to think about it because it's a reality... Lance, I wanna know, have you ever thought about me in the ways that I think about you?"

What the hell, I decided to just blurt it out. I mean I had done enough dirt so why try to clean it up now?

"Toni, when I first saw you I knew that something special was gonna develop between the two of us. Matter of fact I even told you that. And you know what?... That 'something special' is developing as we speak. Baby without a doubt, I know that I love you. I'm passed that stage in my life where I just have sex to be having sex. I've been making love to you, not just sexing you, so you should know that I love you."

Toni, who had to be excited by what I was telling her, tried to keep a serious face as she asked, "Well where do you see our relationship going?"

Toni stumped me with that question. But I knew that I owed her an answer. I understood fully that Toni was just like any other female. She was holding on to all of that emotional female crap. She needed her emotions to feel at ease.

"Toni I'll be honest. And I'm not gonna just say this just because I know that this is what you wanna hear, I'm saying it because it's how I feel about you. I know that you said you hate talking about the fact that I'm married and so do I. Now I'm not saying right away or anything like that, maybe in a year or so, but I know things are gonna end between me and Nicole. And when that happens it'll make room for me and you to be together the way we want to be."

I was waiting for Toni to respond but she didn't. I didn't know why I'd said what I'd just said because I didn't mean it at all. I knew that if I kept talking I was bound to keep putting my foot in my mouth. Trying to put a lid on all of the love talk, I hugged Toni and asked her did she really believe that I loved her. She told me that she did and with the snap of a finger, we were kissing. When we took a pause from kissing, Toni let me know that she had been anticipating making love to me for the past week. She smiled like a little devil and told me that the reason she'd let my phone ring for so long was because of that same anticipation of having sex with me.

I began laughing as I said, "Oh, so you used me!" Then I playfully pulled the bed sheets up to my chin and said, "I feel dirty and cheap."

Toni slapped me and laughed as she said, "I'm just trying to keep it real! A sista does have her needs and Lance you know you got that 'butta-love.'"

We both began laughing and Toni turned on the bedroom light. With the room bright, she informed me that she was going to the kitchen and she asked me did I want anything to drink. I placed an order for a glass of water. After placing my order I watched as Toni's naked body walked towards the kitchen. While I watched her walk towards the kitchen I was really feeling like the man. When she returned with my water she sat on the bed and after thanking her, I reminded her that I still had to wrap her hair for her so she could see my skills.

Sounding excited, Toni replied, "Oh that's right! I have to see what kind of skills you got. You're coming over tomorrow night right?"

"Yeah I'll be here."

Toni added, "Alright bet. Tomorrow night I'm gonna see what kind of skills you got... Tomorrow it's on!""

Toni and I talked until about three in the morning. She didn't have to get up for work in the morning but I did. I knew that I would only get about three good hours of sleep so I was definitely ready to hit the pillow and be out.

By the time I laid my head on the pillow for the night, it was five past four in the morning. I was hoping that two hours of sleep would be enough to carry me through the next day. So far, my adultery plan with Toni had been working to the tee, but the all night sex thing was bound to wear a brotha down!

NINETEEN

The guilt of not having my wife by my side as I slept every night lasted for about three nights. The guilt was replaced with the rekindled excitement of being around Toni. For the past two and a half weeks, my plan continued to work like a charm. Nicole hadn't been suspecting a thing. The fact that Nicole was still in the dark as to my affair with Toni was a testament to my split persona and skilled acting ability. As for Toni and myself, we managed to enjoy each and every moment that we spent together.

Although the majority of the time I've spent with Toni has been at night, we've still been able to live it up. Our nights together have included activities such as romantic strolls on the boardwalk out at Long Beach. Sex on the beach, weightlifting, we've been to the twenty four hour bowling alley, rollerblading, the movies, and much, much more. I also proved to Toni that I did in fact posses a few skills in the cosmetology department. A couple of our nights were spent with me experimenting on Toni's hair and eyebrows.

Over the past few weeks I've also come to learn so much about Toni. I've learned things about her that almost turn me on in the same way her looks turn me on. There is one thing that I know and that I am now convinced of, and that is that Toni is definitely far from a home wrecking whore. Toni's mind is also not on materialistic things. I'm not saying that she doesn't appreciate the finer things in life, but she doesn't let material things consume her. I remember thinking to myself how Toni's non-materialistic quality was such a sharp contrast to Scarlet. Scarlet was always talking about how she had to buy the latest and top designer clothing and accessories. It was always "Gucci this and Gucci that," or "Prada this and Prada that," Manolo, LaPerla, or some $900 snake skin boots or something expensive. I mean there is nothing wrong with wanting nice things but it can't be the only thing that you talk about, and in Scarlet's case it seemed like materialistic talk was always on her brain.

At length, I was explaining to Toni how I have been making over forty thousand dollars since I was nineteen years old, and how I now, with overtime, make close to seventy thousand dollars a year. Toni was shocked to realize that I make as much money as I do, considering what I do for a living. But at the same time she was not all that impressed. I tried hard to impress her by explaining to her how I've used most of my paychecks to invest in Con Edison stock. Speaking like a Certified Financial Planner, I described to Toni how if I kept investing the way that I've been investing, that I should be a millionaire by the age of forty. I was also sure to let Toni know how young I was when I'd bought my house.

I rambled on and on with materialistic mumbo jumbo that most chicken heads would have been salivating over, but Toni wasn't that concerned. In a polite way she told me that if she wanted to, she could have whatever she wanted by simply asking her father to purchase it for her. However, Toni told me that she never wanted to get by life based on the level of success that her parents had achieved. Rather she wanted to go after her dreams and create a legacy of her own.

Besides the fact that Toni isn't about money, one other thing in particular that impressed me about Toni was her expression of a genuine desire to help children. Toni told me that she was in school studying to be a special education teacher and that she only wanted to teach in impoverished neighborhoods. I was curious as to know why, with her father being a doctor and all, why did she want to pursue a career such as teaching? Toni informed me how her father tried to instill in her since she was young that she had to become a doctor. She even wanted to be a doctor, but after failing miserably in school when she was young she got turned off to the medicine thing.

Toni wasn't embarrassed at all to let me know that she had suffered from dyslexia as a child. She told me that she grew up privileged and rich, yet at times she still felt useless because she had a learning disorder. She explained that if as a rich kid she still felt useless, then she could only imagine how low the self esteem levels could drop in terms of learning disabled children that are poor. Toni added that ever since her problem was diagnosed, that it has been her mission to help educate those that were like her but only less fortunate.

With the way Toni had been impressing me, and with the fun we'd been having, it was sad to say, but I had seriously been entertaining the idea of bouncing on Nicole. I mean if things have been this great between Toni and myself, I could only imagine how great things would be if we were spending all of our time together. Plus, Toni is crazy about LL, and LL is crazy about her. She'd bought him exactly what he wanted for his birthday and he was officially hooked on her from that point on, so I know he would have no problem making the transition.

I have been maintaining my sanity throughout this whole spending the night ordeal, but I have been dog tired. In fact during the week there was one twenty four hour episode in particular that really drained a brotha, but I guess in a sick kinda way it was more than worth it. Some how within a twenty four hour period I had managed to have sex with Toni, Scarlet, and Nicole, all at separate times but it was within the same twenty four hour period which was a record for me! I would have to say that that was probably my most crowning and defining day as a dog, and at the same time I had probably never felt more disgusted with myself.

Mainly what fueled me was, well, it was just something that I had wanted to see if I could pull off, I and did pull it off. Doing both Toni and my wife was a relatively easy task. But hitting Scarlet's skinz' that "one last time" was the only minor hurdle that I had to overcome. I overcame Scarlet but it wasn't as easy as I thought it would be. I just had to have Scarlet that one last time so that I could prove to myself that I was still the man and so that I could also end things with her on my terms.

Like I said, sexing Scarlet that one last time proved to be a little tough. I had basically popped up at Scarlet's crib during my lunch break at work. She was surprised to see me but she kept up her defiance in terms of forcing herself to not get close to me. She was properly allowing room for the "permanent space," which of course was something that I had originated and requested. We talked about this and that, basically it was a lot of small talk, but I was straight up with Scarlet and I let her know that I hadn't stopped by to *just talk*, but I wanted to get some booty. I wanted a *quickie*.

Scarlet was really ticking me off because even after expressing to her that I wanted her, she managed to keep up that wall. So I had to kind of force myself on her. Yeah I had to because she wouldn't kiss me or nothing! And in my mind I was like "yo why is she bugging out!?"

I really had to get physical with her and we had basically come to a point of scrapping with each other like boxers and wrestlers. Of course I was stronger than she was so I basically had managed to over power her and get my way. Actually it was more like she had finally stopped resisting me.

So when she had stopped resisting me I literally ripped the zipper on her jeans while ravenously pulling her pants down to her ankles and then I did my thing. Scarlet was not her usual self and I could sense that she wasn't into the sex at all. It wasn't even one of those love-hate-rough-but-good-psycho-break-up-sex type of episodes that we had had on a past occasion. Although I did manage to enjoy it while I was *pounding it*, after I *nutted*, and I was done, I began asking myself, "was this just some rough sex or did I just rape this woman?" My mind was really buggin' because I couldn't tell.

Scarlet had managed to pull her jeans back up and she buttoned them in spite of her broken zipper, and she looked as if she was confused and truly heated but she kept silent. I guess that I felt better about the whole situation when Scarlet consented to my request for a kiss. Despite the fact that she had given me a cold and quick non-wet good-bye kiss which included no tongue action at all, it was still a kiss.

I don't know if she had given me that kiss because she wanted to really kiss me or if because she just wanted me to get the hell out of her crib. But I do know that when I had left her crib and continued on with my work day I was basically feeling like "OK now I am definitely finished with Scarlet. Definitely!"

Yeah that twenty four hour period had really drained a nigga both physically and mentally. Mentally I was all screwed up because now I was feeling like an adulterer and somewhat like a rapist, which was definitely no easy thing to sit with. But like anything and everything else I had to just block it out and not worry about a thing and simply keep things moving. Physically I had never had so much sex in such a short period of time and I was just worn out.

So I informed Toni that Thursday I was gonna be going back to sleeping at home for a couple of weeks just to make sure I didn't wear down my body. Toni had no objections. But at this point in our relationship she had become more than attached to me. I could tell that unlike before, Toni was now more insecure with the fact that my wife was still in the picture. Toni had been making comments such as, "I know you'll probably dump me and go back to only being with Nicole."

And she'd been asking so many "what if" questions. She wanted to know what was gonna happen when she went back to school in August for her last semester. She was convinced that when she was to leave for school that I would automatically revert back to Nicole forever.

As a matter of fact I think it was Toni's insecurity that led her to allow us to have unprotected sex during the past week. I had mentioned to her how sex with condoms just didn't feel as good as sex without them. Toni immediately wanted to know if Nicole and I use condoms. After telling her no, I think she thought I was trying to imply that sex with my wife was better than sex with her. In no way was I trying to imply that, but from that point on Toni and I hadn't used any protection. I know that I was being beyond foolish, but hey, I'm just sayin'.

TWENTY

I don't know how on earth I had managed to slip up, but I had made a major, major error. When I walked through the front door of my house I thought that the world was coming to an end. My heart dropped to my knees as I immediately thought that my wife had some how found out about my multiple affairs. Why else would she be so angry? After all, as far as Nicole was concerned, more than a week had passed since I'd returned to my *normal* schedule and plus, I'd been on point spiritually.

"Lance what is this!?" Nicole yelled while holding up a videotape.

I thought to myself, "Oh my God!... I know Toni didn't set me up and videotape me... Scarlet del Rio! It had to be her ghetto Brazilian ass!" For a split second I thought that maybe Nicole had some Private Investigator tailing me during the past few weeks.

I began my defense, "Baby calm down. I don't know what that is. I mean it's a VCR tape, but…"

Nicole interrupted me, "Lance don't play stupid! Now I asked you a question! What is this!? And why is this garbage in the house!?"

At that point my heart began beating terribly fast, I was about ninety nine percent sure as to what my wife was talking about.

"Let me see that tape," I asked while taking the tape from Nicole's hand. "Oh this," I said very nonchalantly.

"What do you mean, '*Oh this*'?" Nikki barked.

"Nicole calm down, it's just a porno tape," I said while trying to diffuse the situation.

"Lance! Just a porno tape?"

Still trying to down play the situation I said, "Yeah, it's not like I watch it or anything. One of the guys on the job gave it to me."

"Lance, first of all, stop lying! 'Cause you wouldn't have the tape if you weren't watching it! Second of all, do you know that I caught you five year old son watching this crap!? Do you know what this stuff will do to him!?"

At that point all of the energy in my body left me. I felt like I was at a funeral looking into the casket of a dear family member. I think that I was feeling that way because I was wondering if I had just killed LL. Did I just kill my son in the same manner that pornography had managed to kill me? I have been a resurrecting sex addict since I was nine years old. And that can mainly be attributed to my early childhood exposure to pornography.

Nicole was furious and rightly so. With my head bowed from embarrassment, I began speaking in a very low and humble tone. "Honey, I'm sorry that it was in the house... Where is LL? I wanna speak to him."

Nicole ripped into me again, "And Lance what about all of those magazines!? God only knows how long LL has been looking at those things."

"Honey I told you that I'm sorry. They shouldn't have been in the house and I'll definitely throw them in the garbage. But where is LL? I wanna speak to him."

Nicole sucked her teeth, looked at me, and then she told me that LL was in his room. I quickly rushed up to LL and when I stepped into his room the first words out of LL's mouth was "Daddy I'm sorry. I'm sorry daddy."

After watching LL cower into a corner with his hands up, I almost broke down and started crying because he reminded me of a kid that gets physically abused and was and was anticipating a butt whipping.

Mustering up as much mercy and compassion as I could, I immediately began to console LL. I picked him up from the floor and I sat him on my lap. LL was crying and I knew that he felt extremely guilty for what he had done. "LL, daddy is not mad at you... Look at me," I instructed.

LL wiped away his tears and he looked at me. I continued to speak, "LL, I know that your mother probably yelled at you, and she yelled at you because what you were watching is not good for you. See LL, when a person is your age they shouldn't watch what was on the tape or look at the pictures in those magazines because it's not good."

LL was just about done wiping away his tears and he asked, "Daddy, those are grown up tapes right?"

I nodded my head in agreement. With his cheeks still wet from tears, LL asked a very convicting question. "Daddy if it is bad for little kids to watch those tapes, why isn't it bad for grown ups to watch them? You were little before too."

At that point I couldn't help it anymore. I wasn't gonna try to put up a front. If I wanted the cycle to end I had to keep it real with LL. Starting to shed tears of my own, I insecurely laughed and I asked LL had he ever seen me cry before. He was very wide eyed as he shook his head no.

"LL, daddy is crying because I love you so much. You might not understand what I'm about to tell you, but just listen closely. LL, do you remember how I told you that drugs are a bad thing and you should never use them or take them from anyone?"

LL answered, "Yes."

I continued, "LL, the reason I told you to stay away from drugs is because there are people that take drugs and they might want to stop taking drugs but they can't because they get addicted to the drugs."

I knew LL was paying attention because he asked me what did addicted mean. I explained to him that it was similar to how he likes Fruity Pebbles, which is OK. But if he were addicted to Fruity Pebbles then that would be no good because that would mean that all day long the only thing he would think about is eating Fruity Pebbles. He would force himself to eat Fruity Pebbles even if he wasn't hungry. He would eat Fruity Pebbles until he was sick and throwing up. He would sneak and eat Fruity Pebbles even if he knew he could get in trouble by me or his mother. He would steal money to buy Fruity Pebbles or he would steal Fruity Pebbles from the supermarket. LL finally got an understanding of what I was telling him.

I continued, "See LL, when you are addicted to anything whether it's to drugs or cereal, it's no good because being addicted makes you do things that you know are wrong. You know certain things are wrong but when you're addicted you do it any way. LL when you do things that are wrong you start to hurt people that love you and you also hurt yourself. Do you understand me?"

LL said, "Yeah because if I was addicted to Fruity Pebbles then I would get sick and you and mommy would be hurt because I didn't listen right?"

I smiled and replied, "Exactly. Now LL, the reason I am telling you this is because when I was your age, maybe a little older, I looked at magazines and certain pictures that I wasn't supposed to look at. Just like you, I sneaked into my daddy's things. The things I saw were just like the movie you watched and the pictures you saw. But see LL, my father and my mother never caught me. As a matter of fact nobody ever caught me. So I would look at those things whenever I got the chance. I did it because I liked it and it made me excited. But LL I didn't know that those things were bad for me. They were bad for me in the same way that drugs are bad for a person. LL you know what? When I got older I realized that I was addicted to the pictures and to tapes like the one you saw."

As I spoke, LL looked intently at me. I began welling up inside and before I knew it I was balling in tears. I made sure that Nicole didn't hear me and I was hoping that she didn't walk in the room. Literally, for the first time in my life I was being real with someone and admitting that I had a problem with sex. I was trying like crazy to hold back my tears. I told LL that it was not right for a grown up to look at the pictures or watch the tape that he'd seen. I explained to him that grown ups sometimes make mistakes just like little kids.

"Daddy you mean like it would be wrong for me to keep eating Fruity Pebbles, but if I was addicted I wouldn't be able to help it, and I would eat it anyway…and, and…" LL paused then he continued on. "And it's like. It's wrong for you to watch the tape, but you are addicted?" LL ended his statement in a tone that said he wasn't sure if he was saying the right thing. But I knew he understood.

"LL that is exactly right," I told him. "LL, now tell me the truth. How many times did you watch that tape and look at those pictures?... Whatever you tell me I won't get mad at you."

LL paused and looked towards the ceiling. Then he held up three fingers.

"You watched it three times? Are you sure that was it?"

LL answered, "Yeah I'm sure. 'Cause when you were working in the *nighttime*, mommy was on the phone and I was in the basement playing and that's when I found it."

"What did you think when you saw what was on the tape?"

LL shrugged his shoulders, put both of his hands in the air and he said, "I don't know... I thought it was like when you kiss mommy. And like when I got my haircut and you hugged Toni."

Man! I knew that I had been sending LL some damaging messages and I had to change. I only hoped that he hadn't been permanently scarred.

"LL, now I want you to look at me. LL, I promise you that I will throw those tapes and those magazines in the garbage. But LL, just like I made you promise me that you would stay away from drugs, I want you to promise me something else. LL, promise me that you will never ever watch another tape like the one you saw and that you will never look at pictures like the ones you saw."

LL promised me that he wouldn't. I slapped him five and I told him that he didn't have to tell his mother what we'd talked about and that I would make sure that she didn't yell at him for what he'd done. I didn't mind if LL knew about my perverted past, but I didn't want to expose myself to Nicole just yet. I knew that I was gonna eventually have to come out of the closet and tell her about my sexual addictions, but I just didn't know how she would look at me.

I wished like heck that LL was older so I could explain to him how, indirectly my addictions were hurting his mother and she didn't even know it. See, if I could just be truthfully open with someone about my feelings then maybe I could stop creeping around and lusting the way I do. At least I had the courage to speak to LL.

I'm probably a lost cause, but if by me talking the truth to LL is gonna prevent his adolescence from being sexually screwed up and full of pornography and masturbation, well then I feel justified for having let him get dragged into my stupid addiction.

After LL and I finished talking, I went to make peace with Nicole. Nicole was on the telephone in the kitchen. I quietly overheard her yapping all this mumbo jumbo about how she couldn't believe that I would even have that garbage in the house. After eaves dropping for five minutes and listening to her bash me, I didn't know if I felt like crying or screaming out in anger. I proceeded to abruptly walk into the kitchen and I asked Nicole if she could get off of the phone.

Nicole ignored me and she spoke on the phone for another two minutes. Then when she was ready, and only when she was ready, she told her sister that she would call her back.

I was frustrated, but I had to keep it inside of me and I reminded myself that Nikki had no idea of what I'd been through in my lifetime in terms of my distorted sexuality. And there was no way that I was gonna be able to convey that to her now.

"Nicole, do you have to be on the phone running your mouth to your sister about everything that goes on in this house?" I barked.

Nikki, who seemed ticked off replied, "Lance, don't even go there alright!?"

"Nikki, all I'm saying is that I was wrong, but we haven't even spoken about this and you're already spreading my business!"

Nikki added, "What do you mean we haven't spoken about this? There is nothing to speak about! You're getting rid of those tapes and that's it. It's final! I mean if you find those whores on those tapes more appealing than me then that's another story."

Thinking to myself, "Oh boy," I said, "Nicole it has nothing to do with finding those women more attractive than you or anything like that."

Nicole added, "Women!? You mean sluts!" Nicole paused then she sucked her teeth and said, "Well, whatever! Did you speak to your son?"

"Yeah I spoke to him and everything is cool. I explained to him how it was wrong for me to have pornography in the house and how I didn't want him looking at things like that anymore.

Nicole, he promised me that he wouldn't look at things like that anymore and he told me that he'd only looked at it three times."

Nicole yelled, "Three times! Lance do you realize how smart LL is? He knows how to operate that VCR and everything. Who knows how many times he actually watched that garbage? I have a Masters in psychology, so I know how damaging just one glimpse of that stuff is!"

"Nicole look. He watched it and it's over a'ight!? It's not gonna happen again and that's the end of it! I don't wanna hear another word about this!"

As usual, Nicole had to get in the last word and she uttered, "I don't know what kind of Christian you call yourself."

With that sarcastic remark, rage ran down my body. I just wanted to run and grab my wife and ram her skull upside the kitchen wall. She had no right to be making statements like that, especially since she didn't know the amount of years that I'd struggled with pornography. As far as I was concerned, my struggles had no bearing on my Christianity and neither did it have anything to do with my degree of love for Nicole and LL. Nicole's sarcasm had me bent. I felt like storming out of the house, but I knew that running wasn't gonna change anything.

For the remainder of the night I chilled out with LL. As LL and I chilled, I thought about coming clean with every sexual sin that I'd ever committed. I was trying to see how I could tell Nikki everything about my sexual past, up to and including Toni. As I sat and pondered, I realized that I really didn't care about a divorce and all that nonsense. I just wanted to be set free from my skeletons and demons. I can pray to God and I can go to church, but I know that I will never be set free until I truly confess my iniquities to Nicole, who is my heart and soul.

Later that night when Nicole and I lay in bed, my heart was racing. I thought about at least telling Nikki about some of my past. Yeah, maybe it wasn't the right time to hit her with the reality of the affair, but at least I could start unlocking the door to my horrid past.

As I was gearing myself up to voice the sounds of confession, my wife asked me a question.

She asked, "Lance, I don't know how to say this, but, is there *anything* on those tapes that you see those porno queens doing that you would like me to do?"

Once again, all of the strength left my body. As I was getting ready to respond to Nicole, she abruptly added to her statement, "Lance, I just don't ever want you to think about the whores on those tapes more than you think about me. I mean, I can dress up in high heels and garters and all that. I'll strip for you or whatever. Lance, if there's some special sexual favor that you want me to perform just let me know."

I began feeling dejected as hell because Nicole simply didn't have a clue. I guess she was only asking the normal questions that any woman would ask after finding out that their husband has been secretly watching pornography. But still, she was clueless.

Sounding despondent I replied, "Nah baby, believe it or not I'm satisfied. Just keep doing what you've been doing."

TWENTY ONE

To me, LL is the most important person in the world. He is my seed and I didn't want my seed to grow up and bear rotten fruit. For LL's sake, I knew that it was time to go cold turkey and put an end to all of the foolishness. When LL gets older how am I going to teach him that certain things are immoral if I myself have not abstained from them? One thing I know for sure is that actions speak a whole lot louder than words.

My actions over the past month have been phenomenal. It's been hard, but for LL's sake, I have managed to stop going to the strip clubs. I have cut down on the number of times that I masturbate and I have thrown away and stopped looking at all forms of pornography. I've even thrown away phone numbers of females that I've flirted with. My lusting has also been on the decline.

I had managed to see Scarlet a couple of times but that was because I had wanted to make sure that she was ok, both physically and mentally. I mean I had kind of forced myself on her the last time that I was with her and that just wasn't sitting right with me. Little did I know, but I had managed to re-open a whole other can of old worms and emotional baggage and skeletons that were in Scarlet's past as it related to sex abuse and rape. So it was like although I had promised myself that there would be no more sex between Scarlet and I, I knew that now she needed me to be around her because of the old wounds that I had managed to stir up in her mind, plus I felt guilty for stirring up those old wounds. But yeah, I guess that was all just a minor setback in my quest to free myself from my cheating ways.

On the flip side, I would say that my biggest accomplishment has been that I have gone a little over one month without visiting Toni.

Yeah, Toni and I have spoken on the phone but even that has been limited to short conversations. Toni is no fool and I know that she realizes that I have been purposely trying to distance myself from her. LL's future sexuality played a major role in me abstaining from Toni, but there was another major scare that I had which also told me that enough was enough.

About a week or so after LL got busted watching the porno tape, I noticed something odd about my wife's vagina. Nicole had this sort of thick and slimy discharge coming from her vaginal area. And needless to say, she wasn't exactly smelling like a bed of roses down there either. In fact, Nicole's vagina smelled a lot like the low tide at Jones Beach! Anyway, I'd noticed the discharge before my wife had noticed it. I wanted to bring it to her attention but I was scared as hell.

The first thought that came to my mind was that I had contracted some sexually transmitted disease from Toni, and had infected my wife. Man, I was panicking like crazy. When I saw that discharge, I immediately wanted to get on the horn with Toni. But at the same time I didn't want to jump the gun and automatically assume that Toni was at fault. I also wanted to run to the doctor to get myself checked out, but I was too damn scared to do that. What I did was I simply remained quiet.

Nicole and I haven't used condoms since our first year of marriage, but due to fear of the unknown, I felt that it was time to revert back to the old way of doing things. I had no clue as to what kind of disease Nicole had or if I had given one to her. So I figured that by using condoms it would at least keep a bad situation from getting any worse. I was creative in my reason as to why I wanted to start using condoms again, and fortunately for me, Nicole shrugged it off and didn't object to it.

About a day or so after I'd noticed the discharge, Nicole started to complain that her private area was very itchy and irritated. To my surprise, Nicole informed me that she too had seen the discharge but she didn't know what it was. In my heart I knew that Nicole, although she didn't show it, was very alarmed. I was thinking that with this whole pornography episode now lurking in my past, that Nicole surely wouldn't have put it past me of having gone behind her back and also having caught something.

Surprisingly, I'd managed to be up front with Nicole. I explained to her that I had noticed the "white stuff," but I'd chose not to say anything. I also told her that the discharge had alarmed me and that was the true reason that I'd decided to bag up and wear a condom. Nicole was concerned and so was I. So without delay we marched our butts down to the doctor's office.

I was never secure with the fact that Nicole's gynecologist was some middle aged handsome black dude. But hey, she had to see him in order to figure out what was wrong. What ticked me off was the fact that when we got to his office he seemed to be a little extra friendly. Granted that Nicole hadn't been to see him in quite a while, but at the same time it's not like he knew her all that well on a personal basis.

His name is Doctor Timothy Wine, and when doctor Wine came out to the waiting area to greet us, his face lit up with a huge smile.

"Oh Nicole? How have you been?" Doctor Wine happily asked, as he extended his hand to Nicole for a handshake.

Nicole with her ever pleasant smile accepted his handshake and replied that she had been doing fine. It's funny how he'd forgotten my name as he asked, "And your name again sir?"

I just turned my lips and looked the other way so that he would know that I was purposely trying to dis him. For the sake of peace, Nicole interjected and reminded him of my name. Although there wasn't a damn thing funny, doctor Wine started smiling and laughing this fake laugh as he patted me on the back and said, "Oh that's right?...Lance" After doctor Wine realized that I had a very serious face and that he was the only one laughing, he quickly donned a serious face and tried to change the subject as he asked, "And how's the little one?"

That was it, I had had enough of this "punk-ass-brown-nosing" doctor! I rudely blurted, "LL is fine! Now doc if you don't mind can we get started?"

Doctor Wine took the hint and he requested that Nicole follow him into his office. I made sure that I followed right behind the two of them. Nicole pushed me as she tried to persuade me to go back into the lobby, but that wasn't happening. Then doctor Wine tried flexing his authority as he told me that no unauthorized people were allowed into the examination area.

I quickly stepped up and flexed my authority and I explained that the fact that I'm married to Nicole gave me the authority to go with Nicole. To Nicole's extreme embarrassment I added that, furthermore there wasn't a man in the world who could poke and probe my wife's vagina without me being present!

When I was done flexing on the doctor, his position had changed. And without any further delay, all three of us found ourselves sitting in his office. Nicole explained to him her symptoms and he took very studious notes. The doctor then explained to Nicole that he was sure that she had nothing more than a yeast infection.

While Nicole was dropping her pants, the doctor explained that when women have their first yeast infection, it is very often mistaken as an STD. He advised that, just to be sure, he was gonna perform a Pap smear, and he was also going to draw some of Nicole's blood and have it tested for STD's.

After he'd drawn the blood, Nicole was instructed to sit on this table where she had to place her feet into this stirrup like concoction. I was highly teed off as Nicole lay there with here legs wide open and her goods exposed to the world.

The doctor slipped on some plastic gloves and he began pulling back skin, poking, sticking, swiping, and trying to peek at every crevice of Nicole's private parts. Nicole, who had to feel humiliated, wasn't complaining, nor did she look as if she was receiving any pleasure from all of the doctor's poking. Therefore, I remained in my seat and let the doc do his thing.

When he was done he told Nicole that based on his years of experience he was certain that she only had a yeast infection. He prescribed her some medication that she had to inject into her vagina for three days. And he added that after three days of using the medicine that everything should be back to normal.

Man, I can't begin to explain how relieved I was when after a week had passed Nicole told me that the results from her pap smear were normal and her blood test showed that she didn't have any STD's. Without Nicole's knowing, I too had ran out and gotten tested just to make sure everything was on the up and up with me, which thank God it was.

That whole yeast infection episode just made me think. I realized even more so that it just wasn't worth it for me to be running around sexing different women and risking my life, and my wife's life at that.

TWENTY TWO

By the time the middle of August rolled around I found myself being tempted by some of my same old demons. Yeah, I had no porno tapes at my disposal but sadly to say I found myself watching the X-rated channel on cable TV. No, my wife and I weren't subscribers to that channel. But see, I went as far as watching the channel even though the screen was scrambled. I couldn't even get a clear shot as to what was being displayed on the screen. To me just hearing the sounds of people having sex was enough to wet my appetite. Although on a good night, every now and then the picture would clear up for about three seconds which enabled me to see all of the meat and potatoes.

Like a fiend I was exhausting all of my options. I even managed to benefit from the computer age that we're living in. I found myself on the Internet looking at all kinds of X-rated material and talking to people in sex oriented chat rooms. During my sexual excursions on the Internet, I came to realize that there are some major sex freaks in this world! On the Internet I was actually able to meet people kinkier than myself. With me exposing myself to new forms of sexual material, I again had to combat that age old demon of mine, which was masturbation.

I had also been seeing Scarlet more frequently. We had kind of worked out a new arrangement where we both agreed to limit our sexual contact with each other to just oral sex. And it wasn't just selfish oral sex where only I benefited, but I also returned favors to Scarlet. It was a good arrangement for me because to me, oral sex was not really like a form of cheating. At least it wasn't in my mind. Plus my relationship with Scarlet was just *different,* so slipping up with her wasn't too bad, because like I have been saying from day one, what I have going on with Scarlet isn't really wrong, at least, in my mind it isn't.

I have been able to toot my success horn in one area, and that was the fact that I've continued to keep away from Toni. However, with each passing day the urge to see Toni has been growing stronger and stronger. I've been praying to do the right thing and for the most part I have been doing the right thing. But I know that until I actually open up to my wife and tell her the truth about my past, that I'm gonna continue on in my same sad pattern of behavior.

I had called Toni on August 16th just to see how she was doing. When I spoke to her it was as though I had been hit by a moving train. See, to my disappointment Toni told me that she was leaving for D.C. in three days. The fact that my real life fantasy was about to end, well, that didn't sit good with me. Immediately I thought back to the first time that I had ever seen Toni. I thought back to pulling her over and asking her to cut LL's hair. I thought about the numerous times I had visited her in the shop. I thought about all of the sexy outfits that I'd seen her in. I reminisced about the first time we kissed. I got chills thinking about the first time we made love. I tried to go back in time and relive the nights that I had spent sleeping over at Toni's crib, and all the fun we had.

Although common sense had already told me that Toni would eventually have to go back to school for her final semester, it was still an unpleasant dose of reality to have to swallow. I looked back on the last month and a half and realized what a fool I was to have let all that time pass by without even seeing my girl. Sadly to say, I knew that I had let Toni slip out of the grip of my paws. I also knew that very soon she would be fair game to any cat that she would meet in D.C. Inside my heart I agonized as I wished that I could just always have Toni in my hip pocket and pull her out whenever I needed a hit of her.

My obsessive feelings for Toni overrode my common sense. When August 18th pulled in I managed to find my way back over to Toni's place. I had unexpectedly popped up at her crib. When Toni answered the door her jaw dropped to the ground. She seemed shocked and excited to see my face. Although it had only been a little over a month since I'd last seen Toni in person, she looked as if she had matured for the better. She had a slammin' new short hair style and her eyebrows were done up in a very exotic way.

In the doorway of her crib, I hugged Toni. Feeling how good her body felt, made me want to just kick myself for not having experienced more hugs and sex from her. I asked Toni, "You didn't think that I was gonna just let you leave without saying goodbye, did you?"

Toni replied that she knew I would call her but she had no idea that I would take the time out to come by.

"Toni I hope this doesn't mean goodbye forever."

Toni remained quiet. She didn't know what to say. Then I asked, "It doesn't right?"

Toni who was in the midst of packing her clothes, unzipped a suitcase and said, "Lance, I can't front… I'm crazy about you. Like I had told you in the past, in the short time that I've known you I've found myself doing things that I can't believe I let myself do. I don't regret the time we had together, but Lance, come on… I mean I haven't seen you in like almost a month and a half and I think I know why."

I hated hearing that type of talk from Toni. I wanted to put a halt to it. I walked over to her and I tried to hold her. I was trying to make a move to kiss her, but I think she knew what I was up to. Toni pushed me away as she told me no.

"Come on, what's wrong?" I asked.

"Lance, I'm not gonna kiss you because I realize that all I'm doing is letting my emotions dictate how I feel about you. I have to start exercising some common sense."

Playing dumb, I asked Toni what was she talking about.

She replied, "Lance, I don't have to explain because you know exactly what I'm talking about. For the past month and a half I've desperately wanted to speak to you and see you everyday. My heart was telling me to do whatever I had to do to be happy. But my mind was telling me that I had no business whatsoever wanting you like that. Lance, I don't think that I have to tell you that this *is* goodbye forever, because you should already know that."

Feeling like a kid who was told he couldn't have a new toy, I added, "Toni I know what you're saying, but all I'm saying is that I want to keep in touch with you."

"For what?" Toni asked in a somewhat rude manner.

I knew that this conversation wasn't going good, so I tried switching subjects. "OK Toni listen, at least let us depart on a good note. I tell you what, why don't I help you pack?"

Toni answered, "Actually Lance I'm almost done and I really don't need that much help. Plus I have to get dressed 'cause me and Kim are going out tonight."

Feeling like an unwanted roach I replied, "Oh, OK. Well where are y'all going?"

Toni handed me a flyer. On the flyer there were pictures of two cock diesel male strippers. When I saw the flyer I got so vexed that I almost wanted to crumble it up and throw it at Toni.

I barked, "Strippers! Y'all are gonna go see some male strippers!?"

Although I wasn't fond of the idea, Toni expressed her excitement which drove me absolutely bananas! Toni took the flyer from my hand and held it up in the air and began twirling it around as she, being happier than a peacock said, "Yeah we're gonna see Mandingo and oooh, I can't forget about Flava! Both of them have got it going on!"

I was so heated. Here I was trying to spark the last bit of passion between Toni and myself and she was running off at the mouth about Mandingo and Flava, two male strippers that had her salivating at the mouth.

Trying to hold back anger, I asked, "So that's how you're gonna spend your last night in New York?"

Toni continued packing her clothes and she nonchalantly responded, "No doubt, I'm young and I gots to get my groove on! You know what I'm sayin'?"

Man I didn't know what to make of the situation. I have to admit that I was jealous like crazy, but what could I do? I wanted to grab Toni's full attention for one more night. I thought about bringing the conversation towards God and asking Toni about her spiritual life, but how absurd and hypocritical would that have been? I was convinced that Toni still had feelings for me but she seemed as though she had made up her mind to erect this emotional wall in order to leave me out of her life.

I had over stayed my welcome and Toni began hinting that it was time for me to leave. As I hesitantly made my way to the door I asked one last question.

"Toni look... I know that you're gonna be turning twenty five in a couple of weeks. Can I at least have the privilege of having your address in D.C. so I can send you something nice?"

Toni looked at me and smiled, as she nodded her head up and down. I wanted to let out a sigh of relief. At least she wasn't telling me that she absolutely positively didn't want to have anything at all to do with me. Toni quickly jotted down her address and handed it to me. I looked at Toni and wondered would that be the last time that I would ever actually see her.

"Can I have one last hug?" I asked.

Toni quickly complied and gave me a very warm hug that lasted for about thirty seconds. That hug proved to me that Toni was going to be torn on the inside after I'd ceased to be a part of her life. I didn't want the two of us to depart feeling awkward, so I decided to make the situation funny and relaxed.

"Toni take off your socks," I commanded.

"What?" Toni asked as she started laughing.

"Take off your socks... If I never see you again I wanna make sure that I remember exactly how your toes look."

Toni continued laughing as she said, "Lance you are so crazy." She then did as I requested and took off both of her socks and wiggled her toes around. "Are you happy now?" She asked.

"Very happy," I replied with a smile.

Then I gave Toni one last hug and a peck on her ear. While still hugging her I felt like shedding a tear as I told her that I was going to truly miss her. After which she'd looked me in my eyes and told me that she was going to miss me too.

I sadly left and headed home.

TWENTY THREE

With Toni off to D.C. and out of the picture, the relationship with my wife had been so much more pleasurable. Spiritually, I'd been doing better than ever. I'd been able to spend much more quality time with LL. Also, I'd been combating many of my sexual hang-ups. But I have to admit that since Toni's departure, I still felt the need to be with her. To me, I greatly perceived a need to make love to Toni "one last time." It was like in my mind things just wouldn't have been complete between the two of us until that happened.

I had been trying to come up with all kinds of excuses to tell my wife why I would have to take a trip to Washington D.C. Unfortunately I hadn't been able to come up with a plausible enough excuse. I figured that my only option would have been for me to take a plane to D.C. early one Saturday morning, spend the day with Toni and then fly back to New York around eight or nine in the evening. But see, I still had another hurdle to leap over. That hurdle being Toni. My gut feeling told me that Toni would object to the idea simply because she was trying to put me behind her.

To me, jumping a hurdle was not that big of a deal because if I didn't make it over the hurdle, I'd simply try again. I'd keep trying until I was successful. Yeah, I might fall and scrape my knees but even the pain of that would eventually subside. I had to remind myself that women are an easy hurdle to jump if you get at their emotional side. For me I couldn't think of a better way to get at Toni's emotional side than to write her a love letter. I'm not the best one with words but I at least had to try. So writing her is exactly what I did. My letter went:

Dear Toni,

I know that you are probably surprised to be receiving a letter from me, but I just had to write you. Toni I don't know if I made it clear to you when you were in New York, but so that you'll know, I'll tell you now. Toni I love you. I'm not trying to run game on you and I hope that you don't take offense to me saying that I love you, but I really feel as if I do.

I understand what you were saying when you told me that you didn't want to be led by your emotions. I'll admit that when we first met I was definitely driven by my hormones and emotions in the sense that I was only physically attracted to you. Toni I'll even admit that maybe it was a mistake for us to have made love as soon as we did. But the fact remains that we did make love several times, and Toni each time we made love I felt that much closer to you.

Toni, I didn't fall in love with you based on superficial reasons. Rather, what I learned is that you are more of a beautiful person on the inside than you are on the outside. Toni it was during the three weeks or so when we spent every evening together that I learned what a special person you are. I found out what drives you, and that you are far from shallow. Toni, I could go on and on in terms of how much I'm drawn to you, but I don't want you to think that I'm trying to sell you something or trying to gas you.

I know that you probably feel the same way about me as I feel about you. And Toni you have to be honest with yourself in the same way I had to be honest with myself. What I mean is, could only our hormones and emotions be pulling us towards each other? Or is there something that goes deeper than the surface? Could that something deeper be called love?

Toni it's funny how it's been like two months since we've really hung tight with each other. Yet we still have strong feelings for one another. What I'm trying to say is, I know that it was me that chose to distance myself from you. And Toni I also know that you said before you left that it meant goodbye forever, but I can't go on if it really means goodbye forever. You told me that you would be finished with school this December and that you would be coming back to New York to live. Well Toni, December is only a few short months away.

I take the blame for letting you slip out of my life, but now I want you back in my life. Toni I also want to fly to D.C. one

*Saturday and see you. That's if it's alright with you. Let me know.
You have the number and you don't have to be afraid to call.*

Love Lance

*P.S. I know that you told me that you make good money doing hair
in D.C. because women down there get there hair done like it's a
religion, but I want you to keep the three hundred dollars that I've
sent along with this letter. Keep it as a birthday present. Thought
I forgot didn't you? Happy twenty fifth birthday.*

About a week had passed since I'd mailed Toni that letter
and she hadn't called me or anything. I was wondering what on
earth was going on. I began to think that she really did just want to
end the situation between the two of us. In a way I needed Toni to
hammer it through my thick skull that things were over, finished,
kaput, period, end of story. See, if Toni didn't end it I knew that I
was too weak to even try.

As the days strolled along, I began to look back and I
realized that my obsession with Toni was causing me to lose focus
on what was important in my life. Take my relationship with my
friends as an example. It had been a while since Steve and I had
our falling out, yet I was more worried about Toni than I was about
mending things with Steve. I was more focused on which airline
had the cheapest airfare to D.C. as opposed to which restaurant I
should take my wife to on Saturday night. I realized that I was a
sick man, but that's just me.

When Saturday afternoon came upon us, I found myself
mowing the lawn. Again, just like the past couple of days, I was
eagerly anticipating a phone call of some sorts from Toni. The
phone rang off the hook all morning long, but Toni never called.
Even as the early afternoon was in full gear the phone continued to
ring, yet no Toni.

Early Saturday afternoon did however bring one thing. It
brought the mailman to my house with a handful of bills. Along

with the bills, there was a small envelope that was addressed to me. Despite the fact that the letter was in a small envelope, what was odd was that the letter didn't have a return address on it. I knew that many junk mail letters came in that fashion just to throw people off. I was tired of receiving junk mail and I was just about to throw the letter in the garbage, but something told me to just open it.

To my complete shock and surprise, when I opened the envelope I realized that it was a letter from Toni. I quickly turned off the lawn mower. I put my rake to the side and with my dirty hands I began to read what Toni had to say.

What's up Lance?

I hope that you are reading this letter and that it didn't get into the hands of the wrong person. For obvious reasons I left out the return address information. Lance I was glad to have received a letter from you. I had been meaning to speak to you for quite some time now. Actually I wanted to speak to you before I left to come back to D.C., but I didn't know how to approach you.

Before I get into what I want to say let me say this. Lance I believe you when you say that you love me, and I believe that I love you too. But one thing is for sure and that is we can't have a relationship that goes beyond just being friends. I've thought things over, and I feel that we should definitely remain as friends. However, Lance there is something that is probably going to pull us to be closer than friends...

Lance I'm going to get straight to the point. I have been extremely troubled by something. Like I said, I wanted to tell you but I didn't know how, and when you wrote me, I figured that putting my words on paper would be the best way to tell you. Lance, I'm two months pregnant and I am positive that the baby is yours...

I took a pause from reading the letter. I took a deep breath, and I slowly re-read what I thought I'd just read. "Oh man!" I thought. Toni better be joking or else I have some serious problems on my hands! I had to take a seat on my front steps just in case I fainted or something. When I sat down I quickly scanned the letter one more time. I was looking for the spot where Toni would tell me that she was just joking. When I realized that there were no references to a joke, my heart started beating a hundred times per second. I felt a fear that I had never, and I mean never, felt in my life. Before I continued reading on, I thought about what I had just read, "two months pregnant and it's my baby."

> *So Lance, to answer a question that you had asked me in reference to coming to visit me, I think that you know that you have my approval to come to D.C. Lance, I am so sorry that I didn't tell you this when I suspected it in New York. But please don't be upset with me. I just want us to speak about this face to face in person.*
>
> *Lance, I am so scared. I am worried and I am confused. I know that I have to keep this baby because abortion is not in my vocabulary. I just don't know how I'm going to work out a lot of other personal issues. I know that my father is going to disown me, but in time that'll work itself out. I don't have the slightest idea as to what I'm going to do about starting my career and all that. I mean I won't have to leave school or anything like that because I'll be done with school in December. But I don't know what I'm going to do in terms of working and taking care of a baby.*
>
> *Lance, I hate to be telling you this but it's real and I would never joke with you like this. I know one thing and that's that, the both of us can't really worry about what the past has meant or how this or that should have been different. What we have to do is concern ourselves with what we are going to do with the future. Lance call me as soon as you read this letter.*
> *Love Toni,*
>
> *P.S. My number is ………*

I memorized the number and quickly shredded all of the incriminating evidence. I had never felt worse than I was feeling after having read that letter. It was so weird how just that quick, all my talk about how I loved Toni and how I wanted to see her had vanished. As scared as I was feeling, I knew that there was no way on earth I could truly love someone and then in a split second view them as if they had the bubonic plague. Forget about catching a shut eye to D.C. I felt like catching a plane to the nearest desert where I could be alone and not have to deal with all of the drama.

Although the grass was not yet complete, I managed to wrap things up. A beautiful lawn was the last thing on my mind. While putting the lawn mower away I almost broke out into a cold sweat as I thought about my wife. I began to hyperventilate just thinking how I was going to reveal this to Nicole. Nicole wasn't home and although I was terrified to pick up the phone, I had to call Toni just to make sure I wasn't dreaming.

When I dialed Toni's number, she picked up on the first ring. I left out all that hello how are you doing crap, I wanted to get down to business.

Breathing heavy due to my nervousness I said, "Toni I just read your letter. Tell me that you're not serious?"

Toni quietly replied, "Lance I wish I could but I can't."

I cried out over the phone, "Oh no! Toni don't tell me that! Please Toni don't tell me that!... Don't you know that I'm married!?"

Toni quickly became apologetic as she said in a velvet baby tone of voice, "Lance, I wish I could tell you I was lying; I wish I could but I'm really pregnant and I know it's yours."

There was dead silence on the phone for about a minute. I contemplated what I should do. All kinds of thoughts ran through my head, I wanted to ask Toni why she had waited so long to tell me. I also wanted to demand that she get an abortion. In the worse way I wanted Toni out of my life but now more than ever, she was a very big part of my life.

Toni broke the silence and said, "Lance I'm sorry."

I sucked my teeth and said, "Toni you don't have to be apologizing. Listen, next Saturday I'm coming to D.C. I'll call you and let you know what time to pick me up from the airport."

Toni agreed to the plan. We spoke for another minute or so and then we hung up.

I had never felt so lonely in all my life. I felt as if I had nowhere to turn. I couldn't call Steve. I couldn't talk to my wife. LL was too young to give me any advice, and I definitely couldn't call anyone from the church. Also, I hadn't analyzed the situation enough as to speak to any of my immediate family members. Feeling hopeless and with no options. I began sobbing like a baby. Through my tears I glanced at the family photo of my wife, LL and myself. How on earth was I gonna drop this bomb on Nicole?

I immediately dropped to my knees and began praying to God because I really felt like slitting my wrist. The only thing that stopped me from slitting my wrist was that I didn't want LL to come home and see such a gruesome sight.

TWENTY FOUR

Although I was deeply bothered as to how I was gonna handle this baby situation, I knew that the sooner Nicole found out, the better things would be. There was no way to make this situation easy for anyone involved. Two days after I'd found out that I was a father to be, for the second time, and under some real thick conditions I might add, I started hinting to Nicole that I had something important to tell her. Nicole begged to know what was on my mind but I had to keep her in the dark until I had all of the details. It was sad because Nicole thought that I was hiding some sort of pleasant surprise from her. If only she knew.

I managed to put my pride aside and I trooped over to Steve's crib. Steve didn't even want to open the door for me, and I can't say that I didn't blame him. I spoke to Steve through his front door, and I begged him to hear me out. I told him that I was sorry for having played myself. I also apologized for yelling at him. Fortunately for me, Steve opened the door and he reluctantly entertained my sob story.

I reached to give Steve a pound, but he just looked at my hand and did not extend his in return. "Yo Steve, I'm sorry for flipping on you like I did. You don't have to say anything and I know you probably don't even feel like talking to me, but Steve I'm in big trouble."

Steve who has been my man for years couldn't help but be concerned. Although he tried to disguise his concern, Steve looked away and mumbled, "What's up? Get at me. What are you talking about?"

I shook my head but I didn't say a word.

Steve then asked, "Yo L what's up? You got beef with somebody or what? What's up?"

I answered, "Now Steve, we've been tight for years, and I know I was in the wrong and I should have come to you and apologized earlier but…"

Steve interrupted me and said, "Yo Lance, I ain't sweatin' that. Now what's up man? Get at me!"

I made. another attempt to let Steve on to what was bothering me. "Steve promise me that what I tell you is gonna stay between me and you."

"Lance come on, you're my man."

"A'ight check it. Remember that chick Toni?"

Steve sarcastically replied, "Nah, I'm not sure if I do… Help me out, how does she look again?"

I paused and then I let it out, "Yo she's pregnant and guess who the father is?"

Steve looked at me and said, "Nigga you have a… Ah man… Yo… Yo… Kid are you serious?"

"Hell yeah I'm serious!"

Steve replied, "Ah man, I'm sayin'… Man you ran up in that piece raw dawg!?"

If this had been normal circumstances I would have been bragging at this point. But not today, I sadly had to admit that yes, I had ran up in Toni with no protection.

"Steve, man what do you think I should do?"

"Well I'm sayin', if I was you I'd give her the dough and tell her to get rid of it."

"Yeah, but she wants to keep it."

"What!!! She knew a nigga was married. Yo, was she trying to trap you or something?"

"Nah Yo, she ain't like that. It just happened."

Steve shook his head again and said, "Yo all I can say is that if she wants to keep that kid then I hate to say it but you can hang things up with Nikki."

Scared as hell, I wanted Steve to confirm what he'd just said, "Word? You think Nicole is gonna flip?"

"Nigga, what do you think she's gonna do!? Imagine her coming home and telling you that she's pregnant by some other cat, what would you do? It would be over, right?"

I knew that Steve was right and that's why I'd started to plant seeds in Nicole's head, seeds in the form of informing her that I had something to tell her.

"Lance, man how many months pregnant is she?"

"Two months."

"Two months? Man you got time, but I tell you what, just ask for a divorce. Don't mention anything about a baby or anything like that. Just tell Nicole that you aren't happy anymore and it's time to end things."

I jumped in, "But Steve everything is on the up and up with our marriage, and plus what about LL?"

"Lance listen. You ain't working with too many options. Matter of fact if Nicole finds out that you got someone else pregnant, she's probably gonna do an O.J. Simpson on a nigga. I know that Nicole is religious and all but watch how quick she'll lose her religion when she finds out what you did."

Steve had a point. See, the main reason I was so filled with anxiety was due to the fact that I didn't know how Nicole was going to react. But one thing was for sure, and that was the fact that her reaction towards me wanting to get a divorce was sure to be less volatile than her would be reaction to the news that I'd impregnated another woman.

****

Before I knew it, I found myself getting off of flight 702 at the Ronald Regan international airport. It was 8:30 on a Saturday morning. Toni was waiting at the flight gate for me when the plane arrived. When I stepped into the passenger terminal I saw Toni wearing a jean jacket and a pair of jeans along with a pair of the new Air Jordan's. Although I was a mental wreck, I immediately became happy when I saw Toni's beautiful face.

Toni ran over to me and gave me a kiss on the cheek.

"How was the flight?" She asked.

Due to the changes in altitude that I had experienced while I was on the plane, my ears had that clogged popping feeling to them that I hated. But I didn't comment on that, I simply replied, "It was short and quick. It was like before I knew it I was here. I mean they didn't even serve us any food, they just gave us some peanuts and a cup of soda."

Toni laughed and she advised me that she had food in her apartment if I was hungry. We both walked to the airport parking lot where we hopped into Toni's car. The two of us headed to her apartment. In the beginning of the ride we both were silent. So to break the tension Toni popped in a CD into her car's stereo system. It was a base thumping hip-hop mix tape. I wasn't really in the mood for no hip-hop and I asked if she could put on something a little softer. Toni complied and while she was switching CD's she asked what time was I planning to head back to New York."

"My flight back leaves at five thirty this afternoon," I informed.

"That soon?"

"Yeah, I told Nicole that I was working overtime today, so I have to be back at a reasonable time."

Toni understood and as we drove she informed me that she had to stop at a store to pick up some orange juice. When we reached the supermarket I stayed in the car and Toni jumped out and ran inside the store. I started to run in behind her and ask her if we could stop at a pharmacy and pick up a "hoe pregnancy test,"… I mean a "home pregnancy test." After all, what if she was just gaming a nigga? I decided against asking her that because if she wanted me that bad she knew that she didn't have to stoop as low as telling me she's pregnant.

It's funny because whenever I go to another state it just seems so much more peaceful as compared to New York. I always have thoughts of what it would be like if I actually picked up and moved out of New York. The horrid thought of me just breaking out on my family and moving to D.C. crossed my mind. As I sat in the car and waited for Toni I really began to consider that as a natural solution to all of my troubles. I didn't want to be tied down in another marriage but I could definitely see myself living in D.C. with Toni and raising the baby.

Before long Toni had returned to the car.

"That was quick," I said. "A woman never comes out of any store that fast."

Toni smiled and reminded me that she had only gone to buy orange juice. She then advised me that we were only like two minutes away from her apartment.

"Lance, do you eat omelets?"

I replied, "As hungry as I am I'll eat anything."

Toni laughed and she let me know that she was gonna cook us some French toast and omelets. As Toni slowly maneuvered the car over two speed bumps I realized that we must have been at her apartment complex.

I asked, "Is this where you stay?"

Toni informed me that we had in fact reached our destination as we pulled into her personal parking spot. The complex was very nice. I would say that it held fifty or so apartments. It wasn't a high rise complex, it was only two stories high. When we walked into Toni's apartment I immediately noticed that she kept the place just as immaculate as she'd kept her apartment in New York.

"Toni your place is just as nice as your place at home."

"Oh you like it?"

"Yeah it's cool. But you need to take down that poster of Maxwell."

Toni laughed as she told me that the singer Maxwell was the man. Toni also began to show me around the place and when we reached her bedroom I flopped onto her bed and I let out a groan. Who was I fooling? Since the airport I had been behaving as if I was visiting Toni on an ordinary visit. But I knew and she knew that this was no regular visit.

After groaning, I smothered my face into Toni's pillow and I asked, "Toni what are we gonna do?"

Being that the pillow was muffing my voice Toni couldn't make out what I had asked. So I sat up, removed the pillow from my face and I looked at Toni and asked again, "What are we gonna do?"

Toni sat next to me and suggested that we talk over breakfast. I agreed, so as Toni went to the kitchen to cook I stayed in her room on the bed and rested. Again, a stupid thought passed through my mind. With everything going on I still managed to think about realizing the possibility of having sex with Toni one last time. My rationale was that I was already in her apartment and sex would be a great way to relieve some of the stress that I was feeling.

While I was thinking to myself, Toni yelled from the kitchen and asked me to come join her. I sluggishly made my way to the kitchen and Toni remarked, "What's wrong? You scared of me or something?"

Toni was standing in front of her stove, and while I pulled out a chair to sit in I said, "Nah I'm not scared of you, I was just trying to get some more rest... With all that's been going through my head lately I haven't been able to get a lick of sleep at night."

Toni sympathized with me and her sympathy led us into deeper conversation.

"Toni, I've been thinking this whole thing through, and I have to admit something. When I read your letter I knew right away that you wasn't lying and I got mad scared. People usually think irrational when they are afraid. And to be honest, the first thought that came to my mind was that I wanted you to get an abortion."

Toni who was sautéing onions, immediately interrupted me and said, "Lance I already told you in the letter that I ain't getting no abortion! I don't believe in that."

"No. Nah, I understand that. I'm just sayin', that was the first thought that came to my mind when I initially found out. I mean I don't believe in abortion either. It probably doesn't seem like it but I am a *Christian*."

Toni took a pause from preparing the food and she told me, "Lance you know what?... I can't even believe that we are discussing this. For real, I mean in my wildest dreams I never thought that I would be mixed up in something like this. In the past whenever I watched Jerry Springer or some other trash talk show, I always wondered where on earth do they get such jacked up people from? And now here I am having a married man's baby. I need to call one of those trash talk shows and try to get on."

Although Toni was being sarcastic, I could here a sense of pain and some regret in her voice. "Toni believe me, this episode that we're going through is not going to be anything like Jerry Springer... But on the serious tip, what I was thinking was, I'm just gonna divorce Nicole before she even finds out anything about this baby."

Toni again took a break from preparing the food and she commented, "See Lance, that's exactly what I'm talking about. I never could have pictured myself as a home wrecker! And that's exactly what I feel like I am."

"Toni you ain't no home wrecker. This whole thing is my fault. I dragged you into this hook, line, and sinker. You didn't have any intentions of messing with me. That's the difference, see a home wrecker sets out with a motive of destroying a family, and you never had those intentions."

"Still, but Lance I don't want you getting no divorce."

Raising my voice a bit I asked, "Why not!? What do you expect me to do? When you have this baby it's not like I can just bring the kid home to play with LL. And I want to be around any baby that I helped create."

Toni became defensive, "No, Lance I understand that you would want to be around the kid, but I don't know… Just forget it, I don't even know what point I was trying to make."

I was ready to comment but Toni quickly retracted and said, "Oh OK, I know what I wanted to say. Lance, I know things are gonna be difficult but all I want from you is to help me financially with the baby. You don't have to get a divorce in order to do that."

I turned my lips and just looked at Toni for a few seconds. I was disgusted as I said, "Toni what is wrong with you? I don't know about you but my idea of helping to raise a kid isn't just sending the kid money for some new sneakers."

Toni looked at me and she didn't respond. Both of us stayed quiet for about two minutes. The wheels were spinning in my head and my blood pressure was starting to rise because of the silence.

Toni finally cut into the quietness as she said, "Alright. I guess I can see where you're coming from. But Lance, one thing that I say is that you should just tell Nicole what's going on. I'm a woman and all I'm saying is that from a woman's point of view, I know that she would much rather know."

I remained silent and I thought about what Toni had just said. Toni then added, "I know that it's going to be a hard thing to do, but Lance there isn't any easy ways around this whole thing."

I continued in my silence. I guess Toni was feeling uncomfortable because she continued to break the silence, "Lance, I don't know how I would do this, but if anything, I mean I'll tell Nicole what happened. I'll apologize and the whole nine. Woman to woman."

My silence was finally interrupted as I replied, "What!?"

Toni reaffirmed what she had just said. "Toni, if that is not the dumbest most ass-backwards thing that I have ever heard in my life!" I began to use some of Steve's logic as I added, "Nicole is religious and all, but I don't know if there is enough religion in the whole world that would keep her from murdering you if you told her that you're pregnant by me."

Toni was just about done preparing breakfast. She added, "See Lance, I know that I am here in D.C. cooking breakfast for you and it's easy for me to say that I am willing and actually would want to speak to Nicole and all that. But I know that if I were ever face to face with her I wouldn't expect the situation to be a calm one. Lance, I stepped way beyond my bounds. I slept with another woman's man! Better yet, another woman's husband! That's not something that I am proud of, but if I am woman enough to sincerely apologize to Nicole's face, regardless if she accepted my apology or not, I would at least feel a bit more respect for myself."

Both of our breakfast plates were prepared and on the table. I took a sip of my orange juice and I told Toni, "Toni look. I guess I see where you are coming from. I mean deep down I know that I have to tell Nicole what the deal is. Somehow I'll muster up the courage to tell her because I couldn't respect myself if I didn't. The main thing that has been eating at me lately is the fact that I feel that Nicole more than deserves to know the truth. I know that my marriage will most likely end up in divorce court but I have to keep things real. I can't just hit Nicole with divorce papers. First of all if I did that I would have to literally become the most cold, angry, and split personality person in the world to really pull the

divorce thing off.   Second of all by me just hitting Nicole with
divorce papers that would be like I'm trying to hint that I want to
end the marriage because of her.   When in reality I am the one who
did the dirt."

Toni had her mouth full of food, so she nodded her head up
and down to show her agreement of what I'd just said.   I then
informed Toni that it would kind of be out of place for her to speak
to Nicole.   However, if she insisted that she speak to Nicole, then
at least let me confront Nicole first.   Toni agreed that I should
definitely be the first one to speak to Nicole, but she also insisted
that she be allowed to apologize.

The breakfast was on point and I complemented Toni on it.
I wanted to switch the conversation to a more relaxed tone.   So
while switching gears, I smiled and said, "Toni even with all the
turmoil that is going on, the fact remains that there is a child inside
of you.   The baby has nothing to do with the mess that we caused,
and that's why I'm not shy to admit that I would love to have a
little girl that looks just like you."

Toni laughed and asked, "Lance, how could you be
thinking of that now?"

"I'm sayin'!   What's wrong with thinking like that?   I'm
keeping it real, I want a baby girl that is the splitting image of you.
I can picture a little girl in one of those white dresses with white
shoes and those ankle high white lace dressy socks that little girls
wear."

Toni began laughing and she said, "Lance you are so
crazy."

"I'm crazy?" I asked.   "Come on Toni admit it, you know
that it would be fly to have a little girl walking around trying to be
as sophisticated and sassy as you are."

"Sassy? Who you calling sassy?" Toni asked.

I smiled and said, "You know I'm just playing."

Toni finally gave in and admitted that she did in fact want a
little girl.   She explained that she'd always envisioned having a girl
before having a boy.   Her desire for a girl was due to her reasoning
that with little girls there is so much more to do, such as creating

new hairstyles and the like. I informed Toni that the only reason she thought like that was because she's a beautician.

We both were just about finished eating our food. As we prepared to do the dishes together I wanted to make sure the mood remained up beat.

"Toni do you have any candy or gum?" I asked.

Toni pointed to the top of the refrigerator where there was a bowl full of candy. I reached my hand in and I got a peppermint ball. As I made my way back to the sink to help Toni, I made sure to hand her the peppermint candy. Toni smiled and asked what was the candy for.

"No offense baby, but I'm sayin', the onions in that omelet didn't do you any justice."

Toni broke out into laughter. She covered her mouth and slapped me on the arm.

I continued on, "Well you wouldn't have wanted me to let you walk around with stink breath, now would you? Just like if I had a booger or something I would want you to tell me."

Toni continued laughing, she was embarrassed as she said, "Oh my god, I can't believe you played me like that." Toni then ran out of the room.

"It's all good baby, don't sweat it!" I yelled to her.

While Toni was out of the room, I continued washing the dishes. See although I was in D.C. for a serious reason, there was no need to not be loose. After all, there was going to be plenty of time for seriousness in the future.

Toni returned to the kitchen and she blew her breath in my face. "You happy now?" She playfully asked.

As I was forced to inhale a whiff of Toni's breath, I realized that she must have gone to brush her teeth and rinse her mouth with mouthwash.

"Yeah, you good now," I replied. "Your breath isn't as hot. You're good."

Toni then handed me a bottle of Scope that she had used and she recommended that I use it as well. I took the mouth wash and we both began laughing. In an instant we'd both totally forgotten about the dishes and we started snapping on each other and telling "mother jokes."

The mood was definitely where I wanted it and where I preferred it. In the back of my mind I knew that I could get some butt from Toni if I pushed up. And as we made our way to the living room, the thought of having sex with Toni became an even more compelling thought. So I decided to keep the mood relaxed by continuing to joke with Toni. I asked her did she know that my uncle had invented Nacho Cheese.

She looked at me and twisted her lips.

"He did!" I exclaimed.

"Yeah right."

As Toni looked at me and smiled I said, "A'ight you don't believe me, so I'll explain to you how it happened and prove to you that I'm not lying. See one day my uncle was in the park eating crackers and cheese. Then from out of nowhere this bum comes up to him and asked him for the time. He gave him the time and then the bum walked off. So my uncle continued eating his crackers and cheese. Then about five minutes later the bum came back and asked for directions to somewhere. My uncle gave the bum the directions and the bum walked off. My uncle continued eating his crackers and cheese and before you knew it, the same bum came back a third time. My uncle who was sitting on a park bench asked the bum what did he want this time. The bum didn't say anything, he just kept walking around the bench like he was plotting a scheme. My uncle paid him no mind and before you could blink, the bum had snatched my uncle's cheese and he ran off! So my uncle who was left sitting there with only crackers in his hands stood up on the park bench and yelled real loud, 'Hey come back here! That's NachYoCheese!'... And with that came the invention of Nacho Cheese."

After verbalizing the punch line of that joke I fell out in laughter. Toni looked at me and I could tell that she wanted to laugh simply because the joke was so corny. However, she managed to hold in her laughter. I on the other hand was balled over in laughter.

"Toni, you know you wanna laugh," I said.

Toni looked at me like I was stupid. So I ran over to her and began tickling her. "Oh you're gonna laugh, you gonna laugh…"

Toni finally gave in and she started laughing.

"See, I told you that you were gonna laugh," I said as I continued to tickle her.

Toni replied, "Yeah, but I ain't laughing at that stupid joke. Lance… Ha ha ha… Lance, stop tickling me. Ha ha ha…"

As we were both laughing, I decided to stop tickling her. I didn't want to be too childish. The two of us paused and caught our breath, after which we made our way to the living room to watch Soul Train. As we made our way, I stopped and pulled Toni close to me and I hugged her.

"Toni we don't have to act like we both have some kind of disease or something. We can still get close to each other."

Toni tried to push me off as she explained that getting close was exactly what had got us in the mess that we were now in.

"Baby don't fight me. All I want to do is kiss you. I mean we both have fresh breath and all so what's the problem?"

As Toni began to smile, I made my move and I kissed her. As we kissed I began feeling all over her body and kissing on her neck. I knew she was enjoying it but she pushed me away. I moved closer to her and I whispered in her ear that it had been such a long time since we'd done "*it*."

The look on Toni's face after I'd whispered those words told me that she wanted to go further. Unfortunately she exercised self control. Reluctantly, I too told my hormones to calm down and we both sat and watched Soul Train. As we watched I was commenting on all of the slammin' female dancers that were on that show. With Toni right next to me, I found myself getting a little too excited due to the tight and revealing clothing that the dancers had on.

When a commercial came on, Toni took the remote and turned off the television. "Lance, you came here so we could talk, and we aren't doing that, so what's up?"

Realizing that Toni was right, I paused and thought for about a minute. I sighed and said, "OK this is the deal. When I get back to New York I'm gonna make sure that I tell Nicole what's going on because I want to get this off my chest. Matter of fact if I don't get this off my chest I'll probably have a stroke or something."

"Now after I tell her, I have no idea what her reaction is gonna be but if you still want to speak to her then by all means go ahead. But Toni one thing that I want you to know is that no matter what happens between Nicole and me, I am going to make sure that you and the baby are always taken care of. I can't promise how much time I am going to spend with the kid but I can promise that I am going to make the best effort possible to be a big part of the kid's life."

Toni and I continued to hammer out, "what if" scenarios. We came to the conclusion that at this early stage, it was gonna be hard to predict just exactly how all the little details would be handled. But regardless of whether or not the future would go according to how we envisioned it, we both simply solidified the fact that we were going to be committed as a team to giving the best of everything to the baby.

The remainder of the day flew by. When it was all said and done, I found myself on the plane heading back to New York. Yeah, I was wondering how I was gonna open up to Nicole. I didn't know how I was gonna bring myself to open up to her or where I was gonna get the courage from, but at least I had achieved one moral victory for the day. That being, although I'd wanted to hit "it," Toni and I had managed to keep our pants on.

TWENTY FIVE

When Sunday arrived on the scene, I found myself in church. However, I couldn't even concentrate on what was going on. Everyone seemed to notice that something was troubling me but I played like all was OK. Nicole also noticed that I wasn't my normal self and she wanted to know if it had anything to do with what I had to tell her. At that point, there was no sense in lying, so I told her that in fact that was the reason I was in such a lethargic mood. Nicole begged and pleaded to know what was going on and I told her that in a couple of days she would definitely know.

Nicole was upset, and rightly so, due to the fact that I was hiding something from her. But see, that was the exact reason that I had pushed myself to even mention that I had something to tell her. By Nicole knowing that I had to talk to her, I knew that she was gonna keep the pressure on me to tell her what it was that was bothering me. If I didn't have that pressure on me then I would have more than likely let the whole situation drag on, which in turn would have only led me into telling more lies and causing more stress on everyone.

Monday after I'd picked LL up from the daycare center, I found myself at my sister Tiffany's house. I had already called her and told her that I had something very important to discuss with her. Therefore, Tiffany was expecting my Monday afternoon visit. When I got to Tiffany's house I put LL in another room where he could be entertained by the television, while Tiffany and I spoke.

I looked away from Tiffany as I spoke, "Tiffany, I know that you are not going to believe what I have to tell you but it's the truth. Matter of fact I don't even know how to say this to you."

Tiffany knew that I had something serious on my mind and she said, "Lance, I'm your sister so you know that you can tell me anything without worrying about me tripping."

I continued to look away from my sister as I said, "A'ight, I'm gonna be straight up real and just spit it out." I sighed and I felt myself beginning to form tears, as I said, "Tiffany, you know how much I love Nicole, that's why this is so hard."

"Lance what? What is going on? Are you and Nikki having problems?"

I sighed again and then I let it out, "Tiffany, I messed up big time! Nicole has been on point since the day we got married and there was no excuse for me to do what I did but I …"

"Lance, but what?" Tiffany eagerly questioned.

I spat out, "But… I got this other woman pregnant."

With sounds of disbelief, Tiffany covered her mouth which was wide open. Her eyebrows were also raised as she said, "Lance! I can't believe what you just said."

Tears ran down my face as I finally looked my sister in her eyes and said, "I can't believe it either."

Tiffany, who knew that I wasn't lying, asked how had this all come about.

"Tiffany, I don't really want to explain all of that. I mean I'm a dog and I messed up... It's as simple as that."

Tiffany then said, "Lance, like I told you, I'm your sister and I'm glad you came to me with this. But is there anything specific that you want me to do in order to help you? Because really, I don't know what to tell you, but I do want to help you out if I can."

Wiping my tears away I said, "Tiffany, I haven't told Nicole yet. I have no idea how she's gonna react and I don't even know how I'm going to drop this on her. But I just want you to be there when I tell her."

Tiffany assured me that that was not a problem. All I had to do was let her know when.

I then added, "See Tiffany, what makes this so hard is the way people are going to look at me and Nicole. On one hand I'm gonna have to deal with people calling me a hypocrite. I know people are going to be saying I'm supposed to be a Christian and all that and I'm always kicking this religious crap, yet I'm running around cheating on my wife. Plus Tiffany, it just makes Nikki look bad. She has been the best wife in the world and I messed up. What's gonna make things even harder is the fact that there has always been people, especially some of Nicole's friends that have been jealous of our relationship since day one. We're educated, we have careers, the house, the cars and the kid and to everyone we seem like we're totally in love. Now all of those jealous people are going to be laughing and feeling some sort of redemption. But Tiffany..."

As I stopped speaking and I started to cry, my sister came and sat right next to me and began to console me. Tiffany and I were never very affectionate towards each other, and I was surprised that she'd put her arm around me and rubbed my shoulder.

"Lance, let me tell you something. I don't know all of the details. And Lance, I'm sure that you know as well as I do, that what you did was beyond wrong. But this is between you and Nicole to work out. If you start worrying about what everyone is going to think, Lance you'll drive yourself crazy. I'm here for you if you ever need anyone to talk to and I am not going to look at you in a judgmental way."

I remained silent. Although I would be turning twenty eight years old in two months, I had never felt so young and pitiful. I felt like I was re-living a scene from my youth. Here I was crying and being consoled by my sister due to a mistake that I had made. Tiffany went and got me a moist paper towel so I could properly wipe my face. Then she asked when did I plan on telling Nicole.

I paused and thought for a moment, then I said, "Tiffany, I figure it's just like taking medicine. It's disgusting and all, but you just have to swallow it and get it over with. No matter how bitter it might taste, if you ever want to feel better then you have to go ahead with the process. So I was thinking that maybe tomorrow I should tell her if that's OK with you."

Tiffany agreed. I finalized things by letting Tiffany know that I would call her tomorrow once Nicole came home from work.

"Tiffany, I just hope that everything works out. I mean I never wanted to hurt Nicole."

"Lance, let me ask you something. You're religious and all, right?"

Having no clue where my sister was going with her line of questioning, I said, "Yeah, why?"

Tiffany added, "I mean you're not just religious on the surface are you?"

The truth of the matter was, as of late, I in fact had been "just religious on the surface." I mean who was I fooling? For the past six months or so I have definitely been Satan's child. Although I was starting to realize that it was time to get serious about repenting and truly representing as a child of God, I didn't want my sister to know that my religious ways of late had been very hypocritical, so I answered my sister, "Tiffany you know I'm not just religious on the surface. What's up? What are you getting at?"

"Lance, all I'm saying is that I am not as religious as you are, but one thing I know is that God wants us to come to Him when we are feeling troubled or anxious. Lance, you probably know this better than I do, but God is not like your friends on this earth. Your so called friends will sell you out in a second. Your friends will let you come to them with your problems a couple of times. But if you keep coming to them with your problems they'll soon want nothing to do with you. Lance, God is exactly the opposite. He'll never sell you out and He'll never get tired of you. See, sometimes religious people forget the hope that they have in Jesus. Lance, I'm going to stop preaching to you, but what I want you to do is, go home and get on your knees and pray about this whole situation. Pray like you've never prayed before!"

Tiffany paused and then she added, "Lance, I can't tell you how Nicole is gonna take this, but I can tell you that with God, all things are possible. So if you earnestly pray about this, God will see to it that things work out. I promise you that."

I took to heart everything that my sister had just told me. I hugged her and I thanked her for being there for me. LL and I departed and we made our way home.

The remainder of the evening went like any other typical evening. Nicole, LL, and I ate dinner like a loving family. Nicole and I watched a movie after dinner and we talked. I was glad that not once did Nicole ask me about what it was that I had to tell her.

When the lights were out and when Nicole was fast asleep, I snuck out of the bedroom and made my way to the basement. I dropped to my knees and prayed with everything ounce of feeling and emotion that I had in my body.

Dear Lord,
Lord, I know that out of all sinners on this earth I probably take the cake as chief sinner. Lord you see everything that goes on. I can hide things from people, but Lord I can't hide things from you. That's why I beg you Lord, if there is anyway at all, I beg you for your forgiveness. Lord I know that you call us to confess our sins to one another, and Lord I want to let my wife know what I have done. The guilt inside of me is tearing me to pieces. I realize that the wrongs that I committed were done on purpose. I can't blame Satan or anyone else for what I willingly chose to do. Lord, I am a rational thinking man, but I continually gave into the desires of my flesh and I committed adultery in the worst way. Lord, in no way do I expect Nicole to forgive me, and I can only imagine the enormous pain that she is going to feel when she finds out what I have done. Lord, please, please, please, comfort Nicole when I tell her what I have done. Please ease her pain and wipe away her tears. Lord, I did not intend to hurt Nicole or LL. Lord, I know that I have hurt You and I am sorry. Please give me the courage to admit to Nicole what I have done. Lord, please take away from me that desire to be with other women. Remove my desires to lust and masturbate, and the desire to want to look at pornography. Lord those terrible desires have helped to pave my road to adultery. Never have I owned up to my weaknesses, never have I admitted that I need help in overcoming sexual evils. Lord as I kneel, crying and praying to you, I feel comforted because You promised that You would never leave me. Teach me Lord what it means to be loyal as You are loyal. Teach me Lord what it is to love as You love. Lord I wish that I could sit here and talk to You until eternity, but one thing I realize Lord, is that I should have been this honest and earnest with You before I committed my terrible acts. Thank You Lord for allowing Tiffany to remind me that I should come to You with all my problems. For if I had come to You sooner, I would not have been in this situation. Lord, I realize that I am one big perpetual screw up when it comes to adultery,

but there is a child inside of Toni. Lord, somewhere in the mist of all that has happened I know that Satan played a part in my sin that has now blossomed out of control. But Lord, Satan can not create life. You and only You Lord can create life. Although I don't fully understand it now, Lord I know that you allowed Toni to become pregnant for a reason. Satan was behind it, but You Lord saw fit to allow the pregnancy to happen, and in time I know that I will understand why. But for now I pray that You protect Toni and the baby. Lord let that baby grow up healthy and strong so that whether boy or girl it can grow up to serve You. Lord as I end this prayer I want to say that I am so sorry for what I have done. Lord I want to ask You to please have mercy on me and somehow forgive me. And Lord please help me with my struggles. Most importantly, Lord comfort Nicole throughout this whole ordeal. Lord help me and teach me to change and to know what it is like to love as You love.

In Your Son's Graet Name, Jesus Christ, I pray all these things. Amen.

When I was done praying I sat on the floor and just meditated in the dark. Since this whole ordeal began to unravel, I'd never felt as peaceful as I was feeling after that prayer.

When I was done meditating I made my way back upstairs and into my bedroom. Nicole looked so peaceful and beautiful as she slept. I knew that telling her what I had to tell her would be as difficult as driving a knife through her heart. But I had to do it.

TWENTY SIX

The last time that I had butterflies this bad, had to be the night before my high school city championship basketball game. It's ironic that Nicole was a cheerleader in that game. In fact it was Nicole, my high school sweet heart, who told me to relax and concentrate just before I took the game winning free throws.

My current real life crisis far exceeded the pressure and drama of any high school basketball game and I definitely wouldn't have Nicole in my corner cheering me on. I made those two game winning free throws the day my high school won the city championship, but the question now was how was I gonna fare in the present moment under the intense pressure of admitting to adultery.

For the most part I had been holding up well throughout the day. I had already called Nicole at work and told her that Tiffany would be coming by for dinner. Nicole didn't object. As a matter of fact she was kind of annoyed that I would even go out of my way to call her and tell her that Tiffany was coming over. See, her and Tiffany are pretty close, so to Nicole it's like Tiffany could drop by unannounced at anytime she felt like it. I knew that Nicole wouldn't object to Tiffany coming over, however I was just trying to cover all of my bases. I didn't want this to be a night where Nicole decided to go to the mall after work or what have you.

When I came home I was crazy antsy. But I remembered my sister's words, so every time my anxiety became overwhelming, I began to pray. The prayer therapy was working but I decided to cook in order to keep myself busy. Staying busy would be a good way to keep my mind off of the adulterous topic. I couldn't remember the last time I had cooked dinner for Nicole. I didn't go all out with a gourmet meal but what I cooked was baked chicken wings, baked potatoes and some broccoli.

By the time six forty five rolled around, Nicole was walking through the door. My heart was pounding as I greeted her with a hug and a kiss. I took her jacket and put it on a hanger. Nicole then asked what it was that she was smelling.

"Lance, what's that smell? It smells like food."

I chuckled and said, "It is food."

Nicole sarcastically replied, "No, but I mean it smells like it's coming from this house."

"Baby, stop playing. I decided to cook today," I informed her.

Nicole's mouth dropped wide open as she walked towards the kitchen to confirm the unbelievable. Before I knew it, I heard a scream come from the kitchen. I ran to see what was going on. When I reached the kitchen Nicole was smiling and standing with her arms wide open and waiting for a hug. After the hug Nicole expressed her gratitude for me having helped out with dinner. Then she became suspicious. "OK so what's the occasion?" Nicole asked.

I was still feeling nervous as I said, "Why does it have to be an occasion? I'm sayin', I just felt like cooking for you today."

Nicole informed me that she was going to change her clothes. But before she left the kitchen she said, "Lance I know something is going on. You haven't cooked dinner in I don't know how long, plus your sister is coming over. So do you want to tell me now and get it over with?"

My heart was in the bottom of my stomach. But I side stepped everything. I slapped Nicole on her butt and said, "Nicole just go and change your clothes. I'm sayin', can't a brother cook for his wife once in a while?"

When Nicole left the room I immediately grabbed the phone and called Tiffany. I frantically instructed Tiffany to hustle her butt over to my house so that I wouldn't lose the nerve to spill my guts. My sister pleaded with me to calm down and she informed me that she would be at my house within the next half hour.

While I waited for Tiffany to get there, I began to think about how I was going to spill the beans. I rehearsed comments in my head but nothing was coming out the way I wanted it to sound. Thinking of what to say and how to say it was really making me nervous. I decided to just block that issue out of my mind as I realized the best thing to do would be to concentrate and remain calm.

When Nicole returned to the kitchen she walked up to me and gave me a kiss. She also took my hand and suggestively put it inside her pants. I don't know why I was shocked by Nicole's actions but I was. Feeling as though I was doing something wrong, I snatched my hand away.

Nicole frowned and asked what was wrong.

"Nothing," I quickly replied.

"Well why did you pull your hand away like that?"

"Oh because I want to hurry and fix LL's plate so that he can eat his food now."

"Lance, why don't you just let LL eat with us? Tiffany is still coming over, right?"

At that point, I told Nicole that I didn't want LL to eat with us, the reason being that tonight I wanted to discuss what it was that I had to discuss with her.

As I prepared to fix LL's plate, Nicole came close to me and she kissed me on the neck. She was trying to get frisky, but sex was far from my mind. I mean as nervous as I was, I probably wouldn't have been able to get it up anyway.

I was glad that Nicole was behaving frisky because that took her mind off of asking me about what we were going to discuss. Nicole whispered in my ear that she had been thinking about me all day long. She then kissed me and playfully told me how turned on she gets when she sees her man making his way around the kitchen.

Nicole had on sweat pants and bare feet. That combination usually turned me on like crazy. Normally, with the way Nicole was dressed, coupled with the way she was coming on to me, we would have been in our bedroom with the door locked and going at it like two horny rabbits. But at that present time I was functioning only on one track like I had tunnel vision. I kept declining my wife's advances and I quickly got LL's food.

I called LL into the kitchen and informed him that it was time to eat. While he was eating I made sure to remove myself from the kitchen. I went upstairs to the bathroom and locked the door. I was trying to stall and give my sister time to get there.

While I was in the bathroom I sat at the edge of the tub and said another prayer for courage.

When I was done praying I sat in the bathroom and again I tried to rehearse what I was gonna say and how I was gonna say it. While I was pondering, I heard Nicole laughing and talking real loud. She sounded like she was having one of those "Sister-Gal," conversations. I knew that that could only mean one thing. I made my way out of the bathroom and downstairs where I saw Tiffany and Nicole talking.

"What's up sis'?" I asked.

Although Tiffany had only been in our house for about two minutes, she was heavy into dialogue with Nicole, and she basically paid me no mind.

I yelled, "Hello Tiffany!"

Realizing that I had been trying to get her attention, Tiffany stopped in mid stride of her conversation and began laughing as she said, "Oh Lance, I'm sorry. How you doing?"

I smiled and shook my head as I said, "I'm fine, but man! How on earth could the two of y'all be into such a deep conversation that quick?"

The three of us began laughing. With a million butterflies floating around in my stomach I instructed that we go to the kitchen and start eating. LL was basically playing with his food and I wanted to tell him that he could leave, but Nikki beat me to the punch. She yelled at him and told him that he couldn't leave the table until he had eaten everything, broccoli and all.

So as LL toyed with his meal, Tiffany and I sat at the table and Nicole politely fixed our plates for us. When we were all sitting I said grace and we began to eat. Tiffany began to talk about how stressful her job as a school teacher was. I was glad that the ice had been broken in that manner because it allowed things to flow naturally. Before I knew it Nicole began talking about events that happened on *her job*. Just that quick the two of them were again engrossed into another lively conversation.

I let the two of them converse and I tried to eat but I was behaving worse than LL. I was so nervous that I couldn't even eat. When there was a pause in Nicole's conversation she sought of noticed my nervousness and commented on the way I was handling my food.

Nicole said, "Lance you're acting worse than LL with the way you're playing with that food." Then she joked and asked was it that my own cooking was so bad that I couldn't even eat it?

Realizing that it was time to get serious, I didn't laugh or acknowledge my wife's joke. I told LL that he didn't have to finish his food and that he was excused to go to his room and play. LL knew that he had to quickly capitalize on that opportunity, so he didn't hesitate. He bolted from the table and made his way to his room. With LL out of the way I told myself, "now or never."

My heart was pounding and my hands were ice cold. My palms were extremely sweaty. I pushed my chair away from the table and looked towards the floor. After bracing myself I spoke up.

"Nicole, I know that I've been hinting to you that I have something to tell you, and I am about to tell you right now." I wanted to be a man and look Nicole in her eyes but I knew that if I did, then I would surely break down and start weeping.

The room was silent and all eyes were on me. Although my heart was pounding, it was as if I could hear Nicole's heart rate beginning to pick up as well.

I inhaled very deeply. And after slowly exhaling I began to talk. "Nicole, before I say anything, let me start by saying that I love you and you mean everything to me."

Nicole started to get nervous as she apprehensively asked, "Lance what is going on? Just spit it out. Tell me what's up?"

Still beating around the bush, I said, "Nicole, I already told Tiffany, and the only reason that she is here is because I didn't know how you would react to what it is that I have to tell you."

Nicole started to get ticked off and she said in a stern tone, "Lance spit it out! Stop stringing me along!"

I finally mustered up enough courage to look Nicole in her face. She had the most concerned look that I had ever seen in my life. I could see her chest rising up and down as she was nervously but eagerly anticipating what I had to say. Tears came to my eyes and I went back to looking at the kitchen floor. As I shook my head I simultaneously rubbed my head with my left palm.

Nicole then began to raise her voice as she asked, "Lance, what's wrong? Did you get diagnosed with some sickness? No, wait a minute, did somebody that we know pass away?... Lance you are driving me crazy! Just tell me what's going on!"

Through my tears and while looking towards the white tiled kitchen floor, I mumbled, "A'ight. Oh man... Oh God... Nicole... Baby... I cheated on you."

Nicole screamed out, "What! Lance what did you say!? Speak clearly, I can't hear you if you're mumbling."

Mustering up a bit more courage, I again exhaled and said as clearly and coherently as possible, "Nicole, I cheated on you."

Trying to be brave, I gave Nicole a "thug-life" look, as if I was preparing to scream out, "Yeah I cheated on you! What!?"

Nicole insecurely looked at Tiffany. Then she looked at me. She'd definitely heard what I had said, but she rhetorically asked with a frown on her face and a little ghettoness in her voice, *"Lance, repeat that for me one more time."*

I immediately went on the defensive as I said, "Baby, I'm so sorry. Please just let me finish."

Nicole was breathing hard and she was at the edge of her seat. I continued. Through my tears I added, "Nicole, I cheated on you and there is no easy way to say this... But, Nicole... The other person... Nicole, I got someone else pregnant."

Nicole immediately and violently stood up, and in disbelief she looked around. Not really knowing what to say she asked Tiffany was I joking. With the somber mood of the room, Nicole had to know that I was telling the truth. Tiffany confirmed the matter.

Then Nicole calmly, but in a desperate sounding tone said, *"Pregnant*!? Lance, I can't believe you!"

Within a split second Nicole went crazy! She flipped her plate of food into the air and she began screaming and crying and asking, "Lance, how could you do this to me!? Lance how could you do this!? I trusted you! How could you do this!?"

Nicole then picked up my plate of food and threw it at me. I attempted to shield off the plate. I too was crying and I tried to explain, "Nicole I'm sorry! Baby I am so sorry! If there was anything I could do to change this I would!"

Nicole looked at me through her tears and she had a look of death. She charged at me and started kicking me and punching me as she continued to ask, "Lance, how could you do this to me!? What about your son!?"

Tiffany tried to separate the two of us but I wanted Nicole to hit me and let all of her frustrations out.

I kept yelling and telling her that I was sorry. The whole scene was like a very dramatic and climatic movie scene.

"Sorry!?... Sorry!?... Lance, sorry don't count now! Are you trying to ruin my life!... You must want to ruin my life!... Answer me! Are you!?... I can't believe you!... I'm gonna ask you again, what about LL!? Did you think about him!? How could you do this to us!?"

Fortunately Nicole had stopped trying to hit me. She had given in to Tiffany's restraints. I didn't know what to say or do, so I remained silent. Then Nicole asked, "Who is the Bitch!?"

I was shocked because I had never in my life heard Nicole use a curse word. But what did I expect? Nicole was truly heated, she was breathing heavy. She looked as if she had just been in some type of street brawl. Her un-tucked shirt had become slightly wrinkled and her hair was a bit messy. Nicole demanded to know who my mistress was.

"Lance who is she!? Who the hell is she!?"

By this point my tears had subsided and I mumbled, "Toni."

In disbelief, Nicole screamed out, "What!? I know you are not talking about that Bitch that you brought to my house? Lance, I know you are not talking about her! Don't tell me you disrespected me like that!"

I remained silent. My silence confirmed that I indeed was talking about "*that bitch* that I had brought to the house."

Nicole began to whale and weep very loud as she threw a ceramic cup at me. The cup clocked me right upside my head, and it hurt like crazy. The cup shattered to pieces as it landed on the kitchen floor.

"Lance you had that whore around my son! You even had her in my house eating my food and talking to me!"

Nicole paused. I didn't say a word, and I didn't dare to look at Nicole. Then I heard the sound of a person that was coughing and choking. I looked up and I saw Nicole standing over the garbage can holding her stomach. A split second later she began to throw up right into the garbage can. Tiffany ran to Nicole's aid and I began to cry. I didn't think things would get this ugly. I wanted to console Nicole but I knew that she didn't want my hands touching her.

While trying to wipe the spit that was hanging from her mouth, Nicole spoke again, this time in a very despondent tone and while sobbing, she said, "Lance, look at me... How could you do this to me? I thought I did everything I could to please you."

Nicole finished vomiting but she was still crying. When she'd gathered herself, she managed to tell me to get the hell out of the house and that she didn't ever want to see me again. She also threatened that I would never see LL again either.

I tried to run upstairs and speak to LL because I knew that he had to have heard everything that had transpired. But Nicole was insistent that I leave right away. She made it clear that I couldn't get a lick of clothing or anything. She just wanted me out!

At that point I felt that the least I could do was to comply with Nicole's wishes. I searched for my shoes and for my jacket. When I found them, I slipped them on and I prepared to leave. I walked passed the kitchen one last time and I saw my wife sobbing with her head buried into the kitchen table. Tiffany was caressing her back trying to comfort her.

I motioned for Tiffany to walk me to the door. When Tiffany and I made it to the front door of the house I asked her if I could stay at her place. She said that it would not be a problem. Tiffany also told me that she would probably spend the night with Nicole just to make sure that she would be alright.

My life was a mess and I looked like a mess. Before walking out of the house, I hugged and thanked Tiffany for being there for Nicole. I didn't want to let go of that hug, but Tiffany told me to get going. She also sternly reminded me to remember to pray.

TWENTY SEVEN

It had been two weeks since I'd last saw either Nicole or LL. Thankfully, Tiffany has kept in contact with the two of them and they are doing fine. Tiffany has been reporting to me on Nicole's emotional state of being. My sister has been telling me that this entire ordeal has been affecting Nicole like I wouldn't believe. She explained to me that Nicole can get over the fact that I've been unfaithful, but just the mere thought of another baby is too devastating for her to handle.

Like me, Nicole had also been dipping in and out of depression for the last two weeks. Tiffany told me that Nicole went as far as taking a week of sick leave from her job. She wanted to use the week to get her head straight. Unfortunately, I did not have that same luxury. But even if I had the luxury of taking a week off, I probably would have declined to do so. I couldn't see myself taking a week off, because that would have given me too much time to think and condemn myself.

With no surprise to me at all, I found out that everyone on Nicole's side of the family had been updated with the news and details of my affair. The consensus of her side of the family was that I was *a no-good man* and that Nicole should leave me, but not before she took me to court and sued the pants off of me.

My most dominant thought of late had been in relation to my son. In my wildest dreams I never imagined that LL would grow up without a daddy. It saddened me deeply just thinking that I would only be able to see him every other weekend. Since he was born I'd dreamed about taking him to the park and teaching him how to be the next Michael Jordan, or the next Reggie Jackson. With being limited to seeing him every other weekend, I told myself to wash those aspirations down the drain.

With everything that's been going on, I've managed to speak to Toni on a few occasions. I made it crystal clear to Toni that in no way shape or form did I want her to speak to Nicole. I guess Toni had noble intentions by wanting to personally apologize and all, but come on. With Nicole agonizing over this ordeal, I really didn't think that her hearing Toni say sorry was going to help. If anything it would just help to inflame the entire situation. Toni understood and she gave me her word that she would keep her distance. I assured her that when the time was right she would have an opportunity to apologize to Nicole.

During the past two weeks, I'd say that I have been down, but at the same time my thoughts have been extremely sober. Sober in the sense that for the first time in all of my years of being a dog, I was beginning to realize the emotional devastation that Dogism can cause. Yeah, I always knew that adultery was wrong and that pornography, lusting, and the like were not good for me. But I never understood the depths of devastation that the destructive mental programming from those acts could bring to the lives of others.

My sober thoughts caused me to look at myself as a murderer. See, it's easy for a murderer to pull a trigger, shoot someone and walk away with no remorse because that murderer has no real emotional connection to the victim. But if you take that same murderer and let him feel the pain of the murdered victim's family members then everything changes. Force that murderer to sit through the funeral service of the one he has murdered, and suddenly it's a whole new ballgame. When things become real and attached to that murderer and he can make an emotional connection he can no longer simply remain as a coward and continue to hide behind the trigger of a gun. Now he has to face the reality of what he's done. I am convinced that if everyone who was ever convicted of murder, had the opportunity beforehand to feel the emotional devastation that murder produces, then the number of murders around the world would be a fraction of what they already are. And the same holds true for cheating and adultery.

****

In two days, it would mark three weeks since I'd last spoken to Nicole. I was convinced that she really didn't want to have anything more to do with me. I hadn't even dared to venture home in order to retrieve some of my clothing. During the past three weeks I've spent almost four hundred dollars on new clothes. However, my clothes were not my main concern. LL was my main concern. I'd spoken to Tiffany and asked her if she could speak to Nicole on my behalf and try to persuade Nicole to let me see my son.

Fortunately for me, Nicole didn't flex her position of authority when it came to allowing me the right to visit our son. Nicole's pain probably will never go away, but I was grateful that she hadn't allowed that pain to block me from seeing LL. She OK'd my request and when Monday night rolled in, I found myself feeling very uncomfortable as I approached my own house.

The door locks on the house hadn't been changed, so I was able to freely let myself in. I wasn't that nervous per se, but at the same time I didn't know what to expect from Nicole. When I walked in I went straight to the kitchen where I found a mountain of mail and a stack of bills that had went neglected during my absence.

LL must have heard me because he came running downstairs. When he realized it indeed was me, he screamed out, "Daddy!" The biggest smile was plastered across my face as I knelt down to hug LL. LL ran and jumped towards me. After I'd caught him I picked him up and just looked at him.

I hugged him as I told him, "LL, daddy has missed you so much."

LL asked where I had been.

"I've been staying at your Aunt Tiffany's house."

"Why?"

"Well LL, remember how you used to tell me stories of kids in the day care center that got into fights over toys and things like that?"

LL nodded his head and replied, "Yeah."

Then I explained, "Well, I did something that was very wrong. It was something that your mother really didn't like. So just like those children at your old daycare center, your mother and I got into a fight. LL, arguing and fighting is wrong, I want you to know that. I also want you to know that daddy was completely wrong, and your mother was completely right. LL, mommy was so upset with me that she told me that I couldn't sleep here anymore."

LL replied, "But daddy I want you to sleep here. Please daddy, I don't like it when you're gone."

Statements like that were the statements that I had been dreading to hear. I had no idea how to respond, so I said, "LL, listen to me. I can't promise you that I'll be able to stay here, but you have to promise me that you are going to take care of mommy. OK?"

LL whined as he said, "No daddy. I want you to come back home... Daddy I promise that I'll be good if you come back home, I promise."

LL was bringing tears to my eyes. For some reason I think that he felt as though he might have been the cause of the break up. I had cried in front of him before and there was no need for me to hide my tears from him now. As I continued to hold him, I looked at him and I kissed him on his cheek. Through my tears I said, "OK, LL I'm gonna see what I can do."

I put LL down and I asked him where was his mother. He told me that she was in her room.

"LL, go to your room and turn on Playstation. I have to speak to your mother and then I'll come to your room to play with you, OK?"

As I wiped my eyes with a piece of tissue, LL nodded his head up and down, then he darted to his room.

Looking over the pile of bills that had come, I separated the over due bills from the bills that didn't have to be paid right away. While doing that, I contemplated what I was gonna say to Nicole. While I was contemplating, I remembered my sister's words, and at that moment I said a short and quick prayer.

When the prayer was over I put the bills on the table and proceeded to walk to my bedroom where my wife was. By this time Nicole had to know that I was in the house. But I guess she figured that I had only come to see LL, and therefore she probably didn't want to interrupt our time together. As I approached the entrance of our bedroom, I could hear the sound of the television. I walked as quiet as I could possibly walk, then all at once I became very nervous. My heart started pounding, and I thought about just bypassing the bedroom all together. But instinctively I knew that I had to at least say hello to Nicole.

I braced myself for the worst. As I stood at the entrance of the bedroom I saw Nicole sitting on the bed. Her back was cushioned by a pillow and she was leaning against the head board and her legs were bent at her knees. Nicole looked as if she was reading something that related to her job.

In a shy and humble manner I said, "Hello Nikki." My heart continued to race as I waited for a response.

Nicole looked up from the papers that she had been reading, she slowly turned her head and looked my way. I wanted to cringe because I just felt so uncomfortable. There was a brief deafening moment of silence.

Then Nicole sought of mumbled the words, "How are you doing?"

Her words were followed by more deafening silence, as she continued to read what it was that she had been reading. Nicole could have just totally ignored me but she didn't. So I figured that we were at least still friends.

Still feeling extremely self conscious, I took two cautious steps into the bedroom and I asked, "What are you reading? Is that something for work?"

Nicole was very cold, as she was slow to respond, but she did reply, "Yeah it's for work."

Realizing that after three weeks, I couldn't just pop up and hold a conversation like things between us were normal, I shifted gears.

"Nikki, I don't know about you, but I feel extremely awkward and just being around you is extremely difficult for me. I'm glad that you let me come see LL, and that is why I came. I don't want to interrupt you or upset you, but Nikki I just want to say one thing..."

Nicole made sure to ignore me and not look in my direction. I addressed her actions.

"Nikki please, can you just look at me?" Again, Nicole didn't respond. So again I asked the same question, only this time

I asked in a very meek manner, "Nikki, can you please look at me?"

Nicole pondered my request and after thirty seconds or so she looked my way. Nicole was still as pretty as ever. As I looked at her I remembered Steve's words and the words of so many other men, which were, "Why would I cheat on that?"

With Nicole's attention I said, "Nikki I just want to tell you that whatever decision that you choose to make concerning us, I just want you to know that I won't try to fight it in court. Whatever you feel is best, that's what I'll abide by." I paused and a tear came to my eye. If this had been a movie I would have won an award for, "Perfect timing of a tear." But this was no act. It was a real tear.

I continued on, "But Nikki, I just want to beg you and I ask you to please give me the chance to properly apologize to you."

Nicole sucked her teeth, twisted her lips and looked away from me.

I quickly commented, "No. Nikki, please don't brush me off like that. Please. See, what I'm talking about is me and you and a neutral third party sitting down so I can apologize to you and let you know some things about me that I never told you."

Nicole sarcastically commented, "Yeah, um, I'm not sure, correct me if I'm wrong but I think we already did that about three weeks ago!"

"No Nikki come on, please. I'm serious. What I'm trying to say is, what if we go through some sort of counseling session or something like that?"

Harshly, but in a subdued manner, Nicole responded, "Lance listen! I went to school to learn how to counsel people. I am not going to spend money just so I can tell some therapist that my husband is a dog! What black people do you know that actually pay to go see a therapist!? Now if you want to apologize you can do that right now. We don't need no marriage counselor!"

Nicole was still very bitter and I completely understood. "OK Nikki, I didn't come hear to upset you. I just came here to see LL. But Nikki believe me, all I want to do is apologize the right way. I feel that I at least owe that to you. To me that means more than just saying 'I'm sorry.' Again, I came tonight to spend time with LL, but right now I'm just asking you if I can come by tomorrow and apologize. Is that alright?"

Sounding kind of disgusted, Nicole replied, "Lance, just go see your son."

I wanted to make sure that I was persistent, so I asked again, "Nikki, can I come by tomorrow and talk to you?"

I could here the annoyance in Nicole's voice as she said, "Lance! There is no need for you to come here tomorrow with a rehearsed line of crap that you've had three weeks to make up! Now if you want to apologize like you say you do, you're more than welcome to pick up a phone and call me. Honestly, just seeing your face makes me wanna just kill you!"

Working with what Nicole had given me to work with, I replied, "A'ight, so I'll call you tomorrow."

I walked out of Nicole's presence and I made my way to LL's room. Before I reached his room I paused and said another quick prayer. I needed God's help so that I could block out the problems between Nicole and myself and focus solely on LL.

LL and I had a ball together. While we were playing video games I marveled at his innocence and I became envious of him. I thought to myself about how I didn't know what the future held in terms of a divorce and visitation rights and all that. But I was determined to make sure that LL maintained his innocence. I realized that the loss of youthful innocence is what helps breed Dogism. I couldn't wait until LL was old enough to understand subjects such as sexuality because I wanted to give him the proper perspective on that subject. Yeah, I was never taught how to deal with that subject, and it was my ignorance towards my healthy sexuality that probably led me to my dogist ways. Similar to the way ignorance of true love and humanity is the root of racism. As far as my immediate family, I was determined that the Dogism was gonna end with me.

When it was time for me to leave, LL wept and pleaded for me to stay. It broke my heart to see him like that. Why did he have to suffer because of what I'd done?"

As LL cried, I tried to persuade him to understand, "LL, I need you to stay here and protect mommy, OK? I can't stay with you but I promise you I am going to see you as much as I can. What I want you to do is go get your sword that you got from the circus and keep it by your bed. This way you can protect your mommy for me. OK?"

With tears streaming down LL's eyes he complied and did what I said.

When LL returned with his sword, I instructed, "Now LL go kiss your mommy good night. Give her a kiss for me too. And after you do that I want you to get ready for bed. You're in kindergarten now so you have to be well rested for school."

The saddest thing in the world was looking at LL as he walked off to kiss his mother good night.

As I drove back to Tiffany's house, all I could picture was that toy sword in LL's hand and him walking towards his mother's room.

TWENTY EIGHT

Tuesday afternoon when I got off work I headed to the supermarket and I purchased about $100 dollars worth of food. The food was for Tiffany's house. Tiffany has such a good nature that she would easily let me stay in her house for as long as I wanted to and not pay her a dime. I am not one to free load, so buying food and paying for the phone bill was my way of earning my keep.

Somehow, with Toni three months pregnant, my marriage in shambles and my son crying for his daddy, I found myself making the same stupid mistakes from the past. No, the mistakes didn't have anything to do with Scarlet, I guess it was more subtle than that.

When I reached Tiffany's house I carried about three bags of groceries into the kitchen. Tiffany and a female friend of hers were in the living room discussing a few things. They saw that I was having trouble carrying the groceries and they came to my aid. Being that there were about ten more bags of groceries in the car, they came outside and helped me with those bags as well.

I don't know if it was because I hadn't had sex in a month, or if it was because Tiffany's friend was slammin', but her friend instantly turned me on. When we were done carrying the groceries into the house, Tiffany introduced me to her friend. Her name was Naomi. Naomi was more bangin' than Naomi Campbell. I have nothing against dark skin women, but I usually don't find myself attracted to them. However, Naomi was dark skin and she had it going on! Her body was on point, as was her hair, but I think it was her sexy lips that took the cake. Although I didn't know her from Adam, I wanted to just walk up to her and slob her down right in front of Tiffany.

After we were introduced, Naomi remarked on how I looked so much like my sister. Tiffany replied that everyone that meets us always says the exact same thing. I on the other hand wasn't trying to get into no small talk. I held back no punches as I charmingly said, "Naomi, I'm not trying to be obnoxious or anything, but I just have to give you a compliment... You are a very, very, gorgeous woman."

Naomi smiled and I know that she was a bit embarrassed as she thanked me for the compliment.

Tiffany looked at me with an annoyed look and she abruptly interrupted by saying, "Anyway! Um Lance, Naomi and I have a project that we have to get done by tonight, so if you don't mind can you please give us some privacy?"

I complied with Tiffany's wish and I vanished to the bathroom. As I took a shower I plotted as to how I was gonna make my next move on Naomi. I knew that I had scored with that compliment, so I just had to back it up with one more move and I would be in there like swim wear. I thought about doing some push ups to get my muscles stimulated and perky. Then all I would have to do was take my shower, wrap a towel around my waist and accidentally but on purpose, walk into the living room and ask Tiffany if she wanted me to start cooking dinner. If Naomi were to see my sexy body still slightly wet from the shower, she would be salivating over me.

As I showered, I was thinking about Naomi. As I thought about her attractive attributes I started receiving rushes of excitement. Then before I knew it, and thank God, 'cause it helped me to wise up, I felt as if a cinderblock had hit me square in the head.

I couldn't believe that I had just flirted with another woman! "What is wrong with me!?" I thought to myself.

As if all that I'd been through wasn't enough, here I was contemplating exacerbating the situation with another female. That little demon in my head was trying hard to convince me that I would soon be getting a divorce so it really wouldn't matter if I kicked it to Naomi. But I decided to be wise and I listened to the voice of the angel that told me that it wasn't about being divorced. Rather, it was about exercising self control, and if I knew what was good for me then I had better stay as far away from Naomi as possible.

Realizing how pitiful I was, I remembered to just pray. So right on the spot, with my body lathered in soap, I prayed for God to give me some self control, which He did. When I was done washing the filth off of my body and my soul, I headed straight towards Tiffany's room where I changed my clothes. When I was done changing I started watching game shows, but in the back of my mind I knew that I had to call Nicole.

So without hesitation I picked up the phone and dialed my home number. I didn't know what I was gonna say but I did know that I was just gonna shoot from the hip. I was prepared to lay out all of my dirty laundry for Nicole to see.

Nicole answered the phone and I said, "What's up Nikki?"

Nicole obviously knew my voice so she didn't ask who was calling. She simply said, "Yeah."

"Nikki it's me Lance."

Nicole rudely blurted out, "And!"

It didn't take a rocket scientist to figure out that Nicole really didn't want to talk. But I was perfectly capable of mustering up enough things to say which didn't need any responses from Nicole.

"Nicole, I know that you don't want to talk, but please just hear me out." I paused, took a deep breath and I continued on. "Nicole, I want to say that I am terribly sorry for what I have done to you and LL. What I did was foolish, it was selfish, it was stupid, and it should have never have happened. Nicole, I know that I can't even begin to imagine the pain that you must feel. But believe me, I know that I hurt you very bad. And baby I am sorry. What I've been doing in order to sympathize with you is, I've put the shoe on my foot and wondered how I would feel or how I would have reacted if you told me that you had cheated and that you were carrying someone else's baby. Nicole, I would be beyond devastated to say the least, and I know that you are devastated.

I have been praying that God can make this as easy on you as possible. Nicole, I know that things are over between us. I mean even the Bible tells us that once the bond of marriage is broken due to adultery, then and only then is it justifiable and permissible to get a divorce. Baby, I wasn't loyal to you, and yet you always treated me like a king. I just want you to know that now more than ever, I appreciate all that we had. I appreciate all that you have done and all of the sacrifices that you have made for the sake of our marriage. Nicole, believe me when I say that I've put my mind through torment while trying to figure out a way to change the mistake that I made. Unfortunately, I just can't change that mistake. I can't change the past.

Baby, yesterday you said something to the affect that I have had a lot of time to prepare a line of crap. But Nicole listen, I am not dropping a line of garbage to you. I just want to tell you some things that you never knew, things that might shed light on this entire mess."

I took another deep breath and then I continued, "Nicole, ever since I was about ten or eleven years old, maybe even younger than that, I've been sneaking around and looking at anything that was pornographic. I started by finding my fathers dirty magazines, and as I got older, the VCR became a big thing and I started sneaking and watching porno movies. Nicole, even as a kid I knew it was wrong but I loved it and my mind, body, and soul craved it. It was like a drug. Looking at pornography gave me the biggest rush in the world. By the time I was 11 years old, I started masturbating. Nicole forget about it, when I discovered masturbation, it was over. I became deeply addicted to it.

Nicole, when I say addicted, I mean at thirteen years old I was masturbating as much as three times a day. I knew it was wrong but I loved it. No one in my house knew what I was doing and I figured that I wasn't hurting anyone so I kept doing it. As I got older that same pattern continued. In fact it intensified. I would try to go cold turkey and stop masturbating, but like an addict I just couldn't stop. I would go for a maximum of two weeks without doing it, but then I would be caught up right back into it."

As I continued to explain my ordeal I began to cry. Never before had I opened up and exposed myself to an adult in the manner in which I was now opening up. I was hoping that Tiffany didn't walk into the room.

Through my pain and tears I added, "Nicole, when I got older things got much worse. I mean I started going to strip clubs

and getting blow jobs from hookers and the whole nine. Baby it
hurts for me to even tell you all of this. I mean I never wanted to
let anyone into this dark closet of mine. But baby I now realize
that because I've kept that closet closed for so long that it only
made my problem intensify. Baby, I'm so sorry. I didn't mean to
hurt you. It's just that I'm so messed up and you never knew..."

At that point I broke down and started weeping harder. I'd
finally broken through Nicole's wall of defense as she said,
"Lance, I believe you. Believe me I do... But why didn't you ever
tell me any of this? We're married Lance. We don't have to hide
things from each other, no matter how bad it may seem."

I continued to cry as I explained, "Baby, you don't know
how shameful I've felt all of my life. I mean it was only like a
year ago when I realized that other people actually masturbate.
Since I was young I always felt so ashamed because I thought that
I was some kind of sexual freak or something. I mean
masturbation and taboo things like that is something that people
never discuss. And since it wasn't ever being discussed, for like
twenty something years I felt as though only I had that problem.

And baby it even hurts me to tell you any of this. See,
another reason I hid things from you was because I always knew
that if I told you about my past that I would have to tell you
everything."

Nicole asked what did I mean.

"See Nicole, we have been together for God knows how
long. I mean we met in high school for crying out loud. I know
that when we met we were both virgins and all that. And although
we had sex before marriage, things were still special because
neither you nor me had ever been with anyone else."

I paused as more tears were shed, then I kept flowing with
my history, "Nicole, what I meant by I would have to tell you
everything is that I had cheated on you before we were even
married."

In disbelief and astonishment Nicole said, "What! Lance
how could you? I've been trying to handle this pregnancy thing
and you mean to tell me that this whole ordeal gets worse? Lance

what in the world did we ever have?... It definitely wasn't a *marriage*!"

As Nicole sighed, I could sense that she was getting ready to start crying. But before she broke down, I wanted to make sure that I got everything that I'd wanted to say off of my chest.

"Nicole, I'm gonna let you speak but please just let me finish. This is very hard for me and I just want to get it all out. Nicole, we were young when we met and we were young when we got married. But ever since I graduated from high school I've always had money and a nice car. Baby, back in the days, none of my friends were married or even thinking about settling down. They were all about hanging out, partying and whoring around. Now Nicole, I'm not saying that my friends made me do anything, but just being around them put me in situations where I met other women and things happened."

Nicole was now crying, and at that point she asked, "Lance, what kind of things?"

I sighed and said, "Nikki, I mean, well I'm sayin', I had sex with like thirty different women before we got married."

Nicole said in disbelief and through her tears, "Lance! Thirty!? But we've been together since high school so how Lance!? How!?"

"Nikki just hear me out. Like I said, I was young, I had money and my mind was already screwed up sexually. So I just went ahead and did stupid things. I have read many books and I realize that pornography had my mind so screwed up that I was trying to live in the fantasy world that pornography portrays. See baby, most people, especially women, have to connect emotionally before they can have sex with someone. But as for me, pornography had my head so screwed up that I lost all sense of the emotional connection that goes along with sex. For me, sex has always been purely physical, I didn't love any of those women that I had sex with. Nicole I have always loved you and only you. See, pornography made sex seem so easy and harmless. With every porno movie that I watched, I would see women walk into a room, take off their clothes and with no kind of attachment they would start getting it on with some nigga.

Nicole, I tried my best to live out what I saw in those movies. The funny thing is that I didn't even realize what I was doing. I mean subconsciously I was making decisions based on sexual fantasies that I wanted to play out. Nicole you just don't know how bad it was. The struggle between wanting to do good and having evil right there tugging at me. It still is bad at times."

Nicole, who had stopped crying but was still sniffling a little bit, asked, "Lance, before this chick Toni, did you ever cheat on me with anyone else during our marriage?"

"Nicole, no," I immediately responded.

Nicole raised her voice as she demanded to know the truth, "Lance, tell me the truth! Did you!?"

"Baby, no. I'm telling you the truth. I never cheated while we were married, not until Toni. Nicole, if I had done anything at all I would tell you now. I wouldn't hold nothing back, not at this point."

I could hear the pain in Nicole's voice as she added, "Lance, I really can't believe what you are telling me. I mean with everything that has been going on, this is a lot to swallow... One thing I realize is that I have never known you, *Mr. Lance Thomas*! Who are you!?... I mean I have been in the same house with you, I went to school with you. I have eaten with you, I have slept with you, I have given birth to your son, but I still have never known who the hell you were! I thought I knew you. But I only knew the top layers of you. I now realize that I have never gotten inside you. And the funny thing is that I thought I knew you inside and out, but I didn't. I don't know... I mean... all I can say is that it's sad, it's really is sad to say, but you are *good*! I don't know how you pulled it off for all this time. You must be two people 'cause I don't know..."

"Nicole, let me say this, I know that I have a remarkable talent, remarkable, but at the same time horrible. That being that I can deceive anyone. I can do such a good job at it, that at times even I forget that I am being deceptive. I have another ability to just block out my feelings. Like in the past when I cheated on you, I never consciously and deeply thought about how you would feel. If I had thought about your feelings, then I wouldn't have been able to go through with my dirt. What I would do is, I would always block out of my mind, the thought of you and LL, and I would proceed to do that which I knew was wrong."

When I was done speaking, Nicole didn't say a word, she just blew some air into the phone.

"Nicole, it's the same thing with God. I mean I love God and I love the church but at the same time I would block out what was morally and spiritually correct and do that which I knew was wrong. Baby, it goes so much deeper than you could *ever* imagine! I mean my sexuality is so jacked up that it's like my every thought is of something sexual. I think about sex twenty-four-seven. If I see a woman's toe, that could turn me on and spin me out of control, the slightest things are like poison to my mind. Nicole, all the working out and the weight lifting, that's all done so that women will lust over me in the same way that I lust over them. Yo Nicole, I laugh because women talk about 'Waiting To Exhale,' but men are also 'waiting to exhale.' I say that because, nine out of ten men are going through what I have been through. Maybe not on the same level as me, but most men have a screwed up sexuality and they are not letting anyone on to that fact."

Nicole then sighed and asked, "So Lance, what does all this mean?"

I answered, "Honey, I really don't know what all this means. But I'll tell you one thing. Right now I feel so light. For my entire life I have been carrying around so much baggage and guilt. The guilt always intensified as each day passed. And that guilt just kept me seeking more and more immoral behavior so that I could sort of get high off of that behavior, but then, right after the high would wear off, the guilt would return. It was like a vicious cycle. It was like a cycle. But finally I've let it out. Finally I feel free! I mean I still have sexual problems that I have to work out but just knowing that I have opened up to someone, especially to you, is going to help me so much."

Again my wife blew air into the phone's receiver. I knew that she probably had a million and one thoughts running through her head. I had already said my peace and I didn't want to annoy Nicole by keeping her on the phone.

"Nicole, I ain't gonna keep you on the phone any longer. But I just want to tell you this one last thing." My voice cracked with emotion as I said, "Again, Nicole I know what I did was horrible and I can only imagine the pain that you feel. I wish that I could change the past but I can't. All I know is that I can try my hardest to positively affect the future. Nicole, I am sorry for putting you through this and if it takes fifty years for you to forgive me, I'll understand. I mean even if you never forgive me I'll understand. But baby, I say this with the fullest sincerity, God doesn't make women like you anymore. Honey, I know that I've thrown away the best thing that this side of life had to offer me, which was having you as a lifetime mate. But Nicole, please... Please, no matter what happens, please let me continue to be a part of my son's life. Please."

Nicole responded to me in a very soft and gentle tone. She sounded as if she was beginning to develop a sense of closure. "Lance, I'm gonna hang up by saying this. I believe what you have told me and I am glad that you told me all of this... I do wish you had of not waited so long to tell me this... But I mean I guess that now that's neither here nor there..." Nicole paused and then she added, "LL should never get caught up in our problems. You know that I'm a rational person so don't worry about me removing LL from your life. That wouldn't be fair to him."

I smiled as I thanked my wife. After I hung up the phone, I regretted that I hadn't ended the conversation by telling my wife that I loved her. For all I knew that could probably have been the very last time I would have had the opportunity to tell Nicole that I loved her.

Anyway, after hanging up the phone I got dressed. I was in the best mood that I had been in in weeks. I walked into the living room and I let Tiffany know that I was stepping out for a minute. Tiffany acknowledged me. I also told Naomi that it had been nice meeting her. She smiled and said likewise. I made sure not to flirt with Naomi and I kept it moving and I walked out of the house. I realized how easy it was for me to exercise self control if I just simply focused my mind.

Still feeling as if the weight of the world had been lifted off of my shoulders, I jumped in my Lexus and I blasted music as I cruised the streets of Queens. The radio blared as as I listened to FunkMaster Flex spin on the ones and twos I felt so elated.

Yeah, the music was slammin', but I was elated because finally, a huge floodlight was placed into my dark closet of skeletons. True was the fact that my marriage was shipwrecked, but I felt like at least I had managed to fight off the angry waves and was able to make it to the peaceful shore.

TWENTY NINE

I had made plans to hang out with Steve this coming Saturday so that we could go to this Comedy / Jazz club. So when Saturday arrived, I found myself at Steve's crib. It had been a mad long time since the two of us hung out. I take the blame for that. Anyway, as Steve was getting dressed I began to fill him in on all that had been transpiring between Nicole and myself. Steve was adamant about the fact that I should have never told Nicole about the baby and that I should have just went through with the divorce.

I explained to Steve that I was trying to turn over a new leaf. I let him know that, my new leaf would no longer contain the drama, lies and deception of old. Unfortunately, I didn't get any encouragement from Steve.

Steve's outlook on the situation was somber. He asked, "Lance, do you like having money in your pocket?"

"Of course," I replied. "Who doesn't?"

Steve added, "Well you certainly must not, because you're gonna be a broke man in about six months to a year."

I knew exactly where Steve was going with his line of thinking.

He continued, "First of all, you know all that money that you have in stocks and in that 401K crap?"

"Yeah, what about it?"

Steve explained, "Well, Nicole gets half of that. Oh yeah, and that nice house that you have in Cambria Heights, guess what?"

Sarcastically I asked, "What Steve?"

"Oh, nothing really, I mean I just wanted to let you know that you will no longer be living there. That goes to Nicole as well. You'll probably be living in some one room flat. Lance, you're gonna be mad as hell when you go to visit your son and you see some big belly nigga with crusty feet, laying up in the bed that you used to sleep in."

"Anything else Steve?"

Steve replied, "Oh yeah. Um, those fat paychecks that you're used to, well they're going to get small very quickly.

Nicole will be getting something like 17% of your paycheck for LL. And that bad chick, uh, I think her name is Toni. Yeah that's it... Well when she spits out that kid she'll also be getting 17% of your check. That money comes straight off the top! It goes directly from Con Edison and right into their bank accounts before you even see it!"

"Yeah whateva. All I know is that I'm not even thinking about that. I'm sayin', like I told you before, I'm turning over a new leaf... But Steve you know what? With everything that's been going on, I've still never felt so peaceful in all my life."

After I said that, Steve began laughing. He started laughing with this loud, long drawn out laugh. He sounded like he was some wine-o on the street corner who was hoarse and trying to cough up phlegm.

Through his laughter Steve replied, "Peaceful? Nigga when them pockets get empty we'll see how peaceful you are. All I know is that Toni was one expensive piece of butt. Man you're gonna be paying for them few nights booty for the next eighteen years. You better start getting Scarlet to hit you off with some cash because you are definitely gonna need it in a minute."

Steve just didn't get it. He didn't fully understand that I was done with the cheating and the lies and the deception and the strip clubs and all of that. I was completely done with it all, including Scarlet.

Steve continued in his laughter as he added, "Lance, you're gonna be just like the rest of those New York cats. Yeah, you're gonna be riding around flossing in a fifty thousand dollar car but you're gonna be broke as hell living in a one bedroom basement apartment."

With more sarcasm I remarked that we didn't have to go to the Comedy / Jazz Club, for the simple fact that Steve was funnier than any comedian that we were gonna see. Steve added a few more of his one liners, but we finally did manage to depart for the club. Before we got to the club I made sure to tell myself to keep the right focus for the evening. During the entire ride to Manhattan, I kept telling myself, "Lance, have some self control tonight."

When we reached the club there was no doubt that the Honeys were in full "fly mode." The Jazz music made the atmosphere on point. The club was definitely a prime stomping grounds for picking up a couple of high maintenance chicks. And Steve was true to form with his game. As soon as we stepped into the place, he found himself at the bar buying a drink for some bad ass looking chick.

I just parlayed and did my own thing. I even surprised myself when I ordered a plain orange juice. I just didn't want to get alcohol flowing through my body. I knew that if I were to start drinking, that I would quickly loosen up and start doing things that I would live to regret. I was trying hard to maintain and at the same time I was thinking to myself "What the hell am I even doing in here?"

It was places like this one, along with the parties and the hanging out until the wee hours of the morning without Nicole that had added to my dogish mentality.

Thankfully, the comedians were very funny, so they took my attention away from all of the good looking women.

Before long, the club started to get too smoky from all of the cigarette smoke, and I really wanted to bounce. I couldn't fake it. I mean my mind just wasn't feeling that player non-sense. I hated playing party pooper, especially considering that we had only been there for about a little over an hour. Although I knew that Steve wouldn't be ready to leave, I didn't care because I had had enough and I was ready to bounce.

I spotted Steve coming towards me with this "Mac-Daddy Big Baller" look in his eyes. When he reached me he was like, "Yo Lance, you see those two chicks over there, the ones with the white high heels on?"

"Yeah, what about them?"

"Yo Playa' I'm sayin', the one on the right is all on my biznalls! And Yo, her friend was checking you out, so I'm sayin' go kick it to her get the math from her. I think we can probably take them both back to my crib and hit that tonight! You know what I'm sayin'?"

Steve held out his fist for a pound. I didn't acknowledge his hand and I replied, "Yo Steve, shorty has definitely got it going on, but I'm just trying to maintain right now. Matter of fact, I was thinking about bouncing up outta here."

In disbelief, Steve replied, "What!? Yo, do you see the thickness on those chicks? And you ready to leave? Man Lance, are you crazy!? Yo, you better hurry up and get over that Toni and Nicole nonsense!"

Steve looked at me and waited for a response, but I simply ignored him.

After sighing in disgust, Steve angrily said, "Man I'm sayin', I ain't leaving! So if you wanna act like a homo then go right ahead, but you gonna have to bounce on your own."

I was sitting at a small lounge table and I took one of the toothpicks from the dispenser that was on the table. I slowly placed the toothpick inside my mouth and I twirled it around. I contemplated what I should do. I looked over at the chick that Steve was talking about and I confirmed that she definitely had it going on. She was thick in all the right places and she looked good. She waived at me and I knew that that was my cue to get up and go over and kick it to her. So I exhaled and stood up...

"Yo Steve, I'm out kid."

"What!? Lance I'm sayin', at least go speak to her. You're gonna make me look bad in front of them!"

As I made my way to the coat check, I looked at Steve and said to him, "You'll be a'ight. Just tell shorty that I'm a married man."

After retrieving my coat I headed out the door, Steve replied, "Ah man! See that's that BS! Nigga what's wrong with you!?"

I paid him no mind. I kept my focus and I kept on walking. I was in mid town Manhattan and being that I had driven to the club in Steve's car, there was no way that I was gonna hop on a train at such a late time of night. Although it was gonna be expensive, I attempted to hail down a yellow cab. When one stopped to pick me up, I asked how much would it be to take a brotha to Queens. I could barely understand the foreign cab driver's accent but it sounded like he said fifty dollars. I had a feeling that the fare would be in that range, so I just hopped in the cab and headed to Queens.

When we reached Queens, I directed the cab driver to Steve's house. I paid him the fifty bucks and I jumped into my Lexus and headed back to Tiffany's crib. I took the scenic route to Tiffany's house. The scenic route led me pat my house in Cambria Heights. When I drove down my block, I really wanted to just park the car and go inside my house and cuddle up next to my wife. I couldn't remember the last time that Nicole and I had made love.

I pulled up in front of the house and I noticed that all of the lights were off. The house was in total darkness. "Nah," I decided against going inside. I didn't want to wake up anyone.

I chuckled as I imagined myself walking into the house and trying to sneak into the bed with Nicole, only to be confronted by LL and his toy sword. I chuckled once more, then I shook my head in sorrow. Yeah, it was like one O'clock in the morning so I decided to just head to Tiffany's and call it a night.

When I reached Tiffany's, I made sure to be as quiet as possible so as not to wake anyone. From the time that I started staying at Tiffany's I'd been sleeping on the sofa bed in her living room. So after I took off my clothes and brushed my teeth and took a shower, I made my way to the living room. As I attempted to open up the bed I saw a note that was left for me on the cushion of the couch. I picked it up and read it:

Lance, Nicole called around ten thirty tonight. She told me to tell you that she expects to see you in church in the morning.

Good night. Love Tiff.

I was overwhelmed with joy after reading that note. I realized that I desperately needed to be going to church especially considering that I hadn't been to church since I'd told Nicole about Toni's pregnancy. I guess I'd kinda forgot about worshiping God. Or should I say, I stopped going to church because I feared the embarrassment that I would feel from having my business publicly exposed. And I was sure that by now Nicole had let someone in the church know what was going on between us. Even if Nicole had only told one person in the church, that would have been the same as telling the entire congregation. I say that because, that one person that she could have told, would turn around and say to someone else, "Keep this between you and me, but guess what happened between Nicole and Lance?..." Then that someone else would turn around and say to someone else, "I shouldn't be telling you this so make sure that you keep this between you and me. But guess what happened between Nicole and Lance?..."

As I continued to prepare my bed, I thought about not facing up to the embarrassment of seeing church members. Then I quickly realized that all my life I'd been afraid of being exposed. In fact it was that fear of exposure that helped wreak such havoc on my sexuality.

I paused and thought for a moment. I pondered about how exposure to air helps to heal wounds. If a wound is consistently hidden under a band-aid then it leaves the sore less of a chance of ever developing a scab. Without exposure, an ugly scab would not form and if there is no scab then proper healing can not take place. I needed to forget about using band-aids in my life, those band-aids of two-faced living. "So what if I'm exposed?" I thought, "At least I would be free."

I sighed and I convinced myself to be like a sore that was in need of exposure. I continued to talk to myself as I said, "Lance, go to church so that you can help that scab to form and begin the *true* healing process."

Before I laid my head on the pillow of the sofa bed, I got on my knees and prayed to God. I just thanked Him for so much, and I repented of so much wrong doing. I especially made sure to thank God for sending me my own angel in the form of Nicole.

As I waited to fall asleep I realized that what separated Nicole from all of the other women that I'd either been with or fantasized about being with, was that Nicole always held my best interest close to her heart like no other person could or would attempt to do. Even now with everything that we've been going through, my wife was again, still willing to put her pride aside in an effort to ensure that I wouldn't turn my back on God at a time when I needed Him most.

"Man!..." I just wished that I hadn't screwed up such a good thing.

THIRTY

I had purposely arrived ten minutes late to church. The reason being, I didn't want to have to answer a million questions from people who hadn't seen me in a while. I also arrived late because I wanted to sit towards the back of the church. Although I didn't know what kind of reception I was going to get from Nicole, I still felt very good about coming to church.

When I walked through the doors of the church, I immediately saw a brother that I knew. Like I'd guessed, he started right away with the questions. He wanted to know where I'd been, and was everything alright between Nicole and myself. In a non-rude manner, I brushed him off by telling him that I would get with him later. As I continued to make my way to the pews I saw another cat that I knew. He wasn't in close proximity to me so he put his fingers to his mouth and ears, signaling that he wanted me to call him. I nodded my head and just walked to my seat.

When I reached my seat I looked in the direction of where I usually sat, and there I saw Nicole. She was sitting in the exact same row and the exact same seat that she usually sits in. LL was seated to the left of her. Someone was missing from that picture, and I knew that it was me. I contemplated taking a seat next to Nicole, but I just didn't know if she wanted me to be next to her. I mean yeah she'd requested that I come to church, but that didn't necessarily mean that she wanted to be seated next to me.

Five minutes went by and I realized that I wasn't paying any attention to the church service. My mind was completely distracted by Nicole's presence. I braced myself, blew some air from my cheeks and I proceeded to make my way to my normal seat. When I reached the pew that Nicole was in, I tapped her on the shoulder to request that she scoot over and make more room for big daddy.

Nicole's face lit up with a smile as did LL's face. LL waved and excitedly whispered, "Hi daddy."

I smiled, then I reached out my hand for LL to slap me five. Whispering, I asked him, "What's up?"

LL excitedly asked his mother if he could switch his position and sit right next to me. Nicole complied and LL relocated and he planted himself right smack in the middle of me and Nicole. LL used his left hand to grasp my right hand, and with his right hand he took a hold of his mother's left hand. LL's legs weren't long enough to reach the ground, so as he sat he freely swung his legs back and forth. I knew exactly what LL was trying to do and I thought to myself, how it's so funny how kids instinctively know what love is. They are smart enough to realize when the love between their parents is fading and when it is peaking. LL was doing his best to bring the love between his parents to its highest point.

Nicole reached her body over LL's and she planted a kiss on my cheek. Goose bumps ran up and down my body. My wife whispered and said, "I thought you weren't gonna make it."

I smiled and said, "Nah. I'm here."

After that kiss on the cheek I felt so relieved. Throughout the service I felt as if I was on cloud nine. Sadly, I don't remember what the preacher was preaching about, but I really didn't sweat it. I was more concerned as to what would happen once the service was over. One thing that I was going to suggest was that Nicole and I take LL to get some ice cream. I knew that if I asked Nicole right in front of LL, that she would be hard pressed to say no. After all, she was the one who told me that LL shouldn't get caught up in the middle of our problems.

The service finally ended and as everyone stood up and gathered themselves and their belongings in preparation to leave, I sprung the question on Nicole.

Making sure that LL was in good hear shot, I spoke very loud and clear. "Nicole I don't know what you had planned for later, but I was thinking that we should take LL to go get some ice cream."

Nicole looked at me with this sly look because she knew that I had put her on the spot. LL helped my cause by pleading with his mother to accept my invitation. As Nicole adjusted her over coat, she took about ten seconds before she replied. However, she did accept the invitation.

I wanted to take both Nicole and LL by the hand and lead them out of the church, but at the same time I didn't want to over step my boundaries. Nicole seemed to be in a good mood as she smiled and spoke to the brothers and sisters of the congregation. As people came up to me asking me how I was doing and where I'd been, I gave them all generic responses.

I brushed everyone off as I would reply, "Oh I've been alright. I mean, I have been going through a few rough things but God is working everything out. I'll be OK, but hey listen, thanks for asking, I can't really talk right now so I'll catch you later."

Nicole and I both made our way out of the church at the same time. As we stood on the church steps, I told Nicole that we should take LL to the Carvel's that was on Jamaica Avenue. She didn't object as she told me that she would follow behind me in her car. So together we made our way to the church parking lot and we got in our cars and headed out.

When we reached Carvel's and were walking to the entrance, LL continued in his role of match maker as he said, "Daddy hold mommy's hand."

Feeling uneasy, I replied, "LL we're almost inside the store."

LL knew that I was trying to duck his command so he grabbed my hand and pulled it towards Nicole's hand until they touched. Although I felt uncomfortable I had to look at Nicole and smile. She returned my smile with a smile of her own and we walked into Carvel's hand in hand. Nicole's hand had never felt better.

The two of us stood on line holding hands while trying to decide what we were gonna order. Nicole and I both probably wanted to make it seem as if we were only holding hands in order to please LL, but if we both had to confess the truth, I'm sure that we would have both admitted that the hand holding was very therapeutic.

When we were done ordering and the lady was handing us our ice cream I thought about how clumsy LL was. Being that I was in such a good mood, I could have cared less if he dropped his ice cream cone ten times. But surprisingly LL was good. Not only had he not dropped his cone, but on the way to our seats, LL managed to properly lick his cone without spilling anything.

Nicole and I had soft Vanilla Sundays. Our toppings included strawberry glaze, walnuts and rainbow sprinkles. As we ate I joked with LL so that I could ease the tension of feeling forced to speak to Nicole. But to my surprise Nicole began a conversation with me.

"Yeah, Lance like I had said, I didn't think that you would show up, I didn't see you when church started and I know that you're never late."

I answered, "Well to tell you the truth, I came late on purpose. I just didn't wanna have to answer any questions from people."

Nicole nodded her head as she placed some ice cream into her mouth. When she'd swallowed the strawberries she looked at me and said, "Lance, I wanted you to come to church because there are some things that I wanted to discuss with you."

My nerves were instantly on edge as I asked, "Things like what?"

Nicole looked at LL and she told me that she didn't want to talk in front of him. Once she said that, I knew that she probably wanted to talk in terms of a divorce or legal separation. It had to be something to that affect.

Nicole continued, "Lance, I already cooked so when we leave here just come by the house and we can talk then."

When we were done eating our ice cream, I decided to buy some more ice cream for LL to put in the freezer at home. Nicole advised me that he didn't need it, but I was like, he's a kid let him enjoy innocent things like ice cream. Besides, I was also thinking that it would probably be a while before I would again get the chance to do something nice for my son.

I purchased three quarts of ice cream for LL and I had the lady behind the counter put it in a bag for him. LL was extremely excited. I handed him the bag and I instructed him that he was not to rush and eat all of the ice cream in a day or two. I told LL that I wanted him to make the ice cream last for at least two weeks. LL gave me his word that he would make the ice cream last.

The three of us made our way out of the store and LL asked his mother if he could drive with me. Nicole had no problem with it so LL jumped in the Lexus and we navigated our way to Cambria Heights.

As we drove, LL asked, "Daddy are you coming back home today?"

I turned the music down and I said, "LL, I'm gonna eat dinner with you and your mother, but after that I have to leave. I already told you that I would love to stay but I can't. It's not up to me."

LL slumped and pouted in his seat while simultaneously crossing his arms. I informed him that I was sorry but there was nothing that I could do. I relayed to LL that he probably wouldn't understand everything that was going on until he was older.

LL and I reached the house about a minute before Nicole. As I made my way to the front door of my crib, I felt like I was one of Jesus' disciples marching to the last supper or something. LL asked me if I would play video games with him but I declined. Being that it was Sunday, I suggested that LL and I watch football together. LL was elated over the idea. LL's elation made me feel good because I knew that athletically, he would follow in his daddy's footsteps.

As LL and I talked about football, Nicole made her way up to her bedroom and she hollered for me to come up to the room. I told LL to hold his football questions and that we would continue our conversation in a minute.

When I reached the bedroom I saw Nicole taking off her clothes. She was preparing to change into something more comfortable. It was bugged because I felt like I was doing something wrong by seeing her naked. Nicole even suggested that I take off my suit and relax. I had to tap myself to remind me that I did have a whole wardrobe of clothing in the closet. It was weird but I was just feeling like a total stranger in my own home.

As I changed my clothes, Nicole advised me that the food was ready if I wanted to eat. However, I suggested that we wait being that the ice cream had probably messed up our appetites.

Plus it was only one O'clock in the afternoon which meant that even for a Sunday it was way too early to be eating dinner.

Feeling like I should just ask for my whipping in order to just get it out of the way. I asked Nicole if she wanted to talk. We were in the privacy of our bedroom so she replied that it was in deed a good time to talk. I knew that LL was waiting for me so I yelled to him that I would be a while. I closed the door to the bedroom and Nicole and I both sat on the bed in our sweat pants, tee shirts and tube socks. Nicole played with a piece of loose thread that was on the bed sheets and before I could blink, she was in tears.

"Baby what's wrong?" I asked.

Nicole wiped her tears and sighed. Then she said, "Lance, it's just so hard... Every time I think of the fact that you got someone else pregnant I just break down and start crying."

I didn't know what to say. I mean, I understood the harsh reality of what I'd done but I didn't know what to say. I remained silent because I knew that it was healthy for Nicole to get all of her emotions out.

Nicole continued to cry as she looked at me and said, "Lance, you don't know how bad you hurt me... This hurts so, so, soooh bad! You just don't know!"

At that point I lost the desire to look Nicole in her eyes as I told her that I was sorry.

Nicole was beginning to calm down, and she asked, "Lance, do you know how much I love you?"

"Baby, believe me I know and I am so sorry, but I can't change the situation."

Nicole shook her head and she blew some air out of her mouth as she said, "Lance I just wish this pain would go away, I really do."

Again I remained silent. Nicole continued, "Lance, during the past couple of weeks I've been thinking about everything imaginable. Things like the first time we met, the first date we went on, our first kiss, the day LL was born. I even watched our wedding video a couple of times. Lance, with all of the love and memories that we've built together… I just come to so many tears whenever I think about you taking care of a baby that's not ours.

Lance, it probably would have been a little bit easier had it just been some kind of one night stand type of thing and no baby was involved."

"Nicole believe me, I know how complicated a baby makes this whole situation. Plus, we don't believe in abortions so… And like I said before, I'm willing to accept whatever you want out of me. I realize that I caused all of the pain. I washed away the special love that we'd built together."

Nicole paused and she didn't say anything. She remained quiet as she began to form tears in her eyes. Then she said, "Lance, throughout this whole ordeal I have been reading my Bible and praying like I have never prayed before. And it's like God has helped me to realize a couple of things.

Lance I read about King Solomon, the wisest man that ever walked the face of the earth. The ironic thing about King Solomon is that, with all of his wisdom, he did something that God didn't really approve of. What he did was he married hundreds of women and he had hundreds of other women as concubines. Lance, it's weird because although King Solomon was very wise, he almost did a very foolish thing. For the sake of his desire to be with many women, he almost forsook his relationship with God. He practically was ready to spit in God's face despite the fact that God had richly blessed him. Lance, God was angry with King Solomon. But you know what? When King Solomon realized that his actions and his selfishness was hurting God and that he was causing a huge mess, he repented and he changed his life big time."

As I sat and intensely listened to my wife I replied, "Yeah baby, that's why King Solomon wrote the book of Ecclesiastes. In that book he was basically repenting of all the wrong he'd done throughout his lifetime."

Nicole nodded her head and said, "Exactly." Then she added, "Lance, and look at King David. The Bible says King David had a heart like that of God's. Lance, I know that you already know these stories, but I've just personally learned so much from them in the past couple of days... But back to King David, here was a man with a heart like God's heart, yet he still did wrong by committing adultery with Bathsheba, Lance, he went as far as having Bathsheba's husband killed. So you know that God was extremely angry with him. However, when David came to his senses and realized what he'd done, he repented. And Lance, David wept bitterly about the wrong the he'd done. And you know what? God restored him to his full honor."

I nodded my head in agreement with Nicole as I smiled a half smile. I smiled because in the past Nicole and I had both heard sermons about King David and about King Solomon. So we were both familiar with the stories of the two men. It was bugged that during this trial in our marriage, Nicole and I both had been re-familiarizing ourselves with the sins of the father and son patriarchs.

I let Nicole know that I too had been reading and studying a lot about King Solomon and King David during the past few weeks.

Nicole began to cry as she asked me, "Lance, what is the main message of the gospel of Jesus Christ?"

Not knowing what Nicole was getting at, I replied, "Well... It is um... How should I say it? Well, I'll put it like this, 'Jesus died for sinners so that if people believe in him and confess His name as lord and savior and are willing to repent and begin a new life then He will guarantee them eternal life."

Nicole began to weep very hard as she said, "That's right... Lance, Jesus lived a sinless, perfect life, and yet people brutally murdered him for no reason. But as He was being crucified by the people, He asked His Father to forgive the people that were torturing Him. Jesus asked His Father to forgive them because He knew that those who were crucifying Him, really didn't know and understand what they were doing."

I intently looked at Nicole. I was trying hard to understand where she was taking me. Nicole had to know that I already knew the account of Jesus. Through her tears, Nicole added, "Lance, when I think about what you did, I get unbelievably angry! I cry, and all kinds of emotions run through my mind and soul. But then

I think about King Solomon and King David, and how they made mistakes. I also think about how they were willing to change. Then I look at Jesus and I see how He is so willing to forgive."

As Nicole sighed she said, "Lance, I just want to tell you that I know you are sorry for what happened. And I know that you really want to change. So Lance, I just want to say that... I truly forgive you for what you did... I mean believe me, I don't know how I am bringing myself to say this, but I do forgive you Lance."

When I heard those words come out of my wife's mouth I can't begin to describe the feelings that ran through my body. I instantly began crying. I grabbed hold of Nicole and I thanked her, and thanked her, and thanked her like there was no tomorrow. The two of us sat hugging and embracing each other and we soaked our clothes with each other's tears.

As we hugged, Nicole who was teary eyed and all, kinda pushed me away from her and she said, "Lance, I want us to make this marriage work."

I cried and I shook my head as I told Nicole, "Baby no. I don't deserve you. I don't deserve to have someone as special as you. Just leave me... Really, baby just leave me. It hurts me like crazy to say and to think this but I know that there is somebody out there that can make you happier than I can... Somebody that wouldn't put you through what I put you through."

Wiping her eyes, Nicole responded, "Lance I don't want anyone else. What's wrong? I said I forgive you."

As I continued to cry tears of joy, I replied, "Baby, I don't deserve to be forgiven"

At that moment Nicole got up from the bed and went to her closet. She seemed as though she were searching for something. When she returned to the bed she handed me a card and told me to read out loud what was on the card. I looked at the card. Very carefully I examined the card. I realized that it was the card from 1800FLOWERS that I'd hypocritically sent to Nicole a couple of months ago.

"Lance, read that card out loud," Nicole demanded.

I fought back tears and I read out loud, *"Love is patient, love is kind. It does not envy, it does not boast, it is not proud. It*

*is not rude, it is not self-seeking, it is not easily angered, it keeps
no record of wrongs. Love does not delight in evil but rejoices
with the truth. It always protects, always trusts, always hopes,
always perseveres. Love never fails."*

I placed the card on the bed and I hugged Nicole and I said,
"Thank you! Baby, thank you so much! Thank you! I was
overwhelmed with emotion. It was hard for me to even get out
those words of thanks as the impact of the words that I'd just read
simply blew me away."

Nicole held back her tears and with red puffy eyes, she
said, "Lance, a couple of things hit me from the scriptures that are
on that card. One thing that hit me is that, I know that I am going
to have to be extremely patient throughout this whole ordeal.
Another thing that hit me from those scriptures, were the words
that say, 'Love keeps no record of wrongs.'"

Nicole paused, then she said Lance, I know God is helping
me to say what I'm about to say, and that is, "I love you and I
don't care what people will think and I know that everyone will
have plenty to say, but Lance as far as I'm concerned, your slate is
clean with me… If you truly repent Lance, and change, then your
slate will be clean with God so therefore it has to be clean with
me." Nicole took another pause.

She slowly stroked the bed sheets as she added, "Now I'm
not saying that I will never even think about the affair, because to
be honest, I'm going to think about it everyday. But what I'm
saying is that, I'm not gonna be throwing the affair up in your face.
Because if I do throw it up in your face, it won't help things to get
any better. Lance, I want you to know that because of God, I trust
you. I am human so I don't completely trust right now. But I know
that with hard work on both of our parts that I will one day come to
the point where I'll be able to completely trust you 100%. But
Lance, I hope that you will persevere through your struggles and
weaknesses and try to do the right thing. I also hope that you will
trust me, and put hope in God… Also, for my sake, hope and pray
for me that I will persevere through all of this."

Nicole suddenly became silent. She blew out air and she looked towards the ceiling and repeatedly blinked her eyes in an effort to hold back her tears. "Lance, there are many things that we are gonna have to work out. For example, Lance I don't ever want to see that child! I mean, I know that you're gonna have to take care of the kid, but I'm telling you now that I'm not gonna be able to deal with seeing pictures of the kid or having the kid in my house for visits and all of that.

And as far as Toni is concerned, I know that she might have to call here at times, but I don't want to speak to her and I don't want to see her, especially not in my house! Lance, I know that it's wrong but I have so much anger in my heart towards that woman and towards this whole thing in general! I have to ask God to help me out on that.

See I'm not saying that I'll never be able to confront Toni or that I'll never be able to see the baby. I'm just saying that it's gonna take time until I feel comfortable enough for that to happen. As a matter of fact I don't know if I will ever feel totally comfortable being around Toni or the baby. It might take years for that to happen, but that's just how it's gonna have to be...

Lance, something else that I have to say is I don't ever want to know the details of the affair. I mean, I actually want to know, but I know that it is probably best that I never know the intimate details... But I don't know because my mind flip-flops on that subject. I mean, a part of me needs to know all of the details so that I can put complete closure on the topic. But... It's like I think back to the way you were dancing with Toni at the party we had back in May. Lance, I think back to you asking me had I ever cheated on you, and I wonder what exactly was going on back then."

As Nicole sucked her teeth she said, "Lance, see, like right now, I had to catch myself because I can tell that I was starting to get heated inside... Lance, again, all I can say is that I don't think I ever want to know the ..." Nicole stopped in the middle of her statement and just stared into space. Then she looked as if she was gonna cry as she asked, "Lance, do you have love for Toni?"

I thought before I began to speak because I wanted to give Nicole the most honest answer that I could give. In my heart I sensed that Nicole really didn't wanna know the answer to that question and that's probably why she asked another question before I could give her an answer.

"Lance, like I said before, with God, I know that I can trust you. But I want you to tell me, Lance can I *really* ever trust you again?..."

By this time in the conversation, my tears had left my face, and I said in a compassionate tone, "Baby listen. Let me just say this... I understand fully what you have been saying. And believe me, whatever you want, however you feel things should be, that is how it will be. Nicole, I am just so thankful that you can even find it in yourself to forgive me. Baby, you don't know what it means to me to know that you want our marriage to work out. Nicole, I promise you that I am going to give more than a one hundred percent effort in every aspect of our marriage. And I promise you that together we are going to work out all of my sexual hang ups so that nothing like this will ever happen again. Because I realize now that I should have just spoken up much sooner, I could have come to you for help and support in fighting through all of my struggles. I never came to you for help and support and that was a huge mistake, but I promise you that I will be forthcoming with anything that I think might trigger off something sexually immoral on my part.

Nicole, I understand your pain. And baby I don't want you to ever experience again, what it is that I have put you through... And to answer your last two questions, yes you can trust me. Nicole, I'm willing to work as hard as I have to in order to rebuild that trust... And Nicole, I don't know if my word is worth anything, but all I can say is that I have *No Love What-So-Ever* for Toni. Other than God, you're my first and only love, and I realize that now more than ever."

Nicole and I hugged and deeply embraced each other for about two minutes straight. Then she went to the bathroom and got two wash cloths for both of us to wash our faces. As I washed my face, my body felt tingly and numb. I yelled to LL and let him know that daddy was not leaving and that I would be staying at home.

I had a couple of concerns and questions but I was sure that they would work themselves out. I wondered how I would react if I were to see Toni in person. I wondered how I would behave two or three years from now if I were alone with Toni visiting the baby. I wondered how I would deal with the rest of my dogish ways. How would I stop lusting? How would I stop masturbating? Would I *really* never cheat again?

I knew that only time would answer certain questions. But there was one thing that I knew for sure, that being the fact that Nicole is a one in a million kind of woman. In fact, God doesn't make women like Nicole anymore.

As I finished washing my face, I realized that God had answered a prayer of mine. See, through Nicole, God was teaching me what it was like to love as He loves and to live as He lives. Yeah, there will be many tests for me to pass in the future. But for the first time in my life I earnestly want to pass all of those tests. Not only for myself, but more so because I don't want to hurt anyone else in the future.

Again, I realize now more than ever that first and foremost, my dogish ways hurt not only myself, but they hurt God and those around me that love me. If Nicole can love me unconditionally the way she does, I am sure that if I plug into God and really focus, then and only then will I put an end to my DOGISM.

The Calm After The Storm

It is said that when a person breaks a bone in their body, the bone will actually be stronger after the break has been mended and it has had a chance to fully heel.

With my adulterous ways I had broken the fibers and the inner most sacred parts that Nicole and I had created with our union of marriage. And unlike a bone which is very tangible in the sense that one can touch it, grab it, and physically see it, the fibers of a marriage are totally different, they are more spiritual. And therefore how do you mend those fibers of marriage in a way in which they will properly heel and be stronger than they were before the damage was done to it?

That is a question that only time can truly answer.

During the months after I revealed my adulterous ways to Nicole we have been through every range of emotions known to man. We have been frustrated, sad, remorseful, regretful, angry, depressed and so many more adjectives that are along those lines. There have been countless nights where we have laid in our bed and soaked our pillows with tears.

From my standpoint, there have been times following the affair's revelation in which I would literally feel like I was going to go insane simply because I knew deep down inside that my cheating had never *truly* had any bad intentions. It sounds stupid but I never wanted to hurt Nicole. I never wanted to put her in the position that she was in. At times when we would lay in our bed and discuss why the affair had happened and what were the warning signs and red flags that we both should have noticed, I would just want to ram my fist through the bedroom wall out of pure anger and frustration.

For one, I was truly regretful and mad at myself for having ever let myself trample over the vows that I had made to both my wife and to God. I would also get ridiculously angry and frustrated because Nicole would constantly blame herself for the wrong in which I had done. She would always say things like, "If only I had been more affectionate, or supportive then maybe you would have not cheated." She would also say things like, "If I had of only called you Lance on your cell phone and checked on some of your alibis' for not being in the house at night, then maybe I could have prevented you from cheating."

See, I knew that Nicole could not have been further from the truth. The truth of the matter was that I had wanted to cheat. I had something inside of me that was driving me to do what I did and I acted on it. And there was really nothing that Nicole or anyone else could have done to stop me from being a dog.

One night while we were laying in the bed I gave Nicole the following example in order to get her to fully understand how I was feeling and also to get her to stop blaming herself for what she had no control over.

"Nicole, I am sure that the surviving family members, who have ever lost a loved one due to some sick serial killer, walk around blaming themselves for the death of their loved one. They probably say things like, 'If only we had told so and so to take another route to school that day' or, 'If only I would have taught my daughter not to talk to strangers.' See, Nicole, the family members should not blame themselves for the sickness of the serial killer. The fact of the matter is that when a serial killer is determined that someone is gonna be his victim, that serial killer has a twisted and demented drive that will not let him rest until he kills that victim that he is after. And see, that is how it was with me. I had this sick and twisted drive to be with other women. It was a drive that I could not escape. The only way that I would have been able to escape it would have been if God saw fit to not allow it to happen."

Yeah I remember very vividly giving Nicole that example because while Nicole did get the gist of what I was saying, she focused more on the latter part of what I had said.

"See, Lance that is what I can not understand. Why would God allow something like this to happen? Lance, I wouldn't wish this type of pain on anyone, and that is why I just can't understand why God would put me through this. I've been faithful to God and I always trusted Him and prayed to Him and I continue to do that, I just can't understand why God would allow all of this."

I fully understood Nicole's reasoning behind questioning God. But during the months after I'd told Nicole about Toni, there was no way in the world that I could personally question God, because I knew that it was my reliance on God that had carried me through and allowed me to stay on the straight and narrow. It was like my cheating ways had been a cancerous tumor in my soul and by me plugging into God, God was able to go into my soul and cut that cancer out and keep me in remission from cheating.

Yeah, for the first six months following the revelation of Toni to my wife, I was regularly checking in with God and I saw the benefits. If my cheating ways was like a cancer, then it was as if through prayer I was going to God on a daily basis for Chemotherapy treatments. It was as if the Lord's Chemotherapy treatments were designed to totally prevent the cheating cancerous cells from re-forming again in my body and eliminating those cells which grew back after having been fully cut out during the initial operation of my repentance.

But just like most people when they are sick, as soon as they start to feel better, they stop taking their medication, usually they stop their medication totally based on their own decision making process and their doctor will be totally in the dark about it. In my case I was able to battle relentless pressure from things such as dealing with Toni's pregnancy and subsequently the beautiful baby girl in which she and I had. I was able to deal with losing all sense of integrity and credibility with my family and friends. I was able to properly deal with new and old sexual temptations. I was able to muster up the courage to attend a weekly twelve step program called sex addicts anonymous, which was similar to alcoholics anonymous, only it was for people who felt that sex for them was either out of control or beginning to get way out of control. I was able to deal with all of those things and not crack under the pressure because I was managing to stay plugged into God. However, like the sick person who starts to feel a little better and automatically assumes that they can stop taking their medication, I began to get real cocky in my own mind.

Right around the six month following the revelation of the affair, I noticed that I was only praying a few times a week instead

of multiple times a day. It was like I began to put my guard down.
I wasn't reading the bible everyday like I had been doing when the
affair was first revealed. In other words I began to voluntarily skip
my chemotherapy sessions with the Lord.

And like magic, it must have been a new group or a new
cluster of cancerous cheating cells that managed to work their way
through my blood stream and stop at the part of my brain that
controls my common sense. Those new cheating cells had a way
of disguising themselves very well. In my case they had disguised
themselves real good because they used different tactics in order to
set me up. They didn't cause me to out and out lust and just want
to sex someone per se, and they didn't cause me to want to
masturbate or fiend to look at pornography. Rather, those new
cheating cells that had once again started to form began working
on my ego. They began asking my ego: "What's up with you
Lance? Why ain't nobody calling you? You ain't the man no more
or what?"

See, my ego or something inside of me seemed as if it
always needed to really be stroked and caressed. And that is
exactly what those new cheating cells began to play on. Maybe I
felt the need for my ego to be stroked due to my many insecurities.
I don't know. But I do know that my cheating ways had never
really been carried out simply as a quest to conquer the actual act
of having sex or having an orgasm with fine attractive women. It
may have appeared that way, especially considering how attractive
both Toni and Scarlet are. But the truth be told, my cheating ways
went far more deeper than superficial surface things, it was more
like my cheating ways were done in an effort to *prove* to myself
that I was valuable and *needed*. And I would base my value and
my self-worth on the women that I would want to go after and
eventually conquer.

I could have been super successful in all areas of my life,
which for the most part I was, and yet I would always feel the need
of wanting to feel better about myself, and wanting to cause
someone to feel like they really *needed* to be with me and *needed*
me to be around in their lives, regardless if that "someone" was
another woman and I was a married man.

I don't know if it will prove to be unfortunate, fateful, or whatever, but once again I really began realizing my strong need to feel desired and valuable in the eyes of the opposite sex. I began feeling this way only months after Toni gave birth to the baby.

See, God had been answering all of my prayers. He had been keeping my mind free of that need to want to feel needed. He had even made sure and saw to it to protect me from everything. God protected me so much until it got to the point where certain women like Scarlet and others like her actually backed off of me.

Yeah, that was ill because Scarlet, along with my other female acquaintances had totally, voluntarily, and willingly distanced themselves from me. Me! Of all people, Lance Thomas! And I knew that God had played a role in that because that was what I had been specifically asking him to do for me. God had also been keeping me away from bad influences in the form of people like Steve and many others that did not have my best interests at heart.

Yet it was primarily the thoughts of Scarlet that was really wreaking havoc on my mind. I knew that the best thing in the world that had happened to me was that I hadn't spoken to women like Scarlet for a little more than six months, which had been a record time frame for me not having contact with women outside of my marriage. What was really ironic though was that those cheating cancerous cells had kept a serious poker face during those past six months. They had a huge ace in the hole in that they knew that I had managed to keep *"one thing"* in the dark about my past.

Having had revealed just about everything to Nicole, I always knew that I had never told her about Scarlet. Keeping Scarlet a secret had never been my intentions, I guess that after seeing Nicole react the way she did when I told her about Toni, that I wanted to *protect* Nicole's emotions and therefore I instinctively and completely blocked out of my mind the life of sin that I had carried on with Scarlet. Not to mention wanting to avoid that fear of completely being exposed and feeling like a worthless freak, yeah that also played a part in me keeping my mouth shut about Scarlet. Yeah even when Nicole had specifically asked me had there been anyone else other than Toni, I knew that I could have mentioned Scarlet del Rio but something just came over me and made me lie about it. I lied by keeping the Scarlet thing in the dark.

I know it sounds pathetic and pitiful, but again, I figured that telling Nicole about Scarlet would have been a blow that she would not have been able to handle. Even after having told Nicole about Toni and the pregnancy and living through that, something inside of me told me that Nicole would not have been able to handle the entire truth and details about Scarlet. I mean after all, Scarlet had been in the picture for the entire time that Nicole and I had been married so that would have put things in a completely different league of revelation.

I guess for the most part, after Scarlet began fading out of the picture, which happened to be right around the time I'd met Toni that I viewed it as Scarlet didn't really *need* to be discussed with Nicole. I know that I was using twisted logic but Scarlet had been further in the past than Toni had been. Plus I had met Scarlet and had had sex with her before Nicole and I had actually said "I do." So in my mind I had convinced myself that the Scarlet thing was ok to brush under the rug, especially considering the fact that no baby or no sexually transmitted diseases were involved as it related to Scarlet.

My silence about Scarlet gave so much power to my demons. That one ace in the hole that my cancerous cheating cells held was just waiting to be played. The danger of me having kept Scarlet a secret was two-fold and I knew it. On one hand it was like I had a mistress in my hip pocket and Nicole had no way of helping me to stay clear of that mistress. And on the other hand, if now, more than six months after the fact, I had chosen to bring the Scarlet thing to the spotlight and expose what had been a five year on again, mostly off again, sexual affair then Nicole would have really lost all sense of trust in me and she would have never ever been able to believe another word that came out of my mouth for as long as I lived. Not to mention that everything concerning my marriage would have been down the drain, everything!

So in order to protect myself, Nicole, and LL, I convinced myself that it would be best to keep things quiet for the rest of my natural life as far as Scarlet was concerned. In no way could I put Nicole through that type of drama again. In no way was I gonna lose the battle against my demons that Nicole and I had been fighting together during the past six months.

I had a lot of thoughts waging war in my mind on a daily basis. I knew of all the destruction and pain that I had caused. I knew about all of the new promises and new vows that I had made. I knew about all the repenting prayers that I had offered up to God. I knew about the rosy future that I wanted to re-create with Nicole and LL. I truly, truly, from the inner most part of my being wanted to continue to do right. And from the pit of my soul I had truly been genuinely remorseful and sorry for what I'd done. I knew that I truly loved Nicole and that I truly loved God. I really knew those things!

But still, why hadn't Scarlet at least checked for me during the past six months? I mean she hadn't even called me one time in more than six months! I wondered many things such as; if she was a'ight. I wondered if she was angry with me for not having called her. I wondered if she was angry with me because of my relationship with Toni. Hell, I wondered if she had still been stalking me. I wondered if she was *sexing* anyone else. I wondered if she had completely written me off and had really moved on in her mind as it related to me. I wondered if she still thought that I looked good. I wondered if she would still let me *hit it* if I were to see her. I wondered if she were in a relationship with someone else would she be willing to cut that person off for me. I wondered if she still saw me as an emotional stronghold that would help her deal with all of the baggage in her life. I wondered would she still be excited to hear from a brother.

If it takes me the rest of my natural life to do it, I know that I will one day be able to explain why I would want to entertain the thought of placing fire in my lap all over again. One day I will be able to explain exactly why I would want to behave like a dog that returns to his vomit, sniffs it, and then eats what he has already regurgitated. One day I will fully be able to articulate the reasons why, but I want to be able to articulate it in a way in which I understand it and in a way in which everyone else will understand it.

I had an overwhelming need and I was feeling a lot of pressure. And at the same time I was feeling an intoxicating desire to desperately satisfy, address, and fix my need, that is why I wasn't shocked that after only a little more than six months of *sexual sobriety* I had given in to the *need* and sought out a quick "fix."

I still had Scarlet's phone number memorized in my head. Scarlet was the fix that I felt that I could not do without for the moment. I guess I should have run to Nicole for help, or run to anyone to help me fight off this monster that was approaching me and trying to devour me.

I was nervous as hell and I didn't want to do it, but somehow, and I will explain it later one day, but somehow I did manage to get my sweaty palms and fingers to dial Scarlet del Rio's phone number.

My heart was beating and I had no idea what I was going to say to her, or where and what that phone call would lead to, but I had to at least be assured that Scarlet still *needed* me.

Ironically, the radio was on in my living room and I remember the Aaliyah song "If Your Girl Only Knew" playing on low volume in the background while I dialed Scarlet's phone number. As I dialed, I also remember thinking about a bible passage; Romans 7:15, 17-24 that says:

I do not understand what I do. For what I want to do I do not do, but what I hate I do. As it is, it is no longer I myself who do it, but it is sin living in me. I know that nothing good lives in me, that is, in my sinful nature. For I have the desire to do what is good, but I cannot carry it out. For what I do is not the good I want to do; no, the evil I do not want to do – this I keep on doing. Now if I do what I do not want to do, it is no longer I who do it, but it is sin living in me that does it. So I find this law at work: When I want to do good, evil is right there with me. For in my inner being I delight in God's law; but I see another law at work in the members of my body, waging war against the law of my mind and making